Cair Chaladain
Din Eidyn
BERNICIA
Ubbanford
Stagga
R. Tuidi
Gefrin
Deira Stræt
NORTHUMBRIA
Æscendene
Stanfordham
Hefenfelth
The Wall
NORTH SEA
Caer Luel
Carrec Dûn
Roman Fort
Wentende Street
DEIRA
Inhrypum
R. Usa
Eoferwic
Loidis
Tatecastre
Pocel's Hall
Humber
Engelmynster
ELMET
Heah Street
R. Dun
Maserfelth
R. Scheth
LINDESEGE
R. Maerse
FENS
GYRWAS
POWYS

WARRIOR OF WODEN

MATTHEW HARFFY grew up in Northumberland, England, where the rugged terrain, ruined castles and rocky coastline had a huge impact on him. He now lives in Wiltshire, with his wife and their two daughters.

BY MATTHEW HARFFY

The Bernicia Chronicles

The Serpent Sword
The Cross and the Curse
Blood and Blade
Killer of Kings
Warrior of Woden
Storm of Steel

WARRIOR OF WODEN

THE BERNICIA CHRONICLES: V

MATTHEW HARFFY

An Aria Book

First published in the UK in 2019 by Head of Zeus Ltd

9 7 5 3 1 2 4 6 8

A catalogue record for this book is available from the British Library.

ISBN (HB): 9781786696281
ISBN (ANZTPB): 9781786696298
ISBN (E): 9781786696373

Typeset by Divaddict Publishing Solutions Ltd.

Printed and bound by CPI Group (UK) Ltd, Croydon, CR0 4YY

Head of Zeus Ltd
First Floor East
5–8 Hardwick Street
London EC1R 4RG

WWW.HEADOFZEUS.COM

Warrior of Woden
is for Soelwin Oo,
1974 – 2015
"Dude (I totally miss you)" – *Tenacious D*

ALBION
AND ISLANDS
Muile
Hii
DAL
RIATA
THE
WHALE ROAD
Legend
Settlements
Fortresses
Holy sites
Roman roads
HIBERNIA
MAN
HIBERNIAN SEA
ALBION
AD 642
PICTLAND
DAL RIATA
BERNICIA
Bebbanburg
DEIRA
Eoferwic
ELMET
HIBERNIA
GWYNEDD
MERCIA
WEST SAXONS
CANTWARE
Hithe
FRANKIA
0
50 miles
0
100 km

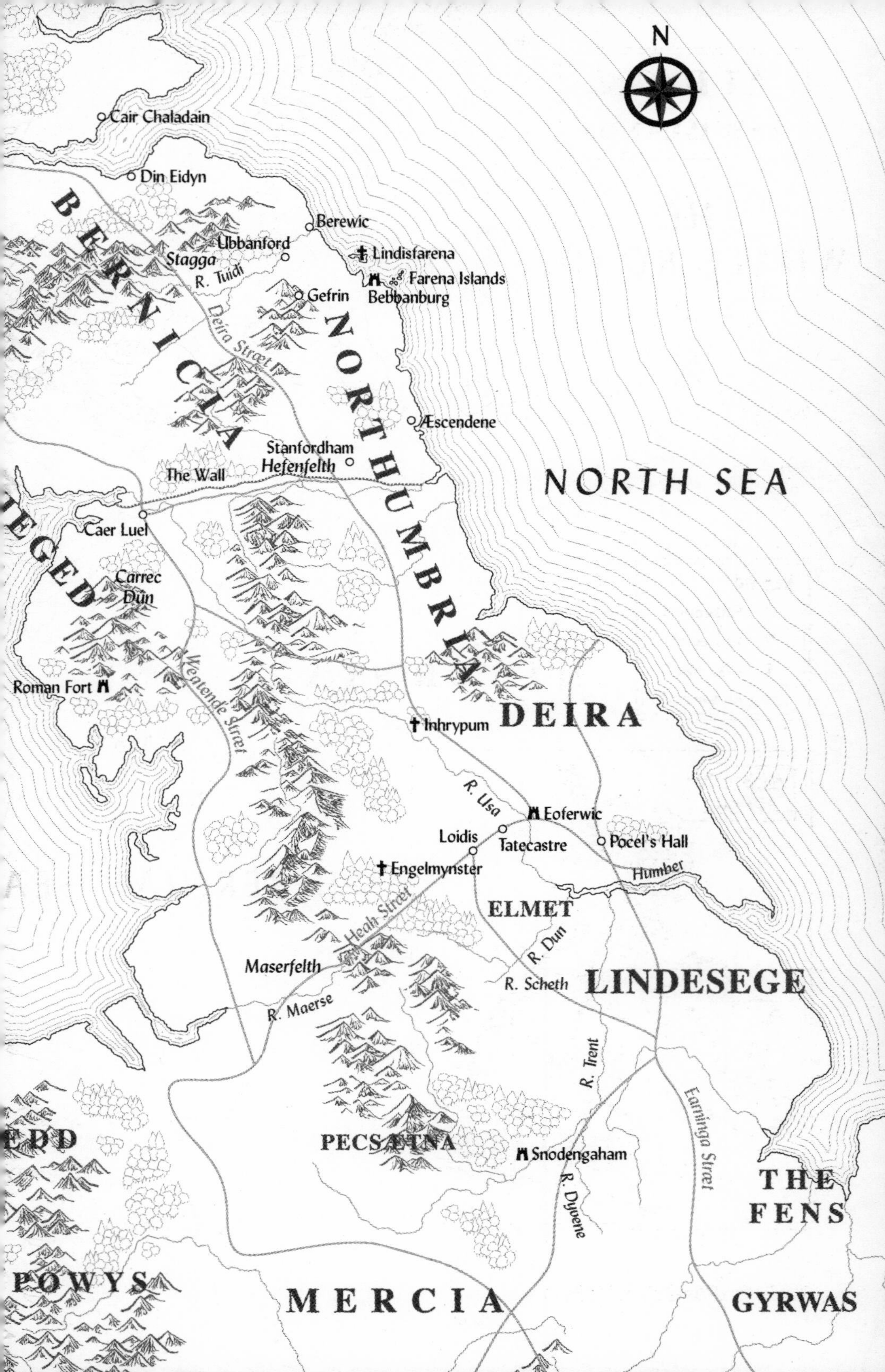
N
Cair Chaladain
Din Eidyn
BERNICIA
Berewic
Ubbanford
Stagga
R. Tuidi
Lindisfarena
Farena Islands
Gefrin
Bebbanburg
NORTHUMBRIA
Deira Stræt
Æscendene
Stanfordham
Hefenfelth
The Wall
NORTH SEA
Caer Luel
Carrec
Dûn
Roman Fort
Wentende Stræt
DEIRA
Inhrypum
R. Usa
Eoferwic
Loidis
Tatecastre
Pocel's Hall
Engelmynster
Humber
ELMET
Heah Stræt
R. Dun
Maserfelth
R. Scheth
LINDESEGE
R. Maerse
R. Trent
Earninga Stræt
PECSÆTNA
Snodengaham
R. Dyvene
THE
FENS
POWYS
MERCIA
GYRWAS

Place Names

Place names in Dark Ages Britain vary according to time, language, dialect and the scribe who was writing. I have not followed a strict convention when choosing what spelling to use for a given place. In most cases, I have chosen the name I believe to be the closest to that used in the early seventh century, but like the scribes of all those centuries ago, I have taken artistic licence at times, and merely selected the one I liked most.

Æscendene	Ashington, Northumberland
Afen	River Avon
Albion	Great Britain
Bebbanburg	Bamburgh
Beodericsworth	Bury St Edmunds
Berewic	Berwick-upon-Tweed
Bernicia	Northern kingdom of Northumbria, running approximately from the Tyne to the Firth of Forth
Caer Luel	Carlisle
Cair Chaladain	Kirkcaldy, Fife
Cantware	Kent
Cantwareburh	Canterbury
Carrec Dún	Carrock Fell, Cumbria

Dál Riata	Gaelic overkingdom, roughly encompassing modern-day Argyll and Bute and Lochaber in Scotland and also County Antrim in Northern Ireland
Deira	Southern kingdom of Northumbria, running approximately from the Humber to the Tyne
Din Eidyn	Edinburgh
Dommoc	Dunwich, Suffolk
Dor	Dore, Yorkshire
Dorcic	Dorchester on Thames
Dun	River Don
Dyvene	River Devon
Elmet	Native Briton kingdom, approximately equal to the West Riding of Yorkshire
Engelmynster	Fictional location in Deira
Eoferwic	York
Frankia	France
Gefrin	Yeavering
Gipeswic	Ipswich
Gwynedd	Gwynedd, North Wales
Hefenfelth	Heavenfield
Hibernia	Ireland
Hii	Iona
Hithe	Hythe, Kent
Inhrypum	Ripon, North Yorkshire
Liminge	Lyminge, Kent
Lindesege	Lindsey
Lindisfarena	Lindisfarne
Loidis	Leeds
Mercia	Kingdom centred on the valley of the River Trent and its tributaries, in the modern-day English Midlands
Maerse	Mersey
Muile	Mull

Northumbria	Modern-day Yorkshire, Northumberland and south-east Scotland
Pocel's Hall	Pocklington
Rendlæsham	Rendlesham, Suffolk
Sandwic	Sandwich, Kent
Scheth	River Sheaf (border of Mercia and Deira)
Snodengaham	Nottingham
Stanfordham	Stamfordham, Northumberland
Tatecastre	Tadcaster
Temes	River Thames
Tuidi	River Tweed
Ubbanford	Norham, Northumberland

PROLOGUE

TATECASTRE, AD 639

"The king is struck. Oswald Whiteblade has fallen!"

Beobrand's stomach lurched at the cry.

"Shut your foolish mouth, Cynan," he snapped.

Cynan, a tall man with haunted eyes, dropped his gaze, abashed.

Beobrand stared over the frost-rimed moor to where the enemy shieldwall stood, linden boards still resting on the ground, spears held aloft, glinting in the early morning sun, not yet lowered and braced for a charge. Their enemies' banners hung limp, unmoving in the still air.

Glancing over to his left, Beobrand felt a stab of anguish, as if it had been him and not his lord who had been injured. Oswald had indeed been hit. A shaft of ash protruded from his shoulder where an unlucky arrow had found its mark and pierced the king's iron byrnie and flesh. Oswald was being held upright with difficulty by two thegns.

The great wooden cross that served King Oswald as his battle standard wavered and dipped in the air as his retainers jostled around him.

Beobrand slapped the shoulder of the stocky man to his right.

"Acennan, take command of the men." Acennan did not speak, but nodded his understanding.

"Cynan, with me," Beobrand said, his tone a sharp bark of command.

Trusting that the younger warrior would obey, Beobrand left his position in the Northumbrian shieldwall and rushed along the lines, elbowing and pushing men aside with his bulk.

"See that the cross is held aloft," Beobrand hissed. "Whatever happens, do not let that rood fall. And Cynan," he gripped Cynan's shoulder tightly, halting his onward rush, "the king has not fallen. Do you hear me?"

Cynan stared wide-eyed at him for a moment before nodding. Beobrand left the Waelisc warrior to his task and pushed forward towards the king. His stomach roiled but he took some comfort when, from the corner of his eye, he noted that the carved wood cross rose once more into the sky, casting its long shadow over the icy ground and the fyrd-men gathered there. He knew he could rely on Cynan. The erstwhile thrall had proven his worth many times over since he had joined Beobrand's warband three years before.

The shieldwall was closing ranks, regaining some order at the bellowed commands of Derian, Oswald's battle-leader. Beobrand thanked the gods for the man. The bearded thegn knew his work. There was no warrior more doughty; none more steadfast. The shieldwall would not be allowed to break while Derian yet breathed.

Two men were half-dragging Oswald back from the front of the line.

"I must stand," Oswald protested, his voice muffled by the ornate faceplate of his grimhelm. "I will not retreat from this rabble. In God's name I must fight. Unhand me! I command it."

The warriors, who had been pulling the king backward, paused, unsure of themselves. They relaxed their grip on Oswald. His legs buckled and he almost fell to the cold earth. Beobrand leapt forward and caught him. Around them, men shuffled back to make room for their king.

"You must sit for a moment, lord," said Beobrand, his face close to the king's helm. "We must see to the wound."

Oswald murmured something that Beobrand could not make out, but he took it as assent.

"Lower him gently to the ground," he said to the two warriors.

Beobrand quickly scanned the faces and armour of those who surrounded them. His heart lifted when he spotted his old friend, Wynhelm. The older man looked on, lips pressed tightly together and brow furrowed, but Beobrand knew he was not a man to lose himself to dismay.

"Wynhelm," Beobrand said, his fingers already tugging at the leather thong that fastened his helm's cheek guards beneath his chin. Wynhelm stepped close. "See to it that nobody beyond your men here sees that the king is wounded. Remember the great ditch. If the fyrd-men see their king fall, we are all doomed." Their eyes met for a heartbeat. They both recalled the morass of blood, mud and shit that had filled the great ditch in the land of the East Angelfolc. How the floor of the dyke had become a swamp of the uneven, slippery flesh of the fallen. Neither wished to be plunged once more into such a savage rout.

Wynhelm turned and addressed his men.

"Keep yourselves close together," he said, his tone quiet, yet urgent, "none must see what transpires here."

Oswald had stopped fighting against the men who had brought him from the shieldwall, and now sat upon the chill mud of the moor. One of the men had crouched beside the king, allowing Oswald to lean against him. Beobrand fumbled for a moment with his helmet strap. His mutilated left hand no longer pained him and he seldom missed the last two fingers he had lost, but he always felt he was clumsier than most. Grunting in annoyance, he finally managed to untie the knot and yanked the helmet free from his head. Despite the cold spring morning air, his hair was plastered against his head, wet with sweat.

He knelt beside Oswald.

"My lord. Let me remove your helm."

Oswald did not speak, but gave the slightest of nods.

Beobrand reached for the leather ties and, after a long clumsy moment, managed to loosen them. He pulled the great helm from Oswald's head. The king's shoulder-length chestnut hair hung lank, his face as pallid as the cloudless dawn sky. His eyes were dark, glazed with pain. Fear gripped Beobrand, but he could not allow his thoughts to show on his face. His gaze travelled over Oswald's fine iron-knit shirt to where the arrow jutted. The goose feather fletchings quivered with each of the king's breaths. The metal head had forced apart the links of the byrnie and buried itself deep beneath Oswald's collar bone. There were flecks of blood on the iron rings close to the wound, but not much. Beobrand knew that when they pulled the arrow free there would be great gouts of dark slaughter-sweat. It would be then that his king might die, if they could not staunch the flow. And even if they were able to stem the gush of blood, he might be elf-shot, the wound-rot eating into his body with its vile corruption.

Despite the obvious pain he felt, Oswald smiled.

"You never were a good tafl player, Beobrand. Your thoughts are as clear on your face as if written by a scribe on calfskin. But no need to hide from me what I already know. It is bad. I can feel it." He closed his eyes for a moment, perhaps offering up a prayer to his god, the Christ. He let out a slow trembling breath that steamed in the air before him. It smelt sour. Beobrand frowned.

Oswald suddenly lashed out with his left hand and gripped Beobrand's wrist. His fingers were pale and fragile against the iron splints that Beobrand wore there to protect his forearm in battle.

"If I die—" Oswald began, his voice intense and jagged.

"You will not die, lord," Beobrand interrupted. He caught the glance of the warrior against whom Oswald still leaned for support. The man's eyes were grim. "You will not die," Beobrand repeated firmly.

"All men die," whispered Oswald. Beobrand made to speak again, but Oswald raised his left hand. "Hush. I am your lord. Your king. And I would have you swear an oath to me."

Beobrand nodded. He did not trust himself to speak, his throat was thick with emotion.

"You must swear to me that if I die, you will serve my brother, as you have served me. Oswiu is a father and husband now." Beobrand recalled how three winters before Oswiu had wed the princess, Rhieinmelth of Rheged. She had quickly borne him a son and was again with child. "Oswiu must not die here today," Oswald continued. "The kingdom will be his. He will need strong men. Men like you. Lucky men."

Beobrand loathed it when Oswald referred to him thus. He was not lucky. But he had long ceased trying to correct his king on the matter.

"You are a father too, lord," said Beobrand, his voice catching. He thought of young Œthelwald and Queen Cyneburg, daughter of Cynegils. "And a husband."

Oswald sighed.

"I am. But I am king first, and I would have your oath before I breathe my last. Would you deny me that, Beobrand?"

Beobrand shook his head.

"Good. Then swear on whatever you deem sacred that you will give your oath to Oswiu when I die."

Beobrand clenched his right hand into a fist. By the gods, how had it come to this? Moments ago, he had been standing in the shieldwall, his gesithas by his side, ready to do that for which Oswald most valued him – to bring slaughter to the enemies of Northumbria in the steel-storm of battle. And now, here he was, kneeling in the gelid mud about to swear an oath that would see him tied to Oswiu atheling for the gods knew how many years. Oswiu. Brother of Oswald, son of Æthelfrith. Oswiu, atheling of Bernicia. A powerful man. A cunning man. A dangerous man.

Oswiu, who hated Beobrand.

Beobrand swallowed. The sun was rising red and burning into the empty sky. The men who crowded around them provided no warmth, only shade.

Of course, his oath would mean nothing should he die today. They had come to this place to fight, to put an end to the coalition between Mercia, the East Seaxons, Powys and Lindesege. The threads of Beobrand's wyrd had long been entangled with those of the sons of Æthelfrith, but he could not have foreseen this twist of destiny.

There was no time for this.

He stared into Oswald's brown eyes. The king was as pale as the snow atop the peaks of Rheged now. No, there was no time.

"Very well," Beobrand said, "you have my oath."

"Swear it on that which you hold most dear."

Beobrand hesitated.

"I swear on Octa's life. I give you my oath, sworn on my son's life." He shivered. Why had he uttered those words? To offer up his son's life so easily. Would that the gods had not heeded him. But he knew it mattered not. His word was iron. The oath was given. It was done. "But, lord, you cannot be seen to have fallen here today, before even a blow is struck. Penda's host will take heart from such tidings. You must stand in the wall."

Oswald gritted his teeth and gripped Beobrand's wrist once more.

"Pull me up."

But Beobrand did not heave Oswald to his feet.

"No, lord, you cannot fight as you are. Have these two take you to the priests, that they may tend your wounds and pray over you." Beobrand had seen the magic the Christ priests could spin. He hoped they would be able to work their miracles for the king. The weight of the new oath weighed heavily upon him as if he had just donned another byrnie over his own.

Oswald looked confused.

"But the men…" he looked about them at the shadowed faces of Wynhelm's gesithas who watched them in silence, "the fyrdmen will know what has happened…"

Beobrand lifted his helm and placed it gently upon Oswald's head.

"No, lord king, for it is Beobrand of Ubbanford who has been struck with an arrow, not the king."

Beobrand picked up Oswald's grimhelm. The faceplate was finely wrought with patterns; images of warriors and beasts embossed in the metal.

"And Oswald, son of Æthelfrith," said Beobrand, pulling the helm over his head and hiding his features completely, "yet stands in the shieldwall, hale and strong." The helmet was tight, pressing against his ears.

He stood, towering over the men around him.

Oswald smiled again.

"It would seem that the king of Northumbria is indeed blessed," he said, "for he has grown in stature by almost a head's height when confronted by this host of Mercians, Waelisc and treacherous men of Lindesege."

Behind the helm's faceplate, Beobrand did not return the king's smile.

"Carry him to the priests," he said to the warriors, his voice booming strangely against the metal of the helm. "Make it quick and see that they heal him. And remember, it is Beobrand who has taken the arrow."

Beobrand reached down and hefted the king's shield from where it had fallen. The handle of the shield boss was cold in his half-hand. He would miss the straps he used in his own shield, but he would have to make do.

The ranks of men parted before him as he stepped towards the front of the shieldwall. He rolled his neck in an attempt to alleviate the tension there, but it was no good. He reached down to his belt and touched the hilt of his sword, Hrunting.

Beobrand took a deep breath. Across the moor, the last vestiges of the morning mists had been burnt away by the rising sun. The frost sparkled like jewels scattered upon the ground. As if they had been waiting for him to take his place, the enemy host let out a huge clamour, hammering their spears and blades into shields and roaring their defiance.

"For Oswald," started the chant around him, rising in intensity as ever more of the Northumbrians took up the battle-cry. "For Oswald! For Oswald!"

By Woden and all the gods he hoped that he was as lucky as Oswald believed. For he must lead these men into battle.

And he must be victorious.

Beobrand drew Hrunting from its finely tooled scabbard and held it aloft to catch the bright rays of the rising sun.

"For Oswald!" he screamed, lending his voice to the tumult. Then, slashing the sword down to point at the enemy shieldwall, he ran forward.

And the men of Northumbria, believing they followed their king, surged forward with him.

Anno Domini Nostri Iesu Christi
In the Year of Our Lord Jesus Christ
642

PART ONE
GATHERING STORM

Chapter 1

"No good will come of this," said Acennan, absently patting his mare's neck.

Beobrand did not answer. Acennan was probably right. Good seldom came from a dark column of smoke on the horizon.

He raised his hand to shade his eyes from the glare of the summer sun and peered into the southern distance. Hills rose there. Craggy and windswept in the summer, when a few peasants grazed their sheep and goats on the dales. In winter they were snow-bound and treacherous. They were home to few men, and fewer still would seek to travel into that tortuous terrain. Especially not Northumbrians. For the hills lay within the northern marches of Mercia.

The sky was clear of clouds, which made the smudge of smoke on the horizon stand out as starkly as a splash of blood on snow.

Beobrand looked back at the men who awaited his orders. They numbered two dozen. All mounted men, bedecked in byrnies and carrying black shields, sharp spears and swords. Spear-men. Warriors. Men of Bernicia. Men of his warband. His gesithas.

Beobrand's mount aimed a bite at Acennan's mare. Beobrand had come to refer to the large shaggy brown beast as Bera, for it more resembled a bear than a horse. Beobrand tugged hard at

Bera's reins. It lowered its ears and snorted. It was a strong horse, stalwart and scared of nothing, but it was as cantankerous as an old woman. For a moment he thought longingly of his great stallion, Sceadugenga. He had lost the horse when fleeing the battle of the great ditch in East Angeln some six years before. The gods alone knew if the stallion yet lived, but Beobrand still missed the animal. He had never known a horse like Sceadugenga. It had been fearless and strong, but more than that, it had seemed to understand its rider in a way unlike any other mount Beobrand had ridden.

Another horse whinnied. The men sat quietly, but Beobrand knew they were waiting for his decision. They had ridden these frontier lands these past two weeks, as they had for a month every year since the great uprising three years previously. Oswald had been caught unprepared then. The forces of the East Lindesege and Mercians had congregated in the lands of Beda of Lindesege and, without warning they had struck north, attempting to destroy Oswald while he celebrated the Christ feast of Eostremonath at Eoferwic. They had clashed at Tatecastre, only a short distance from the ancient capital of Deira. Beobrand still remembered that cold morning when he had donned the king's battle-helm and led the Northumbrians to victory. He remembered the weight of the helm and the pressure of the fateful oath his king had forced him to swear. He had believed they were doomed, but as Oswald had said, Beobrand had again proven his luck. For they had carried the day.

Ever since that day, Beobrand and the other thegns of Northumbria spent a month each year patrolling the borderlands of Deira and Mercia. They would not be caught unawares a second time.

"Whatever burns, it is not our concern," said Acennan, clearly tired of awaiting a response from Beobrand.

Beobrand grunted. Acennan was right, and yet something prickled at Beobrand's mind. He turned to Acennan.

"The weather has been fine these past weeks, has it not?"

"Aye," Acennan smiled, "better than riding through rain and mud, shivering without a fire at night." They both recalled the misery of the year before when it had rained almost every day of their month of riding along this southern border of Northumbria. All of them had been ill by the end of it, and their clothes had rotted on their backs from being constantly sodden.

"You are not wrong there, my friend," said Beobrand. "But do you remember last year, even when the sky was filled with rain and storms raged in the heavens day after day, even then, we caught some of the Mercian brigands raiding into the lands of our king? Remember, there was that fool we caught when he tried to ride Theomund's stud stallion?"

Attor and Cynan, who were near to Beobrand and Acennan, laughed at the memory.

"We were hardly needed then," said Acennan. "That Mercian boy was made to regret stealing a proud Northumbrian horse!"

More men laughed at the memory. One of the few moments of that rain-drenched month that they were happy to remember. The huge stallion had not been pleased to be ridden out of its warm stable and it had thrown the Mercian youth from its back and then, when the boy sought to drag him away by pulling on the horse's reins, the beast had attacked him. The horse had trotted back to its master's stable. The stallion had reminded him of Sceadugenga. Beobrand and his warband had found the Mercian lad trampled and bleeding in the mud.

The boy had still been dazed when they had hanged him.

"There was not much need of us then, you are right," said Beobrand. "That horse was well able to look after itself, it seems. But even then, with the constant rain, men raided from Mercia, seeking to steal what they could. How many men have we seen raiding this past fortnight?"

"We have seen none," replied Acennan, "but I for one am happy of the peace and the good weather. Perhaps I am getting old."

"Perhaps you are at that," laughed Beobrand. "Eadgyth has tamed you when you are at your hall, of that there is no doubt."

Acennan blushed.

"Well, she has her ways of keeping me quiet."

Beobrand smiled.

"I am sure she does."

Acennan was happier than ever. His land prospered, as did his family. Eadgyth had borne him two fine children and Acennan doted on them all. But there was little that could be described as old or tame about him when he rode with Beobrand's warband.

Beobrand stared at the smear of smoke in the pale sky over the southern hills.

"But does it not strike you as strange that this year, when the weather has been fair, and there has been a full moon and clear skies, we have neither seen nor heard of any bands of Mercians striking into Deira?"

Acennan frowned.

"Perhaps you are right, lord," he said. "But what do you think is the cause of the calm over the land?"

"I do not know, my friend," Beobrand answered, smiling to himself at Acennan's use of the term "lord". He only called him thus when he was angry or nervous. "But something is not right and south of here I would wager a hall is burning."

He straightened his back and stretched his shoulders and arms in preparation for a hard ride.

"Attor and Cynan, you are to ride ahead as scouts. Gallop back to warn us if you smell a trap. This could be bait for an ambush." Beobrand raised his voice so that all could hear. "The rest of you, prepare to ride. We will seek out what is the cause of this smoke and mayhap we will find what has kept the Mercians so quiet these past weeks."

Cynan and Attor nodded and kicked their steeds into a canter that took them down the slope of the hill and quickly into the shade of a stand of elm.

Acennan frowned at Beobrand, but touched his spurs to his horse's flanks, trotting forward with the remainder of Beobrand's gesithas.

Beobrand understood his friend's concern and he acknowledged that he was probably right in his appraisal of the situation. Surely no good could come of this.

For Beobrand led his warband into Mercia.

Chapter 2

Cynan kicked his mount into a gallop as he saw Beobrand and the warband in the valley below.

"Come on, Attor, our lord is close." He grinned as his horse sped forward, surging further ahead from Attor. He knew that the older Seaxon warrior hated to be beaten at anything and he prided himself on being the best scout amongst Beobrand's gesithas. And it was true that Attor's eyes were keener and his tracking-craft better than any other's.

But Attor was no match for Cynan when it came to riding. The Waelisc warrior laughed with the joy of freedom as he urged his horse ever faster. When Beobrand had first given Cynan a mount, the erstwhile thrall had been ungainly and unsure of himself. It had been all he could do to stay astride the beast at walking pace. None then would have imagined he would have displayed any ability on horseback. But now, six years later, he was without doubt the best rider in Beobrand's warband and arguably one of the finest riders in Northumbria. He had won many a race with thegns from other halls. The men would bet on the contests and Cynan had become something of a legend in the northern kingdom, with few men now daring to ride against him and risk losing their dignity and their gold.

His transformation from thrall to warrior had happened quickly in that first year after Beobrand had accepted his oath. Acennan had trained him in the use of weapons and Cynan had practised hard and long, becoming adept at spear and sword. No longer resigned to eating the scraps given to a thrall in a mean lord's hall, he had grown strong and hale on the rich diet of meat and mead served to the warriors of Ubbanford. The only thing preventing him from winning every race on horseback was his size. He had grown broad of shoulder and back, and he was taller than most men. A year after coming to Bernicia Cynan had flourished into a strong gesith. When he had first ridden into battle, a skirmish with a scruffy band of Picts who had threatened some of Acennan's folk north of the Tuidi, Cynan had found that he was one of that rare breed of men who seemed more alive in the shieldwall than at any other time.

He was thankful to Beobrand for accepting him and giving him his freedom. He loved him for making him a warrior.

The day was warm, the sun yet hot in the sky and Cynan revelled in the cool breeze made from the speed of his ride. His sweat cooled on his forehead.

Before him, Beobrand raised his hand, halting the column of riders.

Cynan flicked a glance over his shoulder. Attor was some way behind him. Cynan galloped on until it seemed he would clatter headlong into the group of warriors on the valley path. He smiled to see that none of them flinched or made to move aside. They knew him and his horse-skill.

At the last possible moment, he pulled on his reins, bringing his steed to a skidding halt. Then, gripping tightly with his thighs, he made the horse rear up, pawing the air with its hooves. Behind him, Attor slowed his mount and then trotted up to Beobrand.

"What news?" snapped Beobrand, ignoring Cynan's antics.

"You were right, lord," said Attor, wiping his forehead with the back of his hand. "It is a Mercian steading that burns."

Cynan stilled his horse, then nudged it forward.

"There was much slaughter there," he said.

Beobrand frowned.

"Who has done such a thing? Did you see who had attacked the place?"

"We saw," said Attor, "and you too will see them soon, for they ride this way with their spoils."

"How many?" snapped Beobrand.

"Do not fear, lord," said Cynan with a grim smile, "there are fewer of them than us, and besides, they are no match for us if it should come to a fight. Which it won't."

Beobrand's face grew dark.

"Speak clearly, man," he said. "Who rides hence?"

Cynan forced his features into a serious scowl. He had grown used to his lord's moods and had learnt it did not do to ignore the signs of an impending storm.

"Lord Fordraed and his gesithas ride some way behind us, lord," Cynan said.

Beobrand's brow furrowed yet further.

"I see," he said. "Then let us rest the horses. We will await him here and he can explain himself to me."

Some of the men dismounted, stretching and stamping, pleased to be out of the saddle for a few moments. A few wandered off the path to piss into the nettles that grew there.

Beobrand swung himself down from Bera and Acennan also dismounted. Cynan remained mounted, feeling equally at home in the saddle as on foot. He watched as Beobrand and Acennan conversed in hushed tones. He could not hear the words, but could imagine Acennan warning their lord to be cautious, and not to allow his temper to get the better of him. It was no secret that Beobrand despised Fordraed. The man was wealthy and influential, one of Oswiu atheling's favourite thegns. But Fordraed had a vicious streak that had angered Beobrand on more than one occasion.

Ever since Cair Chaladain, Beobrand had loathed him.

It was not long before Fordraed and his men rode into view. They came at a canter, reining in their mounts a spear's throw away from Beobrand's warband. Those warriors who were on foot clambered quickly into their saddles.

Beobrand ordered his men to remain where they were and he and Acennan spurred their horses forward. Cynan joined them. Acennan gave him a sidelong look, but Cynan just smiled. Beobrand ignored him, instead fixing his icy gaze on Fordraed, who rode to meet them, flanked by two of his gesithas.

The thegn wore a fine warrior coat of leather. He was about the same age as Beobrand, perhaps a year or two older, but where Beobrand was clearly a warrior, broad of shoulder and narrow of waist, Fordraed's belly swelled above his breeches, pushing the leather of his jacket taut. His head was uncovered, his long dark hair brushed back from his face, and his thick moustache framed a tooth-filled grin. He was aglow with excitement and Cynan noticed a smear of something reddish-brown on his cheek. Most likely dried blood.

"Well met, Beobrand of Ubbanford," Fordraed said. "What brings you to Mercia?"

"I might well ask you the same thing, Fordraed. I am tasked with protecting the borderlands until the new moon. You know this. I saw the smoke yonder and thought to investigate."

"Oh, that." Fordraed waved a hand carelessly in the direction he had come from. "Don't worry about that, Beobrand."

"What happened there?"

"There is nothing to tell. Truly," he smiled broadly to his men, who chuckled in return, "there is nobody left to tell any tale anyway."

Beobrand took a deep breath, and Cynan noticed Acennan tensing, as if for a fight. Looking behind Fordraed to where the bulk of his men rode, Cynan could see that some of the warriors had women on their steeds.

"What of those womenfolk?" Cynan asked. "Will they not speak of whence they come and what occurred there?"

Fordraed's eyes flashed with anger.

"Do not address me, Waelisc scum. You should not allow your Waelisc dog to bark so, Beobrand."

Cynan dropped his hand to the hilt of the sword that hung from his belt.

"And you would do well not to allow your tongue to flap like an old man's prick," Cynan said, his voice soft but deadly, like the whisper of a blade being drawn from a scabbard.

Fordraed bristled, but Cynan noted that the man did not offer to fight him, keeping his hands firmly on his reins so as not to start a clash of weapons. Cynan was not only known for his prowess as a horseman.

"I am warning you, Cynan," Fordraed said.

Cynan fixed him with a withering, unblinking gaze, daring the thegn to back up his words with metal. Fordraed didn't make a move.

"Enough of this," snapped Beobrand. "Silence yourself, Cynan." Fordraed grinned. "We are in Mercia and this is no place for us to be fighting each other. But Cynan is right, what were you thinking and what of those women you bring from the hall you have burnt? You will start the bloodfeud with the kin of these Mercians. And you are risking destroying the truce. The king will not thank you for breaking the peace."

"Peace?" Fordraed let out a snort of laughter. "The truce is blown away like that smoke on the wind. We are at war, Beobrand. Those women are thralls. Spoils of war."

Beobrand frowned. Something in Fordraed's words gave him pause. Cynan felt the shift in the air, as if a cloud had rolled before the sun, plunging them into shadow at the mention of war.

"War?" said Beobrand. "Why do you speak thus? The borderlands have been quiet for weeks. There is no sign of war. We have heard nothing. Not even a raiding party stealing a goat."

Fordraed's mouth twisted.

"And did that not strike you as strange?" he asked. "I knew something was afoot, which is why I rode into Mercia. And the king will thank me well enough when I bring him the tidings I now bear to Eoferwic."

"Tidings of war? How can you be so sure?" asked Beobrand.

"First, I know why there have been no raids. There were no men of fighting age back at that hall, just women, children and greybeards. No spear-men. No shields. They are all gathering under Penda's banner. He means to strike north with a great host. He has set his eyes on Northumbria again, and this time he means to see the task to its end."

"But how do you know these things?"

"We asked the people of that hall," Fordraed flicked a hand towards the brooding hills and the smoke.

"They might have lied to you," said Beobrand.

"Oh, they did at first," Fordraed scratched absently at the dried blood on his cheek, his eyes glazing as he thought back to what he had witnessed that afternoon. "I asked one of the old men, but he was a tough old nut and would tell us nothing. Even as we pulled out his entrails, he swore and spat at us. Gods, but the old goat was a true fighter. Must have been formidable in his day." Fordraed spat and grinned at Beobrand. "He reminded me of you."

"And yet you are sure of the tidings of war that you now bring?"

"Yes," Fordraed smirked and Cynan wondered for a moment what it would be like to punch the thegn in the face. "You see, I then asked one of the women."

Beobrand hesitated.

"And how do you know she did not lie?" Cynan watched as his lord wrestled with his emotions. Beobrand's knuckles showed white where he clutched his reins in a ferocious grip. "Even if you tortured her," Beobrand said, glowering at Fordraed, "I have known many brave strong women."

Fordraed guffawed.

"You think too highly of women, Beobrand. You always have. And yet, I know some might prove stubborn and refuse to answer my questions. So, I did not inflict pain and torment on the wench I questioned." He pointed to one of his men, who held a slender, fair-haired woman on his saddle before him. Her hands were tied, her face soot-streaked. Her eyes looked blank and unseeing. And yet she seemed whole and unhurt.

"What did you do, you bastard?" Beobrand asked, his voice as cold as a winter frost.

"I did not torture the woman. She could fetch me a good price. She is not ugly. No," Fordraed paused, as if savouring the moment. He rubbed again at the blood on his face and then examined his fingernails. "No, I did not hurt her. I merely threatened her child. That always does the trick."

Cynan thought then that Beobrand would launch himself at the plump, sneering lord. But instead Beobrand took in a long calming breath before replying. When he did so, his words were as sharp and brittle as shattered flint.

"And when she told you what you wanted to hear?"

"Why, I killed the little Mercian brat, of course. I didn't want to have the whelp growing up plotting my death."

"The man is an animal." Beobrand spat into the fire and stood suddenly, unable to contain his ire any longer. All that afternoon he had seethed as they rode east and north. Fordraed had said that he would travel to Eoferwic to give the king the news of the coming war, that there was no reason for Beobrand to accompany him. But Beobrand did not trust him. Besides, he wished to hear what the king said when he heard the tidings.

"Hush, Beobrand," Acennan said, rising from where he had sat beside the fire and joining Beobrand in the darkness. In the distance they could see the shadowy shapes of the sentries Beobrand had ordered to stand watch, despite Fordraed's insistence that they were safe, that this was his land. Acennan placed a hand upon Beobrand's shoulder. "The man's a brute," he said, "of that there is no doubt. But we have known that for years. Ever since Cair Chaladain."

A raucous peal of laughter came from one of the other fires. Fordraed's loud voice carried on the cool night air, though his words were indistinct.

More laughter.

Beobrand did not wish to think of Cair Chaladain. But Fordraed's harsh voice, his men's laughter and the smell of woodsmoke on the wind brought the memories of that dark day rushing into his mind like the tide flooding the sands at the island of Lindisfarena. He closed his eyes and tried to think of something else, but the nightmare of that autumn day in the land of the Picts would not relinquish its grip on him that easily. He would never forget Cair Chaladain, even if he lived for a hundred summers. He had seen much battle in his score and six years. Faced death and the screaming hatred of throngs of foemen in numerous skirmishes and battles. But the horror of Cair Chaladain had stuck with him like no other.

The shieldwall had been terrible. The enemy had fought with savage ferocity and many were the good men that had fallen on that drizzle-washed day. The shieldwall had pressed forward, stepping over the dead and dying, trampling bodies into the mire. Aethelwulf had been gutted by a terrible swing of a Pictish axe. It had not been till long after the fighting had finished that they had found him. Beobrand could still see in his mind's eye the ashen grey pallor of Aethelwulf's face. His gore-slick hands had been locked over his belly, trying in vain to hold in his gut rope, and to keep death from claiming him. Aethelwulf had died alone, left behind the shieldwall as the Northumbrians had pushed forward. The Northumbrians had taken the field, claiming victory, but as Beobrand and his gesithas had stood looking down at Aethelwulf's stricken form, they had all tasted the bitterness of defeat.

The shieldwall that day had been bad, but the night that followed had been worse.

Beobrand opened his eyes, staring out into the gloom. He was accustomed to the darkness now, and he could just make out the afterglow of the sunset over the hills that loomed in the west. To the south, beyond the silhouettes of the guards, there rose a great forest of oak, elm and hazel. They had skirted along its northern edge as the sun had dropped in the sky and now the woodland was utterly black, lacking the light of moon, stars and the last vestiges of sun-glow that lit the heavens.

Another great guffaw of laughter came from Fordraed's men. Beobrand's head snapped around at the sound and he saw a shower of sparks rise up into the dark sky as one of Fordraed's men threw a log onto the blaze.

"I can still remember the burning and the screams," said Acennan. "It reminded me of when we burnt Nathair's hall."

Beobrand nodded. That had been another night of fire and terror and death.

"But Nathair's kin had taken Reaghan," he said, "and killed Tobrytan." He remembered the fury he had felt when learning of the old warrior's murder at the hands of his Pictish neighbours. When he had heard they had carried Reaghan away with them, his rage had been absolute and terrible. "The sons of Nathair brought it on themselves."

"And we fought the warriors," said Acennan. "Not the women."

Beobrand said nothing. He recalled with a pang the ruined face of the woman who had rushed at him outside Nathair's hall. He had slain her without thinking, and the memory of it always shamed him. It was not right for a warrior to raise his hand to women or children.

"You tried to stop it that night at Cair Chaladain, Beobrand," Acennan said. "There was nothing more you could have done."

The night after the battle Fordraed had led the men on a rampage into the settlement of Cair Chaladain. The warriors had been filled with rage and the terrible lust for life that comes of surviving a battle. The darkness had been a welter of blood-letting, flames, torture and rape. If the music of the shieldwall had been the sword-song of battle-play, the tune of that night had been the screams of nightmares.

"I should have prevented it," Beobrand said, picking at the scabs of old memories that he had never allowed to heal.

"You held the men back. And you beseeched Oswiu to order the men to retreat from the village."

When Beobrand had confronted Fordraed, he had scoffed.

"For one with your battle-fame, you are as soft as a woman," Fordraed had said.

Beobrand had seen from the gleam in the man's eyes that he would not pull his men back. This was the part of battle that he truly enjoyed. And so Beobrand had gone to Lord Oswiu, atheling of Bernicia and leader of the warhost.

Beobrand remembered all too well Oswiu's reply.

"Let the men have their reward for their victory. It is the way of warriors, Beobrand. You should understand that."

"It may be the way of some, lord," Beobrand had snapped. "But it is not my way, and it will not be the way of my men. And," he had paused before stalking off back to his men, away from the smoke and screams of the village, "I do not think it would be your brother's way."

Oswiu had bridled at that, an edge entering his tone, as if his voice had drawn a knife.

"But Oswald is not here, is he? I lead here, and I say let the men have their sport."

Beobrand had not been able to sleep that night. The flames from the village had lit up the sky and each shriek of torment had been like a seax in his heart. At first light, he had ordered his warband to ready themselves and they had left that place of death. Some of the men had been disappointed, he knew, to leave before Oswiu could bestow treasure on the thegns who had heeded his call to face the Picts at Cair Chaladain, but Beobrand had not been able to face Fordraed and the others in the light of day. He had been concerned that he would not have been able to contain his anger, if he had seen what the Northumbrians had left of the Pictish village. And so he had returned to Ubbanford with nothing to show but the corpse of Aethelwulf and bad dreams to last him a lifetime.

He sighed. He had enough treasure already.

"I should have prevented it," Beobrand said again, quietly.

Acennan stood close to him.

"You tried, and the men love you the more for it."

Beobrand rubbed at the tension in his neck.

"War should be between warriors," he said. "Women should be no part of it."

As if in answer to his words, the high-pitched screech of a woman's anguish pierced the night.

Beobrand started at the sound.

"No," he said, a terrible finality in his tone.

"Easy, lord," said Acennan. "Fordraed is Oswiu's man."

Beobrand said nothing. His hand fell to Hrunting's hilt and he strode towards Fordraed's warband's fire.

He heard Acennan behind him getting the men to their feet. The sound of battle gear being readied was loud in the flame-licked darkness of the camp. He took in a deep breath of the cool night air as he walked towards Fordraed's men. He would have to be careful here, or he would start something that would only be finished with blood spilt. That way lay bloodfeud and death. The girl screamed again and then Fordraed's men laughed.

Beobrand's anger raged within him now, sudden and bright like oil thrown onto a forge fire. He struggled to keep the beast of his ire in check. He could feel it straining at its chains. He stepped into the firelight. Off to one side half a dozen women huddled, tied and cowering. But none of Fordraed's men paid them any mind. They all looked to where a seventh girl lay on the ground. Her clothes had been ripped, revealing the milky skin of her breasts and belly. Two men held her down and a third was loosening his breeches.

The madness of battle tore at Beobrand's control. He would not allow this. He could not stand by and see another woman defiled. Not since Cathryn, all those years before in the icy forest. Or Tata, murdered in Engelmynster. Or Sunniva. Reaghan. He could not lie in the darkness listening to the howls of torment of another woman. He may share the blood of Hengist, but he would never be like that twisted killer, who had enjoyed inflicting pain on those weaker than him.

"Halt!" he bellowed. All of the men turned their gaze from the object of their passions to the tall warrior lord who was suddenly in their midst. The light from the flames glinted from his eyes and the fine pommel of his sword. That sword was known to them all. Beobrand's hand rested upon Hrunting and they all knew that death would be upon them should that blade be drawn. "Leave the woman be," Beobrand said. His tone rang with the authority borne of leading men in battle.

Nobody moved.

Behind him, Beobrand's warband were hastily forming a shieldwall. He did not turn to see them, he knew their worth and was certain of their mettle. He bared his teeth.

"No woman will be hurt here," he snarled.

Fordraed surged to his feet. His face was flushed, and sweat sheened his forehead. He came towards Beobrand, shouting a torrent of abuse. Beobrand was surprised by the man's rash bravery, but perhaps Fordraed felt sure of the protection afforded him as one of Oswiu's closest thegns. Whether he was brave, believed himself safe, or he was blind to the danger that rolled off Beobrand the way smoke billows from a green log on a hearth, Fordraed rushed at Beobrand.

"How dare you?" he yelled, his voice cracking. "You have no right!" Spittle flew from his mouth like sparks in the gloom. "These are my men. My lands. And my thralls. We will do with them what—"

Beobrand punched him in the mouth. Hard. Fordraed fell back, to sit on the grass, dazed and blinking in disbelief.

A couple of his gesithas leapt to their feet, reaching for their weapons.

"Hold!" said Beobrand. "No weapon has been unsheathed here. None of us wish for bloodshed this night. There is war coming, and we will need all the hale men we can muster."

One of Fordraed's men, a burly man with plaited beard, made to pull a huge langseax from its scabbard.

"Put up your weapon, Heremod," said Beobrand. "If steel is drawn, there will be death before the dawn. Do not doubt that. I know you are a brave man, but do you truly believe that you could best me?" Beobrand let the words hang in the air. Heremod hesitated, clearly weighing up his chances. After a moment, he let his hand fall away from the seax.

"Why, you son of a whore," said Fordraed, his words slurred like a man who has drunk too much strong mead. He spat to clear his mouth of blood. "I will see you before the king for this," he continued, the incredulity at what had occurred replaced by rage. "You will pay me weregild for striking me. You will—"

"How much?" Beobrand interrupted Fordraed's tirade.

Fordraed blinked stupidly. Beobrand towered over him. Fordraed spat again and then heaved himself to his feet.

"What?" he said, his tone dripping with venom.

"How much?" Beobrand repeated. He could feel the tension draining from the camp. The beast within him was retreating once more until a worthy adversary stood before him. "How much weregild? For striking you."

Fordraed's mouth opened and closed, as if he could not find air to breathe.

"No matter," said Beobrand reaching for a solid gold arm-ring he wore. He tugged it down over the bulging muscles of his shield arm. He weighed it in his hand. It was heavy. He threw it at Fordraed. It was not a gentle throw and Fordraed had not expected it. The golden band gleamed for an instant before it struck the portly thegn in the chest. He tried to catch it, but it fell to the earth. He bent and retrieved it as quickly as a heron dipping its beak for fish.

Fordraed licked his lips and wiped his hand across his face. All there knew that the arm ring was worth many times more than the weregild for a single punch when no weapon had been unsheathed.

"Very well," Fordraed said at last, grudgingly accepting the payment. He made to place the ring on his own arm, but quickly realised it was too large for his limb. Frowning, he made to turn and walk back to his men.

"Wait," said Beobrand, halting him. "I think that ring is worth enough to buy me the women too."

Fordraed spun on his heel, his bluster and anger rekindled.

"You go too far," he said. "These thralls will fetch me a better price than this bauble."

"Very well," said Beobrand. "Name your price."

Fordraed's eyes narrowed.

"Three pounds of silver."

There were gasps from some of the watching men.

Acennan stepped forward into the light of Fordraed's campfire.

"That is madness," he said. "We could buy twenty thralls for that much."

Beobrand raised a hand for quiet.

"Very well," said Beobrand. "Three pounds of silver it is. I will pay you as soon as I am able to fetch treasure from my hall. Do we have a deal?"

Fordraed swallowed. This was a fortune. He nodded.

"Yes, we have a deal." He stepped forward, hand outstretched to seal the agreement.

Beobrand fixed him in a stony glare for a moment, ignoring the proffered hand. How easy it would be to pull his seax from its sheath and stab the fat fool. Or to drag Hrunting from its scabbard and take Fordraed's head from his shoulders. With his men arrayed behind him in a shieldwall, they could storm into

Fordraed's warband, slaughtering them all. The idea of it sang to him.

But Beobrand held his arms rigid at his sides. The moment passed.

"Acennan," he said at last, turning away from Fordraed, "bring all the women to our campfires and see that they are given food, drink and blankets."

Acennan nodded.

Beobrand clenched his fists tightly against the trembling that always came after a confrontation. The knuckles of his right hand stung. He felt the gaze of all those gathered there. Gods, he needed a drink.

He walked back to his campfire, the shieldwall parting, allowing him to pass.

"You should have let me haggle," said Acennan, whittling at a stick furiously. The twig snapped and he tossed it into the flames of the campfire. Reaching for another piece of wood, he began shaving slivers of bark from it. "Three pounds of silver! It is madness! Fordraed knows you are rich, that is what it is."

Beobrand watched the flames dance and begin to consume the broken twig. He loathed how he was so often referred to as rich. It was almost as bad as being thought to be lucky. He did not consider himself a man of good fortune. And yet, despite his annoyance, it was true that he had more treasure than most men. He had won battles and been rewarded for it and now he had three chests filled with all manner of silver, gold and jewels. He supposed that men could consider that to be luck. But like all things, his wealth had grown in the telling. The more men spoke of the treasure he had amassed, the greater that treasure had become until now it was believed his hall at Ubbanford rested on a veritable dragon's hoard.

The year before, when he had been visiting Lindisfarena to see his friend, Coenred, one of the other monks had asked him if it were true that his hall's pillars were forged from silver and the roof was thatched with gold thread. Beobrand had thought the man had been jesting, but it had soon become clear he was in earnest. Beobrand had laughed and told him his hall was like any other, made simply of stout timber. The monk had nodded as if understanding, but then had surprised Beobrand by offering him a conspiratorial wink. However much Beobrand had denied his hall was made of precious metals, the man had simply tapped his nose and smiled.

Acennan continued hacking at the wood in his hand.

"Fordraed knows of your wealth and so seeks to rob you," he said, barely containing his anger at his lord being cheated.

"It was I, not he, who sought to purchase those women." Beobrand glanced over to where the women now lay by their own fire. He had ordered men to guard them in the night. More for their protection than to prevent them running. "And it was I who struck him."

Acennan snorted.

"You've been wanting to do that since Cair Chaladain."

"You are not wrong there."

"And," said Acennan, throwing this latest piece of wood into the fire and scooping up another, "what are we to do with seven thralls?"

"I am sure Eadgyth, Reaghan and Rowena will be thankful of the extra hands. There is always more work than the women can cope with. Gods, they never cease to prattle about it."

Acennan gave him a long, strange look.

"You do understand that Fordraed will just spend your silver on more thralls?" He inspected the point he had carved, blowing flecks of bark and wood shavings from the pale, exposed heartwood, and then jabbing the sharp tip into the base of the fire, where it was hottest. "And his men will do what they like to the women they buy." After a heartbeat, he pulled the stick from the embers and blew out the small flame that had begun to consume the wood.

Beobrand watched the dance of the flames for a moment before glancing over once more at the women.

"Aye," he said at last with a sigh, "I know it. And I know it makes little sense. I cannot change everything on middle earth." It was folly, he knew. And the gods had shown him all too frequently that he was often unable to protect whom he chose. He picked up one of the twigs Acennan had set aside to whittle. He bent the two ends of the wood towards one another. The wood was fresh and springy. He pushed harder, and the twig snapped with a sharp crack. "I know it is foolish," he said, tossing the broken twig into the flames, "but I cannot stand by and watch women treated thus." The flames flickered and crackled, heating his face. He thought of Sunniva's pyre, and how her features had been consumed. Now he barely remembered her face. "I just cannot."

Acennan nodded.

For a long while neither man spoke.

At last, Acennan said, "Well, what are we to do with them? We need to make haste. Why not just set them free? They could return to their kin and their homes."

Beobrand shook his head.

"No. I had thought of this already. But Fordraed has destroyed their homes and killed their kin."

"Still," said Acennan, "it is yet their land. They would rebuild. Start again."

"No," Beobrand repeated, "if Fordraed is right about Penda, then we are at war, and for better or for worse now, those women are thralls. They are spoils of war and I own them."

Frowning, Acennan made to say something, then thought better of it. He clamped his mouth shut and focused once more on his knife and the twig.

Beobrand watched his stocky friend for a moment. He could tell Acennan thought his decisions foolish. Perhaps they were, but they were his decisions. And he was Acennan's hlaford, so no more was said on the matter. Acennan would always speak his mind when asked, but he had learnt years before that when Beobrand made a decision, there was nothing to be gained from fighting against it.

"Cynan," Beobrand called to the Waelisc warrior, who was playing dice with Dreogan, Renweard and the brothers, Grindan and Eadgard. Cynan looked up. "Come," said Beobrand, "I would speak with you."

Cynan said something quietly to the men he was playing with and they laughed. He rose, as lithe as a fox, and joined Beobrand and Acennan.

"Lord?"

"I have a mission for you," said Beobrand. "I mean to give you command of six men."

Cynan squared his shoulders and pushed out his chest.

"I thank you, lord," he said, pride and pleasure evident on his face. "What is it you would have me do?"

"You will take the thralls to Ubbanford, keeping them safe from harm and seeing that none escapes. When you have delivered them safely to Ubbanford, you are to seek us out. I cannot say where we will be, but if war is coming, then head towards where the fighting is heaviest. You shall find us there, no doubt."

Disappointment and anger flashed across Cynan's features.

"But, lord. I am your best rider, and one of your best warriors. Surely someone else could be entrusted with this task. My place is at your side in the shieldwall."

"Your place," Beobrand snapped, his voice suddenly as harsh and sharp as splintered slate, "is to do that which I command. You seemed to have forgotten as much this afternoon when you ignored me and rode forward to the meeting with Fordraed."

"But—"

"No, Cynan. You will do what I have ordered and perhaps next time you will be less willing to ignore my commands."

Cynan scowled at Beobrand, wrestling with his emotions. He was a proud lad, and as good a man as any in the shieldwall, but he needed to be reminded from time to time of who was in command here.

At last Cynan took a breath and opened his mouth for what was surely going to be an angry retort.

Acennan interrupted him before he could speak.

"Remember your oath, boy," he said, his voice hard and loud.

Cynan clamped his mouth shut again and without another word, he strode away from the campfire.

Chapter 3

The next morning Fordraed's men were up and ready to leave earlier than Beobrand had expected. Of course, they had foregone their fun the night before, and so there had been little to keep them awake late.

Cursing quietly to himself, Beobrand watched as Fordraed's warband mounted up. His own men were still breaking their fast with oatcakes that Grindan had cooked on a flat stone beside one of the fires. It was a cool morning, and a light mist rose from the earth to mingle with the smoke from the campfire. Beobrand wanted to shout at the men to hurry. He did not wish to be left behind; to arrive at Eoferwic after Fordraed. He wanted to be there and see the king's face when he heard the tidings. But he clenched his fists and tried to remain outwardly calm as Fordraed swung himself up into his saddle and trotted his horse over. He enjoyed a moment of intense pleasure at the older thegn's fat lip and the bruise on his cheek, but managed to hide his smile as the man rode up.

"We shall see you at Eoferwic," Fordraed said, casting a glance over Beobrand's gathered men. "That is, if you ever decide to strike camp and leave. Comfortable, are you?"

Beobrand ground his teeth, but smiled broadly.

"Don't mind us. We'll catch you up soon enough." He took a warm oatcake from Grindan, broke off a piece and popped it into his mouth. It was gritty, but warm and tasty.

Fordraed raised an eyebrow.

"Don't forget my silver."

Beobrand swallowed the piece of cake.

"How could I forget?" he said. "But it may be some time before you will have it. We have a war to fight first."

Fordraed frowned.

"Yes, we do," he said.

Tugging his horse's head to the side, Fordraed wheeled the steed around, dug his heels into its flanks and sped off northward. His men followed him. The early morning mist curled and eddied in their wake.

As soon as the riders had been swallowed by distance and the haze, Beobrand yelled, "Move it, you good for nothing bastards. Strike camp. We ride north and I do not wish to lose this race with Fordraed."

The edge in his voice spurred the warriors into action and they set about the routines they had followed each morning of their patrol. They were well-trained and knew what to do. They would be ready in moments.

Attor was fully prepared. Beobrand had called him over at first light.

"Take three men of your choosing, Attor," he had said, "and ride west. I would know how much truth there is in what Fordraed has heard. You must be our eyes. See if you can find where the enemy is gathering. I believe Penda may plan to strike north into the western marches of Northumbria."

Attor had dipped his head.

"I will ride close enough to smell the Mercian dogs," he had said with a savage grin.

"Keep your distance," warned Beobrand, "and join the king's host when they march, for he must summon the fyrd. Look for me with the warhost."

The wiry warrior was mounted now, and followed by three others who Beobrand knew to be good riders and trackers. The four trotted close and Beobrand raised his hand.

"Be our eyes, but do not get caught," he yelled.

Attor smirked and returned Beobrand's wave. Then, touching his heels to his steed's flanks, he cantered into the west, chasing his shadow that streamed out before him into the mist. Beobrand watched until the four men were blurred specks in the distance before walking to where Cynan, and the half-dozen men Beobrand had chosen to ride with him, were saddling their mounts. He had not spoken to Cynan since the previous night, but did not wish to leave the man without a final word. Cynan's companions were all solid men, serious and dutiful, who would not allow Cynan to stray from his path, even though Beobrand had placed the young Waelisc man in command. The women stared on, pallid and soot-smeared. They spoke the same tongue, so he was sure they had understood that he had forbidden his men from harming them and that he had rescued them from defilement the previous night. But they looked upon him with sullen, baleful eyes from their pale faces. He grimaced. What did he expect? They were still thralls. Women who had lost everything and seen their kin murdered before them, their homes razed. Perhaps they believed his words about their safety, or perhaps they didn't. It was no matter to them. The Northumbrians were still their enemy and they watched him from beneath hooded eyelids as he approached Cynan.

"Watch yourself, Cynan," he said, lowering his voice so that the staring women would not hear. "These women will cut off your manhood and feed it to you, given half a chance. I know you are not happy with this command, but you will need your wits to deliver them to Ubbanford without incident. Do not underestimate them."

Cynan scanned the faces of the women. Some had blank eyes, others looked resigned to what their wyrd had brought them to. One, the slender girl whom Fordraed's men had been ready to abuse in the night, had eyes that spoke of death to the unwary. They burnt with a savage fury. She glowered at Cynan for a long while. He returned her gaze impassively.

"Do not worry about me, lord," Cynan said, a trace of mockery in his tone. "I am sure we will manage to escort these lovely ladies to Ubbanford."

"Each of you should share a horse with one of them. It will make the journey easier."

"Aye," said Cynan, tightening his mount's girth, "and we can better keep an eye on them that way."

"Just be careful. We will leave now with all haste. With your extra baggage we will soon leave you behind us. Travel safe and return as quickly as you are able. I fear I will have need of your battle-skill before too long."

Beobrand reached out his hand and Cynan grinned and clasped it in the warrior grip.

"Enjoy the peace and quiet without me, lord. May the wind be at your back."

Beobrand clapped him on the shoulder.

The camp had been packed up as they talked. The fires had been kicked into scattered embers and ash, horses had been saddled and harnessed and sleeping blankets rolled and tied.

Acennan rode over leading Bera. Beobrand leapt onto the animal's back and gripped the reins.

"Come, men," he said in a loud voice, "we ride with all haste for Eoferwic."

With a wave to Cynan and his half-dozen warriors, Beobrand dug his heels into Bera's flanks, and the mount lumbered forward. His warband fell into formation behind him and they rode northward. Away from Mercia, but towards war.

Chapter 4

They made good time. The days were warm, bright and long, the roads and paths they travelled dry and firm. As they rode north leaving the frontier with Mercia far behind, the shadow of war receded. It was difficult to believe that somewhere, south and west of them, Penda, the great warlord king, might be amassing a force capable of sweeping all opposition before it.

It was the height of summer and many of the men and women they passed were hunched over, surrounded by crops of barley and rye. Weeding out dock, nettles, charlock and other unwanted plants from the precious crops was painstaking and laborious work, but it was vital for a good harvest. Beobrand well remembered the terrible aching in his lower back after a day's weeding when he had been a boy in Cantware.

War was not something that troubled the thoughts of these peasants. They would glance up and watch the mounted and armoured thegns and their retinues ride by. They stood, slack-jawed and gawping at the fine horses and glittering armour. Squint-eyed against the glare of the sun, they looked on in awe at the garnets and gold adornments of the swords and seaxes. But the ceorls and bondsmen in the fields were interested in the way they would be to see a strangely shaped cloud, or the flash of lightning in a dark sky. Their lives were as distant from those of Beobrand and the passing warriors as pigs were to wolves.

And yet should war descend on this land, many would die. If they could not check Penda's advance, it would not merely be those who stood with shield and spear against the foe who would give their lives. Beobrand thought again of Cair Chaladain, and also of the rout after the battle of the great ditch in the land of the East Angelfolc. He looked at the upturned faces of the men and women toiling in the summer's heat and he knew that it was his duty to protect them from the horrors that would wash over the land if he failed.

They rode through the gates of Eoferwic in the mid-afternoon sunshine three days later. They had caught up with Fordraed easily enough and had ridden with him all the way. The two groups of men had seldom talked and at night they had set up separate camps. Each morning, Beobrand had seen to it that his men were ready before Fordraed's. Now, the large band of horsemen clattered into the courtyard before the royal hall at Eoferwic. The city was thriving and the filthy, muck-strewn streets were abuzz with activity. The air was noisome with the waste of the humans and animals who thronged the settlement. Flies flitted around their faces and the men spat and cursed. Beobrand noticed several new buildings each time he visited and the Christ church was being worked on constantly. Artisans and craftsmen had come from over the sea, from Frankia and even further south some said, to work on the buildings of the new capital of Northumbria.

Servants and slaves began to flock out of the great hall to meet the riders.

Beobrand swung down from Bera and stretched. His back hurt and he was glad to be out of the saddle.

"Lords Beobrand and Fordraed," hailed a loud voice, "what brings you both here?"

Beobrand looked up and saw the king's warmaster, Derian, striding towards them, flanked by door wards bearing spears. There was grey in Derian's thick beard.

"I come with grave tidings from the south," said Fordraed. "I must speak to the king."

Derian glanced to Beobrand, who gave the slightest of nods.

"Very well," he said, "I will arrange an audience. But you will have to wait. The king is at prayer. Would you take some drink in the hall?"

Fordraed frowned.

"The news we bring is of the utmost import," he said.

"I understand," Derian said, placing a hand on the portly thegn's shoulder and leading him towards the hall. Over his shoulder, he rolled his eyes at Beobrand.

An hostler approached and took Bera's reins, leading the huge animal towards the stables. Around him, the courtyard was emptying. The men were making their way to the hall, whilst their horses were being tended to.

"Let's wash the dust from our throats," said Acennan. "The king's steward always keeps a good board here. Perhaps they'll have some of that strong cheese I like so much. And there will be nothing to do until the king is out of church."

Beobrand nodded. It was true that the king spent much of his time now at prayer. Beobrand wondered at it, it seemed wrong to him somehow that his lord should give so much praise to the soft god. And yet it could not be denied that the Christ had brought them victories. There was power in the Christ, but it was ghostlike, tenuous as smoke or mist. Beobrand did not understand it. Still, why should he concern himself with the ways of kings and priests? He was a warrior. Nothing more.

He was about to follow Acennan towards the hall, when a squeaking voice cut through the hubbub.

"Mother, look! Beobrand is here!"

Beobrand waved Acennan on and turned towards the voice.

A tiny figure pelted towards him across the courtyard, little arms pumping and feet pounding. The boy had a bouncing shock of auburn hair, the same hue as his father's. His face was slender and his eyes bright. With the energy and trust of childhood, he did not pause his headlong rush, but launched himself into the air towards Beobrand.

Beobrand caught the boy, barely managing to keep hold of the squirming child. He smiled and lifted the boy high.

"I almost dropped you, Œthelwald," Beobrand said, trying to sound sombre and serious.

"You wouldn't drop me!" yelped Œthelwald. "You're much too strong for that. Isn't he, mother?"

Beobrand looked beyond the boisterous child to the blonde-haired woman who followed in his wake.

"My queen," said Beobrand, inclining his head.

Childbirth had not dampened Cyneburg's beauty. Her golden tresses were coiled about her head in a complex pattern of plaits. She wore a blue dress of fine linen and at her slender neck hung an exquisite necklace of gold and garnets.

"Isn't he, mother?" Œthelwald repeated. "Isn't he?"

"Yes. Lord Beobrand is very strong, Œthelwald," Cyneburg said at last.

Beobrand set the boy back on the ground, offering Cyneburg a thin smile. Behind the queen was a young woman, her gemæcce, or perhaps the boy's nurse, and four warriors. Beobrand surveyed the men quickly. They were all tough men, with set jaws and darting eyes. He did not begrudge them the task of watching over the queen and her son.

"I trust you are strong too, young Œthelwald," Beobrand said, "for I need your help."

The small boy gazed up at him with wide eyes. With a pang, Beobrand thought of Octa. His son was not that much older than Œthelwald, but somehow, it was never as easy with Octa. There always seemed to be a hidden wall between them, never this relaxed joking.

"Oh, I am strong, aren't I, mother?"

"Yes, of course you are," Cyneburg replied with a sigh.

"Then you must carry this for me," said Beobrand, handing Œthelwald his waterskin. The boy sagged under its weight, but, clutching it with both hands, he manfully toddled towards the hall with his burden.

Beobrand and the queen followed, with her retinue a few paces behind.

"How fares your wife?" Cyneburg asked, her voice meek and uncertain, as it usually was when she spoke to Beobrand.

"Reaghan was well when last I saw her," he replied, his tone harsher than he had intended it, as so often happened when he talked with Cyneburg. "But we are not wed."

"Oh." Cyneburg was silent a moment, watching her son struggle with the half-full waterskin. The boy puffed from the effort, but offered his mother a beaming smile.

"See, I am strong, aren't I, mother?"

She returned his smile and nodded.

"I saw you arrived with Lord Fordraed. How does Edlyn do?"

The obnoxious thegn had married the lady Rowena's daughter five years previously, something that had made Rowena inordinately happy and yet seemed to bring her daughter no end of sadness. Beobrand could not imagine Fordraed to be a good husband.

"I very rarely see her. Her mother said she was well, when last I asked after her health." He thought that had been at the Blotmonath feast at the beginning of winter. He cared little for Edlyn and her hateful husband.

For a few heartbeats they walked in uncomfortable silence. Then she steered the conversation in the direction she was truly interested in.

"Have you seen your son?"

He sighed. His feelings towards Octa were confused. He had never been close to the boy, and now, for the last year, his son had been taken yet further from him.

"No," he said at last, "not since Geola." He realised with a start that he was saddened by the fact. He watched Œthelwald walk before them and thought of all the time he had wasted. Octa was seven years old now. All too soon, he would be a man.

Cyneburg said something so quietly that he did not hear the words. Perhaps words of commiseration, but he knew she did not really wish to ask after his son.

They were almost at the hall now. Beobrand stooped to retrieve the waterskin from the red-cheeked boy. He ruffled his hair.

"You can help me anytime, Œthelwald atheling," he said. The boy grinned. "And now, my lady, I must bid you farewell. I would slake my thirst, for the journey has been long and hot."

Without waiting for an answer, he strode up the steps, past the door wards, and into the shade of the great hall of Eoferwic.

Oswald, son of Æthelfrith, king of Deira and Bernicia and Bretwalda of all of Albion swept into the hall. Beobrand was gladdened to see him. As with each time they met, Beobrand was amazed that Oswald yet lived. They had all believed he would die after the arrow wound sustained in the battle at Tatecastre against Penda of Mercia and his allies. But the monks had worked tirelessly with their poultices and potions and they had prayed for him night and day. And, after many days where his spirit had been in the balance and the slightest ill breeze could have sent it tumbling into the afterlife, he had begun to recover. And now, here he was, as full of vigour as ever; still filled with energy and ambitions for his kingdom. His long chestnut hair was pulled back from his face and held in place with a silver circlet. Save for a slight pinching around Oswald's eyes, the king seemed to have returned to his former self without a trace of his wound. His brother, Oswiu, walked at his side. The resemblance to his older brother was clear. His hair and eyes were the same hue as

Oswald's, but Oswiu was stockier and shorter, with a harder edge to his features. The atheling's gaze lingered on Beobrand for a moment, but he made no show of emotion.

Beobrand too kept his face expressionless. He still bridled at the oath Oswald had forced from him on the battlefield. One day, he might need to give his allegiance to Oswiu. The idea filled him with dismay. Oswiu was a strong man, and a good leader, but Beobrand had never liked the atheling. And he knew that Oswiu despised him. He could well imagine the misery of being oath-sworn to him. All he could do was to hope for a long life for Oswiu's brother.

The men seated at the boards fell quiet, setting down their cups and knives.

"Now, what tidings are these that I must hear," Oswald said.

Fordraed leapt to his feet, eager to be the one who brought the news of war to Oswald. Beobrand pushed himself up more slowly and stepped over the bench. He followed Oswald, Fordraed and Oswiu to the rear of the hall where servants had set plates of food for Oswald and his favoured guests. Derian joined them and nodded to Beobrand.

As they helped themselves to slices of succulent roast venison and baked pike, Fordraed told his tale of missing men and what he had learnt from the women of the Mercian settlement.

"What say you, Lord Beobrand?" asked Oswald.

Beobrand took a swig of ale to wash down the pike he was chewing. Its needle-like bones scratched his throat as he swallowed, reminding him why he preferred red meat to fish.

"I did not hear what the Mercians told Fordraed, but it is true that the frontier lands are strangely quiet. I have never seen them so free of raiding parties."

Oswald tapped his chin with his knuckles.

"What is your opinion?" he asked. "What is Penda planning?"

"I know not, lord king. But I have sent men westward to scout. If the gods smile on us, they will find where the Mercians are amassing."

"So," said Oswald, "you think they will come from the west?" He flicked a look at Oswiu. "What say you, brother?"

Oswiu narrowed his eyes, as though in deep concentration. He looked at Beobrand sourly for a moment before answering.

"I think it is possible. If Penda is readying for war, he might well try to strike northward in the west, towards Rheged and then turn eastward. He has not attempted such a strategy before and our defences are weaker there."

"Could it be that the men of Rheged have thrown in with Penda?"

"I do not think so, brother," responded Oswiu. "My wife's father is a proud and honourable man. I believe Rhoedd mab Rhun's word is good and he is a proud grandson of the great Urien. He would not sully his name by breaking his oaths."

Oswald took a draught of wine from a green glass clawed beaker.

"And you have heard nothing of Penda's plans, Oswiu?"

Oswiu flashed Beobrand a sharp look.

"No," he said, "I still have some men I trust within Mercia, but alas, I have heard nothing. And of course, I have lost some good men."

Beobrand drank more ale and said nothing. He knew that Oswiu was referring to his killing of Wybert, who had confessed to being a spy for Oswiu before Beobrand had slain him. Wybert had not been a good man and Beobrand felt no remorse at having exacted the blood-price from him for Sunniva's defilement.

Oswald drained his glass of wine and held it out for a thrall to refill.

"Thank you for bringing me these tidings, Fordraed. We will assemble the warhost and march to meet Penda."

Fordraed smiled broadly.

"I live to serve," he said.

"Now leave us," Oswald said.

Fordraed scowled, but he had no response and so, after a moment, he stood abruptly, turned on his heel and stalked back to his men.

"So, Beobrand," said Oswald, "what is this that Derian tells me of you striking Fordraed?"

Derian sipped at his horn of mead, but offered Beobrand a wink. It seemed that word travelled fast.

"It was nothing, lord. A simple dispute. I have settled the weregild for the blow I struck."

"Truly?" Oswald sounded surprised. "Could it be that the mighty Beobrand is growing up? Paying a weregild… well, I never thought I'd see the day when you admitted you were in the wrong."

"Oh, I don't think I was wrong," said Beobrand, "but I did not wish to start a feud. Besides, I can afford it."

Oswald laughed.

"Did you hit him hard?"

"Oh yes, he fell down with a bump and sat there like a beached fish, his mouth opening and closing."

Oswald tried to look disapproving, but he could not.

"I can't say I am too surprised. Fordraed does have a way about him that can infuriate one. Isn't that right, Oswiu?"

Oswiu frowned, but said nothing.

"Now, enough of this levity," Oswald said, his expression serious once more. "If what Fordraed says is true, we are soon to be at war, and there is no time to be lost. Penda has had his eyes set on Northumbria ever since the rule of my uncle Edwin, but he shall not take my lands. I sense that this will be the end. Derian, send out riders to call on the fyrd. Have every thegn and ealdorman bring his spear-men to a gathering place of your choosing. We are to make for the Weatende Stræt in the west and there we will stop Penda once and for all. Oswiu, you will ride with all haste to Rheged, to Rhoedd mab Rhun mab Urien, and you will call upon his oath to lend us his fighting men."

Beobrand watched the sudden change in the king's demeanour with awe. It was easy when he spoke so friendly to him, as to an equal, but Oswald was a great man.

Oswald turned his attention back to Beobrand.

"And you, brave Beobrand, I have something for you to do also."

"Lord, I am your man. I will do what needs to be done."

"I know," Oswald said, patting Beobrand's arm. Ever since the battle at Tatecastre, when Beobrand had saved the day by donning Oswald's helm, the king had treated Beobrand with great affection. Not only had he showered him with gifts, but it was as though the king almost looked upon Beobrand as one of his brothers. It embarrassed Beobrand and filled him with pride in equal measure.

He was sure that the king's favour merely antagonised Oswiu further, making him dislike Beobrand more than he already did. Oswiu watched the two men now over the rim of his cup, his eyes deep, his emotions hidden.

"It is time," said Oswald, seemingly oblivious of his brother, "to call in other oaths and favours, for I feel we will need all the aid we can muster if we are to defeat Penda."

"Lord?"

"The time has come, Beobrand, for you to visit your son."

Chapter 5

"Cynan," the voice hissed, "wake up." A hand roughly shook his shoulder and Cynan opened his eyes, groaning. He felt as though he had only just wrapped himself in his cloak by the fire. Surely he had not slept enough to be woken yet. All around him, figures were stirring in the gloom. It was not yet dawn. Cynan sat up, clutching his cloak around his shoulders against the predawn chill. His breath steamed in the air.

"By the gods, Bearn. What is it that cannot wait till dawn?" His head was still clouded with sleep, but they were far into Northumbria. He couldn't imagine they might be under attack. Maybe there were brigands, lordless men who lived in these hills and had decided to slink down into the camp, drawn by the light of the campfire. Perhaps they had watched them during the day and had seen their precious cargo.

"Sulis has gone," Bearn said.

"What?" Cynan was suddenly fully awake. Beobrand had given him just one command – get the women to Ubbanford. Was he truly going to fail such a simple task? He stood, peering into the shadows surrounding the camp, as if he might be able to see the woman where Bearn and the others had failed. Sulis was the Mercian who had been riding with him. The other women had told them her name. It was her child that Fordraed had tortured and killed. She had ridden these last three days in silence, barely eating and not responding to the Northumbrians or the other women. It was as though her body walked and functioned, but her soul had died when Fordraed had taken her son's life. Cynan had ceased attempting to speak to her, but he had grown accustomed to her warm body pressed against his back as his mount carried them northwards.

"Where could she have gone?" he asked.

Bearn shrugged.

Cynan cursed.

They were far from any settlement and days' travel from Mercia. He conjured in his mind the land that he remembered from when they had set up camp. A dense forest lay to the east and north. To the west, the land rose into hills and moors, dotted with trees and outcrops of rock. Cynan looked up at the sky and saw light in the east.

"How long has she been gone?" he snapped.

Again, Bearn shrugged and held up his hands.

"By Christ's bones, man," Cynan spat. "Do you know nothing?"

He drew in a deep breath of the cool morning air, forcing himself to calm.

"Very well, as soon as it is light, I will try to find her tracks. I'll follow her and bring her back. The rest of you, strike camp and continue north. I will catch up with you. And, Bearn," he said, the jagged edge of ice entering his tone, "do not lose another one."

Cynan was not the best tracker in Beobrand's gesithas, but he was able to follow the tracks of a woman who had traipsed through knee-high, dew-damp grass. As the sun had filled the cloudless sky with light, Cynan had walked the perimeter of the camp, looking for sign, while the men were saddling the horses and packing away their things. The thralls had remained huddled in their whispering group, watching him. Probably each plotting their own bid for freedom.

It had not taken long to find Sulis' tracks. The wet grass had been crushed by her passing, leaving a clear path that led towards the woodland in the east. Where she was hoping to go, he had no idea. Her home lay south and west.

He swung himself onto his mount's back. Around him, the rest of the men were ready to ride and were helping to lift the women onto the saddles. None of them seemed prepared to attempt an escape, but he had warned Bearn again to be careful.

"I will find you on the road north," Cynan said, touching his heels to his horse's sides and trotting eastward, into the bright summer sun.

He followed the tracks all the way to the edge of the woods. Sulis had walked as straight as a spear-throw, never once deviating from her path. Wherever her final destination, she seemed set on reaching the trees as quickly as possible. She probably wanted to be within the shelter of the trees before light. Mayhap she hoped she could hide from pursuit in the shadows. Well, she could hide, but she would not remain hidden for long.

Cynan dismounted. He would need to lead his horse under the tree canopy. There was no trail or path here, and the low branches would impede his progress if he rode. Besides, the sign would not be as clear, without the furrow she had cut through the long grass.

The horse nickered quietly and lay its ears against its head as they walked into the quiet cool shade of the forest. The trees soaked up the light and warmth of the day. The jangle of the horse's harness and the clump of its hooves on the loam were loud in the stillness beneath the leaves. Cynan led the horse further into the dappled darkness. The signs of Sulis' passing were still clear. She had snapped twigs, leaving the pale, fresh wood exposed, and trampled the bracken that grew thick around the base of the oak, hazel, elm and ash. The forest was eerie. Oppressive and still, as if it was holding its breath. Or perhaps it was waiting for him. Suddenly, he became sure that someone was watching him. He shuddered and dropped his hand to the seax he wore at his belt. The seax Acennan and Beobrand had given him the first time he had met them, all those years before in Mercia.

His hand fell on empty air.

He looked down and cursed. The seax was gone. Gods, how had he been so stupid? Sulis may have been quiet and still, easy to deal with, but she was yet alive and a prisoner. A thrall. He had all but stopped thinking about her as a woman with a mind, she had just become a burden to place on his saddle; a warm body that pushed against his back. But now he recalled how the day before he had been surprised when she had wrapped her arms around him. It had not been unpleasant, and he had been snoozing as they rode. He cursed himself for a fool. She must have been planning her escape and taken the chance to steal his seax.

He loved that weapon. It had become a symbol of his freedom. It reminded him of who he had been before meeting Beobrand beside that midden outside Grimbold's hall. Thralls were not permitted to carry blades, and yet Beobrand had given him that fine seax, with its garnet inlay and golden adornments, and in that act, a spark within Cynan had been fanned into life. He would be a thrall no longer. He would be a great warrior and he would carve his own destiny. It had not been his wyrd to be beaten and abused at the hands of Grimbold's household. No, his wyrd was that of a warrior of legend. A free man. And he had been free ever since.

He must find Sulis now. It would be bad enough to have to admit to Beobrand that he had lost one of the women, but he could not bear the thought of losing that seax.

Cynan paused, breathing silently through his mouth and listening.

Silence.

His horse snorted and scraped a hoof against the soft leaf-mould of the forest floor. Cynan absently stroked its neck, quietening the beast. He closed his eyes for a moment and strained his ears for any sound. There was no birdsong. No buzz of insects. The day was still. No breeze rustled the leaves above him. Opening his eyes, he spat and continued into the hush of the forest. Wary now, half-expecting an ambush, he walked with one hand on the hilt of the sword that hung at his belt, the other on the horse's reins. The path was still easy to follow. Bright heartwood where a branch had been snapped by Sulis' clumsy progress. Flattened bracken. There ahead something caught his attention. Reaching out he pulled a thread from the bark of a gnarled hazel. He held it up to catch a shaft of light that sliced through the foliage. It had a sandy yellow hue. The colour of Sulis' peplos.

A sudden cackling cry made him start. Looking up at the sound he spied the white-and-black of a magpie. The bird stared down and scolded the interloper in its domain. Cynan let out a long breath. Gods, but he was wound as taut as a bow string. The forest was warming up now in the light of day. A trickle of sweat slid down his neck. He shuddered.

He wiped the moisture from his brow with his sleeve. She can't have gone far. But he listened again and heard no sound of movement in the forest. Perhaps she was far ahead of him. He cursed silently, as much at his own foolishness as at his fear of the strange atmosphere of the wood.

There was light ahead. A glade where a fallen tree had created a clearing. Was that a splash of yellow? He edged closer to the light and saw that on the other side of the clearing sat Sulis. Her back was propped against the bole of an old ash. She was unmoving.

The horse snorted and pulled back, shying from the glade. Cynan looped the reins around a low branch and left the mount. There was something wrong here. For a moment he believed that Sulis was sleeping, but then he saw that her peplos was stained red. Her skin was as grey as ash.

"Sulis?" he said, his voice hesitant and timid, and yet loud in the still of the forest.

She did not move.

He drew his sword and stepped into the clearing. His eyes flicking from the still form of the thrall to each of the trees around the glade. All was still. There was no sign of an enemy. But who had done this? Sulis' assailant could not be far, the blood that soaked into her dress was fresh. And then his stomach twisted as he understood what had happened here.

In Sulis' lap lay his seax, its fine blade besmeared with her death-dew. Her hands and wrists were covered in her lifeblood.

Gods, she had done this herself.

His heart clenched. Her grief must have been consuming her. Her life had been shattered when Fordraed rode his men into her settlement. She had lost everything except for her life. He knew what it was to be a thrall, to have no control over your destiny. But he had never been able to recall his family from before. He had been taken as a child and had only ever looked to the future, to the day he would be free.

It seemed Sulis had seen the only way to freedom was in death.

Cynan felt tears sting his eyes. He stared at Sulis' fragile form. If only he had watched her more carefully. If he had not allowed her to take his blade she would yet live. Guilt stabbed him as surely as if had drawn the sharp steel of his seax across her wrists. A terrible tiredness fell over him, like a heavy sodden blanket.

Sulis stirred. Letting out a whimpering moan, she shifted, her head slumping forward, chin resting on her chest.

His weariness fled and he rushed forward, dropping his sword on the earth beside her and catching her frail body as she slid to the side.

"I am here," he said, "I am here." He took up his bloodied seax and used it to cut strips of cloth from her dress. All the while he babbled. "I've got you, Sulis. You have nothing to fear now. I will save you." He bound her wounds tightly. They did not seem too deep. Perhaps she might live. He took in the amount of blood she had lost and the pallor of her skin, and he heard the desperation in his voice as he spoke inane promises to this young woman.

He cuffed the tears from his eyes, smudging blood on his cheek.

Cursing, he lifted her from where she lay and carried her to the horse. Angrily, he lashed her to the saddle with the cords he had used previously to tie her hands. All the while he grumbled and spat, swallowing the bitter ire that threatened to engulf him. He worked quickly, pulling the knots savagely tight and cursing under his breath, not stopping to wonder why he was so full of rage, or what it was that angered him so.

Chapter 6

War was in the air like the stench of rotting meat on a bitter breeze. There was no time to waste. Riders had already galloped out of Eoferwic in all directions to summon the Northumbrian spear-men to arms. Oswald had called the fyrd to gather and it would not be long before he took his retinue, his comitatus of hearth-warriors, to join with the ceorls and peasant fighters who would bring their spears to the warhost.

As the messengers assembled and mounted their fast horses that morning, Beobrand had asked Derian which man rode north to Berewic and the Tuidi valley. The bearded warmaster pointed to a slender, youthful man who was fussing with his horse's saddlebags.

"That's him. Rilberht has family near Gefrin, so knows the lands thereabout."

Beobrand had nodded his thanks and strode over to the man. Rilberht swung up onto his horse's back as Beobrand reached him.

"Hold a moment, Rilberht," Beobrand said. "I would have you take a message to my people in Ubbanford."

The man glanced down at Beobrand, an angry retort forming on his lips. The words died in a sighing breath as he saw who addressed him. Beobrand was well-known. Songs of his exploits were sung in mead halls throughout the land and his battle-skill was legendary. As was his temper.

"What message, lord?" he asked, swallowing.

"Tell my steward, Bassus, that I am joining the fyrd. That he is to leave enough men as needed to protect my lands and then to send all other spear-men to the service of our king."

Rilberht nodded.

"Is that all?"

Beobrand hesitated for a moment and then said, "Tell the lady of my hall that I am well."

When he had left Ubbanford, Reaghan had been angry with him. He wasn't certain why, but of late she was not often pleased with his company it seemed. If only things were as they had been when Octa had yet been a babe. But the years had gone by, and somehow, a distance had grown between Beobrand and Reaghan.

Shortly after the riders had clattered out through the crumbling gates of Eoferwic, Beobrand led Bera out of the stable. The beast rolled its eyes at being saddled, as if it begrudged not being given time to rest after its recent exertions. Acennan and the rest of Beobrand's gesithas were readying their horses and securing hastily packed provisions. They were grim-faced, uncertain of what the future held. They knew that battle was brewing, but they would not be riding west towards the assembling Mercian host. No, they were to ride south once more. South into Mercia.

"Lord Beobrand," a small voice said.

Beobrand turned and saw Cyneburg, as radiant as an autumn dawn. Her overdress and braided belt shimmered in the sunlight, and visible beneath her silken wimple, strands of her hair gleamed like gold. She was out of place here, surrounded by hulking warriors in battle-harness and horses stamping and snorting steam in the early morning. The two guards looked nervous, as if they feared one of the mounted warriors might trample their queen. There was no sign of Cyneburg's gemæcce or of Œthelwald.

"May I speak with you before you leave?" she said.

Beobrand sighed. Handing his reins to Dreogan, he nodded and led Cyneburg away from the horsemen. She gestured for her guards to keep a discrete distance.

"Speak quickly, my queen, for I cannot tarry."

"My husband has sent you to Snodengaham." Her eyes sparkled.

Beobrand said nothing.

"I trust you will find your son well," Cyneburg said.

"I have heard no bad tidings from Eowa," Beobrand said. At the sound of the name, the queen started as if she had been stung by a bee. Gods, how he wished she would not burden him, but she was his queen. And she was so beautiful. Whenever he saw her he was reminded of Sunniva and his heart ached. He recalled the mad love between Eowa and Cyneburg. A love that had threatened to bring war. It seemed the queen still felt the same passion for the atheling of Mercia and Beobrand felt a stab of jealousy. He cleared his throat against the lump there. "I am sure Octa is well."

"Would you—" she began, hesitant and tremulous.

"Do not ask me to bear a message," Beobrand interrupted. He could not face the duplicity. "Oswald has my oath. I am his man." She recoiled, as if he had slapped her. Tears brimmed in her eyes. She looked away, perhaps watching the men and the horses, perhaps just wishing to hide her anguish from him. At last she gave the smallest of nods.

"Very well, Beobrand. I will not ask this of you. But should he enquire, tell him I am well." Her voice shrank and drifted so that he struggled to hear the words. "Yes, tell him I am as well as I am able to be."

"And if he does not ask?" Beobrand said, immediately regretting the question.

Cyneburg stared at him, her eyes liquid and shining.

"You are cruel, Beobrand," she said, before turning and leaving the courtyard without looking back.

Beobrand watched her slender form and the sway of her hips beneath her dress. He clenched his jaw. She was right. But if he was cruel, it was his envy that made him so. For he had once found an all-consuming love and then had it snatched from his grasp.

Cynan made slow progress. He walked, leading the horse as Sulis lolled in the saddle, slipping in and out of consciousness. They could not travel fast, even if he had been able to ride. To go at anything more than a walk would surely kill the woman. As it was, he was uncertain she would live. Her skin was pale and clammy to the touch and she murmured and mumbled nonsense. At times she would cry out, whimpering from some horror only she could see. Cynan gripped the leather of the reins so tightly that his hands cramped. He longed to be rid of this burden. Just as Sulis had longed to be rid of her grief, he supposed. He could sense the rest of his small band riding ever further from them. He wished he could mount up and gallop after them, but instead he swallowed his anxiety and led the horse in a slow, ponderous walk.

The day was warm. He halted for a moment and drank from the waterskin he carried. Then, gently, he dribbled some of the warm liquid onto Sulis' cracked lips. The water trickled down her chin and onto her blood-stained peplos, but he thought that perhaps some went into her mouth. She had lost a lot of blood and would need to drink if she had any chance of survival.

The sun was high in the cloudless sky. A movement caught Cynan's attention some way ahead. Squinting against the glare, he saw wood pigeons flap into the air. Cursing under his breath, his hand went to the seax that he had cleaned and replaced in its sheath. There were figures in the distance. A group of men in the shade of some oaks that grew close to the road.

How many were there? He peered, trying to make out details, but they were yet some way off. He could see no horses, but there were more men than he could fight on his own. Perhaps a dozen. Should it come to a fight, he could leap onto the horse and ride. Even with two riders, he was sure his steed would be able to outrun men on foot. But what of Sulis? If he rode hard, he was certain she would lose her fragile grip on life.

Cynan changed hands on the reins, freeing his right to draw his sword if needed. He continued forward warily.

As they got closer, an unusual chanting reached him. His horse nickered nervously. He could see more clearly now. There were ten men all dressed in long robes. They were standing in a circle beneath the oaks and singing. The sounds drifted to Cynan. The words of their songs meant nothing to him, but he let out a sigh of relief. For he had heard similar chants many times before. He cared little for the preachings of the Christ followers, but he knew they would offer him no harm.

Some of the tension left him and he released his grip on his sword. Stepping forward with more purpose, he approached the monks. As he reached them, they finished their song and all turned to him. One stepped forward.

He was a young man, with keen eyes. His hair, like all of his companions, was worn long at the back, but shaved from the forehead to the crown of his head.

"Well met, Cynan," the monk said, his gaze flicking to the senseless form on the horse. "May the Lord's blessings be upon you. We were expecting you."

They rode with haste southward. Beobrand's face was set as they passed fields of green flowering barley, waving and rippling in the warm summer breeze. He ignored the inquisitive faces of thralls and ceorls, and when his gesithas looked in his direction, they saw their lord in total control. They may have been nervous, worried about riding into Mercia, but Beobrand knew no fear. They had followed him into battle and seen him sweep all enemies before him. He was their hlaford. Their ring-giving lord. The greatest warlord in Northumbria, perhaps in all of Albion, and they were proud to serve him. Where he led, they would follow without question.

Behind his clenched jaw and cool blue eyes, Beobrand's head thronged with dark thoughts. Concerns he could not share with his men. Worries that he alone would dwell on until he knew the truth. He could not burden the men with his anxiety. It was ever thus for a leader of men. He knew this, but it did not make it easy.

Acennan rode close to Beobrand and glanced at his friend's impassive face.

"What troubles you?" he asked, keeping his tone quiet enough so only Beobrand would hear.

Beobrand smiled. Was it so easy for Acennan to see his thoughts?

"You would have a shorter answer if you asked me what does not trouble me."

Acennan nodded and they rode on a while in silence. The men behind them pulled back a few paces, instinctively sensing that the two men at the head of the column did not wish to be overheard.

"Do you worry about Octa?" Acennan asked. "I don't know how I would feel if Athulf were sent away to be fostered so far from Stagga. I am sure Eadgyth would not allow it. She is already so far from her kin in Wessex. To send our son away would break her heart."

Beobrand frowned. He had not spoken to Acennan about his feelings, or those of Reaghan. But her screaming and weeping were still fresh in his memory. Octa may not have been her son, but she loved him as if he were of her blood. And no matter how many times Beobrand had lain with Reaghan, she had never borne him another child.

She had taken the news of Octa's leaving very hard.

"Eowa is a worthy man," Beobrand said. "I am sure he will have treated Octa as one of his own children. Octa will be well."

Acennan glanced at Beobrand, perhaps gauging his mood.

"Still, it has been months since you saw him," he said, "and it is a long ride to Snodengaham. It would have been kinder to foster the boy in Bernicia. Closer to Ubbanford."

"Kindness was not a consideration, I feel," snapped Beobrand. His anger at the order to send his son away to be fostered by Eowa, atheling of Mercia, was still fresh even after all these months. By having Octa become part of Eowa's household, Oswald had seen a way to relay messages directly to Penda's brother and ruler of the northern marches of Mercia. Beobrand had protested, but Oswald had been adamant.

Reaghan had been distraught. She had cried for days, raging against Beobrand.

"You must not do this thing," she had yelled, tears streaking her face. "He is your only son. Your only blood kin. It is too dangerous."

"Do you think I don't know of the dangers?" Beobrand had bellowed, his ire bubbling over. He had gripped the edge of the table in the hall so tightly he had believed the stout wood might splinter. But he did not trust himself not to raise his fists to Reaghan, if he released his grasp of the board. Could she not see that he too was terrified at the prospect of losing his son, the last reminder of his wife, Sunniva? Reaghan had bleated on as if Octa were more hers than his, and Beobrand had been consumed with rage. He knew what he was capable of. He had struck women before. Even killed women. But he had never raised his hand to Reaghan, and he had vowed he never would. As he now knew, he truly was not his father's son.

"Then why do you allow this to happen?" she had sobbed.

"I have no choice!" he had screamed and, unable to contain his anger any longer, he'd turned his back on Reaghan, picked up one of the heavy oak benches, and flung it across the hall. It had clattered into trestles and boards that were stacked against the wall. The sudden violence and noise had silenced Reaghan.

"I have no choice," Beobrand had repeated, his voice catching in his throat. "The king has willed it, and I am his oath-sworn thegn. I must obey."

Reaghan had questioned his decision no further, but from that day forth she wore a melancholic sadness about her like a cloak.

Acennan left Beobrand to his thoughts for a time and they rode on in silence.

The breeze felt good on Beobrand's face. The day was hot. There was a glint of sun on water ahead. They would halt there for a time and water the horses. They had no replacement mounts, so they must keep these animals hale.

"Do you think those Mercians told Fordraed the truth?" asked Acennan after a time.

Beobrand thought for a moment.

"I'm not sure, but it has the ring of truth to it," he said eventually.

"Still, it is a lot to gamble on one throw of the dice."

"Aye, it is. But what else could Oswald do? If Penda has been calling his men to arms for weeks, we cannot merely wait to see what happens."

Acennan nodded. They were near the water now. It was a broad river, its winding path flanked by willows and alder. Close to the water's edge, where the crumbling road forded the river, there was a small hut. A man stepped out of the building. He was hunched, but broad-shouldered. He held a huge hound on a short leash at his side. The wire-haired dog eyed the band of riders balefully, but made no sound. The man blinked in the sunlight, evidently surprised to see so many armed men at his door.

"Would you be wanting to cross the Dyvene and keep your feet dry, lord?" he asked, not meeting Beobrand's gaze, instead looking at the ground somewhere in front of him.

There was a small boat tied to a wooden jetty. The timber of the jetty was moss-covered and mouldering, but the boat looked sound. Beobrand gave the river an appraising look. It had not rained in days and the water seemed shallow enough for them to ride across.

"I think not, boatman, but I would know what your eyes have seen these past weeks."

The man looked up and his eyes twinkled in the summer sun.

"I have seen many things," he said, his voice sly.

"Armed men? Warriors? Riders?"

"How much is this worth to you, lord? A man needs to eat."

Beobrand took a hunk of hack silver from his pouch, weighed it in his hand for the man to see. It was as long and wide as his finger. The jetty-man's eyes widened. Beobrand tossed him the silver. It flashed in the air like a fish darting through clear water. The man caught it.

"I have seen no warriors, lord, not for these past weeks. Been very quiet it has. And the river's been low since Eostremonath. No call for my boat when the river is low." He held the piece of silver close to his face and sunlight glimmered reflections on his dirt-seamed cheeks. "This will go a long way, lord, and I thank'ee."

The men let their horses drink from the slow-flowing river and filled their flasks. Beobrand and Acennan watched as the men rode into the water, sending up great sheets of glistening spray. Even at the deepest point the water did not reach the horses' bellies.

When all of his gesithas had reached the southern bank, Beobrand nodded to the old man who had stood watching the proceedings intently. The man offered him a gap-toothed grin and a wave. Beobrand touched his heels to Bera's flanks and trotted into the water.

The cold water splashed his legs and his hands and face. It felt good after the dusty heat of the road. When they were halfway across, Acennan turned to him and asked the question that had most troubled Beobrand since they had left Eoferwic.

"And what if Eowa has sided with Penda? What if he plans to join his brother in war against Oswald?"

Beobrand wiped the water from his face.

"Well, if that is so, then I fear I am leading us all into the wolf's maw."

Chapter 7

Coenred dipped the cloth into the water and wiped the grime from the woman's face. She was so pale and still, she could have been mistaken for dead. But heat radiated from her like a forge. They had lifted her carefully down from Cynan's horse and laid her on a blanket in the shadow of one of the great oaks. Cynan had wished to press on northward, but Coenred had flatly refused.

"If you ride on, she will die. Is that what you want?"

Cynan had looked abashed and offered a small shake of his head.

"How is it you are here?" Cynan had asked after Coenred had given instructions to one of the other monks to light a fire and boil water.

"We have been spreading the word of our Lord Jesus to the people of these parts. There is a new church at Inhrypum and there is always much work to do there."

Cynan had nodded absently, but Coenred had seen he did not truly comprehend.

"We give help to those in need," Coenred had offered. "In whatever way they need. We might help in the fields, if a man is too sick to plough or sow. We can help repair fences and make furniture. We are strong and some of us have skills that can be put to good use." He'd checked the temperature of the water in the pot over the fire. It had not yet been hot enough. "Have you any spare clothing in your saddlebags?" he'd asked Cynan.

"I have a kirtle."

"Fetch it, please." Cynan had looked bemused, but had gone to his horse and brought back the old kirtle that had been bundled in the bottom of his bag.

Coenred sniffed it and held it up to the light.

"Linen. Good," he'd said. "Pass me your knife. I trust it is sharp."

Cynan had handed him his knife and Coenred had proceeded to cut the fabric into strips. He had placed the strips into the water.

Cynan had looked as though he was going to say something, but then thought better of it.

"One of the other ways we help our flock," Coenred had said, using a stick to stir the water and linen strips in the pot, "is to attend them when they are ill or injured. Abbot Aidan has a true gift for healing. God acts through him and I have seen wondrous feats performed by his hands. My knowledge is nothing compared to that of the abbot, but he has taught me much, and I pray fervently for those I treat."

Once the water had boiled for some time, Coenred had removed a strip of cloth and used it to clean the wounds on Sulis' wrists. First, he'd gently removed the bandages Cynan had tied and threw them onto the fire. He'd bent down close to the woman's arms and smelt her wounds. There was no stink of corruption. He'd then taken more boiled strips and bandaged her wrists tightly once again.

"With the grace of God, she might live," he'd said, "but she has lost much blood. We will make camp here tonight." One of the older monks, Comdhan, had nodded and signalled to the others to begin preparing the camp, even though sunset was still a long way off. For much of the day, they observed the rule of silence, but Coenred had been nominated as the monks' voice.

"You seem to have a talent for talking," Abbot Aidan had said to him with a twinkle in his eye when they had set out from Lindisfarena.

The woman stirred, groaning quietly, perhaps from some nightmare, or from pain. Coenred smoothed her hair away from her face. Despite the dirt and blood on her clothes, he could see she had fine features. Her cheekbones were perhaps too prominent, her lips too thin, but as he stroked her hair and wiped her face, he could not ignore the intimacy he felt with this stranger. The touch of her skin. The softness of her hair. He suppressed a shudder. Would the devil ever let him be free of such thoughts? He only wished to do the Lord's work, but whenever he was near a pretty girl his body responded to seeds of desire sown by the devil into his soul.

"Deliver me from temptation, Lord," he whispered in Latin.

"You said you were expecting me," said Cynan, breaking Coenred's reverie.

Coenred dragged his gaze away from the woman's pallid face.

"Yes. Bearn and the others of your band passed us this morning. They said you would follow with another woman. One who'd escaped."

Cynan looked down at Sulis. She lay still now, and it seemed perhaps a little colour had returned to her cheeks. There was something in Cynan's gaze. Some hidden emotion that caused Coenred to feel a pang of jealousy.

"What is this woman to you?" he asked, keeping his tone flat.

"Just a thrall," replied Cynan, but his eyes lingered on her face for several heartbeats before he looked away. "Just a thrall. I am glad we found you. It was lucky for us that we did."

Coenred stood abruptly, keen to be away from this injured woman whom the devil would use to beguile and tempt him.

"No," he said. "It was not luck that brought us together. It was Christ's will."

He walked away, leaving Cynan staring after him.

Chapter 8

As they rode south, the sky grew muddled with clouds. It remained dry, but the air became dense and thick. Beobrand wondered whether there would be a storm, but none came.

They rode on unimpeded into Mercia until they were less than a day's travel from their destination. Beobrand and his band of gesithas crested a small hill and saw in the valley below a group of riders cantering towards them. Beobrand raised his hand and reined in Bera. His men halted behind him on the brow of the rise. The sun was high overhead and its glare glinted from the harness, weapons and armour of the dozen men who rode up the hill to meet them. These men of Mercia bore spears, but most of their helms were tied to their saddles, their shields slung from their backs.

"Looks like they do not mean to attack," whispered Acennan.

Beobrand said nothing, but nodded. He forced himself to appear at ease. The men who approached were not ready for battle. Besides, his own band, depleted as it was, numbered but thirteen men, so any open fight between the two groups would be hard-won, with no sure victor.

He watched intently as the warriors' steeds carried them lumbering up the slope. Squinting against the sun-sparkle from the burnished iron and steel, Beobrand scanned the men's faces.

They slowed and came to a halt less than a spear's throw from where Beobrand waited with his men. The horses' hooves threw up a cloud of dust in the sultry afternoon air.

Beobrand nudged Bera forward, lifting his right hand in greeting. Without comment, Acennan joined him, easing his own horse out in front of the men.

"Scur," Beobrand said, having recognised one of Eowa's hearth-warriors who rode at the head of the group. "Well met. I trust your lord is well."

Scur glowered. Beobrand knew the man still blamed him for Eowa's treatment at the hands of Oswald and Oswiu. Beobrand clenched his jaw, trying to push from his mind the memories of that dark winter's night in Din Eidyn. That was long ago, and Eowa had told Beobrand that he did not hold him responsible. To judge from the grim expression of Scur, Eowa's gesithas were not so forgiving.

Scur leaned from his saddle, hawked and spat a great gobbet of phlegm onto the path.

"My lord Eowa is as well as ever," he said, his voice as hard and cold as iron. He stared at Beobrand, unblinking.

The few times he had seen Scur, it was ever thus. Eowa's man would attempt to kindle the flame of Beobrand's infamous anger. He longed for Beobrand to break the peace that had been agreed between Eowa and Oswald. Scur's fury had simmered all these years and he would like nothing more than for Beobrand to respond. But Beobrand knew he could not allow himself to be goaded.

He took a slow deep breath.

"I rejoice to hear of Eowa's health, Scur," he said, his tone flat and calm. "What of his good wife, the lady Cynethryth? And Osmod and Alweo?"

Scur scowled, as if trying to think of some response that might cause offence without provoking his lord's ire when later he would hear of it. Apparently, he could think of none, for, after a frowning pause, he said simply, "They are all well."

"And my son?"

"Your brat is as hale as a pig in shit," he said, sneering.

Beobrand gripped his reins tightly. Gods, but he wished he could just charge this man from his horse and fight him, here and now in the dust in front of the men. But Beobrand did not move.

"Well, I suppose you would know what it feels like to be a swine," he said. Then, quickly, before Scur could respond, "I must see your lord, Eowa, immediately. There is no time for this foolishness, much as I would love to trade insults with you until the sun sets."

Scur loured for a long moment, first at Beobrand, then passing his gaze over the dust-grimed riders behind the Northumbrian thegn. The silence became awkward before Scur eventually nodded.

"Follow us. We will lead you back to Snodengaham."

Eowa's gesithas turned their mounts at Scur's order. Beobrand dug his heels into Bera's sides and rode quickly to Scur's side before he could wheel his horse around. Beobrand's left hand lashed out and grabbed the horse's bridle. Scur instantly grasped at Beobrand's wrist, attempting to dislodge his grip. But Beobrand's arm did not move, his half-hand remained clutched on the leather of the horse's harness. His eyes flashed with a cold fire.

"Do not forget who I am, Scur," he said, his voice barely more than a whisper. "I am in haste, and I respect your lord. But know this. I am Beobrand of Ubbanford and you would do well to recall all the tales of my battles. I beat you and your lord once before in the mud by the Afen and I let you both live then. But I tire of your taunting and I have slain men for less. Eowa's man or no, if you continue to cross me, I will cut out your heart and feed it to the ravens."

Scur opened his mouth to speak, then closed it again, with no word uttered.

Beobrand shoved Scur's horse's head away and rode past him towards Snodengaham.

Chapter 9

"Beobrand," said Eowa in a voice filled with warmth, "this is an unexpected pleasure."

Beobrand stood from where he had been sitting by the fire. It was not cold, but he enjoyed watching the flames flicker and dance in the gathering darkness of the hall. Around them thralls and servants were preparing the boards for the evening meal. Beobrand had contented himself with sipping the ale he had been given on arrival at Eowa's hall and allowing the normal activities of life to wash over him. Acennan, sensing his mood, had not offered much in the way of conversation. Beobrand's mind had been wandering, thinking of Ubbanford. They would be preparing food there too. He thought fleetingly of Reaghan. He missed her. But gods, she vexed him with her moods. He was tired. He felt as though he had been in the saddle for months, and he was not a gifted horseman.

His back ached as he stood to meet Eowa. The tall atheling of Mercia strode towards him, a broad smile shining from his dark beard. There was a conspicuous dark gap in the fine line of teeth in Eowa's grin. Beobrand remembered when the Mercian lord had spat the tooth out along with a mouthful of blood onto a hard, earthen floor. The firelight caught the scars on Eowa's cheeks and nose. A pang of guilt stabbed Beobrand. Eowa's full beard went someway to hiding the puckered skin, but both sides of the man's nose bore the jagged reminder of that snow-swept night in the land of the Picts, where, in a cold, dank storeroom, Beobrand had helped to beat and disfigure him.

Eowa's smiled broadened. He reached out his right hand and Beobrand grasped his wrist, forearm to forearm.

"Always so glum, Beobrand," Eowa said. "Do you never smile?"

Beobrand frowned.

"I seldom see a reason to," replied Beobrand, which only made Eowa laugh and slap him on the back.

That Eowa had never voiced any anger or resentment at the treatment he had received at the hands of Beobrand, Derian and Oswiu, merely served to make Beobrand feel all the more guilty. If only he had raged and raved at Beobrand when they had met again after that wyrd-laden night when Oswald had discovered the truth and forced Eowa to swear allegiance to the king of Northumbria. But Eowa had offered Beobrand no recriminations, and Beobrand knew he never would. Eowa was a man of honour, and he believed he had deserved the punishment meted out to him.

Eowa stared him in the eye for a moment, before lowering his tone.

"But I see you are more solemn than normal, my friend." Eowa took in his dust-streaked skin and travel-stained clothes. "And you have ridden hard. I take it you have not merely come to see Octa."

Beobrand nodded, glad that Eowa had led the conversation straight to the point of his visit.

"The time has come—" he said, but Eowa cut him off with a raised hand.

"I would hear your tidings, Beobrand," he said, glancing around the hall furtively at the thralls and bondsmen, the warriors lounging on the benches. "But," he said, his voice now a whisper, "I would not have your words overheard. Let us walk outside awhile. The food is not yet ready, and we can be sure we speak in private there."

Beobrand felt a sliver of unease, but gave a nod by way of answer and drained his cup of ale. Setting it down on the board, he followed Eowa from the hall and into the twilit land beyond. Acennan rose, but Beobrand shook his head and signalled for him to remain in the hall.

Outside, the air was clear and still warm. The jumble of clouds were painted with vivid reds and pinks as though the sun was a forge, heating the clouds until they could be hammered by the gods. Beobrand stretched his back, letting out a groan as it made a series of popping sounds.

"You sound like an old man," Eowa said, smiling.

Beobrand grimaced.

"After all that time in the saddle, I feel like a greybeard."

"We can find somewhere to sit, if you would like."

Beobrand snorted.

"I am not old yet, Eowa. Besides, I have been sitting all day on the back of my beast of a mount. I can stand a while."

They walked away from the hall and the buildings that surrounded it. Men and women nodded respectfully to Eowa as they passed. The two men walked in companionable silence for a time, through meadows where downy birch grew along the path's edge. Looking up at the darkening sky, Beobrand saw the flitting shapes of bats diving and wheeling as they fed on the midges and moths.

Some way behind them, he noticed four men. They carried shields and long scabbards hung from their belts. Beobrand tensed, uneasy. They had walked some way from the hall and he had not brought Hrunting with him. He had believed them safe here, in Eowa's lands. Stupid. His hand dropped to the seax sheathed at his belt. It would have to do. Peering back into the dying light of the day he watched as the men slowly approached. He glanced at Eowa and saw the Mercian was unarmed. Gods, he knew Eowa to be a brave man and a skilled warrior, but they would be lucky to survive a fight against four swordsmen. Flicking his gaze back to the warriors, Beobrand's nervousness fled as quickly as it had come. He recognised two of them. They were Acennan and Fraomar. Of the other two, he now recognised one as Scur. Beobrand smiled at his own anxiety.

Eowa raised his eyebrows.

"It seems you do smile after all," he said, following Beobrand's gaze. Eowa offered a lopsided grin and a shrug. "I said I wished for privacy. This is the nearest thing to alone that an atheling is allowed. Scur has taken it upon himself to guard my person. He does worry so."

Beobrand frowned.

"My men also seem to fret," he said. "Though what they think might happen to us, I am not sure."

Eowa was suddenly serious.

"My men fear treachery."

In the distance, the reflection of the crimson glow of the sky turned the broad River Trent to blood.

"You know I would never cause you ill," said Beobrand. As soon as he had spoken, he felt the hollowness of his words.

Eowa said nothing for a moment. There was no need. The scars on his cheeks and nose spoke more loudly than any words.

"You are oath-sworn, Beobrand," Eowa said at last, his voice tinged with sadness. "As am I. Neither of us is free to make such promises."

Behind them, their silent guards followed at a distance.

For a long while they walked on in silence. The fire from the sun made Eowa's eyes glow.

"Now," Eowa said at last, "before we return to feast and drink, and for you to see how Octa has grown in the months since Geola, you must tell me what has brought you to my hall unannounced."

Beobrand did not wish to speak the words. It felt like a new betrayal. Eowa deserved better. But Eowa had known this day would come, ever since he had chosen to spirit away

Oswald's queen from Anwealda's hall one rain-washed night years before. Beobrand thought of the days of pursuit and the shieldwalls in the mud by the ford of the Afen. He saw anew the deathly pallid face of Athelstan, frozen in a roar of defiance as he had attempted to defend Cyneburg, the queen. Their queen. His queen. As sudden as the wind shifts direction in a spring storm, Beobrand was angry. He liked Eowa; considered him a friend now. But the Mercian had brought this on himself. Good men had died for his actions. It was time for him to pay their blood-price.

"You must answer the call of your oath-sworn lord," Beobrand said, his tone sharp.

Eowa sighed, as if he had known the words Beobrand would utter.

"What does Oswald want of me?"

"You are to summon your spear-men and bring your host to battle."

"Who are we to fight? Why call on me to pay my debt now?"

"We will join Oswald and Oswiu and we will face Penda and his allies."

"Penda marches? I have heard nothing…"

"We believe he is amassing a great host in the west. If we are right, he plans to strike northward from the west of his lands."

Eowa ceased walking and stared into the west. The sun had fallen below the horizon now, but the sky was as red as the fires of war. Despite Eowa's thick beard, Beobrand could see the muscles along his jaw tense and bulge.

"Do you…" Eowa hesitated. "Do you think Oswald would harm her, if I did not answer his call?"

Beobrand remembered how Cyneburg had sought him out as he left Eoferwic. The years had not dimmed the love between these two it seemed. It was a madness that time could not heal.

"I do not believe he would," he said, his voice soft now, unable to hold on to his anger at their actions. Would he not have done the same, if he were Eowa? "No," he said. "She is the mother of his son. She is a good queen. I think Oswald would not hurt her."

Eowa nodded.

"How does she fare? Is she well?"

Beobrand pictured Cyneburg's shimmering gold locks. Her slender form. Her sad eyes.

"She is well enough."

Eowa ran his fingers through his hair and let out a long breath.

"So, you will call your men to arms?" asked Beobrand. "You will march with Oswald to face Penda?"

"What else can I do?" Eowa looked Beobrand in the eye and offered him a twisted, sad smirk. "I gave my oath."

A man's word was everything. Beobrand understood this. The words of an oath for a warrior were links in a chain that bound him to his lord.

Beobrand nodded. Eowa was powerless in the face of the vow he had sworn to Oswald in Din Eidyn.

"And so it comes to this," Eowa said, his voice desolate. "I must bear arms against my brother."

"You will not be the first to stand against kinfolk." Beobrand thought of Hrunting's blade sliding into Hengist's throat. He could still feel the bristling of Hengist's beard against his hand after the sword had cut through flesh, sinew and bone. He had not known then that they were half-brothers. And none save Acennan knew the truth now. Hengist was long dead. But it seemed he would never be free of Hengist's shade. Beobrand placed a hand on Eowa's shoulder. "Many a man before you has slain his own brother."

Eowa shrugged off his touch and turned back the way they had walked. Back towards his hall. The men who had been following them halted, waiting for them to pass.

"That is true," Eowa called back to Beobrand over his shoulder. "But I would not be remembered as one of those men."

*

"This boar meat is tender," Eowa said in a loud voice to carry over the throng in the hall. "I had thought that such a grizzled old warrior would have been as tough as chewing belt leather."

Beobrand took a slice of the dripping meat from a serving thrall and placed it on his trencher.

"No meat tastes better than that which you have hunted and killed yourself," he said.

Eowa nodded.

"It is a shame you did not arrive yesterday, for that is when we hunted this monster of a beast. It was a savage animal. Gutted one of my favourite hounds before we managed to bring him down."

"Did you join the hunt?" Beobrand said in a quiet voice to the boy seated at his side. Octa's eyes were wide. He listened much and seldom spoke, unless asked a direct question. Beobrand felt awkward with his son. He wished they were closer, but he knew not how to speak to the child.

"No, father," Octa said. "I asked to, but the lady Cynethryth said I was too young."

Beobrand looked over at Eowa's wife. She was gazing directly at him, as if listening to his conversation with Octa, but he knew they were too distant and the hall was too noisy for that.

"Well," Beobrand said, cutting a strip of meat with his knife, "I suppose she's right. Hunting boar can be a dangerous business. If you had been there, it might have been you and not the hound that the beast had chosen to gut. But you will be old enough soon. You have grown since I saw you last. And your shoulders are wider." He offered Octa the piece of boar meat. The boy took a bite. "Well, what do you think?" asked Beobrand. "The crispy fat is the best part of a boar."

Octa smiled around the meat he chewed and nodded.

Beobrand shouted to Eowa over the hubbub of the feast.

"The meat is good. I would have liked to join you on the hunt."

He raised his drinking horn and Eowa returned the gesture.

"There will be other hunts," he said.

They both drank deeply. The ale was strong and richly flavoured. A heady brew. Beobrand watched Eowa where he sat with his two sons, Alweo and Osmod, at his side. Neither Eowa nor Beobrand had spoken on the return to the hall, but Beobrand had seen Eowa pull some of his hearth-warriors into a corner of the hall, where they had talked earnestly for some time. The warriors had all glanced in his direction, so Beobrand assumed Eowa had told them of his tidings.

By the gods he was tired. He wished for nothing more than to eat and drink his fill and then sleep comfortably beside the hearth fire. But Eowa had called a feast and Beobrand knew there would be no peace in the hall for a long while yet. He ate a piece of the boar. It was good. He had tasted finer, but after days in the saddle eating sparingly from the provisions they carried, it was a delicacy indeed. He closed his eyes and listened to the sounds of the hall. Men and women talked and laughed. Knives, cups and plates clattered on the boards. Two dogs growled and snapped at a morsel that had been dropped to the rushes. Beobrand swallowed the boar meat and took a deep breath of the air. It was heavy with smoke and redolent of the roasting boar. Beneath that he could make out the scent of wool and leather, the green, lively smell of the rushes that had been freshly cut and laid. The tang of ale…

"Father?" Octa's hesitant voice brought him back. "Are you well?" Beobrand opened his eyes and smiled at his son.

"I am fine." Yes, he was well, but his tiredness washed over him in waves. He had been drifting into sleep. The sounds and smells of the hall had soothed him. This was the atmosphere of safety and the warmth of home. He wondered when next he would know the peace of a safe hall after they left Snodengaham and travelled west.

"How are you finding living in Eowa's hall, son?" he asked, pulling himself upright and taking another bite of meat in an effort to shake the drowsiness from his head.

"Lord Eowa and Lady Cynethryth treat me well."

Beobrand glanced over at Eowa's two sons.

"And Osmod? And Alweo?"

Octa said nothing for a time.

"They do not treat me so well."

"You fight them?"

Octa looked down at his lap.

"Sometimes. But only when they say or do mean things."

Beobrand snorted and ruffled Octa's hair. His fair hair was long and soft under Beobrand's huge, rough hand.

"There comes a time when fighting is the only way," he said. "The secret is not to fight when you don't need to."

"But it is craven to run away," said Octa. "I am no coward. You never run away, do you?"

Beobrand felt a surge of love for his son. He had not seen him for months and the boy had changed so much in that time. He could not recall when they had exchanged so many words before.

"I know you are no craven," he said. "Neither am I. But sometimes a wise man needs to leave a battle so that he can return to face his enemies again. For there is nothing to be gained from dying quickly."

"How will I know when to fight and when to flee?"

"Ah, now that is the real question, Octa." Beobrand reached for the jug of ale, refilled his horn and then poured some into Octa's wooden cup. "You are my son and you and I are alike in many ways, I think. You, too, have a temper that can flare suddenly. And you do not back down when you are pushed. Use this when a fight finds you. Many men will ponder too much before entering a fray. Some would call them wise, but a quick decision can win the day. If you act with speed, you can oftentimes defeat your foe before he is even certain he wants to fight."

"And when should I run?"

"Well, I am not the best person to answer such things, but I pray that you are wiser than me. For I always attack. I do not run from a fight, it is not in my nature." Beobrand gazed into Octa's blue eyes. He saw much of himself looking back at him, but also there was much of his mother's beauty in the shape of his nose, his brow and his lips. "I wish your mother yet lived, Octa," he said, "for she would have counselled you with more thought."

"What would she have said, do you think?"

Beobrand thought for a moment.

"She would have told you never to seek out a fight, but not to shy away from one. Protect those who are weaker than you and be true to your word, for it is the most valuable thing you possess." Beobrand savoured the words he had just uttered, turning them around in his mind. "Yes, she would have said that, and I would have agreed with her."

There was a sudden commotion at the great doors of the hall. One of the door wards stepped into the hall and hammered the haft of his spear four times against one of the great oaken beams that supported the roof. The sound stilled the room and all eyes turned to the doorway.

Eowa rose, placing his hands on the board before him.

"What is this? Who seeks entry into my hall in the dark of night?"

The door ward spoke with a clear voice that carried around the hall.

"My lord," he said, "there is a man here who says he is a messenger. He says he has urgent news he must share with you, and you alone."

Eowa frowned.

"Who is this messenger? And who sends him?"

The warden turned and whispered a few words to the shadowed figure in the doorway who was being prevented from entering the hall by another of Eowa's guards.

"He says his name is Eumer. And he brings a message from your brother, Penda."

Chapter 10

Sulis muttered and cried out in the night. Sweat beaded her face and she shivered, despite Cynan placing his cloak and blanket over her and moving her close to the fire. He sat with her, unable to sleep, but unsure what he could do to help her. He tossed another branch on the small fire, watching as the sparks drifted into the night, like lost dreams. Coenred had returned to minister to Sulis several times during the warm afternoon as the shadows lengthened and the monks prepared food.

The holy men travelled light, with each carrying a meagre amount of vittles and utensils. But they were well-accustomed to outdoor living and they made the campsite more comfortable than Cynan had expected. The pottage they produced, as the sun dipped to the horizon, was simple, yet warm and filling. Cynan had nodded his thanks to the elderly monk who had proffered a steaming bowl to him. The man had nodded in reply, but had not spoken. The men's silence unnerved Cynan at first. He was used to the banter and conversation of warriors. But after sitting at Sulis' side all afternoon in the tranquillity of the Christ monks' camp, he understood how the calm allowed more time for thinking. For much of the day the only sounds, apart from those Sulis made in her troubled sleep, were birdsong and the whisper of the breeze through the leaves of the oak they were using for shelter. All the while Cynan had sat beside Sulis as she shook and whimpered. From time to time he found the stillness and inactivity too much and he would stand and pace around the campsite. Then he would feel foolish in the face of the silent Christ followers and return to sit and brood beside the young woman.

By Tiw's balls, he should be halfway to Ubbanford by now. Not sitting under a tree with a sickly woman who, even if she recovered, would as like as not kill herself at the first opportunity. He was a warrior, not a nursemaid. Many times he contemplated leaving Sulis with the monks and riding north. They would care for her and bring her to Ubbanford.

If she lived.

But then he would glance down at the pallid, sweat-drenched face and something would twist inside him. The feelings he had were not familiar to him. They riled him and he poked angrily at the fire. There was war coming. And his place was at his lord's side. Not tending to this woman. But he did not leave. Instead, he took up the cloth and tenderly wiped the sweat from Sulis' forehead.

At sunset, the monks had broken him out of his tangle of thoughts of impending war and frustration. They all stood and began to chant in their strange tongue. The trees were silent and still now. There was no breeze. The monks' voices soared into the quiet dusk. Theirs was a haunting sound. Cynan did not understand the words, but he could sense the power of the Christ magic in the rise and fall of the voices.

When they had concluded the ceremony, Coenred had come to Cynan and Sulis. He had touched her forehead and nodded.

"I hope Vespers did not disturb you," he'd said.

"No," Cynan had replied. "What did the chanting mean?"

"We prayed to God that when the blackness of night falls, our faith would not know such darkness, but that our faith should be a light in the dark."

"It was beautiful," Cynan had said, surprised at his own words and the truth in them.

Coenred had given a small nod and smiled.

"I am glad that you thought our voices gave glory to the Lord. It is all we seek to do. To honour Him and to spread the good word of His love."

Cynan had said nothing. He knew nought of the Christ god's love. He had seen little in his life to make him believe in love and goodness. But he could not deny that Coenred and these monks were doing their best to save Sulis.

"God's love is endless," Coenred had said. "He loves each and every one of us."

This talk of love made Cynan uncomfortable.

"Is she any better?" he'd asked, keen to move away from talk of gods and love.

"Raise her head," Coenred had said. Cynan had done as he was told and Coenred had picked up the water skin, dribbling a little liquid into Sulis' mouth. She'd swallowed and he'd poured a few more drops. Again, she'd swallowed. Cynan had placed her head gently back on the rolled cloak he had fashioned into a pillow for her.

"That she is drinking is a good sign," Coenred had said. "If it is God's will, and she survives the night, I believe she may live. But she is in God's hands now."

And so Cynan had remained awake by Sulis' side, even as the monks wrapped themselves in their robes and blankets and fell asleep. For a long while, their snoring and Sulis' moaning were the only sounds.

The moon rose and a cool breeze rustled the oaks leaves. Staring up at the great expanse of darkness above them, Cynan saw clouds, gilded with silver light, scudding across the sky. The night was growing cool and dew was forming on the ground. He shivered and yawned.

He reached for another branch. In the sudden flare of light as the dry timber began to flame, he noticed with a start that Sulis was awake. Her eyes were dark pools reflecting the firelight. She stared at him, unblinking.

Cynan felt a sudden wave of relief, but pushed it away as if it had never been. This woman was nothing to him.

Just a thrall. And a stupid one at that.

"Are you thirsty?" he asked, keeping his voice quiet so as not to disturb the slumbering monks.

She did not answer for a long while, then gave a small nod. He reached for the skin and held it for her. She raised herself up, wincing against the pain in her wrists.

"Careful," Cynan said. "Do not open your wounds again."

She stared at him with her dark eyes, and then opened her mouth to drink thirstily from the skin. Before she had drunk her fill, Cynan pulled it away.

"If you drink too quickly, you will puke it up."

Sulis ignored him and lay back down.

"Why should I not wish to open my wounds again?" she whispered. Her voice was almost lost amongst the murmur of the leaves above them.

Cynan swallowed.

"I know you are in great pain," he said.

"What can you know of my pain?" Sulis spat the words. "Have you carried a child in your womb? Raised it with love? Seen your son grow into a fine boy…" Her voice cracked. "Only to see him… To see him…" She sobbed, unable to utter the words that told the story of her anguish.

Cynan sighed.

"And now I am to be a thrall," Sulis said, her voice rasping and ragged, like a chipped blade. "Someone for men like you to do with as they wish."

"I am truly sorry for what happened to you," Cynan said. "You are right. I cannot imagine the pain you feel. But I had no hand in that."

"Did you not?" she snapped, anger colouring her tone. "Are

you not a gesith of a Northumbrian lord? Are you not enemies of my people?"

"It was my lord who saved you from violation at the hands of those who attacked your steading."

"And I suppose you believe I should thank you and your lord for that? For making me a thrall?"

A branch shifted in the fire, falling into the embers and sending sparks wafting upwards. Cynan stared for a moment at the flickering dance of the flames. He could feel Sulis' glare on him.

"No," he said at last, "I do not expect your thanks. But I would not see you die."

"What is it to you? It was your lord's silver that bought me, not yours."

Cynan rubbed a hand over his eyes.

"I don't know," he said. "Gods knows it would be easier for me if I'd let you die."

"Why did you stop me then?" she asked, her tone pleading. Tears glistened on her cheeks. Her suffering stabbed at Cynan like a blade under a shieldwall, getting past his defences all too easily. His eyes prickled and his throat felt thick.

"I know what it is to be a thrall," he said.

Around them he was suddenly aware of the sleeping men rousing themselves quietly. Their shadowy forms rose like wraiths from barrows. Cynan shivered again.

"What would you know? You are a warrior..." Her voice trailed off as she noticed the shapes of the men awakening all around them. Her eyes were huge in the gloom. "What...?" she said, unable to find the right words for her question.

"They are friends," Cynan whispered. He did not wish to draw attention to them. Perhaps the holy men meant to perform some rite in the dark of night. Tiny fingers of fear stroked the back of his neck. "They're holy men of the Christ god. They've helped you."

For a time they were both silent, watching as the monks gathered and moved some distance from where they rested beside the campfire.

"I was a slave once," Cynan said. "I was beaten and treated worse than my lord's dogs."

Sulis turned her gaze back to him.

"And how come you to be a sword-man now?" Her voice cracked and broke. He held out the water skin once more and she drank.

"Lord Beobrand took me in. Heard the oath of a thrall. He is a great man."

"And now he adds me to his household. Another thrall."

"It is not Beobrand, nor I, who weaves your wyrd, Sulis. But Beobrand is a good lord, and fair. You will be treated well at Ubbanford. But please don't try to run again. Or to take your life."

The monks began to chant in the darkness, their voices eerie and otherworldly in the still of the night. Cynan and Sulis fell silent and listened to the magic song of the Christ followers, each lost in their own thoughts.

Chapter 11

"Allow Eumer to approach," Eowa said, his voice ringing clear in the hall. He reached for a cloth and wiped his hands. All conversation had died. The hall was silent, and all there peered with interest at the newcomer.

The door wardens had him remove his sword and seax. The decorated scabbard and pommel ornaments glittered and shone. They then made him unbuckle his belt and even relinquish his eating knife. The polished buckle flashed as he handed over the belt. When they were satisfied he bore no weapons, they ushered him forward. The messenger stepped into the light and walked nervously towards the high table, where Eowa awaited him. Eumer's clothes were shabby, dust-streaked and worn, in stark contrast to the fine blades and belt he had left with the door wards. His hair was cropped short. He was a stocky man, broad of shoulder, but more like a farmhand than a warrior. His gaze darted around the room.

"Do you think Eowa will switch his allegiance?" whispered Acennan from where he sat at Beobrand's left. "The messenger comes from Penda and blood is blood, after all."

"I know not," said Beobrand, without turning his gaze away from the messenger, "but I think with Eowa his word is stronger than blood."

There was something about Eumer that Beobrand did not like. He shook his head. There was nothing to fear here. They were safe in Eowa's hall. War would come all too soon, but for tonight, they were in no danger.

Cynethryth poured mead into a cup and stepped around the table to intercept Eumer before he reached Eowa.

"I bid you Waes Hael," she said, offering the cup to Eumer.

The man's features clouded with anger for a moment. But he took the cup and drank deeply of the liquid.

"I thank you, Lady Cynethryth," he said. His voice trembled. Beobrand noticed that drops of sweat glimmered on his forehead. He must be nervous to be addressing the lord and lady of the East Mercian marches before so many watching faces of thegns, gesithas and their families.

Cynethryth took back the cup and bowed to Eumer, who stepped forward to Eowa.

"Well, Eumer," said Eowa, "what message do you bring from my brother?"

Eumer glanced around him.

"My lord Penda ordered me to give the message to you alone."

Eowa frowned.

"Very well, let us step away from the tables where we can talk." Eowa turned to the expectant faces. "Continue with your feasting, friends," he said. "If this news is important, I am sure you will all hear of it soon enough. But for now, the message is for my ears alone it seems."

Conversations slowly started up again. Men spoke of this messenger from Penda. What tidings could he bring? He must have ridden hard to arrive so dishevelled before a great lord, and to come to the hall so late into the night the news must surely be portentous.

The drone of voices enveloped Beobrand. He watched keenly as Eowa and Eumer stepped towards the rear of the hall, away from the long boards and benches. Little light from the hearth reached the dark corner, but Scur scooped up a candle and followed them. The warrior placed the candle on a stool near where Eowa and Eumer conversed in hushed tones. He then moved a few paces away to allow them to speak without being overheard.

"I wonder what message he brings," said Octa.

"I know not," said Beobrand, reaching for the pitcher of ale once more, "but as Eowa said, we shall find out soon enough." He was pouring the last drops of ale into his horn when a sudden, violent movement snapped his attention to the darkened corner where Eowa, Eumer and Scur stood. For a moment, he was unsure what he was seeing, and then, as suddenly as if he had been plunged into the icy waters of the Whale Road in winter, it became shockingly clear.

Beobrand surged to his feet, overturning the board and sending food, drink, plates and cups crashing to the rush-strewn floor. All around the hall other men were leaping up and everyone was shouting.

Beobrand, his tiredness forgotten, leapt over the board and the spilt detritus of the feast and rushed towards Eowa and Penda's messenger. But he knew he would be too late. From somewhere hidden in his dirty clothing, Eumer had pulled a wicked-looking knife. Eowa had been leaning in close to hear the man's words over the noise of the throng in the hall. The blade flashed in the light of the candle, as Eumer swung a killing blow. Beobrand watched all of this in horror. He saw clearly that Eowa would be killed. There was nothing he could do. He was still several paces away and the knife was but an arm's length from Eowa's throat.

Eowa would die here. Killed in his own hall by the treachery of an assassin's blade.

But even as the blow descended towards the wide-eyed Eowa, Scur bounded forward with a speed brought on from the desperate need to defend his oath-sworn lord.

A few more steps and Beobrand would be upon them, but it would be too late. As he watched, Eumer's blade sunk deep into Scur's chest. Scur let out a howl of rage and pain and locked his hands around the throat of the assassin. All three men crashed to the floor.

The hall was in uproar. Men were rushing to their lord's aid, screaming and shouting at the infamy that had unfolded before them. But Beobrand had been the first to react and was the closest. He arrived first.

Scur and Eumer were wrestling, thrashing around on the timber floor, scrabbling and kicking rushes up in their efforts to slay each other. Eowa lay to one side. He looked shocked, his face pale and eyes wide, but he seemed unharmed. Beobrand hauled him to his feet, pulling him away from the fighting men. He pushed Eowa towards his approaching gesithas, and turned back to help Scur.

It seemed Scur needed no help. He had climbed atop Eumer and gripped his head in both his hands. Eumer had yanked his knife free of Scur's flesh and stabbed it again into the warrior's chest. Scur bellowed, but appeared oblivious of the pain. Blood gushed from his wounds, soaking his kirtle and painting Eumer's hands and arms crimson. Scur strained and heaved. Before Beobrand could intervene, there was a crunching crack as Eumer's neck snapped. The messenger instantly went limp, and Scur rolled away from him, to lie panting and groaning staring up at the soot-clad roof beams. Lifeblood pumped and bubbled from his gaping wounds.

Eowa pushed past Beobrand and dropped to his knees beside Scur. He gripped the warrior's hands.

"You have saved me, brave Scur," he said. "You have killed my enemy and saved my life. You are the best of men."

Scur looked up at his lord, but his eyes were already dimming.

"I'm sorry," he said, his voice weak. Gone was the bellowing power of moments before. "Sorry, my lord."

"You have nothing to be sorry for," said Eowa. "You have done your duty as you always have."

"I was too slow..." Scur said. His head lolled to one side and his breath left him with a wheezing crackle. The blood yet flowed from his wounds, but ever more slowly. Eowa gazed down at his trusty gesith, his face full of anguish and confusion. Letting out a ragged sigh, Eowa saw that Scur had departed middle earth. He stood and turned towards the men gathered there. His eyes met Beobrand's.

"What did he mean, he was too slow?" he asked.

For a heartbeat Beobrand knew not what to say to Eowa. And then he saw. Scur had been closest and he had been fast. Fast enough to take the killing blow that had been aimed at his lord. But Beobrand saw a blooming stain of red on Eowa's shoulder. The kirtle was sliced through cleanly there, and blood was trickling from a small wound.

Beobrand pointed.

"He meant that," he said. "He was too slow to prevent you being injured by that bastard's knife. It looks as though the blade went through Scur and the tip nicked you there."

Eowa looked down at the small cut.

"I didn't even feel it," he said, bemused. "It is nothing." Dismissing the insignificant injury, Eowa turned his attention to his people.

"Penda has sought to slay me in my own hall. My brother has long coveted my lands, but he fears me. He sends an assassin to kill me with a hidden blade in the dark. This is not the act of a good king, of a man to be followed and admired. No, this is the act of a craven. Penda fears me. And he fears you. And so he should. For are you not the bravest of warriors?" A growl of assent from the warriors. "I know any of you would have done the same as Scur." He looked down at the blood-soaked corpse, before turning quickly back to his comitatus. He staggered slightly, but found his balance. "You are loyal and strong and you have always stood by me in moments of need. I trust that you are ready to stand once more at my side in the shieldwall." The men cheered and stamped their feet. They had seen one of their number slain and their lord attacked, they were eager for battle now. Such an affront could not go unanswered.

"Good," shouted Eowa, his face flushed, "for we march to war. Penda amasses his host in the west and we will join Oswald and the Northumbrians against him." There was a murmur at this news. Beobrand wondered how they would take to fighting against fellow Mercians. "See to it," continued Eowa, "that riders are sent out at first light to call the fyrd to arms. Send word to all ealdormen and thegns that their lord, Eowa, son of Pybba, is in need of their spears and their shields. We will avenge Scur's death and we will settle this score with my brother once and for all. Soon, I will be king of all Mercia, and we will all be rich."

The men cheered again. But as Beobrand scanned the throng, he saw many faces that were shocked and pale. The safety of the feast had been destroyed by Penda's deadly deceit. And now that Eowa had spoken, they all knew what Beobrand and his men had come here for.

War was upon them. They would once again face the terrifying maelstrom of battle and they would find what their wyrd had in store for them in the steel-storm of the shieldwall. Many would fall to feed the ravens and wolves. Some would rise from the ashes of battle with greater battle-fame and riches. The dice were cast, but as each man talked of what they had just witnessed and their lord's words, none of them knew how they would land. Or who would be winners and who would be losers in this great game played by kings and lords with the very lives of their people.

Some men and women were tending to Scur's body. They were solemn and grave-faced. One of the women was sobbing, her tears streaking her cheeks, but she brushed away the hands of those who offered her help. This was her man, and she would see that he was cleaned and prepared for his final journey.

Cynethryth came to Eowa's side.

"Are you well, lord?" she asked.

Eowa stepped back towards the high table, where people were righting the boards and benches. Acennan had a protective hand on Octa's shoulder. Beobrand smiled his thanks to his friend. As they neared the bench and the lord's gift-stool, Eowa stumbled again. He caught himself on Cynethryth's shoulder and Beobrand moved in to help him.

"What is it?" Cynethryth asked. "Are you hurt?"

"Only a small cut," panted Eowa, "it is nothing. But it does burn so."

Beobrand was suddenly cold, despite the warmth of the hearth fire and the summer's evening.

"You there," Beobrand snapped to one of the door wards. The man was shaken and sombre. He had allowed an armed man within reach of his lord. "Fetch Eumer's blade. And mind you are not cut," he said, "I fear it may be poisoned."

"Ah, yes," said Eowa, "that would explain things."

And with that, he collapsed.

Chapter 12

"Will he live?" whispered Cynethryth.

All was still in the hall now. Men and women had been sent away, leaving only Eowa's closest retinue, who sat in hushed vigil in the main hall. Here, in the sleeping chamber that was separated from the main room with its great hearth and benches, it was silent, apart from Eowa's shallow breathing. Two rush lights gave off a flickering, ghostly light. Cynethryth's face was shadowy and indistinct, but Beobrand could see the strain there. Strands of her hair had fallen from her plaits. She brushed them aside absently, hooking them behind her ear.

Beobrand looked down at Eowa. The atheling was bathed in sweat. He trembled beneath the furs and blankets that were piled atop him, but at least now he slept.

"I cannot say," said Beobrand. "I fear it is in the hands of the gods now. We have done all we can."

When the door ward had brought Eumer's knife to him, Beobrand had examined it closely, holding it out so that the light of the fire caught its blade. It was gore-slick, drenched with Scur's blood, but he thought he could detect the remnants of something else. A thick, translucent liquid. He had sniffed the blade and a pungent stench caught in the back of his throat.

"It is poisoned," he had shouted. The clamour in the hall had risen in pitch. "Stand back," he had commanded, using the voice he employed in battle. "We must remove as much of the venom as possible, before it is too late." He remembered well the burning agony of the poisoned wound from Torran's blade in Din Eidyn, and how Acennan had saved his life.

And so he had fallen to the rush-covered floor of the hall beside Eowa's stricken form. Beobrand had ripped Eowa's kirtle to expose the knife-cut beneath. Above them, Beobrand heard commotion as Eowa's gesithas surged forward, believing he meant to cause their lord further harm. Acennan's voice was loud over the turmoil.

"He is helping Eowa!" he bellowed. "Stand back. Give way."

Beobrand ignored it all, trusting that his friend and his gesithas would give him enough time to do what he must. The cut was small, not much more than a nick. Without poison, Eowa would barely have noticed it. Beobrand took a deep breath, and without pause leaned over Eowa's prostrate body and clamped his lips to the wound. He sucked as hard as he was able, feeling his mouth fill with blood. He rose for a moment and spat into the rushes. One of the hounds pushed through the legs of the gathered men and went to lick where the gobbet of blood and spittle had fallen. Beobrand cuffed the dog and spat again. There was a bitter taste in his mouth. He had tasted his own blood enough times in battle to know there was an evil taint to Eowa's. He fell to again and sucked more blood and poison from the cut. He spat again, feeling some of the liquid drooling into his beard. The dog was no longer there, pushed away no doubt by one of the watching warriors. There was more space around them now too, and more light.

For a third time Beobrand sucked at Eowa's wound, like a carrion crow dipping its beak into a corpse. He shuddered at the thought and spat once more. The acrid taste had gone now, but his mouth felt numb, as if he had filled it with snow. He had stood shakily then.

"Give me mead or ale," he had called out. He felt light-headed, as if he had drunk many cups of strong mead. "Now!"

A hand had thrust a cup into his hand and he had filled his mouth quickly. Strong mead. He swilled it around his mouth and then spat the contents onto the rushes. Again he'd rinsed his mouth with the mead and spat. Finally he'd drained the remainder of the sweet liquid before passing the cup back with a nod of thanks.

Now, gazing down at Eowa shaking and sweating in his bed, Beobrand wondered whether he had been too late. Perhaps enough of the venom had remained in Eowa's body to slay him yet. He remembered that night in the hall of Din Eidyn when his own body had battled Nelda's deadly dew.

"Eowa is strong," he said to Cynethryth. "It is his battle now."

Cynethryth nodded.

"He will survive this," she said, with certainty in her voice. Whether she believed it or was trying to convince herself, Beobrand could not tell.

Beobrand said nothing.

"I have spoken to the men," Cynethryth continued. "The messengers will ride tomorrow. And Eowa will recover from this treachery. And you will ride for war, as you had planned." Was there recrimination in her tone?

"It is not my plan, Lady Cynethryth," Beobrand said. "Penda has provoked this, and my lord Oswald has called in an oath that Eowa swore to him long ago. Before he knew you," he added awkwardly.

Cynethryth brushed the errant strands of hair behind her ear again.

"I had long known this day would come. When Oswald would call upon him for what he did."

Beobrand tensed. He did not wish to be here speaking of these things with this noble lady. His tiredness washed over him again. When he had most needed rest, the night had exploded in a tumult of violence and terror. Now that all was calm again, he felt his hands shaking at his side. He clenched his fists against the trembling.

"I see you are uncomfortable, Lord Beobrand," she said. "You have no need. Eowa told me all. I know about how you met." She looked directly at him, her eyes thoughtful and glimmering. "I know it all." She sighed, and smoothed her dress with her slender hands. "But no matter the past. He is my man now, father of my sons. I need him alive. You must swear to me that you will protect him."

Beobrand swallowed against the lump that had formed in his throat. He wanted to say that he would keep Eowa alive, that he would bring him home to his family safely. But he had seen too many battles; lost too many friends to the spear and the sword.

"If he pulls through, we will ride to face Penda in battle. I will do what I can to protect him. But I cannot control wyrd, and many will fall."

She looked away.

"If he falls," she said, her voice barely more than a whisper in the dark room, "Penda will send his wolves here. He will not allow my sons to live. We cannot remain here hoping that the gods, or the Sisters of Wyrd, will see Penda defeated. When you march to war, I must flee with the children."

Beobrand nodded. He thought of King Edwin's male kinfolk, sent far away to Frankia after his death. They had been killed by Wybert at the behest of one of the royal line of Æthelfrith. Cynethryth was right. Penda would not hesitate to snuff out any spark of a rival claim to the kingdom of Mercia before it could grow into a flame. And of course, Octa was here with Penda's nephews.

"You will take the boys and ride north. I will provide a couple of my men to lead you, and you must take some of your most trusted gesithas for protection. You will go to Ubbanford on the river Tuidi. That is my land and you will be safe there. After the battle, if we yet live, Eowa will come for you there." He rubbed his hand across his face in an attempt to wipe away his exhaustion.

"And if you do not live?"

"Then you will not be safe in Albion anywhere that Penda's hand might reach. If such should happen, you would do well to seek refuge with Eorcenberht, King of Cantware, far to the south. Or with the Christ monks on Hii, in the north and west." Beobrand thought of Yffi and Wuscfrea, slaughtered by Wybert over the Narrow Sea in Frankia. If Eowa fell, would his sons be safe anywhere? A king's power stretches far.

"But let us not think of the worst here in the dark. We all yet live, and in the light of the day, we may see things more clearly. For now, we both need sleep."

"I will stay with my husband," she said, lowering herself onto a stool beside the bed.

Beobrand nodded and made to leave. His eyelids drooped and he could barely think of ought save allowing the darkness of slumber to bring him peace for a time.

"Lord Beobrand," Cynethryth said, halting him with his hand on the door.

"Yes?"

"Thank you."

He looked down at Eowa's pale face. In the dim light of the small rush flames, the scars on his nose were vivid and clear.

"You have nothing to thank me for," he said, and left the chamber.

Beobrand awoke early. The sun was barely in the sky when Eowa's men began to rouse themselves. Men shouted at thralls for food, as they prepared to ride out to summon those loyal to their lord's banner. Outside, Beobrand could hear horses being readied. Snorts, hooves and the rattle of harness were loud in the grey dawn stillness. There was an urgency in the air. The attack on their lord and the announcement of impending war had riled the hall, like a stick prodded into a hornets' nest.

For a while, Beobrand lay still, vainly hoping for sleep to return to him, but his head ached, as it often did since his injury in the great ditch of East Angeln years before. He pushed himself up with a grunt. Gods, he felt as though he had drunk a barrel of the strongest mead. His head was pounding as if it had been used for an anvil by the local smith. His mouth was dry and sour, with the acrid taste of the poison in the back of his throat. He stood, brushing himself down. He had slept where he had found space, wrapped in his cloak like a ceorl, with the hounds. He had been beyond caring, such was his tiredness the previous night.

Acennan saw he was awake and brought over a cup of ale.

Beobrand took a swig, sluiced the drink around his mouth and spat into the ashes on the hearth. A thrall, who was trying to coax the embers back to life, cursed him in the musical tongue of the Waelisc. Beobrand ignored the boy and emptied the cup in three large swallows.

"Any tidings of how Eowa fares?" he asked.

Acennan shook his head.

"Let's find something to eat first. You look as though you drank more than your fill of that poison."

Acennan halted a passing thrall girl.

"Fetch us food," he said.

The girl was pretty, with dainty features, and long, unruly auburn hair. She could have been Reaghan's younger sister. Or perhaps her cousin. Perhaps she was Reaghan's kin, mused Beobrand. He knew not where Reaghan's people had lived. She had been too young to recall, merely knowing that when she had been captured by the Angelfolc, they had brought her east. She had talked little of her past to Beobrand. Could it be that more of her kin had been brought into slavery and sold to other lords? Reaghan had never mentioned any sisters. He had thought all her kindred slain, so he had pried little into the details of her life before Ubbanford. He shook his head. By Woden, this was too much to be fretting about now. There were more pressing matters to attend.

Beobrand handed her his empty cup.

"And some fresh ale," he said, "with our thanks."

The thrall dropped her gaze and hurried away. He watched the swish of her skirts, imagining the curves beneath with a twinge of longing, which was just as quickly replaced with a stab of guilt. He'd been away from Ubbanford and Reaghan for too long.

Acennan and Beobrand walked to the open doors of the hall to stand under the lintel and watch the hostlers and riders preparing their mounts. Some horses were already saddled and harnessed. As they watched, one young man with long dark hair that was held away from his face in long braids leapt onto a grey mare and galloped off to the east.

"Whatever happens now," Beobrand said, "Cynethryth will be travelling north with the boys. A few of Eowa's hearth-warriors will guard them."

"Where will they go?"

"To Ubbanford," Beobrand replied, his breath steaming in the early dawn air, "at least for now. If things do not go well against Penda, they will have to flee further afield. Choose two men to lead them. And," he said, with a hand on his friend's shoulder, "bear in mind that we need the best fighting men with us."

Acennan nodded. He would send a couple of the younger lads with Cynethryth and the children. It would give them a purpose and spare them from the horror of the shieldwall. Beobrand hoped that Cynan and the others had made good progress north and would meet them with Oswald before the clash with Penda. He cursed silently at having weakened his warband thus by sending some to escort the thralls. Perhaps he should have just sent the women back to their burnt homes. He pressed a hand against his forehead in a vain effort to halt the pounding. There was nothing to be gained from worrying about it now. He would have to trust Cynan to return with his gesithas as quickly as he could.

"Lord?" came a voice from behind them.

A young man stood there. A thrall.

"There is some cold meat, cheese, bread and ale awaiting you to break your fast," he said, beckoning them to follow him. Beobrand glanced around for sight of the girl with the auburn hair. There was no sign of her.

"It seems," said Acennan with a smirk, "that your pretty thrall was frightened to return, for fear of falling under the spell of the mighty Beobrand."

Beobrand frowned and shook his head. There was no time for this. He followed the man back inside, but could not stop himself having another look around the hall for the girl.

Behind him, he heard Acennan's laughter.

The chamber was dark. Outside, the summer sun was in the sky and the morning chill had been banished for another long hot day. Through the walls of the room came all the usual sounds of life. Somewhere far off, wood was being chopped. Nearer by, from within the main hall, came the lilting sounds of the women's weaving song. Men raised their voices and there was the clatter of weapons and shields from where the warriors practised their battle-play, out on the open stretch of land that was flanked by birch trees. Beobrand had sent Acennan and his own men down there with Eowa's. If they were to stand against a common enemy, they would do well to get to know one another. There was not much time, he hoped they could build some trust between the two warbands.

"How does he fare?" Beobrand asked in a whisper.

Cynethryth raised her head from where she sat. She was pale, her hair more dishevelled than when he had left her the night before. But to Beobrand's surprise, a response did not come from her but from the man on the bed.

"I owe you my life, it seems," Eowa croaked. His voice rasped in his throat, but he was awake and strong enough to prop himself up on one elbow.

Beobrand smiled to see him so much improved.

"Scur saved your life," he said, "not I."

Eowa closed his eyes and let himself fall back onto the pallet. He sighed.

"He was the most loyal and bravest of gesithas. I will miss him."

"He honoured his oath to you," Beobrand said.

For a long while, Eowa said nothing. Cynethryth reached out her slim hand and he clasped it. The women had stopped their singing in the hall.

"Cynethryth has told me of the offer you have made her. I thank you, Beobrand. It will be easier knowing that my family is far from here, away from the grasp of Penda should the worst befall me."

Beobrand stepped further into the room. It was warm and the air was stale.

"You need not offer me thanks, Eowa. You have cared for my son as if he were your own these past months. I merely offer your kin the same in return."

Eowa looked up at him from the bed. His eyes glistened in the gloom.

"I will not forget this," he said. "You have ever been good to me."

Beobrand shook his head. The scars on Eowa's face told a different tale. Beobrand took in a deep breath. But what else could he have done? He too was bound by oaths as strong as iron.

"I heard horses earlier," said Eowa, breaking the awkward silence that had fallen on them. "Have all the messengers left?"

"Yes. The men have ridden out. There is no time to waste. I feel the weight of the moments passing. Penda has been plotting and planning for a long time, it would seem. I fear any delay will play into his hands. I pray we will not be too late."

"Oswald will already be on the move no doubt. My fyrdmen need time to gather, but we will not tarry. We will march in two days with however many men we can bring to my banner by then."

Beobrand took in Eowa's pallor, the dark rings around his watery eyes.

"Will you be strong enough?" he asked.

Eowa smiled grimly.

"I will have to be."

Chapter 13

Beobrand reined in Bera and looked back at the slow-moving column of men. Most of the warriors who had answered Eowa's call to arms came with spear and shield. A few bore old swords that had been handed down from father to son for generations. Very few came with their own horses. As always, a warhost travelled at the speed of its slowest warrior. And the delay chafed at Beobrand's nerves. The anxiety of not knowing what had befallen King Oswald's host gnawed at him, the way a hound chews and grinds on a bone under its master's table. Eventually, after enough chewing, the bone would shatter under a dog's strong jaws. Beobrand wiped the sweat from his brow with his forearm. He felt close to snapping under the pressure of uncertainty.

The days were long and warm, and he insisted that Eowa's Mercian host march until there was scarcely light in the sky. And he roused them each morning shortly after dawn, shouting and cajoling them until they were on their feet and trudging dustily along the crumbling road that had been laid down generations before by the men from Roma, far to the south. Beobrand knew the men hated him, whispering insults and spitting as he rode past. But they were all careful not to allow him to hear their words, or to witness any slight against him. They may begrudge him pushing them to march at such a pace, but all men had heard of Beobrand Half-hand, and none there would rather face his wrath than take their chances of standing in a shieldwall. Better the possibility of death in the future, than the certainty of it facing the fair-haired giant from Cantware with the frosty blue eyes that loured from a face as hard and scarred as a cliff overlooking the thundering North Sea.

"We should have travelled west," Beobrand said to Eowa, who sat astride a fine white steed. Eowa blew out a long breath and rubbed his face.

"Must we again have this argument?" he asked. "What were your orders from Oswald King?" He made no attempt to hide the frustration in his voice. They had travelled the path of this discussion many times in the last three days and they had always come to the same destination.

"You know the answer to your question," Beobrand snapped.

"I do, but you seem intent on raking over these embers again. As ordered, we will travel north on the Earninga Stræt, then west on Hēah Stræt until we join with Oswald's host and Oswiu's force from Rheged."

"But it only adds days to our journey," said Beobrand. He knew that the moment for such conversation had long since passed, but he could not be rid of this worry that they were wasting precious time.

"To travel west directly," said Eowa, clearly resigned to explaining himself yet again, "would not only have been against your – no, our – sworn lord's command, it would also have been foolhardy. The terrain is rugged, and if you think the men are walking slowly now, you should see armed men walking into the hills of the Pecsætna. They are a strange people, who do not take kindly to visitors. Perhaps they have offered their spears to my brother. And even if we had crossed the hills without problem, what then?" he asked, pushing his long hair out of his face and behind an ear in a way that reminded Beobrand of Cynethryth. "We might have come across Penda's host on the western side of the hills. Do you really think this meagre warband could defeat Penda, if he is arrayed with his Waelisc allies and all his ealdormen and thegns?"

Beobrand sighed and nodded grudgingly. Eowa offered him a thin smile. The Mercian's skin was still sallow, his eyes rimmed with the darkness of illness and exhaustion following his poisoning, but he had not once complained on the gruelling march.

"Besides," said Eowa, "in this way, we know that the path northward is clear." He looked up to where the sun was lowering towards the forested hills in the west. "Come, let us reach that copse of beech trees. We can make camp there, and tomorrow we should join Hēah Stræt." Eowa touched his heels to his horse's flanks and Beobrand nudged Bera forward to follow. Acennan cantered up beside them, bringing with him more dust in a cloud kicked up by his mare.

The three of them rode towards the stand of beech that was hazed in the distance. Their scouts had ridden back to them some time ago and told them of the place as suitable for a camp.

As they rode, Beobrand thought of Eowa's words, and called out to him.

"You think Cynethryth has left already?"

"She gave me her word she would leave the day after us. That is one woman I know I can trust not to break her word to me."

Beobrand nodded.

"Still, I wish we knew they were all safe, far from any battle, and the reach of your brother."

He thought of little Octa and how the boy had clung to him when he had said they were riding to war. He had needed to push his son away in the end and hand him to Cynethryth so that he might mount his great brown horse. There had been tears in Octa's eyes and on his cheeks.

"Be brave, my son," Beobrand had said. The words had been hard to speak over the lump in his throat. "You will be in Ubbanford soon, with Reaghan."

Octa had cuffed the tears from his face, apparently angry at his own weakness.

"May your blade strike true and your shield hold strong," he had said, his face sombre.

Beobrand had laughed with joy at the boy's serious words. Octa had misunderstood his father's response, imagining Beobrand to be making jest of him. Tears had welled in his eyes anew.

"Look for me to the south and I will return to you as soon as I am able." Without waiting for a further reply from Octa, Beobrand had nodded once, curtly to Cynethryth and ridden after the warhost that had already begun marching north.

"Do not forget your words to me, Beobrand of Ubbanford," Cynethryth had called after him. He had not turned, instead he had raised his mutilated left hand in a silent acknowledgement. By all the gods, he hoped he would be able to keep her husband alive. But they rode towards battle and death.

And no man's wyrd was certain.

Acennan trotted close to Beobrand.

"I wonder what Eadgyth is doing right now," he said, staring into the northern distance, as if he thought he might be able to see her all the way in his hall, Stagga. "And Athulf and Aelfwyn. I wonder if they are playing by the stream. It is a hot day, perhaps they have been wading in the water. Aelfwyn loves that."

"I am sure they are all well and awaiting your safe return," Beobrand said with a smile. He hid his envy well. He might be Acennan's lord, with a hoard of treasure hidden in his hall, but he coveted that which Acennan had with Eadgyth. He had no such easy affection with Reaghan. Years ago, he had thought they might find such a thing, but it seemed the longer that went by, the more distant they became. She was still his woman and he did not doubt her fidelity, but there was no closeness now. Perhaps, no love.

"What about you, Beobrand?" asked Eowa. "You have been far from Ubbanford for weeks now, you must miss your woman too."

"Yes," Beobrand said, "I miss Reaghan," he said, but realised something with a start as he spoke the words. He did not truly miss Reaghan.

He missed the memory of her.

Chapter 14

Reaghan hummed a tune under her breath. She was not aware she was making the sound, so intent was she on the weft and warp of her weaving. Maida recognised the tune. It had been old when their grandmothers' grandmothers had woven cloth. Every girl in Ubbanford knew the melody. She added her own humming to Reaghan's. They had been silent for a long while before then, sitting in the porch of the new hall.

Maida and Elmer's sons, Ealred and Frethi, played in the shade of the great oak. Their eldest child, Bysen, sat on a stool beside her mother and wove with a look of rapt concentration on her face. She was a serious girl, and would often sit with the womenfolk. Her weaving was of the best quality. She was quick and controlled, her fingers darting over the threads and the tablets. Bysen did not join in the hummed melody.

Reaghan smiled at Maida as she realised they were both humming the same song. She could sense that the older woman wanted to talk, but she was content to remain silent, or just to hum. There was little to speak of. They sat together most days and shared the tasks of carding, spinning and weaving. Reaghan knew that Beobrand had once ordered Maida to watch over her when he was away, but at some point in the intervening years, the two women had become friends. Sometimes barely a word passed between them, but they had a deep understanding of one another, and Reaghan looked forward to the time she spent with Maida and her children.

Ealred and Frethi screamed and whooped, climbing on the lower limbs of the huge oak.

"Careful, Frethi," shouted Maida, in a voice that expected nothing but obedience. "Get down from there before you break your neck."

The boy swung for a moment, hanging from his thin arms, before dropping to the ground and offering the women on the porch a beaming smile. He turned to his older brother.

"You can't catch me," he yelled and sped off towards the other side of the hall with Ealred chasing behind him.

Maida shook her head and resumed weaving and humming.

Reaghan smiled. She gazed down the hill at old Ubba's hall. There were figures moving about down there in the settlement, but there was no sign of Rowena. Reaghan had half expected her to join them today, but it was never easy to predict the old lady's whims. On the occasions when Rowena did come to the new hall on the hill, Reaghan enjoyed her company. She would often speak of things that were news to Maida and Reaghan. She seemed to have a great supply of tidings of the comings and goings of the nobility of Bernicia and beyond. Some of it came from visits to her daughter, Edlyn, far in the south in the hall of her husband, Lord Fordraed. More came from Bassus and his travels to Berewic for trade. The sailors there bore tidings from all over Albion and even from other distant lands. They spoke of kings of far off Hibernia and the exotic lands of Frankia, where they drank wine in place of mead. Some said they had travelled to lands so distant and hot that the skin of the people there was burnt almost black. They told how the nut-brown merchants rode huge, hump-backed creatures that carried them over endless seas of sun-baked sand.

Reaghan smiled to think of the fanciful tales that Rowena relished recounting.

The lady Rowena was not a consistent weaver. She cared little for the work and, despite having a delicate touch and a fine eye for patterns, the cloth she worked on always took what seemed an age to complete. But she was good company. She was aloof, never truly letting her guard down, but she had ceased to treat Reaghan badly years ago, after that blustery day when they had visited the sacred glade in the forest. There they had witnessed the slaying of Nelda, the cunning woman who had wrought such misery. The witch had almost succeeded in convincing Rowena to murder Reaghan, but Bassus, ever the champion warrior, despite having lost an arm to a Pictish arrow, had stepped from the trees and hacked Nelda down in a savage instant of ferocious power.

Reaghan tried not to think of what she had seen that day, but sometimes, when she lay alone in her bed, with the wind sighing beneath the eaves and the hall creaking and settling in the darkness, the vision of Nelda's dismembered corpse would come to her. On such nights, sleep would elude her and she would lie shivering until the dawn, terrified that outside in the gloom of the night Nelda's rotten body parts had somehow risen from death and were creeping towards Ubbanford to seek vengeance for her murder.

Once, on a bright summer day when Rowena had come to weave at the hall without Maida, Reaghan had brought up the subject of Nelda. They had been sitting in the sun and evil felt very distant, so she had asked Rowena if she ever dreamt about Nelda. Rowena had taken a deep breath and sighed.

"Let us never speak that name again," she had said. "She is gone, and I like to think of her as merely a bad dream that haunted us for a brief time." She had reached out and squeezed Reaghan's hand in an uncharacteristically affectionate gesture. "That witch can never hurt us again." She had offered another squeeze and had turned back to her threads.

They had never spoken of the witch or her death again. But they had shared something that day in the forest clearing that had formed a strong bond. They might never be friends, but Rowena had always treated Reaghan with respect and dignity ever since.

Reaghan glanced over at Bysen who silently brought into existence the patterned cloth from the tablets and the thread. Maida looked up and smiled at her. Reaghan felt a strange feeling of belonging and all at once being terribly alone. Maida and her daughter were very close, and the love they shared was clear to Reaghan. From the way they looked at each other, to casual touches, to the easy laughter with barely a word spoken. The love between a mother and a child was something she feared she would never know.

The boys came around from behind the hall, screaming and hollering.

Reaghan missed Octa. She had been furious when Beobrand had sent him away. She loved the boy as though he were her own. But he was not hers. Her womb had failed to take Beobrand's seed after that first time, when she had stupidly gone to Odelyna to help her rid her body of what she had believed to be a burden. Even now when she thought of it, she felt the echoes of the pangs of pain as her body had voided the unborn child.

She had been so foolish. To think that such a thing would go unpunished. Danu, Mother of all, had made her barren for her terrible act, and now she would never bear Beobrand a child. The closest she would ever come would be to love another woman's son. She had resigned herself to this, and doted on Octa, caring for him and treating him as though he were of her own blood. But it seemed it was not her wyrd to know contentment, for the order had come from the king to send the child away, to be fostered by the atheling of Mercia.

Gods, how she had raved and screamed at Beobrand then. She blushed to think of it. He had suffered her rage, but she had seen the violence building within him, and he had frightened her when at last he had bellowed at her to stop.

Her eyes misted at the memory of his anger and the loss of Octa. She blinked the tears away, not wishing Maida to see her weep. Despite her blurring vision, her fingers knew their work and they continued to deftly push the weft scytel between the warp yarns, rotate the tablets, and then slip the wooden shuttle back through the threads.

How had it come to this? She had been freed from thralldom and become the lady of the hall. The woman of a great thegn. Not the wife though, she thought. Beobrand had never offered to seal their union with a handfasting. And who was she to insist? She had been a slave, and then Beobrand had elevated her to a position she had never even dreamt of. He had treated her well. She had fine possessions and ate rich food. She had servants and thralls now to tend to her needs. And she still yearned for Beobrand. For the closeness they had shared in that first year following Sunniva's death, when Octa was a babe. But those happy days were in the past.

When Beobrand was away from Ubbanford, as he often was, she thought of him regularly and prayed for his return. But when he was in the hall, there was a distance between them now, a wall that she felt as keenly as though it had been a physical thing.

She knew he sensed it too. But they never spoke of it. Was she to blame? What could she do to mollify him? When he was present, he often sat in silence for long periods. He would stare into the hearth fire flames as if seeking to burn away memories he wished he had never seen. When he was in one of these dark humours, nobody would approach him, not even his friends Acennan or Bassus. His ire would wash off him like a stink and, over time, Reaghan had become convinced she was the cause of his anguish. He must feel trapped with this woman whom he had freed in a moment of madness and now, being an honourable man, he did not know how to be rid of her.

It had been months since they had lain together. Perhaps this was the cause of the chill between them. When he next returned, Reaghan vowed she would bed Beobrand more often and with more vigour. She knew he still lusted for her, he could not hide the glances and the way he followed her movements around the hall. But he never forced himself upon her, instead waiting for her to offer herself to him. Surely renewed passion would rekindle his affection for her. And, though she could scarcely bring herself to countenance the thought, perhaps his seed would settle in her womb and she would bring him another child. Then she would be truly useful to him and he would love her.

A horse's whinny and the thump of hooves on the dry, packed earth of the path broke her from her reverie. Reaghan looked up, suddenly alert. Could it be that Beobrand had come home? Her face grew hot. She set aside her weaving and stood. She rubbed her eyes, then pinched her cheeks.

"How do I look?" she asked Maida. She was flustered and breathless.

Maida smiled.

"As pretty as ever," she said, also standing. She brushed her hands over her apron and Reaghan realised Maida too missed her man and hoped that Elmer was returned to Ubbanford.

"Boys," Maida snapped, summoning her sons to her with a gesture of her hand. The two boys ran over and stood beside their mother and sister.

They all stood there in the shade of the porch in silent expectation, listening to the riders' approach. The mounts came at a plodding walk, heavy and lumbering. Reaghan strained to hear more. She frowned. This was not the sound of Beobrand's mounted warband's return. There were fewer horses here. A scratch of worry ran down her back. Could these be raiders? Picts perhaps? She shook her head. That was madness. The sun was high in the sky. No brigands would dare openly attack Ubbanford or its inhabitants. Beobrand was too feared.

The sounds grew closer, the riders were almost in view. She hardly breathed, and Maida and her children stood in hushed silence. Even the two boys, so full of noise and excitement moments before, now waited quietly beside their mother.

Reaghan craned forward, leaning out to catch the first glimpse of the horses. And then, from beneath the rustling shade of the birch and hazel that lined the path, came the riders. The bright sun glittered from harness and spear-points. And for a moment, as the riders came into view, Reaghan was still unsure who it was that rode up to her hall.

Chapter 15

Reaghan squinted against the blinding glare of the sunshine. At first she could not make out who rode astride the horses that plodded towards the new hall of Ubbanford.

"Each horse carries two riders," keen-eyed Frethi said. Reaghan saw immediately that the boy was right. Her stomach twisted. Could it be that this was all that remained of Beobrand's warband that had ridden south to defend the marches of Northumbria? She counted the horses. Seven. Gods, could they truly have lost so many horses? And men?

No, not men. Something about the riders snagged her attention. Each horse carried a man, and a woman. They were closer now, and finally she recognised the face of the leader of the band.

"Cynan," she called, raising her hand in greeting. The Waelisc warrior returned her wave. She scanned the rest of the male riders. She recognised them all as Beobrand's gesithas. None of the women were known to her. Frowning, she stepped from the porch.

Cynan reined in his mount and slid from the saddle. Then, before speaking, he turned to his companion and lifted her down. She was a slight, pale woman, with dark, haunted eyes. She might have been pretty, had she not looked so weary and soiled from the road. As Cynan lowered the woman gently from the horse, the sleeves of her dress fell back to reveal slender, freckled arms. Each wrist was bound in bandages. Behind Cynan, the other warriors were dismounting and helping the other women from their horses.

"Caladh," Reaghan called though the open doors of the hall. A young man was there in an instant, evidently already close, drawn by the new arrivals.

"I am here, my lady," he said.

"See to the horses," Reaghan said. "And find Domhnulla and see that food is prepared for the men." She hesitated. "And these women. They must be hungry from their journey."

The young thrall nodded and went to do his mistress's bidding.

"You are well come home, Cynan," Reaghan said, with a dip of her head. "But what of my lord Beobrand?" She glanced at Maida and saw the hard look of worry etched on her features. Reaghan clenched her jaw. She was sure her own face wore a similar expression. They had both seen that neither Beobrand nor Elmer rode with the newly arrived men and women. "And the others?"

"Do not fear," answered Cynan, "we left our lord and the rest of the men hale and whole still in Deira." Maida said nothing, but she let out a ragged sigh. She must have been holding her breath. Reaghan too, felt a rush of relief, coupled with a prickling of disappointment. She had so hoped Beobrand would have been amongst the men.

"And why do you return now?" she asked. "Without your lord," she flicked a glance around the women who now thronged about the entrance of the hall, "and with these women?"

"They are thralls," Cynan answered. His tone was clipped, he would not meet her gaze. He knew of her past and she of his. Talk of slaves was ever awkward for them.

"I see. And how did Beobrand come by them?"

Cynan handed the reins of his mount to Caladh.

"He bought them," he said. "But there is more to the tale than that. I will tell you all over mead and meat."

Reaghan nodded.

"Very well," she said, but was not ready to end the conversation just yet. Not without learning the thing that most preyed on her thoughts. "But what of our lord? Why did Beobrand not ride north with you?"

"He is needed in the south, Lady Reaghan," Cynan said, his voice taking on a sombre tone. "As am I and the rest of the men. We will not tarry here. We ride south with the dawn."

"Why?" she asked, though she knew there could only be one reason.

Cynan met her gaze at last and nodded, confirming what she had feared.

"War is upon us once more," he said.

Cynan stifled a belch. The warmth of the food and the strong mead soothed him. As they had ridden north, he had become increasingly tense and now, for this brief moment of respite, he felt his body and mind uncoiling its tight knots of worry.

Sulis and he had caught up with the rest of the party a day's ride north of Eoferwic. Gram had decided to rest in the city for a day, allowing Cynan and the thrall time to close the gap. Bearn had told Cynan that, when after the day of rest there was still no sign of him and the missing woman, some of the gesithas had said they should ride back southward in search of them, but Gram had been adamant. They had their orders to ride to Ubbanford and then return as quickly as possible to Beobrand and Oswald's battlehost. Cynan had told him he had done the right thing. Though he was sure that Gram had decided not to push the horses, thus giving the stragglers more chance to reach them on the journey.

The ride itself had been peaceful enough. Sulis had not attempted to run or harm herself again, and the weather had been kind to them. And yet Cynan had not been able to relax. He'd watched Sulis obsessively, scared of what she might do. She had remained sullen, barely speaking. She'd ignored the other men completely, grudgingly accepting food from Cynan and his help to mount and dismount. Cynan cursed himself for a fool at the flush of joy he'd felt whenever the Mercian woman deigned to meet his gaze or utter a word to him.

Once they had rejoined the group, they had ridden as fast as they were able. With two riders apiece, this proved to be more slowly than any of the men would have liked. Despite riding into the familiar lands of Bernicia under clear, warm skies, they could feel the chill clouds of war gathering in the south and west. They followed their lord's command, but even so, they felt the twinge of cowardice at riding away from battle. Were their shield-brothers and their hlaford even now hefting linden board and spear in defence of their king? It was the gesithas' duty to be at their oath-sworn lord's side. They had pledged to protect him, and he would bring them glory, battle-fame and riches in return. Riding away from war, they could neither protect Beobrand, nor weave their own sword-song into the tales that would be told of this conflict.

And so, short-tempered and nervous, they had travelled north to Ubbanford, that they might leave their charges and then rush back south, in search of their wyrd, in which they saw glory and glittering treasure plucked from their foes' corpses.

Cynan had not been aware quite how on edge he had been until that moment. He took another sip of the good mead that old Odelyna brewed. He relished the warmth of it as it trickled down his throat. Stretching out his legs, he arched his back, causing it to pop and crackle satisfyingly. It had been a long ride. He could feel his muscles loosening. Around him the men laughed and chattered with the happiness of coming home.

Home.

Yes, it was good to have a place to call home. And yet, he was not certain he would ever feel completely at ease here. He was grateful to Beobrand and would die before breaking his oath to his lord, but there was always something missing.

Cynan took another gulp of mead. Woden's teeth, he needed a good night's sleep. He must be exhausted to allow his thoughts to become so gloom-laden. He was young, skilled with weapon and shield, a trusted gesith of a ring-giving lord. Before fleeing Grimbold's hall he had been a thrall, beaten and abused. How could he think anything was missing in his life now?

Bassus' great roar of a laugh cut through his thoughts. The giant, one-armed warrior sat beside the lady Rowena. Between them and Cynan, sat Reaghan. She had honoured Cynan with a seat at the high table. He had already given them an explanation of how Beobrand had come to own the thralls. It had proven to be an awkward conversation. He had given little detail, merely saying that Lord Fordraed had acquired the women and Beobrand had offered him payment for them.

"But why would Beobrand do such a thing?" Rowena had asked, incredulity raising her voice's pitch. "We have plenty of thralls. Perhaps we could have done with one or two more," she'd mused. "Ciorstag is old now, to be sure, and is not much use for anything. But seven! Surely my daughter's husband had need of some of them."

Cynan had not known what to say. He felt like a man who has walked blindly into a swamp, and cannot remember the steps he must take to return to dry land.

"I am not sure of my lord's reasoning," he had stuttered. "I think perhaps he meant for some of them to be sent to Stagga, to help Eadgyth with her household." He'd hoped he had not spoken out of turn, but he knew better than to talk of Fordraed's actions with the Mercian womenfolk. Rowena would not care to hear ill spoken of her son-in-law. Bassus had caught his gaze and given a slight shake of his head. The old warrior knew well enough of Fordraed and what he was capable of. When Beobrand had returned from Cair Chaladain, the warriors had told the tale of that long night of violence and violation. But Edlyn had already been wed by then, and Rowena was happy with the match she had found for her daughter. And so Bassus had warned the men never to shine a light on the darkness of Fordraed's character for Rowena. It would only cause her pain and worry, and he would rather have her content and free of anguish.

"Well," Rowena had said, outrage colouring her voice, "I still do not understand how we are supposed to make good use of seven new thralls. However, it is not for me to say," she sniffed. "If Beobrand chooses to be extravagant, that is his concern."

Bassus, no doubt surmising some sort of confrontation between Beobrand and Fordraed, had offered Cynan a smile of thanks. The conversation had moved on to what was known of the preparations for war. Cynan had not been able to offer them much information and his frustration at having been made to ride away became evident in his snapped answers to their questions. For a time they had allowed him to eat and drink in peace. It felt good to allow his nerves to unwind, surrounded by friends and the warmth of the familiar hall. It would not last, he knew. Tomorrow they would ride south to war. But for this one day, he allowed himself to relax.

He glanced over at the edge of the hall where Sulis lay curled up in a blanket. She had been quiet and taciturn as they'd ridden towards Ubbanford and further from the home she had known. She had not complained, but each night she'd fallen into a deep slumber. And when they halted to eat and rest, she would quickly lie down and sleep. Still weak from the loss of blood and subsequent fever he supposed, but perhaps it was something else.

"This one looks to have had the worst time of the ride north," said Reaghan, her voice quiet. Beside her, Bassus and Rowena were deep in their own conversation. He smiled to see them thus, heads close together, eyes shining. Like two love-struck children.

"It was not so much the ride that harmed her," Cynan replied. He looked at the still form of the sleeping woman for a long while, unsure how much to tell. Some things were best left silent and buried. But he would be leaving the following morning. He could not ride away, leaving Sulis with her anguish and Reaghan knowing nothing of the thrall's past.

"She," he hesitated, and took another swig of mead, "she had been sorely used before Beobrand bought her." He lowered his voice. "They... they had questioned her. When she would not speak, they threatened her son."

Reaghan's face paled.

"Did she speak then?"

"Yes," replied Cynan with a sigh. He stared up at the shadows lurking above the soot-stained roof beams. "Yes, she told them what they wanted," he said. His voice was hollow, empty. "But they killed her son anyway."

Reaghan closed her eyes. Her hand flew to her mouth. When she opened her eyes again, there were tears there.

"The poor woman," she said. Her voice was full of sadness.

"You must watch her," Cynan said, surprised at the sound of urgency in his voice.

"Watch her?"

"She tried to take her life. She fled and slashed her wrists."

"I cannot blame her for wanting death." A tear fell onto Reaghan's cheek. "To lose one's child is a terrible thing." Her tone was desolate.

Cynan sipped at his mead. It tasted bitter on his tongue now.

"If we hadn't found Coenred and his monks, she would be dead now," he said. "They tended for her and their skill in healing is greater than mine."

"And you wouldn't want your precious lord's silver to go to waste, would you?" said a new voice.

Reaghan and Cynan were both startled to see that Sulis had pushed herself into a sitting position and now glowered at them from where she sat on the rush-covered floor, the dark-coloured blanket clutched about her shoulders as if sheltering from the cold of a storm. These were the most words she had spoken since they had left the Christ monks in Deira.

"I would not want to see you dead, Sulis," Cynan said. That was the simple truth.

"Nor I," Reaghan said. "I am sorry to hear of your plight."

"I do not want your pity, Waelisc," Sulis spat.

Reaghan flinched, as if struck.

"Very well, I will not offer you my pity," she replied. "But I will treat you fairly."

Sulis said nothing. She loured at Reaghan.

"I will be fair to you," Reaghan said, "I was once a thrall too."

Sulis let out a great burst of laughter, brittle and cackling, like the chattering of a magpie. Cynan shuddered. He had never seen her laugh before. There was no mirth in the sound.

"By all the gods," she said, tears smearing the dirt on her cheeks, "are all of Lord Beobrand's people thralls?"

PART TWO
MASERFELTH

Chapter 16

"Do you think it will rain?" asked Beobrand, shielding his eyes from the bright sunlight and peering into the north. Despite the warmth of the day and the brilliance of the sun, dark clouds brooded there. He sucked a finger and held it up for a few heartbeats. The breeze was slight, but the north-facing side of his finger grew cold.

"The wind blows from the north," he said.

Acennan frowned and patted his mare's neck. "Then I think it likely we'll be getting wet before nightfall," he said. "Still, it might be good to wash some of this dust off. It's been dry for so long, I feel like a loaf that's been rolled in flour."

"Sleeping in the wet is never pleasant," Beobrand said.

"Well, there is nothing we can do about the weather," said Eowa with a twisted smile, "so let us not worry ourselves with it."

Beobrand could find nothing to fault in Eowa's comment, so said, "Let's push on."

He touched his heels to Bera's sides and the three of them trotted forward. Many of the warriors of the host had already passed the point where the three men had paused. Beobrand nodded to Fraomar as they rode past. The young gesith led his horse, allowing one of Eowa's fyrd-men to ride for a while. The grey-bearded man had sprained his ankle and Fraomar had been quick to offer his mount to the man, so that he might recover. Fraomar was a good man.

The host had settled into the rigours of the march well. The complaining had lessened considerably, as the men became accustomed to the pace and realised they only expended their energy by moaning. There were injuries, and that most common, but painful, of problems – blisters. But, as evidenced by Fraomar's loan of his horse, the fyrd – thegns, gesithas and ceorls alike – collaborated and helped one another as they trudged westward.

"Where in the name of all that is sacred is Oswald?" asked Eowa suddenly, his frustration unexpectedly bubbling to the surface. He rarely voiced a complaint or concern, but the pressure of travelling into the unknown was taking its toll on them all.

"If we travel much further west," said Acennan, "we will need a ship soon. Perhaps Oswald has decided against staying on the isle of Albion and has taken to the sea." His jest was a poor one, and nobody responded with anything more than a snort of derision.

Shortly after leaving Snodengaham, as the men had waded across the river Dyvene under the watchful eye of the hunched boatman and his dog, five riders had galloped out of the north. They were Attor and the three scouts Beobrand had sent west. With them came a fifth man whom Beobrand recognised by the name of Ástígend. Attor had been returning with news of Penda's gathering forces and had intercepted Ástígend on the road with a message from the king. Oswald had assembled the fyrd and was making his way westward from Eoferwic. Beobrand and Eowa were to follow with all haste. After Ástígend had rested, they had sent him back on a fresh steed with word of their progress.

Beobrand looked back the way they had come. Great hills rose there, like the backbone of Albion. The warhost had been walking for three days now, following the old Roman road that led south-west from Eoferwic. The road was clear here, with great slabs of stone still clearly paving a straight path across the land. Years of rain and frost had cracked and washed away parts, but here it yet deserved its name of street. Back in the hills, there had been places where the road had disappeared into the heath. The road was always easy enough to find once more though, as long as they continued travelling in the most obvious direct route possible. Eventually, they would see the stones once more through the grass and weeds, just where they expected to find them. Those men of old Roma were clearly single-minded when it came to planning routes across the land.

When they had seen people they had asked for tidings of Oswald. At Loidis they had been told by some boys in a field of nodding barley that a great number of warriors had passed that way four days before. And so they had pressed on, each day hoping to reach Oswald's force. And, as the sun set on every hot, dust-filled day, with no sight of Oswald, the worry that they would be too late scratched at their nerves.

They saw signs of the host's passing each day. An earthenware bowl, cracked and useless, discarded beside the ashes of one of many campfires. A single leather shoe, with a snapped cord. The men had joked about the man who had left that behind. Was he hopping like a lonely mistle thrush following the warhost? Attor even found a small silver amulet. It was the cross symbol of the Christ god.

"Someone will be missing this when battle comes," he had said grimly, picking up the necklace and secreting it in his pouch. Beobrand had not asked whether Attor meant to give it back to its rightful owner if he found him.

At night, whoever was on guard duty, would stare into the west, hoping to see the points of light that would attest to Oswald's host being nearby. But it seemed the king of Northumbria had not yet halted his march and was still some days ahead of them, for they saw no multitude of campfires.

One night, Beobrand had been unable to sleep and so had paced the perimeter of the camp. He had spied, far off in the west, on higher ground, the flickering light of a fire. He had stared at it for a long time. The following morning, he had sent Attor, Garr and Grindan into the hills to investigate. They had returned as the sun reached its zenith with news of a fresh fire and sign that three men had camped in a sheltered cleft in the rocks. Shepherds perhaps, Attor had thought. Unable to continue on horseback into the broken terrain, they had returned to Beobrand and the host.

Attor and the other scouts worked tirelessly, riding out each day far ahead of the column of men. Beobrand would not allow them to be caught by surprise. It was unlikely, with Oswald's force only days ahead of them. But Penda was a wily warlord and Beobrand would take no chances.

Ahead of the main body of men now, Beobrand slowed Bera to a walk. Acennan and Eowa rode at either side. The clouds off to their right had drawn closer. And darker. Smudged skirts of rain painted the sky beneath them. A sudden gust of wind tugged at his cloak. An end to the heat was welcome, but Beobrand did not look forward to a night trying to find sleep in driving rain.

They rode on in silence for a long while. There was nothing to say. They had voiced all of their concerns and worries in the preceding days. They could make no further plans until they reached Oswald and understood where they would face Penda.

The wind picked up, rattling the branches of a stand of hawthorn and elder that stood some way off to the north of the road. Bera snorted and shook its great, shaggy head. On the hot, still days, flies had settled around the horses' eyes and noses. Perhaps rain and wind would be a welcome change for the beasts too.

They cleared a rise. In the west, the sun was low in the sky. It had been hidden behind the dark band of cloud and now it burst forth, painting the hills with gold one final time before darkness and rain would swallow the land.

"Look there," said Acennan, pointing. "Isn't that Attor?"

Beobrand strained to see, but the sun was glaring.

"I expect he is coming to guide us to a good campsite. I hope he's found some shelter." Beobrand looked at the small copses of trees and the rocky scrub land that the road ran through. "But I doubt it. Gods how I hate sleeping in the rain."

"He's not alone," said Eowa.

The atheling was right. There was not one rider, but two. They were closer now, and Beobrand recognised Attor's lean form, and the easy way in which he rode. He kicked Bera forward to meet them.

The other rider was Ástígend, the messenger who had come to them many days before with news of Oswald. His horse was lathered with sweat and its eyes rolled white. He pulled the animal to a halt, and it stood panting and shivering before them.

"What news?" snapped Beobrand. There was no time for niceties.

"Penda has crossed the Maerse," he said.

"And Oswald?"

"He had thought to hold Penda south of the river until you arrived with Eowa and Oswiu came with warriors from Rheged."

"Oswiu has not yet come?"

Ástígend shook his head and spat. Acennan handed him a water skin and he took a draught, spat again and then drank deeply. He nodded his thanks.

"What of Penda's host? How many are they?"

Ástígend's jaw clenched. He looked around to make sure that he would not be overheard.

"He has many allies. Men of Powys and Gwynedd march with him. I have never before seen such a host."

Beobrand touched the whale-tooth Thunor's hammer amulet that hung at his throat.

"The more men to kill, the more battle-fame for us," he said, and forced a grin. But beneath the smile, his mind roiled. Without Eowa's fyrd or Oswiu's warband from Rheged, how could Oswald hope to stand in the face of Penda and his allies?

Ástígend did not return his smile.

"Our lord Oswald King means to hold Penda at a place called Maserfelth. But he is sorely outnumbered. He is in dire need of more men. Riders have also gone out north to seek Oswiu, but I know not how far away the atheling is, nor how long Oswald can hold against Penda."

Beobrand took in Ástígend's quivering, sweat-streaked mount.

"Your horse is spent. When did you set out?"

Ástígend patted the horse's neck, looking down with sadness in his eyes, as if he had only just realised the state of his mount.

"I fear I have killed trusty Léoma. I have ridden him hard since first light this morning."

Beobrand looked back at where the fyrd marched, flanked by the few mounted men of his gesithas and Eowa's hearth-warriors.

"You have done well, Ástígend," he said. "It seems our course is set for us. We will march through the night. And pray to whichever gods you hold dear that we reach this Maserfelth in time to aid our king." He reached over and clapped Ástígend on the back. "Come now, Eowa," he continued. "Let us give the men the tidings. There will be no rest tonight. We will eat and then march into the west. And on the morrow, we will push Penda and his host back into the Maerse."

He swung Bera's head around, ready to canter back to the column, when Acennan stopped him with a shout.

"There is good to come of this, Beobrand," he said, grinning widely.

Bera, excited now, would not stand still and circled on the spot.

"What good is that?" asked Beobrand.

"Well," laughed Acennan, "we won't have to sleep in the rain!"

Chapter 17

The night was dark and miserable. The clouds had rolled in from the north, smothering the land and hiding the light, first from the setting sun, later from the moon and stars. For a short time, the wind had picked up, throwing dust and grit into the warriors' faces before the rain arrived. Then the wind had abated somewhat and Eowa's fyrd had trudged into the west under a constant dousing drizzle.

"You think we will arrive in time?" asked Acennan, leaning over close to Beobrand from atop his horse to make himself heard above the crunch and clatter of the marching host and the steady murmur of the rain.

"Perhaps," answered Beobrand. He tried to pull his cloak more tightly about his shoulders, his left hand clumsy with its two missing fingers. After a moment, he gave up, letting the sodden cloak slip back. He was already drenched. He hated sleeping in rain, but riding and marching in it were no better. "We will know soon enough," he said.

He did not wish to talk of the possibility that Penda had already faced Oswald and defeated the Northumbrian host; that they might march out of the dawn to find their assistance no longer needed. In the rain-soaked darkness it was not hard to imagine a corpse-strewn field and a victorious

Penda, standing beneath his wolf-pelt banner, awaiting his brother.

The host marched in a sombre silence, with none of the singing and conversation he had come to expect from this group of men. They were well aware this was a desperate thing they did. They had known they were marching to war, but now they walked into the drear blackness of night and the force they were meant to bolster might already have been destroyed.

After Ástígend had given his message, with the sun falling into the clouds in the west, Beobrand had ridden to the head of the column, meaning to rally the men with a rousing speech. But he was not their lord. Few of the warriors were his, and his gesithas would fight to the death without silver-edged words from him. No, it was the men who had joined Eowa, the freemen and farmers, who had come from homesteads and settlements of Mercia, who were most unnerved at hearing they must travel through the night in the hope of arriving in time to relieve Oswald's host. Oswald was not their king, and this was not their land. They followed Eowa, and so it fell to the bearded atheling to address them before the night-time march. Eowa had ridden up beside Beobrand and said quietly, "I will speak to my people, Beobrand."

Despite the tiredness and cold rain that wrapped around him like another cloak, Beobrand could not help smiling as he recalled Eowa's words.

"You may think we march towards death," he had shouted, his voice carrying over the tired men. They had murmured and muttered. The news of Penda's host's proximity and the plan to walk through the night had unsettled them. "You are right," Eowa had continued. Stunned silence from the men. "We do truly march towards death." He had paused then, allowing his words to be weighed by the listening men. None had uttered a sound. "We march towards the death of traitors!" Eowa had bellowed. A skylark had burst from the foliage that grew near the crumbling road, startled by the sudden outburst. Eowa's horse had snorted and shied, but Eowa had shaken its reins and it had calmed. "We ride towards the death of oath-breakers and cowards. For did not Penda send a craven to slay me in my own hall?" A grumble of assent from the men, like distant thunder presaging a storm. "My own brother sent a killer to drink of my Waes Hael cup and then to strike me with a venom-dipped blade. Is this how a man fights? How a lord fights? How a king fights? With a knife in the back? With poison wielded by a coward's hand?"

Someone in the throng shouted, "No!"

"No," said Eowa. "And now my brother will know what it is to stand against one of his own blood. A man who leads the best of men. Strong men. Honest men. Men who will stand by their lord because, have I not stood by you? Have I not been a good hlaford to you?" Some of Eowa's hearth-warriors had let out a cheer. "Have I not kept my oath to you in all things?" More men had cheered then. "And I will keep my oath to you now. I will lead you into battle and you will be rewarded with battle-glory and a share of the spoils from our fallen enemies. Penda has broken his oath to me and to Oswald, King of Northumbria, with whom he had sworn a truce. Penda believes he is like a wolf, but he is as a dog. A cur that bites the hand of its lord. And what do you do with a dog that bites?"

One of Eowa's gesithas shouted, "Kill it!"

"Yes," said Eowa, "kill it." He raised his voice and repeated, "Kill it!"

His gesithas took up the chant first, but soon all the gathered men shouted the words.

"Kill it! Kill it!"

Eowa had raised his hand and beckoned for the men to follow him. And so they had set off towards the lowering sun. And towards death.

Beobrand had nodded at Eowa. The men continued the chanting for a few moments, but their voices quickly fell silent.

"Good speech," Beobrand had said.

Eowa had given him a twisted smile and ridden close.

"They believe me wronged," he said, in a quiet voice. "My brother has broken his oath to me and so should be slain."

"And that is true," replied Beobrand.

Eowa had shrugged, a wistful expression on his face.

"Who's to say if one oath is broken, when other oaths have been sworn in secret?"

"You had no choice," Beobrand had said. The setting sun had made Eowa's scars glow as red as blood.

Eowa had shaken his head.

"There is always a choice, Beobrand," he'd said, and pushed his mount into a trot, away from Beobrand and the secrets they shared.

In the middle of the night, the rain stopped. The wind picked up once more, chilling the wet clothes that draped the men. The clouds ripped and tattered above them, allowing the light from the moon to gild the wet stones of the road. Their footing was easier to see then, but the wind was cold. Beobrand shivered as they traipsed on into the gloom of the night.

Bera's rolling gait and the warmth that came from the horse's shaggy back lulled him into a doze. The memory of other night-time marches came to him. He recalled the dazed, exhausted trudge through a night of pain and grief as they'd fled Gefrin in search of the sanctuary of Bebbanburg. He had been little more than a boy then. His body had been numb and heavy from the day of fighting and he remembered clearly the weight of the byrnie Acennan had thrust into his arms as they had set off. He had clung to that iron-knit shirt that had been stripped from a corpse as if it would anchor him to middle earth.

He rubbed his hand against the wet, oiled byrnie he now wore, absently thinking of the work that would be needed to rid it of the iron-rot following this night's soaking. The iron-linked shirt had served him well all these years, saving his life on many occasions. He could still picture the sun coming up behind the crag of Bebbanburg after that interminable night and seeing the Waelisc shieldwall forming before them. That was when he had first donned the metal shirt and marvelled at its heft. Now his body was so used to its weight it could be part of his own skin. Against all odds, they had vanquished the Waelisc in that long-ago dawn before Bebbanburg. And he had finally taken the blood-price from Hengist for all that he had done.

Hengist.

He did not wish to think of Hengist. He pushed thoughts of his half-brother from his mind, instead turning it to Hefenfelth. Then Oswald had led them through a storm-riven night to fall upon the unsuspecting Waelisc host. That blood-drenched night had led to a great victory for Oswald, and the death of Cadwallon of Gwynedd. But Beobrand well remembered the pain that had followed at learning of the death of his lord, Scand, in the battle.

He watched the moon-licked shapes of Eowa and Acennan as they rode some way before him. There were no other men he would rather have at his side in a shieldwall than these and his gesithas. But none save the gods knew what their wyrd would bring with the dawn.

Would the golden light of the morning sun see them victorious over Penda? Or would it only shine its light on tragedy and grief?

Beobrand pulled his damp cloak about him, hunched his shoulders against the cold and let Bera carry him onwards through the dark.

Chapter 18

When the wolf-light of dawn tinged the eastern sky grey, Beobrand called a halt. The men needed rest and to eat something before continuing. Many were almost asleep as they walked, and at the order to stop, these men flung themselves to the wet ground, groaning and muttering. Some had that skill prized by warriors of being able to sleep wherever and whenever needed, and the rasping sounds of snoring were quickly added to the lively birdsong that signalled the impending dawn.

"Gods," said Acennan, dismounting with a grunt and leading his mare over to Beobrand, "I hope we do not rely on surprise. Those snores will alert any enemy from here to the Hibernian sea."

Beobrand offered him a thin smile, and slid from the saddle. He stretched his back, rubbing at the base of his spine to ease the tension there. Acennan always jested at times such as these. Beobrand could feel his skin jangling and a pressure building within his head as they got ever closer to battle. He beckoned to Ástígend. The messenger rode over to them on his new steed. Eowa had ordered one of his gesithas to walk and to give Ástígend his horse. Eowa's man now led the mount that Ástígend had ridden the day before, but the beast looked as though it might never recover from the forced gallop. Ástígend didn't look much better. His eyes were dark-rimmed and sunken, his skin wan.

"How do you fare?" asked Beobrand.

Ástígend straightened his back and squared his shoulders. He took a deep breath, hawked and spat from where he sat in the saddle.

"I am well, lord," he said. His voice was clear and strong. He was a proud man. "I can ride another sennight before I need to sleep."

He looked ready to drop from the saddle, but Beobrand would not shame the man. Besides, he needed him to remain mounted.

"Good man," he said. "Only you have seen this land before, Ástígend. I would have you be our eyes. I would know how far we are from Oswald and Penda."

Ástígend nodded and peered around them. But it was yet dark, and there was little to distinguish one shadowed clump of trees from another.

"The sun will be up soon," said Beobrand. "Ride with Attor to the brow of that bluff yonder and tell us where we are. I would not have us march blindly into Penda's warhost."

They watched as the two riders cantered into the gloom. The sun had not yet cleared the eastern horizon, but the darkness of the night had receded. Around them wisps of mist hung like spectres over the land.

"Do you think Oswald yet stands?" asked Eowa, who had dismounted and stood beside Acennan.

"We must hope he does," replied Beobrand, "for without his host, how do you think we would fare against Penda and his allies?"

Eowa did not reply. He rubbed his hand across his bearded, scarred face and stared after Attor and Ástígend.

Beobrand stifled a yawn and rubbed grit from his eyes. Gods, how he longed for sleep. Close by, Dreogan snored, his mouth open, his scarred and tattooed face, usually so menacing and hard, now soft and peaceful. Acennan caught Beobrand's eye and shook his head. Beobrand wished he could lie down and succumb to the tiredness that tugged at him, but he knew he could not. For the men to see him thus, slack-mouthed and snoring, would not do.

All around them, men were slumped on the ground. Most did not have the luxury of a horse and Beobrand could well imagine their exhaustion after a full day's march followed by the dank night-time trudge through the rain and darkness.

Acennan handed him a chunk of hard cheese and a piece of stale bread. Beobrand was not hungry, but he forced himself to chew, washing the food down with a swig of sour water from his leather flask. Woden knew when next they might be able to rest and eat, and they would all need their strength when they met Penda's host. Of that he was certain.

"They're coming back," said Acennan, staring towards the bluff.

Beobrand swallowed the last of the cheese and bread and pushed himself to his feet with a grimace and a groan. His back still hurt.

The sun had risen, casting warm light over middle earth. His shadow was long and dark on the earth before him as he followed Acennan's gaze. Ástígend and Attor were cantering towards them, the breath from their horses steaming in the early morning air. Beobrand glanced up at the sky. The clouds had blown away to the south. The ground mist would be gone soon, burnt away by the dawn, and it would be a warm, clear day.

"What news?" he called, as the riders reined in.

"We are still some way from the place they call Maserfelth," said Ástígend. "But there are many birds in the sky to the west." He was flushed, as if the ride had awoken in him a new strength. "It will take the best part of the day to walk there." He said no more, but his meaning was clear. If Penda had already attacked they may well be too late, but if he chose to confront Oswald today, there may still be time. But every moment would count. Not a heartbeat could be wasted and they still had a long way to travel.

Beobrand looked about him at the exhausted men.

As if he had heard Beobrand's thoughts, Eowa said, "They are strong men. Their hearts doughty. They will march on and then, despite their tiredness, they will fight."

"I do not doubt the mettle of the men, Eowa," said Beobrand. "But they are but men. They cannot fly. Nor can they run all day after marching since yesterday's dawn with little more than a moment's rest."

Eowa sighed, but said nothing.

"How long would it take to ride there?" asked Beobrand.

Ástígend turned and peered into the west, as though he could somehow see beyond the hills that rose there. He closed his eyes, muttering under his breath. Then with a nod, he opened his eyes and said, "On horseback we can reach Oswald King before the sun reaches its peak."

"Very well," said Beobrand, "you will lead me and my men to Maserfelth." He turned to Eowa. "I cannot bear to walk when my king might even now be beset by Penda and his wolves."

Eowa held his gaze for a long moment, and then nodded.

"Ride then, my friend," he said. "And I will make haste with my fyrd and hearth-warriors to bring our spears to Northumbria's defence."

"I give you thanks," said Beobrand. He was suddenly seized by the urge to embrace the atheling, but instead he held out his hand and Eowa clasped his forearm in the warrior grip.

"I do not seek thanks for honouring my oath to your king," said Eowa.

"You may not seek it, but I give it freely." Beobrand hesitated, and then said, "Friend."

Eowa gripped his arm more strongly.

"Go, Beobrand. Ride to your lord's aid. You are oath-sworn to Oswald and you must protect him. It is as it should be. But,"

Eowa smiled, "look to the east for your friend. For my trusty Mercians will swell your ranks and together we will rid Albion of the scourge that is my brother."

Beobrand swung himself onto Bera's back.

"Mount up, men," he shouted. "For we ride."

He waved to Eowa.

"I will drink with you this night, if my wyrd allows it," called the atheling.

Claws of unease scratched down Beobrand's back and he suppressed a shudder. He hoped Eowa's confidence was well-founded, for they rode towards battle and death. He did not reply, but as he kicked Bera into a trot he could not shake the image of Eowa and him seated side by side and drinking fine mead. But in his mind's eye, they were not sitting on the benches of a local lord, or even in a leather tent after the battle-play was done.

They were raising their drinking horns in the great corpse-hall of Woden, father of all the gods.

"Look, see there." Acennan pointed ahead. He had to raise his voice to be heard over the clatter and thump of the mounted warriors who rode in a tightly packed group along the old Roman road. Beobrand strained his eyes but could make out nothing more than a wooded hill. He blinked and rubbed his eyes with the back of his hand. It was hard to make out details so far away. His eyes were tired and Bera's trotting made it difficult to focus.

"I still don't see it," he said, an edge of frustration in his tone. They had been riding since dawn and the sun was now high in the sky behind them. They dared not push the mounts to more than a trot, for fear of killing them and being forced to continue on foot. Beneath him, Bera quivered and sweated. Fleetingly, he wished he had never lost Sceadugenga. The black stallion had seldom seemed to tire, and its gait was so much more pleasant than this cantankerous beast.

"See," said Acennan, "Ástígend and Attor must have seen them now too."

Beobrand saw the two men, who rode some distance ahead of the main band of riders, spur their mounts forward and speed up the rise towards the trees on the slope. As he watched they slowed and then wheeled their steeds round and cantered back down the hill towards Beobrand and the approaching warband of mounted gesithas. Beobrand did not slow. There was no time to waste. He wished he could urge the horses into a gallop, but sense prevailed. It would do them no good to close a short distance swiftly, only to lose their mounts.

Attor and Ástígend reached them quickly and fell into step beside Beobrand and Acennan at the head of the group.

"Well?" snapped Beobrand.

"We saw riders on the hill," replied Ástígend. His face was set, his eyes dark.

"Who were they?" asked Beobrand.

"Hard to say," said Attor. "But they were armed and rode fine steeds. We gave chase, but their mounts were fresh, ours..." He patted his horse's neck and shook his head, as if apologising for what he was about to say. "Ours are all but done in. We would never catch them."

Beyond the wooded rise, dark flecks spun and gyred in the bright sky. A multitude of birds. Perhaps crows and ravens, bellies heavy with the flesh of fallen warriors.

"How close to Maserfelth?" he said.

Ástígend did not hesitate.

"We are very near, lord," he said. "When we pass this woodland, we will be able to see the Maerse to the south and the hill where Oswald planned to make his stand."

Beobrand shook his head to clear it of the cobwebs of tiredness.

"They know we are coming now," he said. "They will be waiting for us. We cannot follow the road any longer. Ástígend,

Attor, lead us by a different route to Maserfelth and Oswald's hill."

For a moment, Beobrand wondered whether either man had heard him. They rode on for a moment in silence. A glance at Ástígend showed him the man's drawn face, eyes sunken, but bright, almost feverish. He was close to collapse. Beobrand knew he had asked much of the man. Perhaps he would have to rely on another. But before Beobrand could speak, Ástígend tugged at his mount's reins and cantered off the road to the north. Attor was an instant behind him.

"Follow me, lord," Ástígend called. "I will find us a way."

Without pause, Beobrand kicked Bera after them. He gripped the reins tightly. His body thrummed, as taut as a calf skin stretched over a drum. He could almost smell battle on the breeze. They were so close now.

They rode along the base of the hill, skirting thickets of brambles and crossing a burbling stream. Beobrand hoped that the enemy horsemen had not turned back to watch them. If they were still being observed from the shadow of the trees above them, their chances of reaching Oswald without being intercepted would be slim. He pushed the worry from his mind. Without their riders' bidding, the horses had sped up into a loping canter. The animals too could scent the end of their long journey. A journey that would surely end in death and the steel-storm of battle.

Ástígend turned his horse to the east, up the rise following an almost imperceptible track, left by shepherds perhaps. Beobrand had no idea who had made the path, but Ástígend had keen eyes and a clear sense of direction and he seemed to have no difficulty in following the route up the slope towards the trees.

Beobrand kicked Bera's flanks and the horse snorted, powering up the incline. Despite his tiredness, Beobrand grinned at Acennan. His friend smiled back. They knew each other well. All around them, other men showed their teeth and spurred their mounts up the slope. They rode towards the clamour of the shieldwall, towards the uncertainty of a warrior's wyrd when the swords sing and the shields clash. They rode on towards chaos and the great blood-letting of war.

And they were filled with the joy of it.

For these men were gesithas. Hearth-warriors. Shield-men. Spear-men. Sword-men.

Death-dealers.

They rode onwards, knowing that death awaited them and they smiled and snarled at its approach.

They did not fear the end of a life well-lived. They would kill their foe-men or they would die in battle. Either might bring them battle-glory and fame. To die well was all a man could ask for.

Chapter 19

They followed Ástígend and Attor for what seemed like a long time, into the darkness beneath oak, birch and pine, where they had to slow for fear of being unseated by low branches. The forest was dense. Brambles and twigs caught at their cloaks and scratched their hands and faces. Beobrand leaned forward, lowering his body and face against Bera's great neck. The horse's rough, greasy mane was pungent. Heat came off the beast in waves and the rise and fall of its chest reminded Beobrand of the bellows being worked at a smith's forge. Bera may not be as fine a steed as Sceadugenga, but it was a brave creature.

"Come on, old friend," he whispered. Bera's ears twitched, as though in response to its master's voice.

And then, without warning, they were out of the wood.

Beobrand blinked at the bright light of the midday sun. Someway off to their left, was amassed a great battlehost. Banners were held high and fluttered in the wind. Beobrand recognised Fordraed's black horned bull's head on a red background, and to its right the cross of Oswald, King of Northumbria. Beobrand let out a shout of joy. The king still stood.

"Come, men," he yelled at the riders who were leaving the cool gloom of the tree-shade. "Behold, our king."

Ástígend had slowed, waiting for Beobrand to reach him, but Beobrand did not pause. Kicking Bera forward, he waved at Ástígend.

"You have done well, Ástígend," he called. "If we live to see another sunrise I will reward you richly."

Riding on towards the mass of men, Beobrand squinted against the brilliance of the sun that was reflected from hundreds of byrnies and helms. This was a veritable forest of spears, and the wicked steel tips glittered and shone. For a moment he was confused as to what he saw. Where was the enemy? And then the picture made sense to him. Ástígend had said Oswald meant to make his stand atop a hill. He could not see Penda's host, for they were on the other side, beneath Oswald's force. Beobrand and his mounted warband approached from the rear of the Northumbrian lines.

The ground rose gently before them, sloping up to the brow of the hill where Oswald's host stood. Beobrand took in everything as he rode up the shallow incline. The glittering spear-points, pointing at the sky, not forward towards the unseen foe. The banners, held firm, their shafts unwavering. And the stillness, as if all the men on that hill held their breaths.

Oswald had not yet joined in battle.

In that unnatural quiet, the thump of horses' hooves and the jangle of the warriors' harness were strident.

"Hail, Oswald King!" Beobrand bellowed.

Men turned to see who approached from their rear. For a short time, there was uncertainty in the ranks. Spears jostled, as men shifted position and then a figure stepped forth from the mass of men.

He bore a bright shield, freshly painted white with a red cross. The boss glinted in the sun. On his head he wore a fine helm with bronze and garnets glimmering around the eye guards and nasal. Beneath the protection of the decorated helm, jutted a grey-streaked black beard, from which flashed the white of strong teeth. The man planted his feet and roared at Beobrand.

"Well, if it isn't the lord of Ubbanford," he shouted. "You took your time, Beobrand. Did you tarry to pick flowers along the way?"

Beobrand pulled Bera to a halt and slid from the saddle. His black shield, held in place by leather straps, slapped against his back

"Well met, Derian," he said loudly, returning Oswald's warmaster's grin. "I trust we are not too late. My men and I tire of peace and would paint our blades with the blood of some Mercians."

Beobrand untied his helm from his saddle and placed it on his head.

Derian clapped Beobrand on the shoulder, and beckoned for a young thrall to take his horse's reins.

"See to their horses," he said. A short way down the slope, several mounts were tethered and grazing. Other boys came and took the reins of the newly arrived warriors.

"There will be enough Mercian blood for us all, Beobrand, Lord of Ubbanford," said Derian, his voice louder than was needed. Then, in a quieter tone, meant only for Beobrand's ears, his words coloured by anxiety, he asked, "Are these all the men you bring with you?"

"No," replied Beobrand. "Eowa is coming with many score more. They are less than a day away, but they are on foot. I thought you might wish us to hasten here."

Derian nodded, but his grin had vanished.

"The men will take heart at your arrival."

"What of Oswiu?" asked Beobrand.

"No sign, and no tidings," replied Derian, his face grim. "We must pray that Oswiu is close and Eowa arrives in time. Can we trust Eowa?"

Derian had been in that dark hut in Din Eidyn. Both Beobrand and he had beaten the Mercian atheling. Years had passed, but the images from that night were as fresh and raw as recently scratched scabs in Beobrand's mind.

Perhaps their actions that night still preyed on Derian's mind too.

"I do not think we need worry on that score," Beobrand replied, fumbling with the ties to his helm's cheek guards. "Eowa is a man of honour and he gave his oath to Oswald. Besides," he finished tying the helm in place, "Penda has made it easier for him."

"How so?"

"He sent a man to murder him in his own hall at Snodengaham."

Derian nodded.

"Yes, that would make a man less inclined to refuse to stand against his brother."

Beobrand shrugged his shield from his back and slipped his arm into the straps that he used to provide a stronger grip than his half-hand alone would allow. Like all of his gesithas, Beobrand's shield bore no emblem or sigil, it was simply painted black. Years before, Acennan had said that he should carry an emblem or banner for his men to follow. Beobrand had rejected the idea. He did not wish to be one of those thegns who preened and strutted beneath a gaudy standard. When he led his men into battle it was for one purpose only – to slay his enemies. When Acennan had insisted that they needed some way to know friend from foe, Fraomar had put forward the idea of painting all of their shields the same colour. The discussion of which colour had raged long into the night in the hall at Ubbanford. In the end, they had turned to Beobrand for the final decision. "Killing is a black business," he'd said. And so, the colour had been chosen and the battle-fame of Beobrand's black-shielded death-bringers had become the subject of scops' tales.

Derian turned and began pushing his way through the gathered warriors, towards Oswald's cross and the front of the shieldwall. Beobrand followed him. Acennan had dismounted and fell into step beside them. Beobrand dropped his hand to Hrunting's hilt. He absently traced his fingers over the familiar carved pommel.

"How bad is it?" he asked Derian, in a quiet tone, barely more than a whisper.

Derian turned to face him. His eyes shone from behind the eye guard of the helmet.

"I'll show you," he said.

"God has listened to my prayers," Oswald said. His voice was muffled by the intricately wrought faceplate of his grimhelm, but Beobrand recognised well the softly intelligent tone, carrying the barest hint of the lilting tongue of the Hibernians amongst whom he had spent his youth in exile. Oswald had the voice of a Christ monk, but Beobrand knew him to be an implacable warrior. He would not shy away from strife. Beobrand recalled Cadwallon's severed head, lifeblood pumping into the earth while the king of Gwynedd's eyes stared blindly. Again he remembered the cold hut where Eowa had received his punishment for daring to cross Oswald.

Beobrand pushed the memories away. He looked out at the scene below them. Despite the bright sun blazing from a sky of the purest dunnock eggshell blue, this day was dark enough without dwelling on the past.

"If I am the answer to your prayers, lord," he said, "I hope I do not disappoint. I do not see how my meagre warband can make a difference against such a horde."

Below them, the hill fell away to a wide expanse of marshy land. Far in the distance, the sun glistened on the water of the wide Maerse. Several boats were beached on a broad mudflat on the north bank. Pools, meres and bogs dotted the land close to the river, but the ground must be drier closer to the hill on which he stood, for it was covered in tents and shelters. Smoke from dozens of cooking fires hazed the air above the encampment.

Beobrand could see why Oswald had chosen this spot. Having the higher ground would make it easier to defend, and the marshy field before them provided little in the way of cover or protection. There were clumps of waving purple loosestrife and beds of dense reeds, but no trees, save for a solitary ash that rose above the marsh. It was a huge tree, its great boughs heavy with summer foliage. It dominated the landscape and men had set up camp beneath it. The ground must be dry there, and it provided shelter under its soaring limbs.

"Nonsense, Beobrand," came the reply from Oswald. "You are not any man. You are God's instrument and with you by my side, I do not believe the good Lord will allow me to be defeated."

Beobrand looked away, unable to meet his king's eye. Gods, how had it come to this? He let out a long breath.

"You know my sword and my life is yours, Oswald King," he said. "But I have never before beheld such a host. Not at Elmet. Or Hefenfelth. Not even at the great ditch in East Angeln." He swallowed and scanned the men below them. He had no skill for counting, but he saw many banners and standards, and each signified a lord or king. And each brought his own warriors. There, in the shadow of the great ash was the grey, wolf-pelt standard of Penda. Over to the left, he saw the grisly skull-and-scalp totem of Gwynedd. He wondered for a moment whether Gwalchmei ap Gwyar was there in the throng below. Of course he must be. He was a warrior lord of Gwynedd, and what enemy of Northumbria would not wish to be here? This was the greatest gathering of foe-men he had witnessed, and there was no way one such as Gwalchmei would miss it. Other banners fluttered in the soft breeze. A red wyrm and a white eagle, both on black backgrounds, the black lion on white of Powys. He knew not who all of the standards represented, but judging from the horde of men beneath them, they were numerous, rich and powerful.

Then he saw the bear's-head standard of Grimbold and underneath it a flash of red; a mane of flame-coloured hair and bristling beard on a hulking giant of a man. Halga, son of Grimbold. Beobrand had faced the brute twice before, and his body bore the scars as a constant reminder of the huge Mercian's deadly prowess.

"Do you hear that, my brave warriors?" Oswald raised his voice, and it boomed, strangely hollow from behind his great helm. "Beobrand has never seen so many men to slaughter in one place. God has blessed us with a great many enemies that we may smite them all and then find peace." Beobrand had said similar to men before battles. But now, with the exhaustion of the long ride heavy upon him like a wet cloak and the grittiness of eyes that had not known sleep for two days, Oswald's words sounded empty to him. A few of the warriors laughed at the king's comment, but there was no joy in the sound.

"How long have you stood here watching the enemy?" Beobrand asked in a quiet voice.

"We believed they would attack yesterday," Derian replied, "but they just brought more men across the Maerse."

By all the gods, it was no wonder the men lacked the lust for battle. They had stood these past two days watching their foe grow stronger. And they had done nothing to hamper their enemy. How he wished he had arrived sooner. They might have gone down at night and burnt the boats. Such a thing would have fanned the flames of Oswald's host's courage and disheartened the Mercians. Instead, they had stood by, at the mercy of Penda of Mercia, as he gathered his allies to him. They all knew the king of Mercia was a great warlord. He was a killer of kings. A warrior of Woden who had never been defeated in battle. Stories about him were oft told in the mead halls throughout the land. It was said that he was Woden-touched, favoured by the old gods. He yet offered blood and sacrifice to the gods in the way of his forefathers, and many believed the gods had made him invincible as a gift for his faith.

Beobrand knew not the truth of that, but there was no doubt that Penda was a mighty warrior. Death sang to his tune, and it seemed the gods smiled upon him.

To stand atop this hill and offer no resistance to the man as he crossed the river that bounded the frontier between Mercia and Northumbria was foolishness. Each moment that had passed would have seen the resolve of the defenders weaken and wither.

Beobrand took a step out in front of the shieldwall. He could go no further for he would then be lower than Oswald's battlehost and his voice would be lost to those behind the front rank.

"Men of Northumbria," he shouted in the battle-voice he had learnt from his old lord, Scand, "you know me. I am Beobrand, Lord of Ubbanford, who many of you will know as Half-hand." He held his shield aloft, showing the straps on the inside of the board and the severed fingers of his mutilated hand. "You have watched as Penda has brought his warriors across the Maerse. They now camp below us on Northumbrian soil. Do they have a right to be here?"

A few men muttered a response.

"I asked if the Mercian and Waelisc scum," he spat the words as he bellowed, "gathered there on the boggy field of Maserfelth have a right to be on Northumbrian soil. On our soil!"

This time the reply was loud.

"No!"

"No," he shouted. "Penda leads our enemies here to take what is ours. Do men of Northumbria allow their enemies to come into their land?"

"No!"

"No, we fight!" he screamed, his voice cracking. "We fight, and we kill! We will send these dogs back into the river bleeding so hard that the Maerse will run red." The men of the fyrd cheered. An inchoate roar of outrage and anger that had finally been unleashed. His hands shook at his side now. His body trembled, the fire of battle burning away his exhaustion. Acennan grinned at him. Beside him Beobrand saw Dreogan, Attor and the others. They raised spears and swords into the air, adding their voices to those of the men who had stood on this hill watching Penda's force grow.

Beobrand waited for the noise to abate and then he raised his voice once more.

"Hear me, men of Northumbria. Oswald King speaks true when he says there are more men gathered below us than I have seen before. And those Mercian and Waelisc men down there will be quaking with fear as they behold us atop this hill. For know this. They have never before faced the likes of us. We are men of Northumbria and our king is Oswald, son of Æthelfrith, and he has the ear of the one true God. He brought us victory at Hefenfelth, and he will do so again."

Acennan caught his attention, gesturing with his chin that Beobrand should look behind him, towards Maserfelth and the river. He turned and saw that Penda's host was moving. It seemed the men of Gwynedd and Powys were being sent to the eastern flank, while the Mercians were moving towards the foot of the hill.

"The time for waiting is over," said Beobrand, once again facing the Northumbrians. "Penda knows that a great warband marches from the east to our aid. They will be upon them before the day is out, so he can tarry no longer." Beobrand cast another glance back down the slope. There was no question; the warriors were forming a shieldwall to the south of the hill. It would not be long now.

"Prepare to stand strong," Beobrand roared. "Gird yourselves and see to your weapons, for now comes the time of blood-letting. We are men of Deira and Bernicia. Northumbrians all! We stand with our king, and we shall let none pass!"

The men cheered.

"For Oswald!" he cried, repeating the chant until every man took it up.

He returned to the shieldwall and Oswald clapped him on the shoulder in thanks. Beobrand leant in close to the king so that he alone would hear his voice over the cacophony of the host who still chanted his name.

"I hope your Christ god truly listens to your prayers," he said to Oswald.

"Of course He does," Oswald replied. Beobrand could see his brown eyes glistening from behind the elaborate grimhelm that he himself had once worn into battle at Tatecastre.

"That is good, lord king," he said, taking hold of a spear that Dreogan handed him, and looking back at the hundreds of men forming ranks at the bottom of the slope. "Otherwise, I think we'd be as fucked as one of Fordraed's thralls."

Chapter 20

"Shields," yelled Beobrand, raising his linden board over his head as yet another rain of projectiles fell amongst the Northumbrian ranks. Stones and arrows clattered from shields and helms. Something cracked against his unprotected midriff. Looking down, Beobrand saw the pebble fall harmlessly to the grass. It was impossible to remain completely protected by the hide-covered board of his round shield, especially with the angle of the attacking archers and slingers. Some of their missiles arched overhead to drop from above, while others were sent on a straighter path, up the slope and into the first rank of the shieldwall. Beobrand offered up a silent prayer of thanks to Tiw, god of war, for his byrnie. The metal shirt would stop all but the unluckiest of arrows and no pebble or slingshot could hope to penetrate its iron-riveted links.

He did worry about his legs. They were the most exposed part of his body, and being clad only in breeches and leg bindings, should an arrow find its mark there, he would suffer from it. He glanced over at where Oswald crouched behind his own shield, and recalled the stray arrow that had pierced his king's shoulder at Tatecastre. Beobrand had also felt the sting of an arrow's bite before, and his calf still ached in memory of Torran's barb when the weather turned cold.

The arrows and stones ceased falling and the Northumbrians lowered their shields once more to peer over the rims and look at the Mercians below. Thus it had been for a long while. The Mercians shot arrows and stones at the defenders, wounding a few every now and then, but causing no great damage to Oswald's force. Then, they would pause for a time, before starting the process again. Each time, Beobrand thought the shieldwall would advance under the cover of the missiles, but every time when the arrows and stones stopped falling, the grim-faced Mercian warriors yet stood resolutely at the base of the hill.

"This reminds me of the scrap in the ditch," said Dreogan, his savage grin stretching the soot-stained tattoos on his cheeks.

Beobrand grimaced.

At the ditch, Penda had ordered his archers and slingers to pound them before the attack with spear and sword. Beobrand thought of the mud, shit and blood that had formed a quagmire of death at the bottom of the ditch, and how the defenders had broken their ranks and rushed down the slope to their doom.

"Let's hold our position then," he shouted back.

Dreogan laughed.

"That would seem wise," he said.

Beside him, a figure took a quick step out from the line. It was Garr, his slender, tall form in stark contrast to Dreogan's bullish shoulders and thick muscled neck. As Beobrand watched, Garr flung a light throwing spear high and far. Did he expect to hit a target at such a range? If anyone could, it would be Garr. He was a natural with a spear and Beobrand's gesithas had often won wagers on the distance he could throw. The host fell silent and everyone followed the arcing flight of the javelin out into the bright afternoon. The throw was good and true. The weapon seemed to hang in the air for a moment, dark against the blue of the sky, and then it sped down towards the Mercians. They too must have observed the single spear hurtling towards them, for some of them jostled, trying frantically to get out of the path of the deadly dart.

But Garr was the greatest spear-man Beobrand had ever seen, and it was as though he controlled the weapon with his mind even after it had left his hand, such was its accuracy. The Mercians scattered, hastily raising shields, their faces pale as they gazed up at the heavens and the death that plummeted towards them. The javelin found its target, burying itself deep within a bearded archer's chest. He fell to his knees, mouth agape, eyes wide in the shock of sudden and unexpected death. Slumping to the side, he shuddered once, and was still.

The Northumbrians let out a great cheer. They were not toothless up here on their hill. They too could rain down death on their foes.

Garr raised a hand in salute towards Beobrand and the king.

"Well done," Beobrand said, "now get back in line." Beneath them, he could see the Mercians preparing another onslaught.

"Shields!" he bellowed again. And all around him, men lifted their boards above their heads and prepared again to weather the storm of metal and stone.

The first projectiles began to fall, with the patter of hail rattling against the wooden shingles of a great hall. Beobrand chanced a glance from underneath his shield. As he had expected, Garr's spear had goaded the Mercians into action. While the archers tensed and loosed, and the slingers swung their leather straps to fling stones, the Mercian shieldwall surged forward up the slope.

"Shieldwall! Ready yourselves," Derian boomed in a powerful battle-shout from the centre of the Northumbrian line. "The Mercians are coming!"

Chapter 21

"Come to die on my blade, you maggots!" screamed Attor, darting forward from the line. He ducked beneath the wild sweep of an enemy sword and opened the man's throat in a spraying fountain of crimson. As usual the slim scout was unarmoured, moving with lithe, seemingly effortless grace to avoid the clumsy blows of his foes. He wielded a vicious langseax, almost the length of a sword, but single edged, with no guard. Attor was as fast as thought and his langseax flashed in the afternoon sunlight, silver and red, like a leaping salmon. The Mercian's lifeblood spouted forth, covering Attor in gore. Attor grinned, his teeth and eyes bright in the mask of blood.

Beobrand shoved hard with his shield at the burly Mercian before him. The man slipped on the blood-soaked grass and Beobrand hacked down with Hrunting into his shoulder, sundering the man's byrnie and almost severing his right arm. Iron rings and gouts of blood flew into the hot air. The man shrieked and tumbled back, disappearing down the hill to join the dozens of his comrades' corpses that already rested there. Beobrand laughed aloud, the battle-joy upon him now.

"Attor," he yelled. "Get back into the shieldwall."

Beobrand gazed down at the slain; the Mercians who had charged against the shieldwall atop the hill overlooking

Maserfelth. Many were the brave men who had attacked the Northumbrians and fallen to drench the earth with their slaughter-sweat. And yet still more came up that treacherous slope. And behind them numerous banners still fluttered in the breeze. Penda's horde seemed undiminished, despite the Northumbrian host's terrible death-dealing.

The onslaught had been nearly continuous, with barely a moment to take a swig of water or to rest. But despite the weariness of his limbs, Beobrand could not deny the excitement that filled him. He might think he longed for peace when he awoke from the horrific dreams of terror where he saw the faces of those he had slain; blood-splattered and terrible, screaming for a mercy which he knew he would never give. But here, surrounded by the clash and clamour of battle, his nerves thrilled and he knew the truth of it. This was where he belonged. He was a killer, like his father before him. And his brother. He shuddered at the thought, but deep down he knew it was true. He lived to kill.

All along the hilltop, the Mercians were retreating, pushed back down the slope to lick their wounds before the next assault.

On Beobrand's right, Acennan faced a well-armoured warrior who perhaps had not realised he had been left alone before the Northumbrian host. The Mercian was broad-shouldered and powerful; a man of some means, judging by his ornate helm, with its embossed plates of decoration and the fine, pattern-bladed sword he wielded. As ever in the shieldwall, Acennan and Beobrand stood shoulder to shoulder, each seeming to understand the other's movements without words. Attor took a step towards Acennan to offer his aid against the lone Mercian, but Beobrand held him back.

The man was taller than Acennan, with a longer reach. But Beobrand did not doubt his friend's ability to bring him down and he knew that Acennan would not thank Attor for interfering.

The Northumbrians fell silent as they watched the encounter between the rich Mercian thegn and the squat Northumbrian gesith.

With a bellowing roar, the Mercian stamped forward, leading with his shield. Acennan swayed to the side, hardly seeming to move, and yet the attack went harmlessly wide and Acennan hammered his own blade into the man's unprotected shin. Acennan's sword cut deeply, slicing sinew, muscle and bone. The Mercian mewled in shocked agony and lost his balance on the shattered limb, falling to the red-stained earth. Before he could begin to recover, Acennan thrust down hard into the Mercian's now-exposed groin and then leapt back quickly to avoid the man's flailing swings as his life left him. All those who watched knew the Mercian had taken a killing blow, and his blood pumped dark from the artery on the inside of his thigh.

The Mercian screamed and cursed Acennan, but the stocky Northumbrian did not risk getting close to silence him.

Beobrand thrust Hrunting into the earth at his feet, freeing his right hand for a moment so that he could wipe the sweat and blood from his brow. He was unable to use his forearm, as it was encased in metal strips fastened by straps of leather. More than once the armour had saved his hand, so he would put up with the discomfort. Just as he would endure the sweltering heat of wearing his great helm. He well remembered the clang of the slingshot in East Angeln. He still got terrible headaches, but the helm had saved his life that day.

Dreogan proffered a water skin. Beobrand took a long draught and handed it to Acennan. The shorter man drank, spat, then drank again. Beneath them, the Mercians would soon begin sending up more arrows and stones, in preparation for another attack. They appeared to have few arrows and pebbles left now, or perhaps some of the archers and slingers had ventured up the hill already and paid the ultimate price for that foolhardy act. Whatever the reason, each new hail of projectiles was less vehement than the one before.

The Mercian whom Acennan had felled still whimpered and cried out.

"Gods, won't you finish what you started?" asked Dreogan. "The man's whining is making my head hurt."

"He'll be silent soon enough," said Acennan. "I'll have a rest for a moment, then I'm getting that helm. It must be worth a fortune." He took another mouthful of water from the skin, then passed it back to Beobrand. "I was quite pleased I managed not to damage it."

The man's cries were becoming faint, as he faded quickly.

"I don't know what you will do with such a fine helm," said Fraomar. "It will never fit on your big head." The men laughed, the sound jarring against the moaning of the dying man. Somewhere from further down the slope another injured warrior wailed pitifully for his mother. It was the voice of a boy, and Beobrand thought fleetingly of Octa.

"You may be right," said Acennan, "but it will look good on Stagga's wall. Besides," he smiled, "I would not wish to cover my beautiful face. What then would the ladies have to look at?"

The wounded man was silent now. Acennan stepped close to him, placing his foot on the man's sword to prevent an attack. He drove his own blade deep into the man's throat. Quickly, he set about removing the fabulous helm before the next Mercian advance.

"You think we can win, lord?" Attor said in a quiet voice.

Beobrand looked up at the sky. The sun was long past its zenith. To the east, the ranks of unblooded Waelisc yet guarded the road, awaiting the arrival of Eowa's fyrd.

"Aye," Beobrand said, "of course we can win." He hoped the men could not hear the uncertainty in his voice. "We are strong here on this hill. We can hold until the end of time. But we will not need to wait that long, I hope." He forced a grin. "Once Eowa arrives with his host, Penda and his Waelisc allies will have a real fight on their hands."

Acennan had retrieved the Mercian's helm and sword and returned to his place at Beobrand's side.

"But for now," Beobrand said, tugging Hrunting from the earth and once more hefting his shield aloft, "we hold this hill, and we do what we do best."

"And what is that?" asked Fraomar.

"We kill the bastards," shouted Beobrand, as the first arrow flickered into the sky towards them. As one, they raised their boards again and readied themselves to do just that.

Chapter 22

The day wore on in a haze of sweat, blood and death. The steel-storm's song was the ringing clash of blades and the screams of the dying. As the sun slid towards the western edge of the world, the exhaustion of the defenders began to tell. Men stumbled and slipped, or were too slow to parry or lift their shields. The Northumbrians had held firm that long afternoon, but now, with the last light of the sun casting long shadows, the men of Bernicia and Deira began to die.

One of Oswald's hearth-men, a fearsome fighter who stood beside Derian, took a spear to the neck and collapsed, clutching bloody fingers around his leaking throat. His mouth worked silently for a moment until he shuddered and remained still and staring.

The shieldwall trembled like a living thing. Like a wounded animal. Beobrand could sense the signs of impending defeat. Almost imperceptibly the shieldwall had been pushed back, pace by pace away from the lip of the hill, giving the attackers a foothold on the knap of the rise where before they could find none. He had ceased speaking of victory when Eowa's host would arrive, for the atheling of Mercia was nowhere to be seen. How could it be that Eowa had not reached them yet? Was it possible that he had turned back as soon as Beobrand had ridden away with his warband? No, it could not be. He shook his head to dispel such dark thoughts from his mind. Eowa was no craven and he had given his word. He would come.

And yet, when Beobrand looked to the east, at the Waelisc who thronged before the dark forest, there was no sign of Eowa and the men he brought with him.

Again the Mercians attacked, and Beobrand stepped forward to meet them without thinking. Acennan was at his right, Dreogan to his left.

"For Oswald!" Beobrand bellowed, his voice cracking in his throat. The men around him took up the chant.

"For Oswald!" they cried in defiance of the Mercians that crested the hill.

"For Oswald!"

They railed against the defeat they could all scent; against the unfairness of the threads of their wyrd that would see them die here.

A bearded man thrust a spear at Beobrand's face. Beobrand's shield felt as heavy as if it were made of granite, but he heaved it up just in time to catch the spear-point. The steel flickered bright past his eyes and, trusting to his instincts, Beobrand leapt forward. The spear haft scraped along the rim of his splintering linden board and Beobrand hunched his shoulders, dropping his head behind the shield's protection. The spear was over his shoulder now, its point behind him and no danger. Twisting his shield to the left, Beobrand drove Hrunting's point forward and felt the blade bite into flesh. Despite the weariness that threatened to engulf him, Beobrand smiled to see Acennan step forward with him to protect his flank. To his left he sensed without looking that Dreogan had also matched him. Gone was the surge of power that came with the first moments of battle-joy. In its place was the training and battle-skill that had been honed over years.

Beside Dreogan, young Fraomar and Garr were testament to that training, both working with implacable efficacy to dispatch the enemies who dared confront them.

Beyond them, Grindan and his brute of a brother, Eadgard, were still adding to the heap of dead before them. Eadgard lay about him with his huge axe, felling Mercians as if they were saplings that he was chopping for lumber, while Grindan leapt this way and that, parrying and lunging, killing many foe-men and also defending Eadgard, who always seemed oblivious to any danger once battle commenced.

Beobrand's men had been in the front line of the shieldwall all that long afternoon, with the stalwart Elmer, flanked by Renweard and Beircheart at the farthest point from Beobrand. They were all deadly; solid as a cliff-face and as vicious as a winter storm on the North Sea. The ground was slick and gore-spattered before the whole of the Northumbrian host. But the bodies were piled highest on the hill directly beneath Beobrand and his warband.

Beobrand and his black-shield-bearing gesithas were renowned throughout Albion for good reason. There was no deadlier group of warriors in all the kingdoms of the island.

But even such formidable fighters were but men. And no mortal man is invincible.

Renweard, his black raven's nest of a beard bristling from beneath his helm, rushed forward on tired legs to meet the latest onslaught of Mercians. But just before he struck at the warrior who came towards him, Renweard stepped upon the dented iron boss of a splintered shield. His ankle turned and he fell prostrate at the feet of the attackers. Beircheart and Elmer surged forward to his aid. But they were too late. A Mercian spear pierced Renweard's belly. The steel spear-point split the rings of his byrnie and buried itself deep in his body.

Elmer, his usually soft face contorted with rage and streaked with blood, roared and with a savage swing of his sword slew the man who had killed Renweard.

Beircheart did not scream or bellow his anger. He threw himself at the Mercians with abandon, hacking and beating his adversaries down with his blade in a welter of fury.

Beobrand shoved Hrunting under his shield again to saw into the crotch of a monstrously ugly man with a bulbous nose and a toothless maw. The Mercian let out an ululating scream and clawed at the rim of Beobrand's shield, vainly attempting to pull it down so that he might at least take his killer with him to the afterlife. Beobrand leant forward and bit the man's fingers. Hard. His mouth filled with blood and the Mercian let go. Beobrand punched his shield forward, catching the man in his ugly face with the boss. Blood slathered his repulsive face from the shield boss' shattering blow. More blood gushed from the gash in his groin and splattered the ground, and yet the man remained on his feet.

Acennan, with uncanny speed and agility, deftly dispatched the man he fought with a scything blow to his throat and then hacked a backhanded slash into the face of Beobrand's opponent.

"My blade improved his looks," he laughed.

Beobrand did not smile.

He looked over at where Beircheart and Elmer stood forlornly with slumped shoulders over Renweard's body. Beobrand's chest clenched. He had brought them to this place to stand by their king. He glanced to the east. Still no sign of Eowa. Could it be that they would all die here?

He looked down at the banners and standards of the Mercians and the horde of men amassed around the great ash tree below the hill. He swallowed, his throat dry. He feared this might well be the last battle he would stand in and he felt a great sadness. Renweard was dead. How many more would follow him to Woden's corpse-hall or to the Christ's heaven?

He took a shuddering breath of the warm air. It was redolent of the bitter tang of death. Far off in the west, the sun touched the rim of the earth.

Beobrand let out a ragged sigh.

They might all die here, but not this day. For the Mercians were falling back once again. And this time they were not regrouping at the base of the hill, but pulling back to their encampment for the night.

Chapter 23

Beobrand sat apart from his men, gazing over the marshy land towards the shimmering expanse of the Maerse. The last light of the setting sun still burnt beyond the western horizon, but soon it would be night. He had watched as Penda's great horde lit fires and settled down for the night. The smell of roasting meat came to him on the breeze. The laughter and songs of the Mercians and men of Powys and Gwynedd were muted by the distance, but distinct enough in the evening air. The king of Mercia seemed content to allow Oswald's battered force to remain on the hill. Perhaps he hoped they would flee in the darkness. Beobrand frowned to himself at the thought. Maybe some men would skulk off in the night. He could understand why they might do so. A corpse could not plough a field or sow seeds. A dead husband was no use to any woman. A dead man made a poor father. He snorted, thinking of the brute who had raised him. Grimgundi was long dead now, and Beobrand had never missed him.

Sometimes, he thought of Selwyn. He missed that old warrior and wished they'd had longer together after he knew the truth about him. But word had reached him of Selwyn's death shortly after their last meeting. Beobrand still could not think of Grimgundi's brother as his real father. Beobrand had believed the man to be his uncle for too long.

He rubbed his half-hand over his face. It was rough and sticky with sweat and blood.

Looking down at Penda's host, he felt hollow. He could not imagine the Northumbrians would withstand another day's assault. Men might well flee under the cover of the night, but Beobrand would remain. He had given Oswald his oath, and his word was iron. He would stand, and he would give his blood and his life to protect the land and his king.

How would Octa grow without a father? Would he become a warrior? Beobrand scratched at the crust of dried blood beneath his fingernails. Gods, he hoped not. Below him on the hill, in the last light of the dying sun, he could make out the black shapes of crows pecking and pulling at the flesh of the fallen. The Mercians had carried away some of their dead, but they did not seem keen to venture up the slope where they would be vulnerable to Northumbrian spears. In the morning, the bloated, bird-pecked remains of their shield-brothers would prove a stark reminder of the foe they faced. And the need to navigate around the bodies would make the climb all the more difficult.

Beobrand spat. No. He prayed that Octa would never know the terror of the shieldwall. But who was he to wish a soft life on his son? Did he truly hope that Octa would become a merchant or a monk? Would he see the boy denied the thrill and soaring joy of victory over an enemy? Was that not a true man's wyrd?

He sighed, too tired to worry about that which he could not control.

"He will come, Beobrand. God has not forsaken us."

The voice startled Beobrand from his thoughts. Oswald stood close to him. Derian, ever vigilant, scowled from a few paces away; close enough to guard the king, far enough not to overhear quietly spoken words.

For a time, Beobrand did not respond. He stared into the east, at the gloom beneath the trees there. There was no movement, no glint from spear or helm in the last rays of the sun.

"Yes. Eowa will come, my king," he said, at last. "He has given his oath on it."

"And you trust him?"

Beobrand nodded slowly.

"I do, lord. Whatever you think of the man, Eowa is honourable."

Oswald was silent. He had removed his great helm and his hair hung lank with the sweat of the day's fighting.

"And what of your brother, lord?" Beobrand asked. "Is there news of his coming with his warband from Rheged?"

Oswald sighed.

"Oswiu should have been here days ago. I sent men north to seek him out, but I have had no word and I can spare no more riders. I know not what might have befallen him to make him tarry so."

The king's eyes were dark. Beobrand could see his own weariness mirrored there. He worried for himself. For his warband and his son. Oswald also had these concerns to fill his head. He too was a father and husband. And also a brother. And yet, these things were as nothing compared to the fate of the whole kingdom of Northumbria. If it was a game that kings played, pitting their realms and their hosts against each other like so many pieces on a tafl board, had Oswald made a terrible blunder in the move that brought them to this place?

A sudden billow of fresh smoke signalled that one of the men had finally succeeded in lighting a fire. It was windy here, atop this hill, and the smoke blew into Beobrand's face as he looked at Oswald.

"I considered fleeing," Oswald said, his voice not much more than a whisper. "Today, when neither Oswiu nor Eowa came. I looked upon Penda's force and I knew despair."

Beobrand said nothing. He did not breathe. Was it possible he would yet be able to leave Maserfelth with his life. It was not death he feared, but to never see Octa grow. To never again see the way Reaghan's eyes shone when she looked upon him. No, he was not scared of death, but to his surprise, he understood in that moment he wished to live.

Oswald pushed his greasy hair back from his face and gazed down at the numerous campfires on the marshy field beneath the hill.

"My resolve faltered," he said, "but I should not have feared. For God is great. I prayed to Him and he sent me a sign, Beobrand."

"What sign, lord?"

"There was a lull in the fighting and so I prayed and the Lord showed me that we must remain here. Eowa will come and we will prevail." For a moment, the king was silent, his eyes focused on the past, on what he had seen during the battle. "I saw a dove of purest white in the clear sky over the forest there," he indicated the oak and birch woodland to the east. "As the bird flew, a hawk descended on it at great speed, striking it. I could see the blood from its wounds, the red on the white feathers, even at this distance. I thought then that the Lord was showing me my defeat, for it is well-known that the dove is a bird of God. But it does not do to try to understand the ways of the Lord. For even as I watched, another bird, as black as night, a raven, I think, flew out of the woods and attacked the hawk. The dove tumbled in the sky for a heartbeat, and then flew away, injured, but not dead."

"And the raven and the hawk?" asked Beobrand.

"I lost sight of them against the dark of the trees, and then the Mercians attacked up the hill once more and I could look no further. But the message is clear."

"Is it?"

"Yes," Oswald's voice took on a strained tone, as one exasperated with an obtuse child, "I am the dove, Penda is the hawk and Eowa is the raven. Eowa will come and we will be victorious."

Beobrand did not reply. The fire of faith burnt in Oswald's eyes. He would not listen if Beobrand questioned the omen; if he asked why it was that the dove that represented Oswald had flown away, and yet his king chose to stay and face Penda again on the morrow.

Oswald seemed to sense Beobrand's unease.

"Eowa will come, and so I pray will Oswiu. Together we will defeat Penda." Oswald's tone had become more urgent. Did he seek to convince Beobrand or himself?

"I will stand with you, my king," Beobrand said. He knew not what else to say. But his words seemed enough for Oswald, for he smiled and let out a sigh, as if he had feared Beobrand would run, leaving him to defend the hill without his warband.

"You have your luck, Beobrand," Oswald said, his dark eyes sparking with the reflection of the flickering fires of their enemies, "and I have God. With the two, how can we not be victorious?"

Chapter 24

After it was dark, and the moon had risen, gilding the land in silver, Acennan brought some food to Beobrand. But he had no stomach for it. He forced himself to chew and swallow some of the stew he was given, but it wadded in his throat and made him gag. The stench of death was heavy on the warm summer air and he could not rid himself of the knowledge of what awaited them when the sun rose. The sounds from the Mercian encampment wafted to them, making it impossible to forget even for an instant that their enemies rested only a few spear-throws distance from them.

Grindan produced some mead he had somehow managed to save until now and Beobrand's gesithas drank in memory of Renweard, their fallen brother. Beobrand sipped the drink. It tasted sour in his mouth. He always drank sparingly before a battle. As tired as he was, he did not wish to have dulled wits in the morning. Usually, he would have admonished his men, telling them not to get drunk, but they all knew what awaited them, and he would not deny them this night of drinking and companionship.

They set watches and Beobrand wrapped himself in his cloak and tried to sleep. His body ached, the old wounds to his chest and head throbbed, and new scrapes and cuts that he had not noticed during the heat of the day's fighting, now stung and itched. He had not slept for two days and was exhausted, craving sleep as a thirsty man lusts for water, and yet the release of slumber refused to come. He closed his eyes and his mind was flooded with images of those he had slain. His ears rang from the clangour of the shieldwall and the remembered screams of the dying filled his thoughts, allowing him no rest.

He awoke with a start, disoriented and confused, surprised that he had indeed slept. Around him men were talking quietly, rousing themselves. Someway off towards where the horses were tethered, someone was retching noisily. Beobrand sat up, then climbed to his feet with a groan. His breath smoked in the cool air. The sky was cloudless, the eastern horizon the colour of burnished bronze. Dawn was moments away.

Beobrand walked to the edge of the hill and looked down at Penda's host. The land was wreathed in mist, thick over the river and the marshes. The great ash tree rose from the sea of mist like a monstrous leafy island. The banners and standards of the different kings and warlords jutted out of the fog. There was no breeze, but the mist curled and eddied, wraith-like, as Mercians walked about the encampment.

"It is going to be a hot day."

Turning, Beobrand saw that Acennan was at his side. He nodded, but said nothing.

Acennan hawked and spat. There was no mist up here to hide the grisly remains of the previous day's fighting.

"That fog will burn away in moments once the sun is up," Acennan said. "I sent men to fetch water in the night. Killing so many Mercian bastards will be thirsty work."

Beobrand offered him a thin smile, but his attention was elsewhere. The movement in the Mercian camp was strange. He could not make out what was happening down there in the mist by the great ash. As he watched, flames flared up from four fires that had been placed at equal distance positioned around the huge tree.

"I've got a bad feeling about this," said Acennan.

Fear prickled Beobrand's neck.

A horn sounded from the field of Maserfelth then, long and lowing, like a calving cow. Several more times the horn was blown, and now the Northumbrians were gathering atop the hill to look down at what was taking place. Many were donning their helms, and hefting their shields as they came, cautious in case this was some trick and the Mercians meant to storm the hill while the defenders were distracted. Beobrand did not send for his helm or shield. He shivered and touched his hand to the hammer of Thunor that hung at his throat. This was no distraction for an attack with spear and shield. This was power of another sort. Dark and deadly.

The sun pushed itself above the edge of the earth, and the land was filled with light. The mists turned the pink of blood-stained linen.

Beobrand became aware of movement to his side. Acennan made way for their king. Oswald's face was ruddy in the warm light of the dawn, his eyes shadowed and dark as he looked down towards the tree and the men gathered there.

"What are they doing?" Oswald asked.

"I am no priest, Oswald King," Beobrand said, "but I think we are about to see a sacrifice to the All-father. To Woden."

Oswald made the sign of the Christ rood over his chest.

The sounds of conversation from the ranks of Northumbrians died out. They could not tear their gaze away from what was unfolding beneath the ash tree.

Beobrand's mouth was dry. To see this would weaken the men's resolve, but he was incapable of drawing them away from the spectacle. Grudgingly, he acknowledged that Penda was a canny king. Whether or not the old gods paid heed to his offering, the will of the Northumbrian host would be damaged.

The hill was silent now. They watched in rapt horror as a dark-cloaked man made his way to the base of the ash tree. He was followed by another man leading a fabulous white stallion.

Even from this distance, the quality of the beast was plain for all to see. Its muscles quivered and bunched beneath sleek hair. Its mane and tail had been brushed and plaited and the animal walked with its head held high, as if it was accustomed to being the focus of attention and admiration.

It reminded Beobrand of Sceadugenga.

The horn sounded again and the robed figure imprecated and screamed, raising his arms in the air and turning this way and that. He wielded a long staff, which he pointed in turn to each of the four bonfires that raged around the tree. The stallion snorted and stamped nervously at the priest's ranting. The animal pulled at its harness, but the man who led it held the rope tightly.

Beobrand could not make out the words of the priest, but it was clear now to all the onlookers what was going to transpire.

The mist was thinning, burnt away by the sun and the heat from the fires. A few paces from the massive ash tree, the Mercian warriors were gathered to witness the offering of blood to the father of the gods. All men knew that the ash was Woden's sacred tree, and the blood of a stallion was filled with potent magic. Claws of dread scratched down Beobrand's back and he fought the urge to shudder.

Penda's priest came to the end of his incantations and drew close to the trembling horse. There was a flash, as the rising sun blazed from the blade of a wicked knife, followed by the gush of crimson on the beast's white neck. Its pitiable whinny reached them on the hill, thin and tremulous as the stallion faced its own death with terror and agony. The man holding the horse's rope was flung aside, and the horse reared up, pawing the air with its hooves. It shied away from the priest and his sharp knife, but the flames of the bonfires pushed it back towards the tree. Frantic and desperate for escape, it whinnied again. Blood pumped in a stream, painting its neck and flank red. The once proud beast turned a tight circle, eyes rolling in fear, and then its strength fled. It fell to its knees, chest heaving. Its plaited tail flicked and twitched.

From the host stepped a broad-shouldered warrior. The sun glinted from his fine byrnie and the great grimhelm that covered his face. The fur of a massive wolf was draped about his shoulders. This was Penda, son of Pybba, Lord of Mercia. The king of Mercia stood before the dying stallion, and the horse, losing all strength now, dipped its head to the earth. It appeared as though the once proud animal had bowed to the king in the moment of its death.

The Mercian host let out a huge cheer at the sight.

Woden, All-father, had been given a grand sacrifice beneath the sacred tree, and had honoured their lord by having the noble stallion, that king of beasts, make obeisance to Penda.

Their roaring cheer continued for a long time.

As the sound of the Mercian horde subsided, a new voice filled the air. Oswald bellowed in a roaring voice that Beobrand had never heard before.

"Hear me, brave men of Northumbria," Oswald shouted. "You have seen an animal killed under a tree. Any one of us could do this thing. To slay a defenceless creature is nothing. It is what we do at Blotmonath. What the ceorls who work the land do when meat is needed. This spilling of blood means nothing. We stand here atop this hill beneath the cross of Christ," he signalled his standard of the crossed beams of wood. "And Christ is all powerful!" Oswald's voice cracked with the force of his words. "Those who follow the one true God need not fear the magic of the old gods. They have no power over the true Lord."

The Northumbrians shifted and shuffled. Their faces were pale, dirt-streaked and drawn from weariness and the omen of doom they had just observed. Beneath them, the men of Mercia, Powys and Gwynedd were once again preparing for battle.

"Did Jesu Christ not bring us victory at Hefenfelth?" Oswald yelled. "Did we not survive yesterday against Penda's host?" A rumble of assent from the Bernician and Deiran warriors. "Pray with me again, as we did at Hefenfelth, and you will see that the Lord God Almighty will once again grant His children victory."

Without hesitation, Beobrand knelt on the dew-damp grass. He knew not whether the Christ had more power than Woden and the old gods, but he understood that battles were won and lost on the morale of the men in the shieldwall. And the sacrifice had delivered a terrible blow to that morale.

Acennan and the rest of his gesithas quickly copied their lord, and in a few heartbeats all of the Northumbrians were kneeling. Oswald alone stood before them, holding his arms out to his sides in the position it was said the Christ had been nailed to his death tree.

"Fæder ure þu þe eart on heofonum."

Oswald began to speak the familiar words of the Lord's prayer. All of the warriors joined him. The words were known to all, both those who believed and had been baptised into the ways of the Christ followers and those who yet paid heed to the old ways. Oswald had ensured that Aidan's brethren on Lindisfarena always uttered this most holy of prayers whenever and wherever they preached. And he had seen to it that they spoke it in the tongue of the Angelfolc, so that nobody of his kingdom would be unable to understand the word of God. Over the intervening years they had all heard the prayer hundreds of times.

"Si þin nama gehalgod to becume þin rice…"

Many of the thegns and warriors bowed their heads and held small talismans of the Christ rood. Attor was one such fervent believer in the Christ, ever since Aidan and his monks had cured him from a wound that all had been sure would take his life. The slender gesith spoke the words of the prayer with passion.

"…gewurþe ðin willa on eorðan swa on heofonum."

Beobrand said the words, but he did not close his eyes. He watched as the Mercians formed ranks on the field below in preparation for moving towards the hill. Beneath the ash, the dark-robed priest was hacking the recently slaughtered horse apart with a long-hafted axe. If they were victorious, they would eat the horseflesh in a feast that night. There was a wondrous power in such meat.

"...urne gedæghwamlican hlaf syle us todæg and forgyf us ure gyltas swa we forgyfað urum gyltendum..."

Beobrand's skin crawled and prickled. The air felt charged and pregnant with hidden energy, as it does before a storm. The gods, old and new, were looking upon this field of Maserfelth. The intense, quiet belief of the saving grace of the Christ vied against the blood and rage of Woden, who was known as Frenzy.

The dove pitted against the raven.

"...and ne gelæd þu us on costnunge ac alys us of yfele..."

Beobrand watched as the skull-and-scalp totem of the men of Gwynedd and the black lion of Powys once more veered to the east to block the road. And what he saw there made the words of the Christ prayer catch in his throat.

"Soþlice," intoned the kneeling Northumbrians, signalling the end of the prayer.

Beobrand stood, and pointed to the east and the road out of the forest.

Oswald followed his gaze and smiled.

"You see," he said, his voice clear and loud in the crisp dawn air, "the Lord God is good and He answers His servants' prayers. Eowa of Mercia comes with his battlehost."

From beneath the trees came a great throng of warriors. The sun was behind them and they were yet in the shadow of the forest, but they stood out clearly against the dark of the wood. Beobrand spied Eowa's standard of a scarlet boar on black raised high and proud. Perhaps they would survive after all. It seemed the gods had fought their own battle of wills and magic and Oswald's nailed god had won.

"Christ has sent Penda's brother to our aid," Oswald continued, as the men on the hill rose to their feet and stared at the arriving warriors, "and today we will crush the pagans on this hill, as easily as soft lead is crushed against an anvil."

The men let out a cheer, glad to be given hope after the doom-laden vision of the sacrifice under the tree.

Beobrand smiled, despite himself. But he could not dispel the feeling of gloom that had descended upon him in the night. Had the dove truly beaten the raven? After all, it was he, Beobrand, not the Christ, who had ridden to Snodengaham and brought Eowa to this place. He looked upon the twisted, grey-skinned corpses on the slope below them. And it would be men, not gods, who would fall again today, hewn and hacked by sword, spear and axe.

The horde of Mercians was almost ready at the foot of the hill now. Gods, there were so many of them. It would be a long and bloody day.

"Fraomar," he said, his tone brusque, "fetch my helm and shield. Those Mercians are not going to let us dawdle up here all day."

The younger man nodded and rushed back to where they had slept to bring his lord's gear.

Beobrand spat and again surveyed the host of warriors on the field of Maserfelth.

Eowa had come and mayhap they could take the day.

The movement of the priest butchering the horse caught his eye and Beobrand reached up with his half-hand and grasped his whale-tooth hammer amulet. He shivered, but the morning was already warming.

Everyone knew there was great power in the sacrifice of a stallion under a sacred ash.

Chapter 25

That morning, the Mercians attacked even more ferociously than the previous day. There were fewer moments for Beobrand and the others to rest as Penda's wolves pressed up the hill, trampling the corpses of their fallen and assaulting the seemingly unbreakable Northumbrian shieldwall. But like hounds that could scent the imminent death of a stag, so the Mercians sensed the end of Oswald's defence on the hill. Perhaps emboldened by the horse sacrifice, or urged on to finish the defenders quickly now that Eowa's reinforcements had arrived, the Mercians flung themselves upon the Northumbrian shields and spears in a furious and prolonged onslaught that added many more to the heaps of dead and dying. And those who yet survived, reeled, close to exhaustion in the forge-swelter of the hot day.

Beobrand's body ached from the constant fighting. His face was drenched in sweat and he longed to remove his helm, but he would not. Too often had it protected him. Acennan and Dreogan stood at his shoulders and together they slew countless foe-men with an economy of movement that was uncanny, should any have been able to pause to behold it. But all who stood before them died too quickly to marvel at the speed of their killing.

As so many times before that day, the Mercians came again, screaming and spitting their ire. And once more, they were pushed back, tumbling and sliding down the gore-soaked slope towards their waiting shield-brothers. But there would be little respite. Beobrand plunged Hrunting into the earth at his feet and watched as the bulky warlord, Grimbold, erstwhile lord of Beobrand's sworn enemy Wybert, cuffed the fleeing men, bullying them with shouts and curses to return to their task of unseating the defenders from their hilltop perch.

"Water," Beobrand said. His mouth was dry and sour. Attor handed him a flask that one of the camp thralls had filled from a stream in the forest that morning. He filled his mouth and poured some of the liquid onto his face, caring nought now for getting his byrnie wet, heedless of the iron-rot that would set to eating the metal. The rings of his shirt were caked in congealing blood. If they survived this day, there would be time enough to clean the links then with sand and oil.

"Look," said Acennan, pointing to where Eowa's host was sorely pressed by the Waelisc, "there in the vanguard, where the fighting is fiercest. That is Hyfeidd the Tall, champion of Cyndallan ap Cynddylan of Powys. It is said he has never been bested in combat."

For a moment, they all stared into the seething morass of the press below them. Sunlight glinted from the burnished helm of a man who stood at least a head taller than those who surrounded him. This impression of huge height was increased by the jutting plume of white swan feathers that bedecked his helm. Hyfeidd the Tall's sword shone as it slashed in savage sweeps and all those who stood before him fell back.

The champion of Powys had almost made his way to Eowa's boar's head banner. Eowa's fyrd had fought well, but Beobrand could see now that they would be slaughtered. The Waelisc host was pushing them ever back, wholly intent on crushing the newcomers to this battle. They had been unblooded on the first day and it seemed to Beobrand they wished to prove to Penda that they deserved an equal share of the spoils.

He could not bear to watch as Eowa's force was destroyed. He recalled the words of Cynethryth. He would not merely stand by and see the Mercian atheling cut down. A small band of warriors would be able to rush down the hill and assail the Waelisc from the flank. If they were quick about it, they would not be halted by the Mercians. He glanced down the slope to the Mercian warriors. They had yet to regroup and Grimbold and the other lords were still berating them, exhorting them to attack.

"My gesithas," Beobrand bellowed, suddenly filled with a certainty of what he must do. "My brave hearth-warriors, follow me. There is not a moment to waste. We must descend upon those Waelisc dogs and smite them hard before they know what we are about."

Some of the men looked confused, but Acennan, Dreogan and Attor all stepped forward instantly, hefting their black shields and raising their gore-slathered blades. But before Beobrand could lead them down the hill, Derian, Oswald's warmaster shouted, "Halt!"

Beobrand spun to face the older man.

"There is no time to speak of this," he snapped.

"No, Beobrand," said Derian, his tone as sharp as the bloody blade he held unsheathed at his side, "this is no time to speak. And no time to run."

"I do not mean to run!" Beobrand yelled, his anger sudden and hot. "I am no craven. See there," he gestured with Hrunting at where the Waelisc battered their way in a bloody swathe through Eowa's fyrd-men, "Eowa needs our aid. He will not hold without it."

Beobrand made to turn, to lead his gesithas down the slope towards the Waelisc. Acennan, Attor, Dreogan and the others were all poised, awaiting his command. Derian strode forward and grasped Beobrand's shoulder.

"No, Beobrand," he repeated, his voice softer now, but no less firm.

"They will not hold!" Beobrand shouted, his frustration turning to fury.

Derian nodded, his calm expression infuriating. His grey-streaked beard was black and glistening with the blood of his foes.

"You must hold the line here, Beobrand," he said. "You must protect the king."

"But Eowa will fall."

"If Eowa falls is in the hands of the Sisters who spin his life thread. It is his wyrd, not yours. You must stay."

Derian fixed him with a stern gaze. After what seemed a long while, but was merely a few heartbeats, he released his grasp on Beobrand with a nod.

"Come, form the shieldwall again," he said, taking up his shield from where he had let it fall, "the Mercians attack once more."

Beobrand swallowed back the bitter words that formed in his mind. Eowa had come to fulfil his oath, to defend the land of the man who had married the woman he loved. Eowa had lost his love to Oswald. Now he would give his life for him.

"Shields!" yelled Beobrand. His gesithas said nothing, but obeyed their hlaford without complaint. With well-trained speed, they fell into formation once more to face the Mercians that again swarmed up the slaughter-strewn slope.

As the enemy warriors reached the lip of the hill, Beobrand saw the man he would next kill. A portly warrior, red cheeks shining above a full long moustache. He came towards Beobrand, puffing and clumsy after the climb. The man was slow and Beobrand stole a quick glance over at Eowa's fyrd. The white feathers of Hyfeidd the Tall's helm had reached Eowa's black and blood-red boar's head banner.

And then Beobrand had to shift his attention back to the chubby Mercian before him. He caught the man's spear on his shield, twisted his body, and with a savage blow of Hrunting's blade, cut the haft. The man's eyes opened wide in terror and he fumbled at his belt for the seax that hung there in a tooled-leather sheath. But Beobrand did not give him time to rearm himself. Taking two quick steps forward, he buried Hrunting into the man's fat neck. Blood splattered and the Mercian fell. Beobrand moved rapidly back into the shieldwall without thinking, the motion as natural to him as walking.

Another Mercian stumbled on the body of his rotund comrade and hesitated there, fear gripping him in the face of the huge, blood-painted Northumbrian thegn. Beobrand again flicked a furtive glance down towards the road and Eowa's warband. Still he could see the feathers atop the gleaming helm, but with a sinking feeling in his stomach, he saw that the boar standard had fallen.

With a grimace, Beobrand turned back to the Mercian warrior who now faced him. The man yet hesitated, still unsure whether he had the courage to attack the tall lord, bedecked in the finest war gear and with the battle-sweat of many Mercians splashed all about him.

Beobrand made the decision for him. Roaring, he sprang forward. Startled, the Mercian raised his shield and sword. Beobrand beat the man's defences away as if he were a child, and hammered Hrunting's notched blade across his knees. The man howled and collapsed. With barely a thought Beobrand sent him on his way to the afterlife with a downward swipe of his sword.

For a moment, there was no enemy to slay. Once again, the Northumbrians had proven stalwart defenders and pushed the Mercians back down the slope.

But from the distance, the sound of cheering reached Beobrand. Down by the old road, men were fleeing back into the forest. Eowa, son of Pybba, had fallen, and his fyrd was routed. Behind them, the Waelisc, led by their champion, Hyfeidd, pursued them and made great slaughter.

Chapter 26

"I think your famous luck may have finally run out," yelled Acennan over the tumultuous crash of the battle. His face was smeared in a thick mask of mud and blood, but despite the despair and death all about them, he offered Beobrand a broad grin.

A Waelisc warrior, chest bare and screaming in an ecstasy of violence, leapt towards Beobrand. His eyes burnt with hatred, spittle flew from his lips as he spat curses in his own tongue. Beobrand barely registered the man's presence. With the slightest of movements, he swayed to the left, parrying the man's blade with Hrunting, oblivious now of the damage to the sword's already battered edge. With seemingly casual speed and skill he then reversed the direction of Hrunting's movement, slicing into the Waelisc attacker's throat. Fresh blood fountained, crimson and hot, smothering him in yet more gore. The Waelisc halted, still and shocked for a heartbeat, eyes blinking and wide now, perhaps the better to see death's approach. Beobrand smashed his tattered shield forward into the man's face, sending him away and reeling. But the Waelisc warrior did not tumble down the slope, for the Northumbrians had been pushed back and now fought on the hill's summit. The sheer number of attackers, with the men of Powys and Gwynedd adding their weight to the Mercians, was taking its toll on the defenders.

Defeat seemed inevitable. But still they fought on, and the hill above Maserfelth was soaked in the lifeblood of the fallen. The brave and the cowardly bled the same hue and, as that hot day wore on, it became impossible to distinguish the one from the other in the tangle of corpses that riddled the slope and the hilltop.

No new enemy was before Beobrand now, so he took a moment to regain some of his strength. The breath rasped in his lungs. His head throbbed and his chest ached from old injuries. The pungent stink of death, the metal tang of blood and the acrid reek of spilt guts filled his nostrils, making his gorge rise. His arms and legs were as heavy as if they'd been carved from stone, such was his weariness.

"I never was lucky," he shouted to Acennan, spitting up a gobbet of bloody phlegm, "but if we are to die here, there is something I must do first."

Acennan hacked his blade into the head of a man even shorter than him. The man's simple helm dented with a great clang and blood streamed over his brows, nose and cheeks.

"What is that?" Acennan asked, dispatching the short warrior with a savage thrust into his throat.

"I would avenge Eowa before I depart this life."

Ever since he had known that the atheling had fallen, Beobrand had felt the pressure of the anger within him grow. Despite the tiredness that wrapped his every sinew like a sodden cloak, and in spite of the ever-increasing likelihood of his own doom, he burnt at the injustice of Eowa's death. The man had been honourable and steadfast. He had known great love, which he had cruelly lost. But he had kept his word, been a good hlaford to his people, a good husband and father. Eowa had cared for and protected Octa as if he were his own son these last months and he had been repaid with battle and death. Gods, the man's own brother had attempted to slay him.

"And how do you plan to do that, lord?" Acennan called in a loud voice, to make himself heard through the chaotic cacophony of the battle-play.

Beobrand rolled his shoulders in an attempt to free up the seizing muscles.

"You said that Hyfeidd the Tall has never known defeat?"

"That is what they say."

"Well, I will face him this day, and he will know defeat. For he has slain my friend."

"With his height and those ridiculous plumes it shouldn't be hard to find him."

Beobrand nodded. He'd had the same thought. He must see where the champion attacked the shieldwall, so that he might manoeuvre himself into his path. Raising himself to his full height, he scanned the enemy force. There was no sign of the burnished helm with its white feathers standing above the mass of shorter men.

Another Waelisc man rushed towards him screaming. Beobrand deflected the spear thrust and lunged forward, disembowelling the enraged warrior.

Along the line his gesithas were slaughtering the Waelisc, who were lightly armoured at best. The black shields of his warband were scarred and splintered, but his men stood strong, their training and skill making them formidable. As he watched, Grindan and Fraomar parted, allowing mighty Eadgard to step from the line. With three massive strokes of his axe, three more Waelisc collapsed, adding their flesh to the charnel heap before them. Eadgard bellowed and raved, laughing as he killed, but when Grindan called him back, he returned to the shieldwall. Now, after years of drills, he was able to control the madness that came upon him in battle.

Beobrand searched again for the white feathers and the tall champion of Powys. Surely if this flank was where the Powys men attacked, Hyfeidd must be here too. But there was no sign. Could he have fallen? Perhaps. Even the bravest and most battle-skilled met their end at some time. But Beobrand did not believe it was so for Hyfeidd. Not just yet. When he had last seen the man it had been from afar, as he chased Eowa's fleeing Mercians into the forest.

Ever since then, the attack on the hill had been ferocious and terrible, scarcely giving the Northumbrians time for breath or a moment to think. And then it struck him.

By all the gods, could it be? He was suddenly certain.

"My gesithas," he screamed in his battle-voice, "to me!"

Without hesitation, his comitatus disengaged from the battle and formed around their leader in a well-practised movement.

Beobrand saw Derian flash him a scowling glare from where he stood with the king and his hearth-warriors. But there was no time to answer to the warmaster now. Not if Beobrand was right.

"By Tiw's cock," Acennan said, panting, "what are you doing?"

"Saving the day and taking my revenge," Beobrand replied, and without waiting for a reply, he turned and ran, away from the battle.

Chapter 27

Beobrand did not look back. Either Derian, Fordraed and the other thegns would be able to rally the troops to plug the gap left by Beobrand and his warband's departure, or they would not. Derian was a doughty fighter and knew which end of a seax was sharp. Beobrand was confident he would manage to organise the men and remain strong.

There were screams and shouts from the hilltop, but still Beobrand did not turn. He shoved his way through the ranks of men. Some were injured, some taking a moment's hasty rest after having stood long in the wall. Some, no doubt, were cowards, holding back from the fighting in the hope that death would not seek them out.

"To the front!" yelled Beobrand. "To the shieldwall!"

Some of the men, grim-faced and already bloody, obeyed him, heading back to the churning steel-storm of the front line. Those warriors knew their place and knew him. He was Beobrand of Ubbanford, half-handed slayer of Hengist. His bravery and battle-skill were things of legend and scops' tales, and they knew not to question his orders. Others, younger men, some unmarked by war, despite the battle having raged all the previous afternoon and much of this day, saw Beobrand and his black-shielded warband as a possible means of escape. They perceived the Bernicians to be fleeing, having scented that the battle was already lost, and so they fell into step with them, trusting that the tall half-handed thegn had a plan to lead them to safety.

If it was safety they sought, they would be sorely disappointed, for Beobrand did not run from battle. He had merely chosen a new battle in which to fight. One that was yet to begin.

"God's blood, Beobrand," shouted Acennan, as they ran down the slope, leaving the tumult of the shieldwall behind them, "where are we going?"

For a heartbeat, Beobrand wondered whether he had made a mistake. Could it be that he had been wrong? He slowed to a jog, casting his gaze across the slope from the tethered horses to his left then over to the shade of the forest to the east. No, he had been right. There, where Derian had positioned a handful of men for just this eventuality, Beobrand spotted a flash of white, a glint of sun from a polished helm.

"There," he said, pointing with Hrunting's bloody blade and renewing his pace into a run.

From beneath the trees came more than a score of men. These were Hyfeidd the Tall's warriors. Their shields, once bright white, were now daubed with the red of their fallen foe-men; the blood of the Mercians who had come with Eowa. At their centre strode Hyfeidd, champion of Powys, resplendent in his battle gear, bedecked with fine armour. His sword was slick with slaughter, his shield scored and blood-splattered. But his helm seemed untouched by the fierce fighting. It still shone in the bright sunlight, its swan feathers yet proud, waving and taunting his enemies.

The men of Powys pushed the few warriors who guarded the forest path before them. They were outnumbered and outmatched and so retreated.

"Hyfeidd!" bellowed Beobrand, his voice loud enough to tear his throat.

The tall champion paused, looking beyond the men at the forest's edge and spying Beobrand and his warband descending the slope at a sprint. At the sight of Beobrand and his gesithas, battle-hardened, grim and gore-soaked, the few remaining defenders of the forest fled.

Hyfeidd halted and barked a command. His men, just as well-trained as Beobrand's it seemed, slipped effortlessly into a wall of interlocking shields.

There was nothing for it now. To face them shieldwall against shieldwall would be long and bloody, with no certainty as to the outcome. Hyfeidd's men numbered more and they were set to receive them. Beobrand remembered when he had faced Eowa, all those years before, on a dark forest path. Then too they had been outnumbered and he had risked all on one throw of the dice.

"Boar-snout!" he screamed, slowing slightly so that his men could fall into place. He offered up his thanks to Tiw, Woden and Thunor for all the long days of practice in Ubbanford. And thanks to Bassus for demanding so much of the men. Even when Beobrand would have rested, the old warrior would make them go through the drills again and again, until they cursed him and hated him for it. As his comitatus moved into position, Beobrand loved Bassus for his diligence. Perhaps it would save them now.

They formed a spear-head, with Beobrand at the point. Acennan and Dreogan ran at either side, and behind them, the other men lent their weight to the formation. In their wake, the stragglers who had followed down the hill, slowed and marvelled at the skill needed to exact such a manoeuvre whilst running.

"If you ever had any luck," shouted Acennan, "I hope it has not left you yet, Beobrand."

Beobrand did not reply. He fixed Hyfeidd in his gaze and prepared for impact.

"Charge!" he screamed, and felt the men behind him give an extra push forward.

Beobrand's raven-black-shielded warband sped towards the white shieldwall of Hyfeidd the Tall, the undefeated champion of Powys. Fleetingly, Beobrand thought of Oswald's words and his vision of the dove, the hawk and the raven. What had the omen meant?

And then it was too late to ponder such things. Beobrand's spear-head-shaped formation smashed into Hyfeidd's shieldwall and all was clamour and chaos.

Chapter 28

Beobrand's boar-snout charge sundered the Powys shieldwall. The white shields were shoved aside as Beobrand used the strength, speed and weight of his men to carry him through the wall of willow, hide and iron. Beobrand was awestruck at the skill of Hyfeidd. The champion took a swipe at his head and it was all Beobrand could do to avoid it. Too late he saw it for what it was – a clever feint. He had not avoided the blow. Hyfeidd had never meant it to land. Instead his wicked blade slipped past Beobrand and found its true target. Dreogan grunted as the sharp sword found a gap in his defence and sliced deeply into his neck.

But the momentum of the boar's head charge could not be halted now. Dreogan powered on, ignoring the pain, or oblivious to it. Beobrand found himself almost lifted from his feet as his men surged forward, slashing and hacking with their weapons to either side as they went.

Hyfeidd's eyes opened wide in surprise, shocked that the Bernicians had broken through his shieldwall. A heartbeat later, Beobrand reached him.

The energy of battle-lust flowed through him like a torrent, but he knew that his body was close to exhaustion. He had fought all the previous day and had barely slept for the last three days. And he had watched this huge warrior of Powys from the distance of the hill, and had witnessed his easy speed and deadly skill now at close hand. A duel between them would be no sure thing.

Hyfeidd must have recognised Beobrand. His black-shielded warriors were famous throughout Albion. Seeing such a thegn, one whom he deemed worthy of his skills, Hyfeidd took a step back, preparing himself for the sword-play. Here was a man who loved to wield his blade. He clearly relished the joy of crossing blades with another great swordsman, and Beobrand's skill with a blade was sung of in mead halls in all the kingdoms of the land.

But Beobrand did not slow; did not enter into the well-loved game of taunts and boasts before a combat. This was no tourney in a king's hall. No game. Beobrand used the energy from his men to fling himself forward. He smashed into Hyfeidd, and the two huge men fell to the earth in a clatter of shields and swords. All about them stamped the feet of their gesithas. The anvil clash of steel on steel and the straining shouts of the battling men surrounded them. But their world was reduced to each other. Hyfeidd's shock at Beobrand's assault was short-lived. He quickly regained his composure and grappled with Beobrand's right hand, preventing him from bringing Hrunting to bear. Hyfeidd had discarded his shield, but Beobrand's was yet attached to his arm by the leather straps he used. This encumbered him, but also impeded Hyfeidd's movements. They rolled in the dirt, each trying to pin the other to the ground.

Beobrand cursed and gritted his teeth.

Woden, but the Powys bastard was strong. And lithe. Despite Beobrand's efforts and his prodigious strength, he found himself lying on his back with Hyfeidd straddling him. The Waelisc champion had pinned Beobrand's shield beneath his bulk, leaving only Beobrand's right hand free. Hyfeidd produced a slender knife from his belt, thrusting it at Beobrand's face. Beobrand caught Hyfeidd's wrist, halting the wicked-looking point of the weapon a hand's breadth from his eyes. Beobrand struggled and heaved, but he was unable to dislodge Hyfeidd, who leant forward, putting his weight behind the knife. Beobrand groaned. The knife point moved closer. Hyfeidd's left hand lashed out and grasped Beobrand's throat, squeezing, choking the life from him just as surely as any blade would do.

Beobrand's vision blurred.

Gods, he would die now. Not in some great show of skill and sword-play, but in the muck, brawling. Strangled and skewered on a knife like a common brigand. He roared his defiance, but the sounds were cut off by Hyfeidd's ever-tightening grip on his neck. Beobrand tried to hit Hyfeidd with his knees, anything to rid himself of him. But the Powys man smiled as his grip tightened and his knife descended.

All about them, their two warbands yet hacked and battled, shoving and yelling, spitting and screaming.

Beobrand's sight darkened. Sounds receded and grew muffled. His strength waned. Hyfeidd grinned, certain of victory now.

Close to the wrestling men, a white-shielded warrior fell hollering and mewling to the earth. A heartbeat later, a black shield boss clumped into the side of Hyfeidd's helmeted head. The champion fell to the side, releasing his grip on Beobrand's throat.

Beobrand wanted to lie there, to take in great gulps of summer air. His body screamed in agony, his head throbbed and blotches of shadow seemed to swim in the air before his eyes. Would that he could just rest here. Yet he did not pause. With scarcely a thought, he rolled over atop the stunned champion of Powys.

Hyfeidd's eyes were glazed, dulled from their bright intelligence by the great blow he had taken to his head. Even so, he recognised the danger and brandished his knife. Beobrand, gasping and coughing, paid no heed to the weapon. Raising himself to his knees he lifted his splintering shield and, holding it firm in both his hands, he brought it down with crushing strength. Hyfeidd's blade skittered away and the metal rim of the linden board hammered into his neck. Beobrand heaved it up and smashed it down again. A third time he brought the shield down on Hyfeidd's throat. The light had gone from the man's eyes now, and the swan feathers of his helm were smeared with mud and blood.

A strong hand reached down and pulled Beobrand to his feet. It was Dreogan, his soot-marked face set in a scowl. There was fresh blood on his throat. He spat onto Hyfeidd's corpse.

"That'll teach him not to kill me when he had the chance." He reached up and put his fingers to his neck. "Barely a scratch," he said, and spat again.

All about them lay white shields. The remaining Powys warriors, seeing their lord slain, turned and fled at a run back into the forest.

"Let them go," Beobrand croaked. "There is more work for us to do this day on that hill." The distant noise of battle suddenly took on another tone. Gone was the boulder-crash rumble of the shieldwall, in its place came a great roaring cheer.

Could it be that they had seen how Beobrand and his gesithas had turned away the threat from the forest? After all, they had slain the undefeated and protected the Northumbrian host from a deadly attack from the rear.

He looked up the incline to the men massed there, and his heart clenched.

The Northumbrians were not cheering his victory over Hyfeidd the Tall. The cheer did not come from the Northumbrians at all. The Christ rood banner, stark and simple against the brilliance of the summer afternoon sky, no longer rose over the host.

King Oswald had fallen and men were streaming down the slope towards them.

Chapter 29

By the Mother of all, where had Sulis got to? Reaghan poked a stick angrily into the fire sending sparks spiralling up towards the soot-streaked rafters of the hall. To one side of the hearth sat the great pot that she used for brewing. Into it she had poured the malted barley and had been all set to boil it, when she had found there was not enough water. If she was to brew ale, she should make enough to last the household for at least three days. Not that the household would need as much as usual with so many away. Brewing was not something she enjoyed, but it needed to be done, and she would rather be involved than have the thralls do it unattended. She hated sitting idly by doing nothing.

Reaghan jabbed the stick into the flames again and cursed. She had dislodged the logs from where she had so carefully positioned them. She prodded and pushed with the stick, trying to move them back to where the fire was hottest and they would burn best.

Gods, where was that woman? It should have only taken her moments to fetch water from the barrel outside the great hall. Yet Sulis had a way of making every chore take three times as long as needed.

"You should send her to Stagga, to serve Eadgyth," Bassus had said on more than one occasion in the days since Cynan had brought the Mercian slaves to Ubbanford. The day after he'd left with most of the remaining warriors, Bassus and Reaghan had gone to Acennan's hall. Reaghan really had no need for any more servants, in fact she disliked being served at all. It always made her uncomfortable. Rowena had no such qualms, so Reaghan had sent two slaves to Ubba's hall in the valley, and four to Eadgyth on the other side of the Tuidi. She had kept only Sulis in her own hall to help Domhnulla. The Mercian woman was sullen and morose, slow to help and always surly. And yet there was something about her story that spoke to Reaghan. She knew that Sulis despised her because she was Waelisc and also her mistress, but she understood the woman's resentment. And Sulis' despair at what Fordraed had done to her son.

"I do not understand why you wish to keep her in your hall," Bassus had said a couple of days previously, when Sulis had spilt the fresh milk she had been carrying up from the dairy hut. It had been a terrible waste, but the thrall had merely shrugged and not even begun to clean it up until Bassus had shouted at her.

Reaghan didn't really understand it either. It would have been easier to have no thrall than Sulis. Reaghan was convinced the woman actively hindered any work they undertook. But she had seen the way that Cynan had gazed on her, and she did not wish the woman to come to harm. If she could keep a watch on her, have her near, surely Reaghan would be able to ensure that Sulis settled into her new life at Ubbanford.

Bassus shook his head whenever she told him of Sulis' behaviour.

"By Frige," he'd said, "you should give her a good hiding. That is what she needs. You'd see then how quickly she would go about her tasks."

But Reaghan would shake her head and frown at Bassus.

"I will not beat a thrall, Bassus," she had said. "You know this."

Abashed, he had turned away from her, before offering a small nod of comprehension.

"I hear you, girl," he'd said, his voice quiet and gravelly like distant thunder, "but that is part of the trouble. Mark what I say."

Perhaps he was right, but she knew she could never bring herself to strike a thrall. Her own back bore the scarred memories of the hazel switch and she well remembered the long painful nights lying on her belly, trying to find sleep as the blood from the welts on her back soaked into her dress.

Movement by the hall door drew her attention away from the fire. Sulis moved slowly from the warm, bright daylight and into the gloom of the building. Normally, on such a summer's day, the hall provided a welcome shady coolness after the heat of the sun. But today was brewing day, so the fire had been stoked and burnt hot, making the interior sweltering and smoky. Sulis shuffled towards Reaghan, holding the large buckets of water suspended from a wooden yoke over her shoulders. She trod slowly, perhaps taking extra care following the incident with the milk.

Perhaps, thought Reaghan, but more likely she just revelled in making her mistress wait yet further.

Reaghan watched as Sulis approached. The slave's eyes were downcast, watching each step carefully. Reaghan could see why she had captivated Cynan so. She was a pretty thing. Gone was the sickly pallor of her skin from when she had arrived at Ubbanford. Colour had returned to her cheeks; her hair had been brushed clean and braided and Reaghan had given her a new peplos. But despite the obvious return to health, Sulis' eyes were yet dark with barely hidden despair and she moved with a careful, fragile vulnerability, as if she feared she might break something at any moment.

Reaghan sighed.

Bassus might speak the truth that she spoilt the woman by not chastising her for tardiness or mistakes, but Reaghan knew she would never strike Sulis. She saw too much of herself in the woman.

Reaghan reached out and took one of the brimming buckets from her. Sulis frowned and did not reply. They each emptied their bucket into the huge ale pot. And then, without a word, each took hold of one side and hefted the cauldron over the fire. They fumbled with the hook attached to the long chain that hung from the oaken roof beams. For a moment, Reaghan thought they would surely drop the pot. It was heavy and their arms quivered with the strain of holding it aloft. Reaghan muttered a curse. They should have filled the thing after lifting it over the fire. Their eyes met. Reaghan steadied the hook against the handle of the ale bowl, and then, just as she thought they were sure to let it fall, losing the contents and extinguishing the fire at the same time, the hook caught. With visible relief they lowered the vessel.

Reaghan let out a long breath.

"By the all-mother," she said, "I thought we were sure to lose it all then."

"You needn't have worried," Sulis replied, her face expressionless, "it wasn't full of fresh milk."

Reaghan met her gaze and, for a moment, was unsure she had caught Sulis' meaning. Then she noticed the glint in the thrall's eye, the slight twist of the mouth. Blessed Mother, had the woman made a jest?

Reaghan smirked. Perhaps she had been wrong about Sulis. Maybe they merely needed to spend more time together. The Mercian would come to know that Reaghan treated her fairly and they could be friends. She searched Sulis' face for any sign that her icy demeanour was thawing. But she saw none.

"Hail the hall," a voice boomed from the open doorway, startling both women. It was Bassus. His huge bulk almost completely blocked out the light from the door.

"Hail, Bassus," she replied, her voice light and breathless. "What brings you to the hall this fine day? The ale will not be ready for some time." She smiled.

"I do not come for ale," he said, striding into the hall. "But it is good that you are brewing fresh ale. I come with tidings, so that you may prepare."

"What tidings?" she asked.

"We are to be visited by royalty before the sun reaches its peak."

Chapter 30

By all the gods, what had he done?

Beobrand stared in confusion at the Northumbrian warriors who ran down the hill. He stood, solid and unmoving, like a boulder in a river as the flood of fleeing men streamed around him. For several heartbeats he could not think. His battered body trembled and he gulped in great heaving gasps of air. His throat burnt where Hyfeidd had attempted to crush the life from him. Beobrand had slain the champion; avenged Eowa. But at what cost? Slack-jawed and dazed, he stared about him.

His gesithas stood close by, instinctively moving in to protect their lord.

Pale-faced, blood-streaked Northumbrians rushed past them, some running towards the shelter of the forest, others making their way to the tethered horses.

Tears stung Beobrand's eyes.

Woden, what had he done? His lord, Oswald, had fallen and where had he been? He had abandoned his king on the hill and now Oswald was slain.

"Shieldwall," shouted Acennan, bringing order to the warband. The gesithas drew in and interlocked their black-painted boards.

Beobrand shook his head, trying to free it of the shock; the amazement at the sudden shift in the tide of fortune.

"We should get our horses," Acennan said.

Beobrand shook his head. On the hilltop, there yet stood a tight clump of Oswald's hearth-warriors; the king's most trusted thegns. Beobrand should have been there with them. If he had not left his position in the shieldwall, the king might yet live.

"Beobrand," Acennan's voice was urgent, "the horses."

Beobrand spat. His mind cleared at last.

"No, Acennan," he said, "our place is with our king. We will not run like those cravens." He indicated the fleeing men all about them. "Follow me, my brave gesithas," Beobrand screamed, his voice cracking painfully in his throat. Battle-ire once again flamed within him, burning away the confusion and self-pity of moments before. "Oaths are not ended by death," he shouted. "I was oath-sworn to Oswald King, and I will fulfil my vow to my lord. The king has fallen," he swung Hrunting above his head, flicking gobbets of gore and blood in the warm afternoon sunlight, "and we will surely also fall. But what a death we will have!"

Letting out a savage roar, he surged up the hill. Without hesitation, his comitatus followed him. Despite the pain he felt at the loss of Oswald, his heart swelled with pride at their loyalty.

The flow of routed defenders had lessened now, and a few Mercian and Waelisc warriors ran down the hill in pursuit. Easier to face cowards who fled the battle than the hardened hearth-men of a great king. Nobody stood before Beobrand and his grim-faced, black-shielded warriors and soon they were within a spear's throw of the knot of fighting that yet raged on the summit overlooking Maserfelth.

The tight shieldwall of Northumbrians was being forced backwards. Mercians and Waelisc warriors swarmed on three sides of the rough square of shields. Soon they would be totally surrounded, such were the numbers of attackers.

"What now?" asked Acennan, a twisted grin on his face.

"We fight," shouted Beobrand. He had no other answer. He strode closer, trying to find a point in the enemy ranks where his small band could hope to stem the flow of the assault. There were so many of the enemy. It was clear that the Northumbrians would be overrun, no matter where Beobrand directed an attack. But attack he would. He did not wish for death, but a life branded a coward would be worse. He would not flee.

Within the shifting sea of spears to the left of the Northumbrians, he spied Grimbold's bear's-head banner. Beneath the totem, he saw the flash of a red beard. Halga, Grimbold's brute of son. The man had been Wybert's friend. Beobrand's head throbbed still from the memory of the blow he had received from the red-headed giant. Beobrand rolled his shoulders, loosening the tight, tired muscles. He had slain the champion of Powys this day. Now, before he breathed his last, he would slay Halga, son of Grimbold. The man was huge, fast and deadly. It would be a battle worthy of a tale.

A death worthy of song.

They would form the boar-snout once more and smash into the ranks of Mercians. It would be difficult to gain momentum running up the slope, but he did not doubt his gesithas. They would carry him through the enemy ranks and to the focus of his fury.

Filling his lungs with air, he prepared to bellow his defiance. His muscles bunched.

But before he could give the order, a familiar voice rose over the tumult of the battle. From the rear of the Northumbrian shieldwall stepped Derian. Oswald's warmaster waved his blood-smeared sword frantically and bellowed in a massive shout that carried over the battle din.

"Recall your oath to Oswald!" he roared.

What did Derian mean? Beobrand had brought his men back here to fulfil his oath, to give his life for his lord.

"You must flee to Oswiu," Derian roared. "Give your sword to the new king now!"

Beobrand shook his head, though he knew not whether Derian would see the movement. He remembered the oath he had given to Oswald when he had believed the king to be mortally wounded, but he could not run.

"We will stand here and hold them," Derian screamed. "I would not out-live another lord."

A fresh anger filled Beobrand, flaring as quickly as mutton fat dripping into a fire.

"But you would have me marked as a craven?" he yelled.

But Derian did not seem to hear him. The warmaster turned back to the battle and was swallowed into the press of warriors.

Beobrand panted, shaking at the impotent rage that burnt within him. He would fight, and die. A dead man cannot break an oath.

"There is no time for this, Beobrand," said Acennan. "We must go now. We can yet take our horses and leave this place."

"Men will think me a coward. An oath-breaker who flees, leaving his lord behind to be defended by better men."

"But Derian speaks true," replied Acennan, "you gave your word to Oswald. You swore you would serve Oswiu when he died."

Beobrand's head span. Oath upon oath. How should he best honour his king and his word? The gods must be cackling as the threads of his life twisted and knotted.

"Voice your anger at Oswald in the afterlife," said Acennan, "but on this middle earth, stay true to your oaths, Beobrand. It is all we warriors have."

Beobrand let out an inchoate scream at the ways of his wyrd. His cry was lost in the chaos of the battle on the hill above them.

Then, without another word, he turned and headed back down the slope.

Away from Halga.

Away from Derian.

Away from certain death.

He strode towards the horses, secretly hoping that a band of Mercians or Waelisc would confront them. Perhaps then he could leave his life here with that of his king and not need to live knowing that he had allowed Oswald to be slain and then had fled the field of battle.

But no men stood before them, and their horses remained tied and trembling, awaiting their riders, as if the gods themselves had protected the mounts from other deserters. Beobrand had thought that the magic words Nelda had screeched in the dark of her cavern on Muile all those years before had lost their power at her death. But now, as he pulled himself onto Bera's broad back, with the clash and cries of battle wafting to him on the soft summer breeze, he wondered whether he was yet cursed.

Chapter 31

"We are being followed," said Attor, as he pulled his steed from a gallop to a canter, falling in beside Beobrand and Acennan at the head of the mounted warband.

They rode on for a time, none of them speaking. Beobrand could feel his men's gaze upon him. They looked to him for leadership; for guidance. But how could he lead them? These brave warriors deserved better than such as he.

"Beobrand?" Acennan said, speaking into the awkward silence.

Beobrand sighed. His body was a mass of bruises and aches. Around him, the men were dour-faced and solemn. They had all stood strong in the shieldwall. They too had lost their king, seen friends cut down. He felt a sudden pang at having left Renweard's corpse behind. Another failure that would nag at him when he had time to dwell on such things. He squared his shoulders and sat straighter in the saddle. His muscles screamed at him. All he wanted was to throw himself down by a fire and sleep. He prayed he would not dream then, for he did not relish the shades that might come to him in his slumber. Maybe there would be time for sleeping later. But for now, he must be the man his gesithas expected him to be.

"How far?" he asked.

Attor flicked a glance over his shoulder at the rolling hills that lay behind them, as if calculating the distance. Fraomar rode close to him and tossed him a half-filled waterskin. Attor caught it one-handed, unstopped it and took a swig, all without losing his balance or slowing his horse. Never having been a great horseman, Beobrand marvelled at the slender scout's riding skill. He was sure he would have either dropped the skin, or fallen from the saddle, had he attempted such a feat.

"Not far enough," Attor said, throwing the skin back to Fraomar with a nod of thanks. "Our mounts are not yet recovered from the ride westward to Maserfelth. If we push them, they will die."

"How many are there?" Beobrand said. "Can we turn and fight?"

Attor shrugged, clearly thinking such a decision was not his to make.

"I'd say about a score. Mercians by the looks of them."

Beobrand nodded. His warband numbered sixteen men. They were weary and battered from two days of fighting and their horses were almost as exhausted.

"We ride on," he said, touching his heels to Bera's flanks. The horse snorted but did not increase its speed. To their left, the sun was dipping towards the edge of the world. The land was tinged with a golden glow that spoke of firelight and cheery tales with good friends. There would be no comforting hearth fire for them at journey's end. They rode ahead of the tidings of Oswald's defeat. Beobrand knew not where Oswiu and his warband were, but Oswald's brother had been sent to bring aid from Rhoedd mab Rhun mab Urien, the king of Rheged, the land which lay to the west of Bernicia. And so Beobrand and his gesithas had pushed northward, hopeful that they would intercept Oswiu as he marched south towards Maserfelth.

In the distance, the ruddy light of the setting sun picked out the peaks of the great mountains to the north. Beobrand did not know this far western reach of Northumbria well. It was wild, and sparsely inhabited. The scops told tales of spirits and beasts haunting the tarns and meres of the craggy land that rose before them.

Acennan nudged his horse close to Beobrand's.

"It seems those Mercians will be upon us before nightfall."

"How do you know?" asked Beobrand. He had been hoping they could lose their pursuers in the mountains and valleys to the north.

By way of answer Acennan signalled the path behind them.

Beobrand shifted in his saddle. In the distance, the sun glinted on the battle-harness of some two dozen horsemen. They had just crested a low hill and now galloped at great haste down the slope. At that speed, they would catch Beobrand's warband all too soon. He frowned.

"By Tiw's cock," said Dreogan, "why are those Mercians so keen to chase us?" His neck was wrapped in a strip of blood-stained cloth and his tattooed cheeks seemed to pull his face into a permanent scowl. "There were surely pickings enough for all amongst the dead left at Maserfelth."

Grindan craned his neck to study the men who followed them. He had sharp eyes and Beobrand waited to hear what he saw.

"They are not Mercians," Grindan said, at last.

"No?" said Eadgard. "Who are they then?"

"They all bear white shields," replied Grindan. "They are men of Powys."

Beircheart let out a bark of laughter that startled them all. He had ridden in sullen silence until now, but Beobrand knew he had taken the death of Renweard hard. Leaving his fallen friend behind and fleeing must have been eating at him, as it had plagued Beobrand's own thoughts.

They all turned to Beircheart now, wondering at his mirth. There was no humour in his eyes.

"So, we leave behind our king and fallen brothers, unable to do them the honour of dying with them," Beircheart said, each word stabbing at Beobrand like a seax beneath the shieldwall, "and we are to be killed by some Waelisc scum who have more honour than us and come to seek vengeance for their fallen lord."

He guffawed again, but his eyes were as hard as flint.

They urged their mounts on, but another glance at the Waelisc behind them showed Beobrand the truth.

"We will need to turn and fight before the sun sets," he said. He pointed to a tree-topped escarpment someway to the left of the track they followed. "We will form a shieldwall there."

If the men from Powys attacked immediately, the sun would be in their eyes. Beobrand's men would be outnumbered, but with the higher ground, they might yet prevail. Turning towards the bluff, he urged Bera through the thick fringe of nettles and thistles that grew in a tangle beside the road.

"Perhaps you will get your wish after all," Acennan called to him, his expression somewhere between a smile and a frown.

"What wish?" snapped Beobrand. He had no time for Acennan's riddles and games.

"Well, you wanted us all to die in battle, didn't you?"

Chapter 32

The sun had touched the horizon when the men from Powys reached them. The sky had turned the hue of hot iron, but the slope before them was shadowed by a single downy birch on the bluff. They had tethered the horses beneath the tree. Beobrand had told the men to rest, while he stood, watching the road for their pursuers. The land was rough, dotted with heather, sedge and copses of trees, but they would have plenty of time in which to form a strong shieldwall once their enemy came into sight.

Grindan and Eadgard slumped in the shade and Beobrand was sure that the huge axeman was snoring within an eye-blink of lowering his great bulk to the ground. Would that he could find peace so easily. Dreogan and Elmer pulled out their blades, cleaning them of dried blood and then passing a small whetstone over them in long rasping sweeps. Attor, always tense and taut as a bowstring, would not rest, Beobrand knew, and the slight warrior and Fraomar both peered into the south-east for sign of Hyfeidd's men.

"With their sharp eyes," Acennan said, indicating the two men, "we'll know the instant the men from Powys approach."

Beobrand grunted.

"You don't need to keep watch," he said to Acennan. "Sit. Rest your bones."

"You make me sound like a greybeard, in need of a staff to walk." Acennan raised his arms above his head, stretching and then twisting his body to either side. He grunted as his body clicked and cracked. "I am not old yet," he said, "besides, we have been seated all afternoon in our saddles. I welcome the chance to stand again." He drew his seax from where it hung on his belt and examined its blade. With a shrug at what he saw, he slid it back into the hardened leather sheath. "And how can I rest, if you do not? I cannot have you making me look weak."

Beobrand's limbs quivered. He clenched his fists against the shaking of his hands.

"I cannot rest until the men are safe," he said. He glanced over at where Beircheart sat with his back against the gnarled bole of the birch. The man was sombre and silent, staring into the distance with unseeing eyes. Beobrand knew that Beircheart was seeing his fallen friend, Renweard, in his memories. Perhaps he was thinking of whether he could have done more to protect him. It was ever thus after a fight. The victorious relived the moments when their foes were slain, recounting every detail in great, ale-fuelled boasts. The defeated also thought of each moment they had witnessed in the shieldwall. Some sought confirmation that there was nothing more they could have done. Others berated themselves for poor decisions. Most blamed others for their lot. Bassus had said to him after the catastrophe of the battle of Cair Chaladain that it was easier to throw the stone of blame at someone than to swallow it yourself.

Beircheart's dark, grief-stricken eyes turned to gaze at Beobrand. There was no doubt whom Beircheart found at fault. Beobrand looked away. It was right that he should. Gods, he blamed himself for all of it.

"Well, sword-sleep or slumber," said Acennan, his voice cutting through the morose hush that had settled upon them, "you will be able to rest soon." Beobrand followed Acennan's gaze.

At the same instant, Attor shouted, "To arms! They are here."

In an instant, the lethargy fell away from them, and the gesithas leapt to their feet. Beobrand marvelled at the speed with which Eadgard shook off sleep and readied himself. In an instant, he was standing tall, feet apart, chin jutting in defiance at any foe, his massive axe, chipped and nicked from its recent use, held before him menacingly. To either side of the tall axeman, the others took their places without complaint. Moments after Attor had called out, Beobrand stood at the centre of a wall of black shields.

They all watched in silence as the Waelisc cantered towards them. They presented a sobering sight. The golden red of the setting sun reflected dazzlingly from helms, harness and weapons. Many of the Powys men wore torcs of silver and gold around their necks and arms. The horsemen reined in and dismounted well over a spear-throw distant, and with the same well-trained speed as Beobrand's men, they formed a shieldwall.

The warband of Hyfeidd the Tall, white shields stained red by the setting sun, walked in good order up the shallow slope towards the Bernicians.

"I count twenty-five," said Acennan.

Beobrand said nothing. In the warm stillness he could hear the buzzing of insects in the grass and plants that dotted the rocky hilltop. He scanned the Waelisc that approached them. These were hard men; killers. Their eyes were sharp and piercing beneath their burnished helms. And with their superior numbers they were confident.

Reaching his hand up to his neck, he clutched the Thunor hammer amulet that hung there and offered up a silent prayer that the gods had not abandoned him.

The men from Powys continued to slowly climb the hill. Soon they would be within the reach of a well-thrown spear. Beobrand sensed, rather than saw, movement to his left.

"Garr," he said, his voice hard and cold in the summer dusk air, "do not." He glanced over. Garr lowered the javelin he had been poised to throw. The lithe spear-man gave him a curious look, but did not question the order.

Now, well within the range of Garr's spears, the erstwhile warriors of Hyfeidd the Tall halted at the raised hand of the one who must be their new leader. The Waelisc leader took a few steps forward from the line of white-limed shields.

He was slim and quite short, with a close-cropped beard and a handsome face. He wore fine armour and his neck was adorned with a golden torc, fashioned to look like twisted ropes of the precious metal. At his hip hung a long-bladed sword. This was not the huge warrior that Hyfeidd had been, but a man did not rise to lead a warband after a lord's death without being a warrior of cunning and skill.

"Beobrand, the Half-handed," he shouted, his voice lilting and musical in the way of his people.

For a moment, Beobrand did not answer. His mind whirred, full of thoughts and ideas. A bee droned past as it headed for its nest, hidden somewhere in the branches of one of the nearby oak woods perhaps.

Beobrand stepped forth from the shieldwall.

"I am Beobrand of Ubbanford," he said, his voice carrying easily in the stillness. None of the men on either side made a sound.

"You took the life of my lord, Hyfeidd the Tall," the small warrior shouted, "and I would seek vengeance." His sing-song tone made the words sound less dire than their meaning.

"It is true that I slew Hyfeidd," Beobrand replied. "And if you lift your sword against me, you too will die. Who is it that I must kill?"

"I am Mynyddog Mwynfawr and I have bested taller and better men than you, Beobrand of Ubbanford." Mynyddog grinned and pulled his sword slowly from its scabbard. The sun burnt red and hot from its blade.

"Many men have died this day, Mynyddog Mwynfawr. Short and tall." Beobrand could not keep the smile from his tone. There was something about this Waelisc warrior that amused him. And yet this was no matter for mirth. Death was in the air, and blood would once again soak the land before nightfall. Beobrand drew Hrunting from its fur-lined scabbard, absently noting the few places where its notched blade snagged. He began to pace down the hill towards the Waelisc warrior.

"Beobrand," said Acennan, his voice low, but urgent.

Beobrand turned and raised a calming hand.

"All will be well," he said in a hushed tone, "but be ready for a fight." Then, retuning his attention to Mynyddog, "I will give you a chance at the vengeance you crave," he said, halting his downward progress where the land flattened out somewhat. Splashes of purple saxifrage and moss campion grew in thick clumps amongst the rocks, but there was a flattened expanse of meadow where the grass and shrubs had been cropped short, no doubt by sheep or goats. Perhaps there was a settlement nearby. Beobrand cast his gaze over the haze of the valley. A slight breeze whispered in the branches of the birch on the hill. This was a place of peace. He could imagine shepherds bringing their flocks here to pasture. Beobrand sighed. The calm would be shattered soon, the way Eadgard's axe splintered shields. The tranquillity would be replaced by the clash of weapons, and death would descend with the setting of the sun.

"Come," he beckoned to the short Waelisc, "we will fight here. But when I kill you, your men will mount their steeds and ride out of Northumbria."

Mynyddog Mwynfawr said a few words in his own tongue to his men. One of them replied, but Mynyddog cut him off with a sharp word. He made his way to where Beobrand waited.

"*If* you slay me," he said, with a twisted smile, "the men of Hyfeidd the Tall will leave this place and ride south. But what if I kill you?"

"Such a thing will not happen," said Beobrand, enjoying the banter with this stranger, despite the threat of death and the weariness that lurked just beneath the current of energy that flowed through him at the approach of battle. "But if by some twist of wyrd, I should fall, your men may take the weapons and byrnies of my gesithas. You will leave them their lives and their horses, that they may return to their homes. The death of one of us should be enough. Too many brave men have already died this day."

Beobrand heard the grumble from his men at his words.

Mynyddog smirked.

"They do not sound as though they would honour your bargain."

Beobrand scoured his gesithas with his gaze. They fell silent.

"They will do their duty and do that which their lord wills. And if they do not," he said with a grin, "you are more than twice their number. I am sure you could convince them."

Mynyddog Mwynfawr shrugged. Then, with a nod, he said, "We have a bargain, Beobrand, Half-handed. To the death then."

All trace of humour dropped from his face, as quickly as ice and snow slips from a steep roof when the thaw comes. Mynyddog crouched into the warrior stance, sword held high over his shield.

Beobrand glanced at the ground, checking for anything that might cause him to lose his footing. Lichen- and moss-covered rocks were strewn about the hillside, but this flat meadow of cropped grass provided ample space for sword-play. Much more than the space of an extended cloak that the gesithas used for practice bouts.

The instant he looked up, Mynyddog leapt forward, as Beobrand had known he would. He hefted his shield, soaking up the flurry of blows and stepping backward. This was not the shieldwall, where no quarter could be given, this was a duel, and Beobrand was a master with sword and shield. He had tested his skill against the best warriors in the land with a wooden practice blade and many a wager had been placed on him over the years. Those who placed bets on him had seldom had to part with their stakes. And of those who had stood against him with sharp, naked steel, most had become food for crows and foxes. His skill was legendary, the thing of scops' tales and songs.

But as he defended against those first strikes of Mynyddog's sword, Beobrand knew he had perhaps never faced a man as quick. This Waelisc was a true swordsman, his blade like a living thing. Entranced, Beobrand watched Mynyddog's feet as the diminutive warrior skipped and paced, as lithe as any dancer.

This would be no easy fight. Mynyddog's blade was a blur. Beobrand again parried a series of attacks on his splintering linden board, then, as fast as a striking adder, he lanced Hrunting's point at the Waelisc warrior's throat. It was a desperate lunge, and a move that Beobrand had used before, always to devastating effect. But Mynyddog was unperturbed by the assault. He swayed to the side, avoiding the strike and effortlessly lashing out with his own counter-attack.

Beobrand leapt back, his right bicep burning. Mynyddog's sword had found its target. Beobrand flexed his arm and risked a glance at the wound. Blood seeped from a short cut. It stung terribly, but it was not deep.

"Did that wake you up?" sneered Mynyddog. "I had heard tell that you were fast. I've seen the dead move more quickly."

The Waelisc onlookers let out a cheer at their leader's insult and the drawing of first blood.

Beobrand took a deep breath, willing himself to be calm. He could almost hear Bassus' words when they trained together: "Do not let him anger you. Focus."

He stepped forward, and Mynyddog retreated. The man was no fool. He may make light of his adversary with his taunts, but he knew that Beobrand was deadly.

They circled each other, each ready for the slightest movement, the smallest gap in the other's defences.

Without warning, Beobrand roared and leapt forward, hammering Hrunting down, keeping his shield ready for the counter he knew would come. Mynyddog caught the great blow on his shield and attempted to slide his own blade beneath

Beobrand's guard. Beobrand swung his board to intercept the attack, pushing the sword aside. But rather than retreat, he pushed himself forward, inside the Waelisc warrior's reach. Mynyddog was momentarily off balance and Beobrand kicked out at his right knee.

Mynyddog grunted and then both of them were parting, jumping apart as quickly as they had clashed. Beobrand noticed the narrowing of the small man's eyes. That had hurt. Beobrand hoped it would slow him down.

They circled again. Each staring at the other, intent on the eyes and the feet, for those were what would show when and from where an attack would come. Beobrand's Bernicians were shouting their encouragement now too, their voices mingling with those of the men of Powys so that the small patch of grass on the hill sounded like a battle between two warbands, and not just two men. Beobrand ignored the noise. He could not afford to be distracted.

He was panting now, sweat flowing freely from beneath his great helm and trickling into his eyes, stinging them.

"How is it I have never heard of you?" he asked, wishing he could pause for a moment to wipe his brow. "I would have thought one of your skill would be sung of in all the mead halls of Albion."

Mynyddog laughed, but did not cease his stealthy pacing around the grassy patch of ground. Was he favouring one leg? Beobrand could not be certain, but he thought he detected a slight limp.

"You must listen to the wrong bards," Mynyddog said. "Typical of you Seaxons. You believe your kind is better at everything and cannot begin to think that one of my people could possibly best you in anything. Well, prepare to learn, Seaxon."

And with that, Mynyddog pounced as fast as a cat. Beobrand was forced backwards, such was the frenzy of the attack. Blow after blow crashed into his shield. The watching Waelisc screamed and jeered. Beobrand parried frantically, looking for any weakness. If Mynyddog had been limping, there was no sign of it now.

Sparks flew from the blades as they rang together. Beobrand was careless of Hrunting's edge now. This was a foe to be reckoned with. If he did not turn the tide of this fight soon, he would have no need of his blade, save to grip its hilt in the hope that Woden would notice him fall and usher him into his corpse-hall.

Halting his backwards motion, he reached forward and down, aiming a huge blow at Mynyddog's leg. Had the strike connected, it would have slain the warrior from Powys. It was a powerful swing with the fine sword and would have more than likely severed the leg, or at least cut deeply and shattered the bone, killing Mynyddog just as surely as a cut to the neck. And yet the slicing blade did not hit its target. As he reached out, Beobrand's weight shifted and his left foot slipped on the trampled grass, that was now slick from being crushed by the duelling men.

His leg slid from under him, and he crashed to the earth. In an eye-blink, Mynyddog stood over him. Beobrand made to swing Hrunting up into his adversary, but the blade did not move. With a shock, he saw that Mynyddog was standing on the blade. Panic seized Beobrand then. He stared up at the small Waelisc warrior. Gone was the twinkling eye and the ghost of a smile, this was the implacable face of death.

The watching warriors were baying like hounds who scented blood, but the sounds they made receded as Beobrand lay there on the shadowed slope. The green scent of the grass filled his nostrils. The sky above Mynyddog's head was afire with the last rays of the sun. Beobrand drew his gaze away from what would be his last sunset, back to the set features of Mynyddog's face. The Waelisc warrior had placed his sword at Beobrand's throat and he found himself staring along the burnished length of the blade.

He had known this day would surely come, when he would meet his match. He did not wish to die, but he was so tired.

To close his eyes for a time would be welcome. But he would not look away from death. Clutching Hrunting's grip tightly, he ceased struggling to free the blade. He would miss Octa growing into a strong man, but perhaps he would soon see his older brother after whom he had named his son. Maybe there was a place in the afterlife where he would meet again with all those he had lost. His mother. His sisters. Sunniva.

His gaze met Mynyddog's.

"Do it," he whispered. "Make it quick."

But Mynyddog withdrew his sword, shifting it to his left hand, where he held it awkwardly along with his shield. Then, leaning down, the bright sky turning his grinning face to shadow, he offered Beobrand his hand.

Beobrand blinked, unsure and confused.

Mynyddog laughed at his discomfort.

"You tripped, man," he said. "I would not be known as the man who slew the great Beobrand with the help of some damp moss."

For a moment Beobrand lay there panting, drawing in great gulps of air. He could taste the freshly crushed grass in his throat. The air was cool and sweet, revitalising him as if it had been cold river water.

He reached out his hand and allowed Mynyddog to haul him to his feet.

Mynyddog took a couple of steps back, allowing Beobrand to retrieve Hrunting. Beobrand wiped the sweat from his face and readied himself once more to face the Waelisc swordsman.

The cheering from the two warbands intensified. The men of Powys must have been full of pride at the bravado shown by their man. The Bernicians strained their voices in the hope that they would lend their lord the strength and skill to vanquish Mynyddog. Beobrand's mind was reeling. The man had let him live. The shame of it hit him like a slap. How could he fight him now? And yet, did he have a choice? The lives of his gesithas hung by the thread of his wyrd.

Mynyddog ended his moment of reflection with a lightning attack, which Beobrand barely managed to parry.

"Come on," taunted the Waelisc man, "it will be dark soon, and one of us must be dead before then."

And so they continued to duel. The watchers marvelled at the prowess of their two leaders. Mynyddog and Beobrand clashed again and again, each time their speed and weapon skill enough to finish a lesser opponent. But these two men were both masters of their chosen craft, and each attack ended with the strike being avoided. Often this took the form of a block that further tattered and splintered the men's hide-covered linden boards. At other times, the warriors simply darted out of reach of a scything blade, skipping over the grass and sparing their shields and swords further damage. When particularly pressed and desperate, the men would parry with their blades. The clang of steel on steel made the watching men wince. They all knew they risked blunting and chipping their swords, or worse, shattering the metal.

But the blades were well-wrought, and the men were so skilled that neither could find a gap in the other's defences for a long while. They were both panting and sweat-drenched now, taking longer pauses to regain their breath between bouts of vicious fighting.

And they were slowing.

These were the best warriors those watching had ever beheld, but they were not gods. Their breath was ragged, their deflections and dodges ever slower.

Mynyddog danced forward, feinting at Beobrand's head. But Beobrand had been studying the wily Waelisc and anticipated the true attack, that would be a thrust to his groin. When the lunge came, Beobrand side-stepped and crashed his shield rim down into Mynyddog's sword hand. Beobrand timed the move well, but he knew that if his adversary had not been tired, he would never have connected with the shield. And yet, weary as they both now were, it was not merely skill that would win the contest. Guile, chance and luck would all play their part.

Mynyddog's sword fell to the churned grass and mud. Grimacing at the pain in his wrist where Beobrand's shield had struck, he leapt quickly out of Hrunting's reach. Beobrand stepped forward and placed his foot on Mynyddog's blade. The Waelisc warrior, clearly in pain, held his right hand up behind his scarred, white shield. He offered Beobrand a twisted smile.

"Well, about time you scored a hit," he said, his voice coming in gasps as he tried to regain his breath. "After all, I did give you a lie down and a rest before!"

Beobrand returned his grin. Gods, the man was a strange one, to laugh in the face of death. For surely Beobrand must slay him now. He looked down at the sword beneath his foot. Mynyddog had let him live when he had fallen, could he slay him now, as he stood weaponless before him?

They stared at each other for several heartbeats, both breathing hard, glad of the respite, but knowing blood and death were not far away now.

Something drew Mynyddog's gaze from Beobrand. For a moment, Beobrand thought this was some crude trick to make him turn, but then he heard it.

Hooves.

Galloping hooves of many horses. On the hilltop his men were rattling their spears and swords against their shields, cheering more loudly now than the Powys men, who had fallen silent.

Beobrand turned and stared down into the valley. For a moment he was unable to make sense of what he saw, he had been focused for so long on his opponent that it was difficult to take in the wide expanse of land, dappled in shade and the golden light of the sunset. But then his heart soared. From the north came some twenty mounted warriors. Their war gear glimmered and glinted in the sun's dying light. And instantly he knew why his men atop the hill rejoiced. For these were battle-hardened men of Bernicia, warriors without compare. They all carried black-painted shields and followed a fair-haired young warrior who rode as if he had been born to the saddle.

Cynan!

The men from Powys were hastily forming a defensive square, seeing that they would very soon be facing enemies from two directions.

Beobrand rammed Hrunting into the ground, then, stooping, he lifted Mynyddog's sword from the earth.

A movement from the birch on the hill caught his eye. Perhaps startled by the sudden noise of the arriving horsemen, a white bird flapped from the canopy of the tree and flew overhead. A dove. Beobrand frowned, thinking of Oswald and his omen.

He proffered the sword towards Mynyddog hilt first.

"Go, Mynyddog, lead your men away from here with your honour."

There was no smile on the Waelisc man's features now. He fixed Beobrand with a stare as cool as a winter's night.

"But not with my lord," he said.

From below them came the sounds of men dismounting. Shouted orders rang out as warriors formed shieldwalls. Beobrand did not remove his gaze from Mynyddog's.

"No," he said at last, rubbing his calloused right hand over his face and smearing the dirt, dried blood and sweat there, "no one can bring back the dead."

Mynyddog's eyes narrowed. He sighed and took a deep breath. He accepted his sword from Beobrand and sheathed it with a fluid flourish. Nodding, he spat and then grinned once more.

"Until we meet again, Beobrand, the Half-handed," he said, and returned to his men without a backward glance. Mynyddog joined his warband and ordered the men to mount up.

"Let them go!" Beobrand shouted to Cynan, who acknowledged the command with a wave of his hand.

"Oswald was right," Acennan said, from beside Beobrand. The gesithas had descended the hill and now stood around their lord.

"Right?" Beobrand said, almost too tired to speak.

"You are one lucky whoreson."

Beobrand hawked and spat.

"My mother was no whore," he said.

Acennan chuckled.

Beobrand watched as the men from Powys rode away. They cantered south, the white shields strapped to their backs flashing blood red in the final rays of the day's sun.

Beircheart suddenly bellowed after them, "Go on and run, you Waelisc scum!"

"Charming, that is," said Cynan, leading his horse up the hill to meet them. "I didn't expect to be welcomed with a feast, but, after riding to your rescue, I had thought to receive better than that, Beircheart."

Chapter 33

Reaghan took a deep breath, willing herself to be calm. The room was filled with the sounds and smells of a feast. A small boy turned a sheep on a spit over the hearth. Mutton fat dripped into the fire, sending up sizzling sheets of flame. The fresh ale had been served, and more had been fetched by the other women of Ubbanford, who were all present. In fact, there was nobody from the settlement who was not crammed into the hall. They drank, ate and laughed, but Reaghan also sensed their gaze upon her and her guests. After all, it was not every day they got to see a queen.

"She is not a queen," Rowena had told her that afternoon, after sending one of her new slaves down the hill to fetch a large cheese that had been hanging in Ubba's hall, "just the wife of an atheling." That may be so, thought Reaghan, but as she looked over at the beautiful woman, who delicately lifted her eating knife to skewer a morsel of meat, she could not make the distinction. Cynethryth was clearly a woman of breeding.

Reaghan was breathless to think that she, who had once been a thrall, was the hostess here, and Cynethryth, wife of Eowa, atheling of Mercia, a guest. She had hardly believed the number of chests and coffers Cynethryth had brought with her. And her clothes! By Danu, Mother of all, Reaghan had believed that some of the garments she had fashioned from cloth purchased from Aart the peddler were fine. But they were rags when compared to the finery Cynethryth wore.

The Mercian lady seemed to sense her gaze, for she looked in her direction and smiled. Blushing, Reaghan turned her attention to the slices of meat and freshly baked bread before her. She cut a small sliver of mutton and placed it in her mouth, trying to emulate the way that Cynethryth used her knife. She chewed slowly. Don't be so foolish, she told herself. Cynethryth is just a woman, the same as you. But no matter how many times she told herself that, she could not bring herself to believe it. She did not look the same as her, and Reaghan could not imagine she felt the same either.

Still, Cynethryth's smile seemed genuine. And, glancing around the hall, Reaghan could not deny that the feast was going well. Not that she had done much in order to make it happen.

After Bassus' announcement of the arrival of important guests, the day had gone from the usual chores, completed with a practised lack of urgency, to a frenetic rush of tasks.

Rowena had presented herself in the new hall on the hill shortly after Bassus had told Reaghan to expect visitors.

"I have come to help you arrange things, my dear," she had said. But rather than help Reaghan, she had taken over the role of lady of the hall. At first Reaghan had been resentful of the older woman taking charge, but then Bassus had come to her side. His face, as it always did, had softened when he'd looked upon Rowena.

"See how happy she is," he'd said, keeping his voice quiet and conspiratorial. "She loves to organise a good feast."

"We'll need to slaughter a sheep," Rowena had been saying, as much to herself as to anyone else in the hall, oblivious that she was being watched. The thralls bustled about the building, eager to do what the lady Rowena ordered. Reaghan recalled when she had been as quick to do Rowena's bidding. It seemed the Mercian thralls had learnt quickly enough not to cross their new mistress.

The afternoon had been a flurry of activity, with Reaghan fretting that nothing would be ready in time. Thankfully, in the end the visitors did not arrive until the sun was well past its zenith. Apparently it was impossible to travel quickly when laden with so many chests of clothes and possessions.

But looking about the hall now Reaghan could see that the extra time afforded them by the slow progress of Cynethryth's retinue had allowed Rowena and the other women of Ubbanford to lay on a welcome fit for a queen. And for the homecoming of their lord's only son.

She turned to Octa now and beamed, unable to contain the happiness that flooded through her to see him home again. Safe within this hall. As it should be.

"He has grown much these last months, has he not?"

Reaghan started. Cynethryth had set aside her small eating knife and leaned in close to Reaghan.

Reaghan smoothed her dress over her slim frame, conscious that the green woollen peplos, the best and most-prized item of clothing she possessed, seemed coarse and cheap next to the shimmering perfection of Cynethryth's gown. The Mercian wore a blue tunic of the finest wool, decorated at the sleeves with silken purple stripes. Around her slender waist was a woven hemp girdle of white, green and indigo. The ends of the girdle were finished in gold that glittered in the firelight.

Reaghan swallowed.

"Indeed he has, lady," she replied, her voice shaking.

Cynethryth seemed not to notice Reaghan's nervousness.

"He is a fine boy," she said. "He looks much like his father, but there is something softer about him." She looked sidelong at Reaghan. "Something of his mother's looks perhaps?"

Reaghan tensed. Did Cynethryth know she was not the boy's mother? Surely she did. But Reaghan saw no malice in the woman's face.

"He does have something of his mother's features," she replied. "Sunniva was beautiful."

To Reaghan's surprise, Cynethryth reached out and placed her hand on her arm.

"But you are Octa's mother now, aren't you?" she said. "Octa never stopped talking of you. He missed you terribly."

Reaghan felt her eyes suddenly brimming with tears.

"I missed him too," she said.

Cynethryth patted her arm.

"Well, I have brought him back to you."

Octa was playing with Eowa's sons, Osmod and Alweo, on the far side of the hall. They were teaching the hounds to sit and beg for scraps. As the two women watched, one of the dogs got tired of waiting for his reward and jumped up, knocking young Alweo over onto the rushes. Cynethryth and Reaghan both sprang to their feet, but before they could even utter a sound, Octa had jumped forward and pushed the dog away. He helped Alweo up and the three boys were soon laughing again.

Reaghan and Cynethryth seated themselves once more, smiling ruefully at each other.

"It is a woman's lot never to stop worrying, I fear," said Cynethryth. "First for her children, and then for her man." She took a sip of the ale from a small silver cup. Reaghan had taken it from Beobrand's hoard of treasure, keen to honour her guest.

Reaghan smiled now. Cynethryth was not aloof and distant as she had feared she would be. She was a woman. A wife. A mother.

"It seems to me that our men are often worse than the children," she said, emboldened by Cynethryth's friendly demeanour.

Cynethryth offered her a sad smile.

"Unfortunately, the games that men play are oftentimes deadly."

They fell silent then. Reaghan thought of Beobrand. Seeing Octa made her miss him all the more keenly. She said a silent prayer that he would be safe. When he returned, she would make it all the way it had been before. Too long had she allowed the cold distance to build between them.

The boys had grown tired of tormenting the dogs. The other children from Ubbanford had joined them, forgetting their initial shyness, and they were all now engrossed in defining some complex rules to a game they appeared to be inventing. One of them evidently said something humorous, for the throng of children suddenly erupted into gales of laughter.

"We may be very different, you and I," Cynethryth said. "But we are sisters. We have a shared bond. Our men are away, and there is nothing we can do but wait and see that their children are cared for."

Reaghan could scarcely believe she had feared this woman.

"I am glad Beobrand sent you to our hall, Cynethryth," she said, realising with a start that it was true. She had been lonely for so long. Perhaps Cynethryth would truly be her friend.

A sudden angry shout sawed savagely into Reaghan's soft, contented thoughts.

"By all the gods, I can listen no more!"

The furious shriek came from Sulis, who had been standing all the while behind her mistress, ready to attend her when needed. Reaghan had almost forgotten that the woman was there. She was not accustomed to having her own house thrall to serve her, and Sulis had been still and silent.

Until now.

Her scream cut through the warm conviviality of the hall like a sword blade slicing into the plump stomach of an unsuspecting foe. All eyes turned in her direction. Conversation and laughter died on ale-wet lips.

"I am a woman of Mercia!" she shouted, spittle flying from her mouth. Her ire was directed at Cynethryth and for a moment Reaghan thought that Sulis would launch herself at the lady. Sulis' fists bunched and she looked set to throw herself at Cynethryth. "Would you eat and talk with this Waelisc slut while I am held a slave?"

Sulis panted, seemingly shocked at her own outburst. Bassus rose from his seat, his huge presence bringing with it a sense of control to the hall.

Cynethryth gave Sulis a long appraising look.

"I am a guest in this hall," she said, her voice clear and steady. This was not a woman to be cowed by a thrall's anger. "I am sorry for your plight, but it is not of my concern."

"Not your concern?" spluttered Sulis. "You eat and drink here, a guest of these Bernicians. Your sons yet live. Where is my son?" she sobbed. "Where is he?" Tears flowed down her cheeks and it seemed she would speak no more, that the fire of her anger had burnt out. But then she screamed, "I am no slave!"

Bassus strode towards the thrall. His great bulk looming over her. He lifted his one hand menacingly.

"Watch your tongue, girl," he bellowed.

Reaghan surged up, placing herself between Bassus and Sulis. Her neck prickled. Behind her, she could sense Sulis' rage emanating from her like the heat from a forge.

"Hold, Bassus," she said, surprised that her voice did not quaver.

"She needs a good beating," roared Bassus. "I have told you before that this one needs to feel the lash if you are to ever trust her."

"Nobody is going to be beaten tonight," she replied, her tone calm and soothing. The same voice she used when speaking to Octa when he was tired and angry.

She turned to face Sulis.

"Leave now," Reaghan said. "Go to my sleeping quarters and remain there."

Sulis glared at her. Her anger was almost palpable, but Reaghan did not recoil from the strength of Sulis' ire. She held her gaze until, at last, the slave stalked out of the hall through the partition that led to the private chambers beyond.

Chapter 34

Cynan took a deep draught of ale. Usually the warmth of a hall and the rich, heady brew would relax him. But now, as he sat amongst so many warriors in the hall of a stranger in Caer Luel, he could not shake the feeling of anxiety that had settled upon him like a bad odour. He had hoped to be rid of the nagging sensation of doom that had clung to him ever since riding to Ubbanford with Sulis and the other Mercian thralls. And yet it still clung to him, heavy and brooding, like the dark clouds that now covered the land.

The sky had darkened, ushering in angry, gloom-laden clouds from the north as they had ridden northward from Beobrand's duel with Mynyddog. Cynan had been jubilant to find his lord and most of his shield-brothers hale, and he had thanked all the gods that he had pressed on south after meeting Oswiu's host on the road. Oswiu had been taken ill with the sweating sickness and so his comitatus, and the warriors of Rheged who had joined his banner, had lingered at the hall of Rhoedd mab Rhun mab Urien. Rhoedd carried himself with the bearing of a great man, tall and proud, wearing the finest of clothing. But just as the crumbling remains of Caer Luel were a pale shadow of their former glory, so too the grandson of Urien knew that his kingdom's power had waned. Rheged had aligned itself to

Bernicia and Northumbria, and the sons of Æthelfrith were now Rhoedd's masters.

Oswiu's men had urged Cynan and the men who had ridden with him from Ubbanford to wait with them at Caer Luel and later ride south when Oswiu recovered, thus swelling their ranks yet further. But the tugging worry would not leave him and Cynan had firmly refused, leading Beobrand's gesithas away before Oswiu could be roused from his sickbed. He had feared the atheling might order them to remain with him, and once such an order was given, it would take a very brave man or a fool to ignore it. And so he had told the men to mount in haste and they had galloped south, leaving the crumbling walls and cracked, dry fountains of Caer Luel behind.

Cynan glanced at the atheling now. Oswiu had made a speedy recovery and sat at the high table beside Rhoedd mab Rhun, surrounded by his closest thegns and ealdormen. As Cynan watched, Lord Fordraed, drinking horn sloshing its contents carelessly in his left hand, leaned in close to Oswiu. The atheling listened intently, nodding his approval at the words of the plump thegn. Cynan drained his cup and cursed, sure that Fordraed dripped yet more poison into Oswiu's ear about Beobrand.

Beobrand and all his warband, including Cynan, sat at the far end of the boards, in the place of least prestige. Such a thing was unheard of for a thegn of Beobrand's worth, who had served Oswald with dedication for many years.

But of course, Oswald was dead.

A few other survivors from Maserfelth, including Fordraed and a handful of his warband, had straggled into the hall in the day since Beobrand's arrival, but Beobrand had been the first, and the only lord to travel with a substantially intact band of warriors. Cynan had seen the looks and heard the whispers. How could it be that the great Beobrand could ride free from a battle so terrible that the mighty King Oswald, the Christ-anointed lord of all Northumbria and much of Albion, had been slain, along with most of his warhost? They knew the answer, for Beobrand had spoken of what had transpired before them all, as Oswiu slouched in Rhoedd's intricately carved gift-stool. Beobrand had recounted everything in a voice devoid of feeling; the savagery of the battle, the sacrifice to Woden under the great ash tree, the forced march of Eowa's host, the doomed stand upon the hill, and then, how Eowa had fallen, and later seeing Oswald's banner fall, and Derian's order to flee north.

The hall had been silent as men listened to the tale of defeat and sacrifice. Beobrand was no storyteller, no scop. But even those men with little in the way of imagination could picture the scene as it had been on that hill overlooking the marshy field north of the Maerse. The pain of the defeat was plain to see on the faces of Beobrand and his warriors. They were all dirt-streaked, stiff from battle and hard riding, and their eyes were grim and dark. They were exhausted, their bodies had been battered, and they had lost their king. Worst of all, Cynan knew that Beobrand blamed himself for Oswald's demise.

Oswiu had sat as quietly as the rest of them as Beobrand had spoken in his dull monotone of the events to the south, but when he spoke of running from the battle, the atheling's face had clouded and he'd pushed himself upright on the gift-stool and spoken.

"You fled from the battle, brave Beobrand?" he'd asked, his tone dripping with contempt.

Cynan had wanted to scream out in his lord's defence. At least Beobrand had stood in the shieldwall, had taken many men from Mercia and his own warband into danger and death. Oswiu had been convalescing all the while in this comfortable hall, no doubt being fed the choicest of foods and sating his other hungers with the prettiest of the house thralls. Beobrand's gesithas had all bridled at Oswiu's tone, but Cynan had taken a step forward. He could not allow such injustice.

But Gram had placed his hand on Cynan's shoulder and whispered, "You cannot win a fight with an atheling, Cynan."

Cynan had stepped back, but his anger yet simmered to remember the scene.

Beobrand had taken a deep breath and merely nodded, seemingly unable to utter the words that would brand him a coward in the eyes of all the gathered men.

Oswiu had frowned.

"Was it not your duty to defend the king?" he had spat the words. "Were you not oath-bound to give up your life in his defence and if he fell, to take the blood-price from his slayers until you too were killed?"

Again Beobrand had simply nodded assent.

"Then why," Oswiu had screamed, a sudden fury coming over him, "are you not feeding the wolves at Maserfelth?" A hound that had been resting quietly at Oswiu's feet, had leapt up in alarm and slunk off into the shadows. All about the hall, men had shifted uncomfortably. Gram had tightened his grip on Cynan's shoulder.

Beobrand had met Oswiu's gaze then. There was yet flint in those eyes. He had ridden from Maserfelth, and that clearly weighed heavily upon him, but those were not the eyes of a craven. He glared at Oswiu, and something like his usual fire kindled in his stare.

"I did not break my oath, Lord Oswiu." He made the title sound like an insult. "I did not remain at Maserfelth because it was not my king's will."

Oswiu had forced himself to sit back with a visible effort. He ran his fingers through his hair and then brushed invisible dust from the shoulder of his kirtle.

"Explain yourself," he had said, holding Beobrand's gaze, but visibly uncomfortable.

"Derian, son of Isen, reminded me of my oath to your brother." For several heartbeats, neither had spoken further, but then Oswiu's eyes had opened wide in understanding.

"The pledge you swore when he was struck down at Tatecastre," Oswiu had said, his voice small now, disbelieving and surprised at this twist of their wyrd that would see them linked together.

Beobrand nodded once more. There were no more words needed. Whether they had all been there or not, there was no one in the hall who did not know of the tale of the battle of Tatecastre, the battle where he had donned the king's helm and led them to victory; where Beobrand swore to plight his oath to Oswiu upon Oswald's death.

And so it was that Oswiu had stood before them all, an unfathomable expression upon his face. And there, in Rhoedd mab Rhun's leaking hall of Caer Luel, with the smoke billowing from the hearth fire and the driving rain pounding the tiled roof, Beobrand of Ubbanford had knelt in the damp rushes and sworn his oath to yet another son of Æthelfrith. He had spoken the words clearly, but each syllable fell brittle and sharp from his mouth like hammer scale chipped upon a smith's anvil.

"I will to Oswiu, son of Æthelfrith," Beobrand had said, "be true and faithful, and love all which he loves and shun all which he shuns, according to the laws of God and the order of the world. Nor will I ever with will or action, through word or deed, do anything which is unpleasing to him, on condition that he will hold to me as I shall deserve it."

Oswiu had stared at Beobrand for a long while after Beobrand had spoken the oath. It was usual for a lord, upon receiving a man's oath, to raise him up, embrace him, and often to proffer a gift as a token of the treasures they would bestow in the future. Oswiu did none of these things. He merely stared and the silence grew uncomfortable. Rain hammered the roof, and water trickled onto the rushes in several places where tiles had been lost and never replaced. Beobrand, motionless and unflinching, returned his new lord's gaze.

When it had seemed neither man would break the silent battle of wills, Oswiu had lowered his eyes and returned to his gift-stool.

"I accept your oath, Beobrand, son of Grimgundi," he had said carelessly over his shoulder.

Cynan poured more ale into his cup but did not drink. It was good, but he had no appetite for it. And his muscle-clenching anxiety still gripped him. For how could he relax when so much was wrong in the world? After his initial happiness at finding Beobrand and his gesithas alive and riding north, their pervading mood of gloom had settled upon him too. The weather had drawn in, and a cold spiteful rain had pounded them as they had ridden betwixt the huge peaks of that farthest western reach of Rheged.

When they had camped, the men had told him the story of Maserfelth and he had believed he had understood their mood. They were weary, and sorrowful at the loss of their king. But now, thinking back to the previous day when Beobrand had been forced to give his oath to Oswiu, Cynan thought he truly comprehended the full extent of his lord's woe.

Not only had Beobrand lost his lord and king, for which he felt true guilt, but he had now given his word to obey Oswiu, and to stand by him unto death.

Cynan watched as Beobrand, Acennan, Attor and the others methodically chewed their food and morosely drained their cups and horns. Unbidden, the image of Sulis came to him. His mind had often turned to the thrall since he had left her at Ubbanford. He knew it was foolish, but no matter how often he told himself to forget about her, the memory of Sulis would flood his thought-cage. The feel of her arms, gripping tightly about his waist as they'd ridden north, her head leaning against his shoulder. The scent of her hair. The touch of her skin as he had bound her wounds. She despised him, he was sure, but he could not dispel the thoughts of her.

From the high table came a sudden, raucous burst of laughter. But there was no mirth for Beobrand and his men. For the lord of Ubbanford had sworn his solemn oath to a man who might well become the next king of Northumbria, and, in spite of

Beobrand never having said as much within Cynan's hearing, or to anyone else as far as he was aware, it was clear to all that he loathed Oswiu. Cynan knew not if the dislike stemmed from Oswiu's contempt for the suffering inflicted by his men at the battle of Cair Chaladain, or if there was more history between the men, but of the enmity's existence, there could be no doubt.

Cynan looked at Oswald's brother. All round Oswiu, his retinue seemed content. Perhaps pleased at their lord's probable ascension to the throne left empty by Oswald's death. The thegns and ealdormen talked and riddled, and earlier a scop had sung songs of Oswald's great victories and how the Christ would take him into his bosom in heaven. But Oswiu was still and sombre. And he was staring directly at Beobrand.

Cynan shuddered. More worrying than Beobrand's dislike for his new oath-sworn lord, was the obvious hatred Oswiu felt towards Beobrand.

Chapter 35

Beobrand awoke with a start. He stifled the scream that was on his lips, looking about anxiously at the slumbering men who lay about the hall. He felt enough shame already, without Oswiu's retinue hearing him crying out in his sleep. The taint of cowardice had tarnished his name. He could see it in the eyes of the other warriors. Warriors who had never fled from a battle.

"They will think what they will," Acennan had told him the night before. "It is the truth that matters." They had both been well on the way to drunkenness on the ale of the lord of Caer Luel, but were still sombre and grim. As the night drew on, their speech had grown more adamant and harsh, despite the slurring of the words.

"Look where we sit, Acennan," Beobrand had hissed. "We are as far from the high table as it is possible to be without being out in the storm." He'd emptied his cup and held it out for Attor to fill it from a jug. "Truth matters not. Lies ruin a reputation just as well as the truth. Besides, it is not a lie that I fled from Maserfelth."

"You had no choice!"

"There is always a choice," Beobrand had replied, drinking yet more of Rhoedd mab Rhun's strong ale.

They had talked no more on the subject that night. But all the while Beobrand had been unable to pull his mind away from the thoughts of his failure to protect Oswald, from the knowledge that he had been responsible for his lord's death. And that he had then left the battlefield with his life.

Now, as he sat in the gloomy hall and listened to the wind and rain that yet buffeted the building, his dream was still as real to him as if it lay just outside in the driving rain and gusting wind. As if he had merely stepped through a door into this smoke-hazed darkness, sour with spilt ale and the body-stink of dozens of sleeping men. His breathing came in short gasps, as though he had been running. His body trembled, and his brow was beaded with sweat, though the fire had burnt to embers and the hall was cool. This was only the second night they had been in Rhoedd mab Rhun mab Urien's hall. The second chance at restful slumber. And yet, despite the bone-deep weariness of his limbs, which screamed at him to lie back down and attempt to find sleep once more, Beobrand remained seated, forcing himself to breathe more slowly. He would not find rest again this night. Men thought him a craven and perhaps it was so. For he feared to close his eyes; to step through that door from the gloomy reality of this noisome hall and into the death-filled maw of his nightmares.

So much killing. So many dead.

In his sleep he saw them all. He was running down the slope from the hill overlooking Maserfelth. Behind him, on the marshy land north of the Maerse, he had watched in horror as Penda and his men butchered dozens of horses that screamed like children as they were slaughtered beneath the huge ash tree. In his dream the tree was so massive that it could have been Woden's Gallows, the Earth Tree itself. It towered over the hill, so that even when he was far down the northern slope, he could still see its huge spreading branches hung with the dripping carcasses of the sacrificed steeds. He had stumbled on something, a root perhaps, but he regained his balance and ran on. He could not remain in that place, to see Penda bathing in the blood of the stallions, to witness the Mercian horde gorging themselves on the raw, blood-streaming flesh of the beasts.

Again something snagged at his leg and he almost fell. Looking down, his stomach lurched and bile flooded his mouth. It was not a root that had impeded him. The grasping fingers of the fallen warriors reached for him as he passed. They stared up with vacant eyes and blood-filled mouths, reaching out with their dead, clutching claws. Panicking, Beobrand brushed the hands away, pushing them aside, desperate to escape this place of doom.

A hand grasped his ankle, and with rising terror Beobrand tugged to free himself.

"I thought you were my friend," gurgled a voice and Beobrand stared down into the pallid, scarred face of Eowa.

"I'm sorry," Beobrand said then, pulling away. He turned quickly. But where the way had been clear a moment before, now his path was blocked by dozens of corpse-warriors, weapons bloodied and battle-harness beaded with gore and gobbets of flesh.

At their centre, he recognised Oswald. The king of Northumbria walked towards him on stiff, unbending legs, arms outstretched to embrace Beobrand. His great helm had fallen from his head and his blood-wet hair was slathered to his scalp.

"You should not run, Beobrand," the dead king said, his voice rasping against the corruption that clogged his throat. Beobrand had been transfixed by the horror before him. Eowa's hands scratched at his legs.

"You said you were my friend," bubbled up the voice of the atheling of Mercia.

Oswald tottered forward, his mouth pulling open into a horrific grimace.

"Come to me," he held his arms open, "embrace your king." Something moved in Oswald's mouth. With a twist of his guts,

Beobrand saw it was a worm, that wriggled, long and slime-slick, to fall from his king's lips.

That was when he had awoken. He had dreamt the same dream for the last two nights. He had hoped that drinking himself to oblivion might help, but, if anything, the night shades had seemed more vivid.

The wind whistled under the eaves, rattling the clay tiles of the roof. The sound made Beobrand think of the gnashing teeth of the corpses of his dream. He shuddered, and stood. No, he would sleep no more.

Somewhere in the darkness of the hall someone coughed. Another man, his sleep disturbed by the noise, rolled over with a curse. The sounds reminded Beobrand of the ghosts that clawed at him in his dream. His stomach was in turmoil and he feared he might puke. He needed air. Pushing himself up, Beobrand picked his way over the sleeping men towards the hall doors. The guards there eyed him suspiciously, but after a moment, the shorter of the two removed the bar from the door and, without a word, pulled it ajar, allowing Beobrand out into the windswept night.

The rain did not fall as vehemently as it had the evening before, but the wind gusted, slapping his cloak about him, as the drizzle cooled his face. All around him loomed the shadows of the buildings of Caer Luel. Weeds grew from cracks in the cobblestones, and the roofs of some of the buildings had collapsed completely, leaving wall-shells heaped with the smashed remains of tiles and timber. The wind rustled the bushes that grew in the empty buildings, and the branches of a hawthorn, that rose from the crumbling courtyard, creaked above him.

Beobrand gulped down fresh air, willing himself to calm. Try as he might, he could not shake the terror of his dream.

A hand touched his shoulder and he cried out, leaping away and drawing the seax from his belt. Gods, did he yet dream? Or were the denizens of the otherworld here, crawling amongst these stone bones of the Roman city?

"Easy there, Beobrand," said a familiar voice.

Beobrand felt a renewed shame. It was only Acennan. His stocky friend stepped from the hall behind him. This was no night-stalker to haunt his dreams.

"There is nothing to fear here," said Acennan.

Beobrand sheathed his seax and clenched his fist at his side. He felt foolish to be shaking, like a child frightened of the dark. Turning, he walked away from the hall. Acennan followed.

Beobrand looked up at the sky. Clouds roiled there, grey in the wolf-light of dawn. The rain had almost completely stopped. For a time the two friends stood in silence, each seemingly content to listen to the dying of the storm. Birds began to chitter and sing in the hawthorn in the courtyard. The birdsong was echoed from other trees around the city. Morning would be upon them soon. The sky brightened, picking out the details of the crumbling stones that the Romans had left so many years before. Acennan stooped, picked up a rock and threw it into a circular pond, which was surrounded by a low wall. The lord of Caer Luel had said that once water had spouted into the air from this pond, somehow controlled by the ingenuity of the long-forgotten Romans. Beobrand could scarcely believe it. It served as a water trough for the animals now. Acennan's pebble splashed into the brown water.

"I cannot stop thinking about those we left behind," said Beobrand, not looking at Acennan.

For a time Acennan did not respond. He picked up another stone, tossing it into the water and watching the ripples that formed there, reflecting the lightening sky.

"It is as you told Oswiu," Acennan said. "You gave your oath to Oswald. You could not stay. Do you remember after the battle at the great ditch?"

"Of course I remember," Beobrand snapped. He would never forget the shame he had felt at fleeing then. He had been injured, and Acennan had dragged him from the battle, saving his life. But there, as now, he had believed it was his duty to have given his life in battle.

"You were furious with me then. But it was my oath to protect you, Beobrand. I had no other choice. We are bound by our oaths. It is all we can do to fulfil them. And your word has ever been true." Acennan placed his hand once more upon Beobrand's shoulder. This time Beobrand did not flinch. "And you fulfilled more than one of your oaths at Maserfelth."

"Which oath?" Beobrand felt as though his oaths were of little value.

"You fulfilled your oath to Oswald, and you fulfilled your oath to your men. For did you not lead them safely from that place?"

Beobrand took in a deep shuddering breath.

"To safety," he said, his voice hollow. "Do you believe we are safe now that I have sworn myself to Oswiu?"

"I do not know, lord. But what else could you do?"

Beobrand snorted.

"If only I knew the answer to that," he said.

The rain had ceased now, and the wind had subsided somewhat. A tinge of salmon pink touched the clouds in the east. The birds had grown quiet in the trees. A dog barked furiously somewhere off to the south. And then a new noise came to them in the still of the morning air. The clatter of many hooves on the cobbled streets.

And the shouting of men.

Chapter 36

"I have a bad feeling about this," Acennan said.

On hearing the arrival of the horsemen they'd hurried back through the ruins of Caer Luel and had found a half-dozen of Oswiu's warriors, dismounting and rushing into the hall. Oswiu was no fool and he had sent many such small groups of riders out into the lands to the south to watch for sign of the enemy.

Beobrand and Acennan stood at the back of the hall and all was chaos around them. Men, groggy from the night's excesses, groaned to be awoken abruptly from their sleep. Thralls and bondsmen did their best to bring order, coaxing the hearth fire back to life, setting up boards on which to place food and drink, righting overturned chairs.

"Do you think they have spotted Penda's men?" asked Acennan.

"The gods alone know," said Beobrand. "But it seems doubtful. To march an army through the mountains towards Caer Luel would make little sense. Perhaps a small raiding party. Some of those Powys or Gwynedd Waelisc may have decided to chance their luck." They shouldered their way through the gathered men to get a better view of what was taking place. After the fresh, cool air outside, the atmosphere in the hall was thick and pungent, redolent of wet wool, stale sweat and sour ale. Beobrand's stomach churned. At the far end of the hall a door swung open and there stood Oswiu, hair tousled from sleep and face blotchy.

"Where is he?" he shouted, his voice cracking. He coughed and spat into the damp rushes.

One of the riders that had recently entered the hall stepped forward. Beside him stood a slim man. Dried blood and dirt smeared his face, his cloak was ripped and tattered. With a start Beobrand recognised Ástígend, the messenger who had led them to Maserfelth.

"We found him some way to the south," said the warrior, "his horse was almost dead, and he seemed close to death himself. He says he has come from Maserfelth. We tried to make him rest before coming here, but he would have none of it. Said he had to speak to you, lord. To Oswald's brother."

"Indeed?" Oswiu stepped into the hall, peering with interest at the newcomer.

"And what is it you would say to me, Ástígend?"

Ástígend looked shocked that Oswiu had remembered his name, but he raised himself up before the atheling.

Beobrand, Acennan and the other men at the doorway pushed forward, the better to hear what was said. All around the hall, men and women, servants and freemen, set aside their tasks, and turned to witness the exchange.

"My lord Oswiu," said Ástígend in a ringing voice that belied his injured and exhausted aspect. "I grieve with you at the loss of your brother. Oswald was the best of lords, and the best of kings."

There was a murmur through the hall. Oswiu frowned.

"And yet, faithful Ástígend," he said, his tone sharp, "you stand before me, alive. While my brother is dead."

Ástígend dropped his gaze and Beobrand thought he saw the man shudder.

"I fought to the last," he said, his words caught in his throat, "I saw my king fall." The hall was still and quiet. For a time it seemed Ástígend would speak no more, but then he raised his head and looked directly at Oswiu. "We fought then to avenge our lord," he said, "Derian raged and screamed, leading us forward, hacking and smashing into the enemy line. But alas Derian was lost to his rage." Ástígend hesitated. "God did not see fit to grant us vengeance." He sighed. "We fought with the strength and ire of wild boars, but in the end it was all for nought."

"Yes, others have already told me of how my brother fell," Oswiu said, his voice as harsh as a seax blade. "I thought you had something to tell me that I did not already know."

Ástígend licked his lips.

"I was wounded in that final furious fight. A Waelisc axe smote my helm and I was knocked senseless. When I awoke, night had fallen and all around me lay the bodies," Ástígend let out a small sob, but continued quickly, "the hacked meat of my countrymen. The hill was strewn with corpses."

"And yet here you are. Alive," Oswiu sneered.

"Yes, lord," said Ástígend, fixing Oswiu with a hard stare, "the Lord God delivered me from that evil place. But not before I witnessed the horror of it."

"I am sure we would all enjoy hearing the tale of your escape from the battlefield, brave Ástígend," said Oswiu, "but I fear we have more pressing matters to attend."

One of Oswiu's retainers let out a harsh barking laugh. Nobody else joined in.

"I do not come to recount my escape, Lord Oswiu, but to speak of your brother's death."

"I have already heard tell of his passing. I would not be reminded of it now."

"But lord," said Ástígend, "as a man of God, I know you will wish to hear this. It will pain you to hear the words I speak, but they must be spoken." Ástígend paused, as if expecting to be interrupted again, but Oswiu was silent now. "When I awoke, all around me was death. Men had been stripped of byrnies, helms and weapons. Why I yet lived I do not know, but I beheld such a sight then that I can never forget. You have heard perhaps of Penda's sacrifice the day before the battle."

Beobrand suppressed a shudder, his dream still fresh in his memory. Around the hall men nodded, for the tale of the stallion's sacrifice had been told to them by the survivors of Maserfelth.

"Penda is a pagan king," Ástígend said, his tone hard and cold as he thought back to what he had witnessed on that hill. "He is a pagan and he chose to rejoice in the victory the old gods had given him. A great fire burnt in Penda's camp and all around it his men and the warriors of Powys and Gwynedd cavorted and caroused.

"It seemed to me as a scene from hell itself. My skin yet crawls to think of those heathen devils and their celebrations in the firelight." All those gathered in the hall were rapt now, entranced by the tale Ástígend told, and the pictures his words drew in their minds. This was not the solemn, flat telling of Beobrand, Ástígend brought to his tale the gift of the scop. Oswiu too stared on, wide-eyed, hanging on every word.

"As I stood up, the bodies of my shield-brothers all around me moved and twitched. And yet they were truly dead." He let out a ragged breath. "The movement was from the birds and the beasts of the land who gnawed and chewed the flesh of those brave warriors." There was not a sound in the hall and Beobrand wondered whether anyone there yet breathed or if, like him, they held their breath waiting for Ástígend's next words.

"Many were the ravens, their beaks red with gore, and I had to be wary not to send them flying into the night sky, for surely then the warriors below would see someone had disturbed the feast of those birds of Woden. I wanted to be gone from the place, to run, north or east, anywhere but that place of slaughter. And yet something drew me down the hill, towards the bonfire and the great ash where Penda's men celebrated their victory. Perhaps the blow upon my head had made me mad, I do not know. Maybe I was moon-struck, or maybe the one true God led me, guiding my steps, so that I might see and bring you these dire tidings." Ástígend closed his eyes then rubbed dirt-stained hands across his face. Unbidden, the warrior who had brought him there picked up a pitcher of ale from a board nearby, poured it into a cup, and handed it to Ástígend. Ástígend started, surprised by the gesture. But he nodded his thanks and drained the cup in one huge gulp. Nobody spoke for a time, all eyes upon Ástígend.

At last, Oswiu could bear it no longer.

"What did you see there?" he asked. His voice was no longer contemptuous.

Ástígend focused his gaze once more upon the atheling and yet he hesitated, as if, having reached this moment in his tale, he now felt unsure about how to proceed. He drew in a deep breath and continued.

"I do not think I was mad, Oswiu atheling. I believe that God led me down onto that marshy plain. For had I been mad, would I not have been seen by one of the many warriors that roamed there? But no, I walked in a daze, drawn inexorably towards the fire, towards the giant ash tree. I was as Daniel walking amongst the lions, and no Waelisc nor Mercian halted my progress. They were drunk on mead, ale and the dark magic that Penda and his pagan priest had wrought."

"The stallion sacrifice?" Oswiu asked, his voice as expectant as a child's now. Gone was all his earlier belligerence.

"I am sure they gorged themselves upon the flesh of that poor beast," Ástígend said. "The blood of the stallion is a thing of power to the old gods, we all know this. But there is other blood that brings greater strength to the magics of Woden."

Beobrand felt the cold fingers of dread scratch down his back. He feared he knew what Ástígend had beheld there, in that flame-filled night.

"The blood of a king is the ultimate sacrifice," said Ástígend. He did not break his gaze with Oswiu now and the atheling could not look away, like a vole caught in the stare of a swooping night owl. "My path led me all the way to the base of that great tree and there, upon sharpened death poles, waelstengs for Woden, I saw Oswald. His eyes looked down upon me, those clever brown eyes of his, sightless now in death. Penda had taken his head and placed it upon the central waelsteng. And on the other stakes he had placed Oswald's limbs."

A ripple of unease ran through the hall. This was evil magic indeed.

"How did you escape?" Oswiu asked. Were those tears on his cheeks that Beobrand could see?

"I turned away from that evil site," said Ástígend. "And once again the great Lord God was watching over me, for I found my way to the edge of their encampment, where their horses were corralled."

"And you merely mounted one of their steeds and rode from that place unhindered?" The incredulity in Oswiu's voice was clear.

Ástígend nodded.

"Yes, lord," he said. "It was as though none could see me, and so I took a horse and then rode away into the night. I knew not where you were, lord, but again God led me. I headed north, to where your men found me. There," again he rubbed his hands across his face, "I have said my piece."

Ástígend, having imparted his tidings, seemed to wither and crumple. He had been injured and was exhausted, and now, it seemed his strength left him. The warrior at his side reached out and helped him to a stool, where he sat heavily.

For several heartbeats nobody spoke, and then all those gathered began to whisper and murmur at the news they had heard.

"Beobrand, son of Grimgundi," shouted Oswiu, his voice slicing through the hubbub like a knife to the throat.

Silence once more.

Beobrand did not wait for Oswiu to repeat his name. He would not have men believe he was too cowardly to face his lord. He stepped forward, elbowing his way past the onlooking warriors. Oswiu saw him, and turned his tear-streaked face towards him.

"Beobrand," he said, showing his teeth in a broad, mirthless grin, "my newly oath-sworn man, I have a task for you."

Beobrand clenched his fists, but made no other movement. "Lord?"

"You it was who caused my brother's death," said Oswiu. Beobrand said nothing, but his jaw hurt with the force of his bunching muscles there. "Because of you, Oswald..." Oswiu took in a shuddering breath. "Oswald... My brother... His body has been defiled by that pagan bastard, Penda. The Mercian scum has taken my brother from me, but he cannot keep his body. The land of Northumbria will be mine. I will ride to Bebbanburg and I will summon the wise men of the Witena Ġemōt. They will pronounce me King of Bernicia. And then I shall summon my warriors once more to me, and I will ride against Penda."

Oswiu's retinue let out a ragged cheer. Beobrand made no sound.

"Penda may have taken my brother's life," Oswiu said, "but I will not allow his head, his limbs, his body, to be used in his pagan sorcery. No, Oswald's heart belonged to Bernicia and to God, and his body shall be interred on Bernician soil. You will take a dozen of your gesithas, Beobrand of Ubbanford, and you will ride to Maserfelth, and you will retrieve my brother's remains. Oswald died because of you, now you will bring him home."

PART THREE
A SAINT'S JOURNEY

Chapter 37

They rode south under louring skies. The rain held off, but the clouds were grey and heavy, reflecting the mood of the men. When they had heard of Oswiu's orders Fraomar and Bearn had come to Beobrand.

"To do this thing is madness," Fraomar had said. "For surely Oswald's body will no longer be there, or if it is, Penda will have left men to guard it."

But Beobrand had merely shrugged. There seemed to be no fight left in him.

"Oswiu has my oath," he'd said.

Cynan watched him now as he dismounted. Beobrand, never a strong rider, rode stiffly now, his body evidently not yet recovered from the battle of Maserfelth and the long ride. Most of the other warriors were also weary, having stood in the shieldwall atop the hill. When Acennan had asked Oswiu why they could only ride with a dozen men, the atheling had replied that the rest of Beobrand's warband were to join the lord of Caer Luel's men. Acennan had protested, but Beobrand had pulled him back, cutting off his retorts with a harsh word. Beobrand had selected eleven men from his comitatus to ride with him. When Bearn was not chosen he had turned angrily to his lord.

"Have I not proven myself worthy?" he had asked.

"Of course, brave Bearn," Beobrand had said. "But I have another task for you. I entrust to you the rest of the men. You will lead them with my voice."

Mollified, Bearn had nodded his thanks and acceptance of the honour bestowed upon him. Beobrand had clapped him on the shoulder and led him away from the men. Cynan had watched intently as they'd spoken at some length out of earshot. Beobrand's face had been grave and serious. They had gripped each other's forearms in the warrior grip and Beobrand had returned to the men he had gathered about him for the seemingly impossible quest.

"And what of the twelfth man," Cynan had asked. He had counted the heads as Beobrand had named the men: Fraomar, Attor, Acennan, Beircheart, Dreogan, Eadgard and Grindan, Elmer, Garr, Gram and Cynan himself. "I count only eleven."

"If he would join us," said Beobrand, "I would have Ástígend."

"But we were at Maserfelth," said Attor. "we know where the great ash tree lies. Can we not give Ástígend some peace now? I fear he has suffered enough."

"We have all suffered," said Beobrand, "but if we are to dispel this dark magic of Penda's, I would take with us one whose steps are led by the Christ god. I believe it is Ástígend's wyrd to come with us."

And so it was the dozen were complete. Cynan marvelled at the resilience Ástígend displayed. The man's face had been sallow, his eyes sunken and dark, but with each day in the saddle Ástígend's strength returned. He seemed pleased for this opportunity to retrieve that which he'd left behind.

That morning as they'd ridden through the dim light of dawn they'd spotted a lone figure on a hillside. The man didn't see them until they emerged from the shade of the trees where they rode, but when he did, he turned and hastened from their path, clearly terrified of a group of armed horsemen. Cynan and Ástígend had kicked their heels to their mounts and galloped after him. His pitiful flock of sheep had scattered before them and the man had cried out in dismay, cursing at them for frightening his animals, defiant yet at the same time fawning in fear as the riders had run him down. They brought the man back to where Beobrand led the rest of the warriors and there they had questioned him. They had been pushing their mounts hard and in the three days since they'd left Caer Luel they had traversed the rugged country of lakes and rock-strewn crags. The land was softer here, wooded with rolling slopes and meandering rivers. They were close to the hill where Beobrand had faced Mynyddog. Within the day they would reach Maserfelth.

"There was a great battle to the south of here," the man said, tugging at his forelock and bowing before Beobrand. "A warhost led from Mercia. Penda it was. He killed the king." The man sucked at his teeth, seemingly unsure whether to be happy or sorrowful at the death of a king. He looked at the grim faces of the mounted warriors and swallowed deeply. "It was a terrible thing. Killed the king," he repeated, licking his lips. "Dunstan, the Christ priest, said the king is a martyr now. A saint. Hung upon the tree, just like the Christ."

"You have seen him?" asked Beobrand. "You have seen where Oswald has been placed upon the tree?"

The man nodded.

"Yes, lord, they did not mind the likes of me. I was afeared to go there, but Dunstan said the blood in the soil could cure any ill, and my wife has had a terrible cough these past months. So, I made my way there, down beside the Maerse. There is a huge ash and that is where he is."

"You said 'they'," asked Acennan. "Who do you mean?"

The man's eyes darted this way and that. Like a frightened animal, Cynan thought. The man wet his lips, spat to ward off evil, then made the sign of the Christ rood over his chest.

"Men like you, lord," he said.

"Like us?"

"Warriors."

"Whose warriors?"

"Penda's," the man frowned. "At least I think they served the king of Mercia," he said. "But they were men of Gwynedd."

"You are sure?"

"I'd swear that on the life of my best sheep. Their lord was a haughty one. Rode a great black stallion and had a white cloak." The old man shook his head. "I could hardly believe he had kept that cloak so clean. The ground around there was all mud and muck. I suppose that is why he stayed up on that big horse of his."

When they had pressed him for how many men there were at the ash tree by the river, he'd scratched his head, frowning. But then he'd closed his eyes, tallying up the men he had seen on his fingers, as he would count sheep. After what seemed a long time and many muttered grunts, his eyes had flickered open and he'd said, "There were somewhere between one and a half score to two score, when I was there not three days ago."

Beobrand had tossed him a hunk of hack silver for his help and the man's eyes had grown wide.

"Perhaps you can trade it for something for your wife," said Beobrand.

The man had looked bemused.

"You think a trader might heal her?"

Beobrand had looked into the distance where a flock of starlings swooped and swarmed in a shifting cloud.

"Perhaps," he'd said at last, "if the magic earth doesn't work."

Cynan had frowned. He wondered whether the soil from beneath the tree really was magical. Whether the earth there could cure sickness, as the man's Christ priest had said it could. Without warning, he thought of Sulis. Perhaps he could bring back some of the earth from the tree for her. Maybe this magic could cure the pain she felt. He cursed silently then at his foolishness. The Mercian slave wanted nothing from him. And yet he could not dispel her from his mind. Whenever they had ridden in silence, his thoughts would stray to Sulis. He wondered what it was she did back in Ubbanford. Was Reaghan keeping watch on her? Had Sulis softened, or did she still brood and dwell on her dark past? How could she not? Such a thing could not be forgotten in weeks or months. The loss of a son would never be healed.

In the end Beobrand sent the old man on his way. They watched as he hurried back to his sheep, whistling at his dog to herd them together. He cast a glance back at them, raising a hand. Then he turned and led the sheep and his dog away from the armed men, up the slope of a hill that was topped with a copse of beech.

"You think he spoke of Gwalchmei?" asked Acennan.

Beobrand looked up at the sky, thinking.

"I know not," he replied at last, his face stern. "But if Gwalchmei ap Gwyar is back at Maserfelth and stands between us and our king's body, we will settle our scores once and for all."

"From the sounds of it, he still rides Sceadugenga," said Acennan.

"If he does, I will slay him and take back what is mine," replied Beobrand, his voice as hard as the rocks of the crags of Rheged behind them.

"Well, it was his horse first," said Acennan with a smirk.

Anger flashed across Beobrand's features and, for a moment, Cynan thought he would strike Acennan. But instead Beobrand shook his head and sighed.

The starlings still murmured in the distance. The sun was low, the cloud tinged a bruised green and yellow.

"Come, men," Beobrand said at last, pointedly ignoring Acennan. "If we ride hard, we can be at the forest that rests at the foot of the hill of Maserfelth before nightfall. There we will hide the horses, and we will see whether the shepherd speaks the truth about the men who guard our king's remains." Beobrand kicked his heels into Bera's flanks and the huge, shaggy horse started off once more at a lumbering canter.

With a last glance at the shepherd, who was now almost lost in the shade of the beech woods on the rise, Cynan kicked his own mount into motion and followed his lord south.

Chapter 38

Darkness pressed about them like a shroud. Beobrand shuddered. They had tethered the horses beneath the canopy of the trees that lapped against the skirts of the hill. The hill where they had stood in the shieldwall against Penda's horde. The night was dark, the cloud, low in the sky, hid the sliver of moon and only a thin silver light permeated to the dark earth below. Beneath their position, where they crouched on the hilltop, they could see the great ash tree and there beside it, just as the shepherd had said, huddled a cluster of tents. Flamelight flickered there from the campfires. From this distance they could see no more detail, but Beobrand could think of no reason for changing the plan. He shuffled forward, trying to get a better view of the tree and those who guarded it. Peering into the gloom he strained his eyes to pick out more, but the night was too dark.

As he shuffled forward he touched something cold and pliant. Looking down, he saw with a shock that his hand rested upon the mottled, corrupt flesh of a corpse. He jerked his hand back, as if he had placed it on the glowing hot metal pulled from a smith's forge. The hillside was strewn with the scattered remains of those who had fallen in the great battle that had taken place there. When they had ascended the slope from the forest below,

Beobrand had not looked at the pallid shapes that lay there. Now he could not draw his gaze from the corpse before him. The gaping maw of the gash in the dead man's throat was black in the thin moonlight. Beobrand shivered. Whether the dead warrior was Waelisc, Mercian or Northumbrian, he could not tell. The unfortunate man was stripped of any war gear, and his features were bloated. His eyes were dark, open voids where the ravens had pecked at the tender morsels.

Beobrand backed away from the corpse.

Despite not having had the dream again since they had set off southward, the nightmare was as vivid and real to him as any memory. He frowned at his foolishness. The dead did not rise from the earth to assail the living. They did not stagger up from the cold ground, reaching for the warm flesh of those who yet walked under the sun, gurgling their recriminations at those who had forsaken them. And yet, who knew what power, what dark magic, may have been woven from the blood of a fallen king hung from a sacred ash? The stench on the hill was overpowering, pungent with the sickly corruption of death.

"We stick to the plan," he whispered. He feared he would gag, shaming himself before the men.

Acennan, Attor, Ástígend and Garr all stood silently. They had tethered their own mounts someway off to the west and had then crept up this slaughter-strewn hill to meet their lord. There had been some debate on where best to commence the plan, but in the end they all agreed that nobody else would be out amongst so many corpses. It seemed they had been proven right. Beobrand spat in an attempt to free his mouth of the taste of death that hung in the cool air. Breathing shallowly, mouth open, he rose and grasped Acennan's forearm in the warrior grip.

"May the gods smile on you," he said.

But which gods held sway here? Woden had accepted the gory offering of a king's blood that Penda had offered at the sacred ash. And the Christ god had turned away from Oswald, his faithful servant. And yet had not the Christ guided the steps of Ástígend as he had descended to gaze at the tree? Had he not kept the lean messenger safe, as he had beheld the grisly totem on the waelstengs, and brought him safely northward to Oswiu?

"Good luck, my friend," Beobrand said. They would need to rely on their wits, their luck, and hope that their wyrd would see them through.

"And to you lord," said Acennan, his teeth flashing white in the darkness. "We will meet you at the place we agreed." And with that, the four of them were gone, descending the hill until they were lost to the night. The four men were silent as shadows and Beobrand strained to hear their movements. But all was quiet in the still of the night.

For a long while Beobrand waited with the remainder of the men on the hilltop. They crouched in silence trying not to breathe of the foul, foetid air. Beobrand pictured in his mind how long it would take Acennan and the others to reach their position. He reached down and touched the hilt of his seax, then Hrunting's finely wrought pommel. Lastly, he fingered the hammer amulet at his throat. Perhaps the gods were not watching, or if they were, they cared nought for Beobrand and his small band of gesithas. And yet, he offered up a silent prayer to Thunor and Woden, who loved mischief. Perhaps the All-father would appreciate what they were about to do.

Rising up, Beobrand beckoned for his men to follow him down the hill. Without a word, the men got to their feet and as quietly as they could, they slipped past the mounds of pale, rotting corpses, down the slope towards the marshy land below. Towards the campfires, the great ash tree, and their king's remains.

Beobrand felt no fear. He was glad to be leaving this doom-heavy hill. Whatever the outcome now, there was no turning back.

He thought he saw the dark shadows of Acennan and the others flitting before the fires. He increased his speed. They had left their shields with the horses. They needed stealth for this to work. With his maimed left hand he once again reached for the comforting touch of the whale-tooth hammer amulet.

As suddenly as lightning streaking from a storm cloud, the night blazed into light, making Beobrand blink at the glare. The tent furthest from the ash was aflame, and the camp was plunged into a chaos of shouting, followed shortly after by the clash of metal on metal. Acennan and the others were doing their part.

Beobrand sprinted forward, his feet squelching in the moist earth.

"For Oswald," he hissed, and his gesithas matched his pace.

He offered up a final prayer to any god who might listen. The plan was simple, he just hoped it might work.

Beobrand sped forward out of the darkness and into the flame-flickered night. The ash reared above him, its great branches spreading out to the moon-gilded clouds above. Beyond the shadowy form of the tree the camp was in uproar. A second tent was on fire now and men screamed and called out in the night. All was confusion, but there were too many for Acennan and the others to face for long. Beobrand cursed himself for not sending more of the men with Acennan. But he could not change the plan now.

Without warning a figure loomed before him in the gloom. It was a large man, but Beobrand had no time to discern his features. All he saw was a shadowy shape and before the man could utter a sound Beobrand drew his seax and, without slowing, plunged the blade into his chest. The man grunted and fell back to the soft earth. Fraomar, who was closest to Beobrand, quickly knelt at the man's side and sawed a blade across his throat.

They pressed on. There was no time to waste. Beobrand did not know how long Acennan and the others would be able to engage with the guards of the camp before they were either slain or forced to retreat.

"Quickly," he hissed and they rushed on.

At the base of the great tree two more warriors stood and Beobrand thanked whichever gods were looking down, for the guards had their backs to him. They must have been told not to leave their post, but were unable not to be drawn to look towards the flames and the fighting on the other side of the encampment. Cynan, as fleet of foot as a wolf, and as deadly, sprinted past Beobrand. The flame light glimmered on the seax blade he held. To Beobrand's right Beircheart leapt forward and together he and Cynan made short work of the two guards, who crumpled onto the ground with a whimper and a gurgled scream.

Beobrand slowed his pace, scanning the dancing shadows of the night for what he sought. The ash was massive and menacing in the gloom, its bark rough and moss-covered, like a rock. As old as time itself. Perhaps not a living thing at all, or maybe it had been planted by the gods themselves at the dawn of middle earth. Beobrand shook his head to free it of such thoughts. There was no time for this. They had come for one thing and if they did not retrieve it soon, it would be too late and all would be lost. It was a simple plan, but it relied on luck. For an instant Beobrand could hear the voice of Oswald himself telling him he had always been lucky. Perhaps his king had been right, for in that instant he saw the waelstengs, the great sacrificial death poles, that Penda's pagan priest had erected before the sacred ash. And there, in a mockery of the tale of the death of the Christ, was Oswald.

Beobrand recognised his king, the long brown hair that hung in matted tendrils, the high cheeks, the strong forehead. But gone was the intelligent man whom Beobrand had served these past eight years and in his place was the mutilated corpse of Penda's blood rite to Woden. Oswald's head, gazing down from sightless, hollow eye sockets, was impaled on the central stake. To either side his arms and hands had been skewered on shorter stakes, giving the appearance that he was welcoming Beobrand into an embrace.

Beobrand shuddered. Anger swelled within him. Oswald had been a great king and had given him everything. That he should die like this, to be displayed thus by his enemy filled Beobrand with rage. Gone then was his anger at Oswiu for sending him south on this mission, which he'd believed must surely end in his death and that of his men. For now he saw that he must bring back Oswald's remains. Oswiu had been right in this. It was he who had caused Oswald's death, and it should be him who brought back his body.

"Cut him down," he said, "gently." Grindan, Eadgard and Elmer stepped forward and worked at the stakes until they brought them down and placed them with reverence on the ground beneath the ash. The flames of the tents were dying down now, and the sound of fighting had abated, replaced with the shouts of men seeking a quarry in the dark. Acennan and the others had fled into the night and were being pursued.

There was no more time. They must be gone from this place, or they would be found, and slain.

Kneeling on the wet ground Beobrand shook out the sacks they had brought for the purpose of carrying Oswald away.

"Help me," he whispered to Elmer, who nodded. Elmer gripped the stake in his large hands, and Beobrand, taking a deep breath, reached out and took hold of Oswald's head. It was cold, heavy, lifeless. The touch of it made Beobrand's stomach twist, but he clenched his teeth and pulled. The head came free from the wood easily enough and Beobrand placed it within the sack. Eadgard and Grindan, with the help of Fraomar and Beircheart, had done likewise with Oswald's arms.

"What about the rest of him?" asked Cynan, his voice jagged with tension. Oswald's torso and legs were displayed on other stakes that jutted from the ground.

Beobrand scanned the camp. The chaos and cacophony had gone now. The fires had all but died out, and the yells of those pursuing Acennan and his band were far off and faint with distance. If they lingered here a moment longer, they would be caught.

"There is no time," he said. "We have Oswald's head, and his arms. That will have to do."

He turned his back on the huge ash, still feeling its brooding presence behind him. He half expected to feel its gnarly twig fingers scratching at his back as it reached out with its limbs to lift him up and hang him high from its branches, like a mouse left by a shrike on a thorn. He remembered the way the stallions had dangled from the branches of the giant tree in his dream. But this was no dream.

He suppressed the urge to glance over his shoulder, and ran into the night, with his men at his heels.

Chapter 39

They were all panting when they reached the forest where they had left the horses. Beobrand had shaken off the horror of his dream memory and, the further they ran from the ash, the more possible it seemed that they might actually survive the night. It had been a simple plan, and relied on luck, but it appeared that his luck had held. The sounds of pursuit were distant and growing ever fainter as Acennan led their enemies into the west.

Beobrand would not again cross the hilltop, with its charnel stench and fish-pale corpses, so he had led the small band around the base of the hill. And then they had sprinted, breathless and gasping, along the tree line to their mounts. When they had rounded the hill, they had halted for a moment, breathing through their mouths as quietly as possible, and listened to the night. The mass of the hill almost completely cut off the noises from the camp and, save for a couple of shouts that seemed to echo from a long way off, the night was silent and still.

As they jogged into the clearing, one of the horses nickered softly. Beobrand recognised Bera's whinny, and walked to the shaggy beast.

"Easy there," he whispered in the voice he always used with animals. It was so dark beneath the trees that Bera was just a black shadow in the gloom. Beobrand stroked his half-hand through the thick mane, soothing the nervous beast with his voice. Reaching for the saddle, he cursed the lack of light as he fumbled to secure the sack he bore to the pommel. But they could not risk a flame so close to the enemy that guarded the ash and Oswald's remains. Who could say what eyes might be watching them from the dark? The sack was heavy and every time it had bumped against his leg as they'd run, Beobrand had winced. This was no way for his king to be treated. But there was nothing for it.

"I am sorry, Oswald King," he whispered, as he finally managed to tie the precious burden to his saddle. He hoped the son of Æthelfrith could hear him from the afterlife. For he truly was sorry. For so much.

Around him, the others were mounting up. There was no time for regrets now. Beobrand swung himself up onto Bera's back.

But before he could urge the steed forward, someone tugged at his foot.

"Lord," said the voice of Grindan. It was too dark to make out the face.

"What?" hissed Beobrand. "We must ride hard. We can talk when we are far from this place."

A hesitation.

"We cannot ride."

"Speak sense, man," Beobrand snapped. There was no time for this.

Another pause. Silence in the dark. One of the horses stamped and snorted.

"My horse," Grindan said, his voice flat, "and Eadgard's. They're not here."

"What do you mean?"

For a brief moment, Beobrand had believed he might truly be lucky. How the gods must be laughing.

"They have pulled their reins free of the tree and they have gone." Grindan sounded desolate. He knew their success lay in their ability to flee at speed.

Beobrand took a calming breath. Suddenly he knew what had occurred.

"Did you leave the task of tethering the horses to your brother?" he asked in a hard, hushed tone. Eadgard was good for many things. Lifting enormous weights, breaking a shieldwall with his great axe, but not those tasks that relied on wits and dexterity.

"Aye," answered Grindan. "Sorry, lord."

"If we escape from this with our lives, I will make you sorry."

Eadgard did not respond. Beobrand's mind was racing. Without the horses they would not be able to make up the distance they had hoped for before the sun came up. He peered into the gloom, but all was as dark as his mood. The horses might be very close. It was unlikely they would have wandered far from the rest of the animals, but it was too dark. They had no time for thrashing about in the undergrowth. Besides, any noise they made would just as likely scare the horses further as well as attract any of the Waelisc that might be pursuing them. There was nothing for it.

"Bera is the strongest of the mounts," he said swinging his leg over the pommel of the saddle and sliding to the ground. "You and Grindan will share my horse." He had been whispering, keeping his voice as quiet as possible, but now he spoke more loudly, so that the others would hear him. "Grindan and Eadgard have lost their horses."

"How can any one man be so stupid?" said Dreogan from the darkness.

"Enough," snapped Beobrand, his voice sibilant and sharp. "There is no time now. We must ride. The brothers are sharing Bera. I will take Fraomar's mount. Fraomar, you will ride behind Dreogan."

He heard Dreogan spit. But he said no more. Fraomar, a slim shade in the gloom, slipped from his saddle without a word and pulled himself up behind Dreogan. Beobrand mounted Fraomar's chestnut mare. The horse was much smaller than Bera, but he was sure it would bear him well. Fraomar was the lightest of the gesithas and Beobrand calculated that Dreogan's dappled stallion would cope with the two of them. At least for a time.

"Now, come men," said Beobrand in a firm but hushed voice, "we have far to ride before the dawn. We will walk the horses for some time until we are sure that those Waelisc bastards will not hear us, and then we will push the horses as fast as we can."

He touched his heels to the mare's flanks and was surprised at how quickly she responded. He was used to Bera's lumbering gait. The mare trotted forward out of the clearing and into the cool, silvered darkness beyond the trees. He tugged on her reins, conscious of riding too fast and betraying their position with the noise of their passing. The men followed him out into the night, the hooves and the jangle of their harness loud in the dark stillness. Beobrand swung the mare's head to the north. He strained to hear any indication that they were being followed, or whether Acennan had been captured, but he heard nothing. When they reached the stream that ran some way to the north of Maserfelth he would increase the pace. It would be risky to push the horses in the dark, for an uneven piece of ground, a tree root or a badger's sett, could break a leg. But with any luck the horses would remain hale, and they would put some distance between them and Gwalchmei's men.

Beobrand frowned in the darkness at the thought of luck. Within the coarse sack tied to Bera's saddle rested the rotting head of the man who had always claimed Beobrand had been lucky. Oswald had also believed that Beobrand was the hand of God on middle earth. He felt neither like the hand of God nor lucky. He wondered, as he rode into the dark, whether whatever luck he possessed had been given to him by capricious gods who revelled in watching his failures.

Chapter 40

Acennan cursed silently and placed his arm around Ástígend's shoulders.

"Come on," he hissed, "lean on me. It's not much further. But we cannot stop."

Ástígend grunted, but did not reply. He clung to Acennan and matched his pace, running clumsily, feet squelching in the marshy earth. He had taken a deep cut to the side, and before they had fled into the darkness, Acennan had seen that Ástígend's leg was slick with blood. And yet the wiry messenger pushed on without complaint.

Behind them, the shouts, cries and heavy footfalls of their pursuers were loud in the still night air. Acennan did not know how many followed them, but it sounded like at least a dozen. Too many for them to face.

They had rushed out of the night and hit them hard. Attor had managed to torch one of the tents, scooping up a brand from the campfire and tossing it into the shelter. Acennan had no idea what the burning wood had landed on, but perhaps some of Beobrand's fabled luck was with them that night, for the tent had burst into flames in a matter of moments. Like a pine cone thrown into a hearth fire, it had blazed, sending a sheet of fire into the night and lighting up the camp in an instant. In the confusion that followed Acennan and the others had added to the chaos, leaping this way and that in the dancing light to strike down any man who showed his face. They must have slain half a dozen that way, perhaps more, before the Waelisc formed a defence. Once their enemies had brought their shields to bear in a rudimentary shieldwall there had been nothing for it but to hope that Beobrand had been successful in his mission and that they had bought him enough time. They had turned and sprinted into the night, swallowed once more by the darkness like nihtgengas returning to their dank, tomblike caverns.

It was when they had run that Ástígend had taken the unlucky blow from a spear flung after them.

Ástígend stumbled and would have fallen if Acennan had not been gripping him tightly. He heaved him to his feet.

"Not much further," he said. "We'll have you in the saddle in no time and you can rest."

Ástígend did not reply. He pulled himself upright using Acennan's shoulder, and pressed on. Acennan hoped he would make it to where they'd left the horses. If they didn't bind his wounds soon, he feared Ástígend would lose too much blood.

The sounds of pursuit were growing louder. A torch flared in the gloom. It was very close.

"Get him to the horses," whispered a voice in Acennan's ear.

Attor.

The man was as silent as a ghost.

"I will slow them down, and catch you up." The slender scout did not wait for a reply but disappeared into the darkness. Acennan was sure he saw the flame light of the distant torch glimmer on Attor's grin before he was gone. The man seemed to know no fear, relishing the thrill of this night-time attack.

Acennan increased his pace, pulling Ástígend with him. Garr, whose long legs had carried him further than Acennan and the wounded messenger, returned to them now. He positioned himself on the other side of Ástígend and helped half carry the ailing man forward.

"We are almost there," he whispered. His breath came in gasps. "The horses are where we left them."

Back in the darkness came a sudden ululating scream, followed by the familiar voice of Attor.

"Death awaits you in the darkness, you dog-fucking Waelisc pigs!" he roared.

Acennan smiled grimly. Once Attor's blood ran hot, there was no holding him back. Acennan hoped Attor would make it to the horses to join them as they fled, but there was nothing he could do. It was in the hands of the gods now.

Another scream, this time further away. Several men shouting angrily words that Acennan could not comprehend. Whatever Attor was doing, it did not please the Waelisc.

Before them loomed the shadow of the woodland where they had left their mounts. The shouts and cries of the Waelisc were still clear, but there was no doubt, they were further behind them now than they had been.

"Find some cloth to bind this wound," Acennan said. There was nothing for it. Ástígend was barely conscious. If they did not staunch the flow of blood, he would be dead long before the dawn.

Garr and Acennan lowered the wounded man to the ground propping his back against the bole of an oak. Garr said nothing but hurried into the darkness and returned moments later with what seemed to be a cloak. Pulling a knife from his belt, he cut into the cloth and then ripped a long strip. The sound was terribly loud in the gloom of the night. One of the horses whinnied, quietly. If they were not gone from this place soon, they would be overheard and discovered.

Reaching for Ástígend's kirtle, Acennan winced to feel it soaked and sticky. He peeled back the linen and between the two of them they managed to tie the bandage around Ástígend's midriff. The wound was deep and blood still welled within it.

"Cut another strip," Acennan said. His voice was as jagged as a notched blade. His worry snagged at his thoughts. The plan they'd come up with had been simple. Simple enough to end in their deaths. By Christ's bones, how had it come to this? Eadgyth had always warned that following Beobrand would lead him to his death eventually. But who else would he have followed? No man was perfect. No hlaford either. But Beobrand had entered his life like lightning from a cloudless sky, unexpected and sudden. He had given the young man his oath, but they were more than that. They were friends, and Acennan's heart swelled with pride to think of how far his friend and lord had come. And what they had achieved together. He would change nothing. But, by God, he missed Eadgyth and the children.

Garr tore another strip of cloth, the rasping rip pulling Acennan from his thoughts. Silently they worked to tie the new dressing over the first bandage that was already wet with fresh blood.

Far off now, perhaps towards the south and the Maerse, Acennan could hear the angry shouts of their pursuers. It seemed Attor had led them away. But there was no time to lose. They would surely turn back when they reached the river. For he doubted they would believe their assailants had the means to cross the broad expanse of water. And it would make no sense for them to have come from the south, for there lay Gwynedd and Mercia.

"Ástígend," said Acennan. No reply. He gripped the man's kirtle and shook him gently. "Ástígend?" A groan. Acennan slapped his face.

"Can you not let a man die in peace?" hissed Ástígend, his voice slurred and groggy.

"You are a warrior, Ástígend. Is it really to die in peace you wish?"

Ástígend snorted.

"You make a good point," he said.

"Let's get you into the saddle," Acennan said. He nodded in approval as Ástígend grunted and pulled himself to his feet. The man was a warrior alright. They heaved him up onto his steed, and then mounted their own horses.

"What about Attor?" asked Garr.

Acennan hesitated for a heartbeat. He listened to the night. All was quiet now.

"Attor will have to take his chances. We'll leave his horse here, and we ride."

"Well, it is good to know that you value my life so," said Attor, stepping into the blackness beneath the trees and quickly swinging himself into his saddle. He had entered the copse as silently as smoke. "So tell me, what are we waiting for?" Acennan could hear the smile in Attor's voice. The man was pleased with himself and whatever fresh mischief he had dealt the Waelisc.

Despite his raw nerves, Acennan grinned in the gloom.

"We had heard tell that the dawn was beautiful from this spot," he said, "but since you are clearly desperate to be gone from this place, let us ride."

Without waiting for a response, Acennan dug his heels into his mount and cantered westward.

Chapter 41

They reached the stream that flowed to the north of Maserfelth without incident. Beobrand held the mare in check, forcing it to walk, despite the nervous energy the beast seemed to sense from its rider. Beobrand was nervous, there was no denying that. He tried to listen into the darkness, beyond the clump of their horses' hooves on the earth, straining to hear anything more than the jingle and creak of harness, weapons and saddles.

But he heard nothing.

Perhaps Acennan had led his pursuers far away. But maybe he had fallen, along with Ástígend, Attor and Garr. Beobrand tried not to brood on such dark thoughts, but the night pressed around them as black as a tomb, and whenever he peered into the gloom he saw the face of Oswald, slack jaw hanging open above the ragged cut of his neck. The gaping sockets of his eyes staring accusingly down at him. He shuddered to recall the sight of his erstwhile king's head, impaled on the stake beneath the sacred ash. And now, to think that his lord's head rested within the rough sack tied to Bera's saddle filled him with sadness.

And rage.

None of them spoke. Grindan had nudged Bera close to Beobrand's mount and Eadgard had tried to stutter an apology from where he rode behind his brother.

"Sorry, lord," he had said, his voice shaking like a frightened child's, "I should have... I should have tied a better knot."

Beobrand had cut him off.

"Silence," he had hissed. "You have done enough this night, without leading the enemy to us with your flapping tongue."

He had felt a moment's guilt at his anger. Eadgard was brave and stalwart, he had killed more than his share of enemies in the shieldwall at Maserfelth. And yet Beobrand could not hold his anger back. He could feel the beast of his ire tugging at its fetters within him, seeking a moment in which it could break its bonds and launch itself onto an unsuspecting prey. Beobrand gripped the reins tightly and led the small band of warriors onwards into the darkness.

They splashed through the shallow stream and the horses clambered easily up the northern bank. Beobrand had judged that from this distance they would be free to gallop or canter northward. He had hoped to put as much distance as possible between them and possible pursuers before the dawn. He squeezed his horse's flanks and the mare, pleased to be allowed its head, sprang forward into an easy canter. The other riders followed him, but he knew it could not last. And after only a few moments, he slowed the chestnut mare to a trot. It was risky enough to ride in the dark, but to push the mounts that already carried two men apiece was foolish. He looked at the eastern sky. Could dawn be upon them already? He could not be certain, but he thought the first paling of sunrise brushed the eastern horizon. An owl shrieked in the darkness, making Beobrand's horse shy and step to the left. Beobrand clung to the reins and managed to hold his seat. He patted the mare's neck.

"Easy there, girl," he whispered. "It's only a bird."

In his mind he heard the echo from the past of those same words, in Acennan's voice, reverberating in the dark cold of a cavern, far to the north on the isle of Muile.

Beobrand hoped Acennan had managed to escape from those who had guarded the tree and Oswald's remains. With any luck, he would be waiting for them when they arrived at the agreed spot in the north.

He kicked the mare into a trot once more, urging the mount forward and offering up a silent prayer to any god that would listen that, come the dawn, they would be far enough away from Gwalchmei's Waelisc not to be spotted.

Chapter 42

Acennan ground his teeth. It was all he could do to keep his anxiety from showing. He sat astride his horse and watched as Attor rode his stocky grey stallion, slipping and skidding down the steep river bank before plunging into the cold waters. It was not shallow here. They had ridden west in an attempt to throw off their pursuers and there was no ford over the river. But they must cross it if they were to have a chance of reaching Beobrand within the land of cloud-veiled mountains that lay on the northern horizon. Attor was the first into the river. For a moment his mount floundered, losing purchase against the rocks before kicking out strongly and swimming for the other bank. Attor clung to the horse's reins and mane and reached the far bank without incident. His horse scrabbled and kicked, sending up great clouds of spray that caught the light from the midday sun. After a heartbeat, Attor's horse clambered up the bank and at the top he wheeled it around, halting there and raising his hand.

"I will cross with you, Ástígend," Acennan said. The messenger had been lolling in his saddle for some time now and Acennan feared that he would fall. He had lost a lot of blood. They had stopped shortly after dawn and Garr had replaced the sodden bandages with which they had bound his wound. But with the constant movement, the deep cut had no chance of healing. Blood still oozed freely from it when they peeled back the dark, sticky cloth. Ástígend had winced, but had offered no complaint.

He was a proud one, that was for certain.

"I can cross a river without your help," replied Ástígend, his voice curt and brittle. Without awaiting a response, the injured man kicked his heels into his horse's sides and it leapt down the bank, splashing noisily into the deep water. Acennan cursed under his breath. By Christ bones, the man was full of pride.

He watched as Ástígend controlled his steed, driving it forward through the water. He had swung himself from the saddle and clutched the pommel tightly, allowing the horse to drag him beside it through the water. Acennan grimaced to see the water billowing pink where Ástígend had passed. Surely the man would not live much longer without rest. And yet they could not halt. Shortly after they had re-bound Ástígend's wounds they had continued on their way. The sun had painted the low cloud in the east the dappled pink and grey of a trout's belly. They had slowed their pace then, hoping to be able to allow Ástígend some respite. But Attor had ridden close to Acennan and spoken the words none of them wished to hear.

"They are following us."

"You are sure?" Acennan had asked. Perhaps Attor had been mistaken. He turned in his saddle, gazing back the way they had come. He saw nothing there to indicate there was anybody in pursuit. And yet he did not take Attor's word lightly. The man knew what he was about, and his eyes were keen. Acennan had ridden with the man enough times to know that he was ever vigilant. He trusted Attor's judgement completely. And yet he hoped he was wrong.

"Just now," Attor had said, indicating to the south with a nod, "I saw the sun glinting from metal. A spear-point perhaps. Or a helm. But there are armed men behind us, and I think it is likely they are not friendly." He had grinned then, showing his teeth like a wolf that scents its prey. "If they were angry after we attacked them in the night, I think my little dance with them will have annoyed them even further." He let out a barking laugh then, and Acennan had frowned. He wished he could find the mirth in the situation. He often jested with Beobrand about how serious he was, and yet now, having to lead these men, and facing the stark reality of what would befall them if they could not throw their hunters off their scent, he could find nothing to laugh about.

"And if Beobrand and the others managed to take Oswald's body," said Garr, who had overheard the conversation, "I expect those Waelisc bastards are as angry as bees who have had their hive kicked."

Acennan had not answered. He had stared southward at the forested slope they had passed earlier that morning. Still he saw no movement. Could Attor be wrong? And then he saw it. A flash of light. Bright against the darkness of the trees. Gone in an instant. But there was no denying it had been sunlight reflecting from a burnished piece of metal.

"They are on our trail," Acennan had said, keeping his voice steady, despite the panic he felt threatening to engulf him. "We will lead them further west. Further from Beobrand's course. Then return north, and we will lose them in the high lands."

And so it was that they had ridden hard into the west, veering north as they went until they reached this river.

He sighed with relief to see Ástígend had made it to the northern bank. The horse clambered up through the bushes that grew thick along the river's edge and Ástígend tenaciously hung on to the saddle and was dragged up the bank a way. There, his strength seemed to leave him and he lost his grip, falling into the foliage. His horse, free of the awkward burden of its rider, surged up the slope to join Attor and his grey stallion.

Perhaps Ástígend had finally succumbed to his wound, thought Acennan darkly.

"Come on," he said to Garr. "Maybe we will lose them at the crossing."

He kicked his horse forward through the clouds of midges that thronged the river's edge. Garr followed without a word.

The day was warm, the air damp and heavy. Acennan's horse jumped from the bank with a great splash and Acennan was instantly drenched. He gulped in a sharp breath at the shock of the chill water. He wrapped his hands in the horse's mane and gripped its flanks with his legs. The horse snorted and rolled its eyes in fear. Beneath him, Acennan could feel its body working, its powerful legs kicking as it swam through the deepest part of the river.

Close behind him, Garr's horse followed, swimming well.

On the far side of the river Attor jumped down from his horse and scrambled down the bank to where Ástígend had fallen. Acennan let out a breath to see Attor help the man up. Together, with Attor pulling Ástígend, the two men climbed the bank.

"By the gods," said Garr, "I was sure that he was dead."

"He is a tough one," replied Acennan. He chose not to mention that he had thought the same moments before. He wondered how much longer the man could hold out. Still, it would matter little if those Waelisc caught up with them.

His horse's hooves once again found the ground beneath them and the beast pulled itself out of the water. Acennan leaned forward in the saddle and kicked the horse onwards. It bounded up the bank easily enough, following the track through the foliage that had been left by Attor and Ástígend. Garr followed close behind.

"We thought we'd lost you there for a moment," Acennan said to Ástígend.

Ástígend was once more astride his mount. He was bedraggled and pale, his eyes dark.

"It'll take more than a nick from a Waelisc blade and a cold river to finish me," Ástígend said. He spat into the nettles that grew in abundance there. "Now," he said, grinning, despite the obvious pain he felt, "are we going to stand here all day talking, or are we planning on out-riding those Waelisc bastards?"

Acennan did not return the smile. He scanned the land to the north. A few spear-throws distant lay a dense wood of beech and oak. He turned back and gazed over the river and at the hills that lay to the south-east. The sun again caught the bright iron that adorned armed men. But now they were closer and Acennan could make out a score of riders, perhaps as many as two dozen, riding towards the river. The lead horseman rode a huge black steed. His white cloak streamed behind him as he galloped ever closer. So, Gwalchmei ap Gwyar himself rode on their heels.

Acennan looked up at the haze of cloud that hung low in the sky and cursed that they would not bring rain any time soon. A downpour might have made the river impassable, but such was not to be their luck.

He tugged his mount's reins, turning its head towards the north. The low clouds wreathed the mountains that rose beyond the forest, hiding their summits.

"Come on then," he said, forcing a light, jovial tone to his voice. "It seems old Ástígend thinks we can outrun them. So who am I to disagree?"

He spurred his horse forward towards the gloom beneath the trees.

Chapter 43

They continued riding the horses hard throughout the rest of that long, muggy, late summer's day. They rode until their horses were lathered in sweat and the four riders could barely remain in their saddles. Attor led the way and Acennan trusted his instincts and his sharp eyes to find the best path north and to spot any danger that may await them on the journey. Somehow, with a strength that Acennan could not help but admire, Ástígend had managed to stay conscious and to keep up the pace with the others. Acennan and Garr rode to either side of the wounded man. They made no offer to help any longer, for when they had, Ástígend had snapped at them that he was a man and not a child.

"I can ride better than both of you, even if I left half of my blood behind at Maserfelth," he had said through gritted teeth.

Acennan had watched him closely as the sun began to drop into the west and the shadows lengthened. Ástígend was pale, his features drawn. But his pride and his strength kept him going and it was true that though he was clearly exhausted, weakened by blood loss, and in pain, he rode as well as any man, keeping his seat even when his horse was forced to jump a fast-flowing stream that traversed their path.

They had ridden through the forest of oak and beech for a time. But it was slow going beneath the dense canopy of leaves. There were thick stands of snagging brambles and deep gullies that were hidden beneath tangles of bracken and nettles. Acennan had hoped that the woodland would allow them to pass unseen. But it soon become clear, as they had become forced to walk the horses cautiously through the undergrowth, that all that would be achieved would be to allow the Waelisc to close the distance with them. For a time Acennan had agonised over what to do, but in the end he could see no option.

"I'm sure they will have seen us enter this wood," he had said, cursing as yet another thorn snagged his cloak.

"What should we do then?" Attor had asked. His face was grim, his jaw set. Gone was his smirk of earlier. They all knew now that each decision they took could as easily lead them to their doom as to safety.

"We leave the forest as quickly as we can," replied Acennan. "Our best hope is to outrun them on the open land."

"Hiding from our hunters," Ástígend had croaked, "is a good idea. But not if they know where we are hiding."

Acennan had gazed at the injured messenger in the dappled light beneath a broad beech tree. He looked Ástígend in the eye for a long while and then nodded. The man spoke sense. He prayed he would be able to lead them to somewhere where they could hide in secret from the pursuers. He hoped he could lead them to safety.

But as they had ridden through the hazy heat of the afternoon, the Waelisc could always be seen riding in their wake; unerring in their pursuit. Acennan cursed silently to himself. By Christ's bones and Tiw's cock, all they needed was a little luck. Just a moment when Gwalchmei and his Waelisc dogs could not see them. And yet each time he turned in his saddle, there was the white cloak of Gwalchmei, streaming and resplendent in the sun. And behind the Waelisc warlord followed the score of horsemen.

Acennan began to know despair then. They were close to the hills; the broken land before the earth rose into the mighty peaks of Rheged. But the horses were blowing hard. Acennan's mount stumbled and for a moment Acennan thought it would not win the struggle to keep itself upright. If the men were exhausted, the horses were close to collapse. He could see no way out from this. To turn and face the Waelisc would bring certain death, but soon that would be the only option open to them. The horses would not last much longer.

They were following a well-trodden path now, a track worn in the earth that stretched northward into the hills. They had seen thin wisps of smoke on the eastern horizon not long before and this track was almost certainly what the locals used to take their cattle and livestock to pasture and grazing. The packed earth of the track made the riding easier, but also signalled their route to any follower. Acennan glanced back. Their followers were strung out into a line now but at their head rode Gwalchmei on his huge black steed. Was it possible it could be Sceadugenga, the stallion he had stolen from Beobrand? It was no matter. It was only a horse. Acennan could never understand why Beobrand felt so strongly about the animal.

The path led them up an incline and into a valley between two steep hills. The air was suddenly cool here, shaded from the sun that dipped in the west. As they entered the shadow, Acennan's horse stumbled again, tripping on an unseen rock. It staggered for several paces and then fell to its knees. There was a moment of confusion but there was nothing that Acennan could do. He soared over the horse's head. He saw a flash of clouded sky and then the jarring impact as he crashed into the cool, hard, dusty earth of the path.

For a moment Acennan could not breathe. The air had been forced from his lungs. His vision blurred, darkening at the edges. And then, without warning, Attor was by his side, reaching for him and heaving Acennan to his feet. Attor slapped him hard on the back.

"There now," he said. "Get some breath back in you."

Acennan gulped in a shuddering breath of the cool air and looked about him, dazed and confused still from the fall.

Attor, seeing that Acennan would not collapse, rushed over to his leader's horse. With the practised skill of the natural rider, he calmed it with soothing sounds, holding out his hand for it to nuzzle. The horse dipped its head and Acennan snatched up the reins. The beast quivered and shook, snorting and blowing. Its chest heaved from its exertion and the fear from the fall. Acennan cast an experienced eye over the creature.

"It won't run much further," he said, "but it is not lame."

Acennan shook his head to clear it. His thoughts were jumbled. Ástígend and Garr had both reined in their horses and were waiting patiently for their leader to remount. Attor led the shaking horse back to Acennan, handing him the reins.

"Can you mount?" he asked in a quiet voice meant only for Acennan.

Acennan nodded.

His thoughts were clearing now. There was no time to waste. They could not tarry here. Not with their pursuers so close behind. Anxiously he looked back down the path in the direction from whence they had come. The hillside hid Gwalchmei's band from view. But he knew they were there. All too soon they would round the skirts of the hill and be upon them.

Acennan swung himself back into the saddle. The horse whinnied and trembled.

Savagely, Acennan kicked his heels into the horse's ribs. The beast lurched forward and rolled its eyes. But there was nothing for it. He would push the beast to its death, if he thought he might be able to lead the men to sanctuary. And now, with the shadowy valley rising into the tumbled, craggy land ahead, Acennan thought there might just be a chance of that.

He urged his horse into a gallop. The others followed him and they sped into the hills, as fast as their tired mounts could carry them. They crested a rise and the path dropped down into a broad meadow, surrounded by hills. And there, in the distance at the end of the meadow, he saw what he had been looking for. His moment of luck. The slim chance of saving the men.

He rode close to Ástígend, but before he could speak, the gaunt man said, "Yes, it is a good place for what I'm sure you have thought of. I will join you."

Acennan did not stop to ponder how it was that Ástígend had known what he planned. After all it had been the messenger's idea that hiding would only work if their pursuers did not know where they hid. And who was he to question the luck that God had sent him?

The meadow was lush with cropped grass. Scattered dark droppings of sheep attested to its use as a pasture by local shepherds. They galloped down the incline towards what he had seen. There, running across the path from east to west, flowed a broad, shallow, rocky stream. The earthen path they followed continued on the far side, winding upwards before it turned east and was lost from sight behind a spur of the hill. As they neared the stream, Acennan could see that God must surely have led them here. Perhaps it was as they had said and Ástígend's steps were guided by the Christ. For the stream ran from the right of the path and in each direction it was shadowed by trees and bushes and the streambed was hidden from view as it curved down the rocky course it had carved between the crags.

Acennan cast a glance back up the slope behind them. No sign yet of Gwalchmei and the Waelisc riders.

"Garr, Attor." Acennan barked their names. This was the voice of the shieldwall, of command. There was no time for argument. "You will both ride along the streambed to the east. Do not stop. Ride until you are out of sight of this place and then, when you can, head east and north. Find Beobrand and the others at the agreed place."

"And what of you?" asked Attor. His glowering expression showed he expected the worst for the stocky warrior and the wounded messenger.

Acennan looked again up the slope. Time was short. If the Waelisc saw them here, their only chance would be gone as quickly as a handful of snow thrown onto a hearth fire.

"Ástígend and I will follow the path into the hills. With luck they will follow us. And if God is watching over us, we will escape them and join you at the meeting place."

"But if they catch you," said Garr, his voice coarse with emotion. "You are only two men."

"Then pray they do not catch us," Acennan spat. His shoulder and neck hurt from where the horse had thrown him. "Four of us, or two of us, against more than a score of Waelisc. I fear the end will be the same. But there is no time for talking. Go, now! Godspeed, friends."

For a heartbeat Garr and Attor hesitated.

"Now!" yelled Acennan, making the horses flinch. "Ride!"

Attor and Garr needed no further prompting. They pushed their horses into the stream and splashed their way eastward.

For a moment Acennan watched them go before swinging his mount's head towards the north and kicking the horse forward into the burn. Ástígend was at his side. The water splashed up around them, cold as winter on their skin. As he crossed the stream, Acennan looked to his right. Already Garr and Attor were lost to sight. There was no sign of their passing. For an instant, he wished he had said more to them before parting ways. There were words he could have spoken that they could have carried back to Eadgyth and the children. But it was too late for that now.

The horse clambered out of the stream and he smiled to see the wet tracks that Ástígend and he had left in the dried earth of the path. Without speaking they both wheeled their horses once more into the stream and then, turning full circle, they cantered out of the water and up the path into the hills.

For the first time that long day, Acennan hoped that Gwalchmei and his warband would find the trail and follow them.

Chapter 44

For a time Acennan thought they might actually be able to shake off their pursuers. His horse laboured on, breathing heavily, but eating up the distance with its lumbering canter. Ástígend, dour and grey faced, rode silently at his side. They travelled into the hills for some time and whenever Acennan glanced over his shoulder, there was no sign of the Waelisc warband. The sun slipped towards the horizon in the west and Acennan began to hope. If they could remain unseen until nightfall perhaps they could escape their followers.

As the land rose so the wind picked up. It shook the stunted bushes of the hilltops and drove tears from Acennan's eyes. If only they could ride until dark, then surely they could make their way stealthily away from this place, and if their luck held they would be free of pursuit and able to join Beobrand and the others.

His horse stumbled once more. It had done so many times now. Its breathing came in great rasping gasps and Acennan thought he saw flecks of blood around the beast's nose and mouth. He would be astounded if the animal lasted until night. Looking at Ástígend, Acennan noted how the wounded man was hunched in his saddle, gripping the reins with white hands. His face was drawn and pallid and, not for the first time, Acennan marvelled at the man's strength of will. Even if their horses made it to dusk, Acennan could see no way that Ástígend would survive much longer. But what did he know? He had thought the man would be dead long before now and here he was, still riding without complaint. Whether the Christ god directed his steps, or it was simply the man's savage warrior pride, Acennan did not know. But Ástígend defied expectation at every turn.

The wind gusted, tugging at his cloak with chill fingers. Several crows flapped and cawed against the windswept clouds that rolled in from the north. Acennan sniffed. Perhaps it was raining in the north. He wondered whether it was raining near the Tuidi. It was getting late in the day and Eadgyth would have already prepared the evening meal. Would Athulf and Aelfwyn be bickering as they so often did when hungry and tired at the day's end? Their moaning whine always rankled him. And yet now he thought their voices would be the sweetest of sounds. It had been so long since he had seen them. Had they grown? When he had left with Beobrand all those weeks ago, Aelfwyn had been ill with a hacking cough. Every night, before he slept, he offered up a silent prayer that they were all hale and that Aelfwyn had recovered from her illness. It was stupid he knew; the girl was young and strong. And yet he could not keep himself from worrying. He still remembered all too keenly the sharp pain of loss when his first wife and their son had both died of the pestilence. He had never thought to know such love again. For many years he had thought he would grow old alone with nothing but the company of his lord and his shield-brothers. But who could fathom the ways of one's wyrd?

Beobrand often said to Acennan that he thought he was cursed. Perhaps Beobrand was. Who was he to say? But to Acennan it seemed his friend had so much. And he was grateful for the share of Beobrand's good fortune that had come to him. He never would have believed that he could find one such as Eadgyth. Let alone that she would marry him. Her raven hair and piercing blue eyes all but stopped his heart whenever he looked upon her. That she would give him two strong children was a gift beyond all measure. He loved them all and he was proud of the hall he had built for them. Stagga, he had called it and above its broad doors he had lofted the great antlers and skull of a huge stag.

He still recalled clearly when he had first seen the magnificent beast. He had taken Eadgyth to view his new lands and the stag had been standing near the charred ruins of Nathair's hall. It was as though it warded against intruders. The land had been wreathed in fog and the animal had bellowed at them, its breath steaming as it roared its defiance at Acennan. It had turned away and been swallowed by the mist. After that day, Acennan had scarcely been able to think of anything save the huge creature and how it had stared at him. It had felt as though it had been waiting for him. As if, within that shaggy-haired animal, there resided some malignant spirit; perhaps that of Nathair, the Pictish lord who had once ruled there.

It's only an animal, Acennan had told himself, and yet he could not shake the strange sensation that the stag was a malevolent force.

After a few days, Eadgyth had sent him out to hunt the beast.

"You're no use to anyone," she'd said with a smile, "while you dwell on that deer. Go. Hunt it, and bring back its meat. Only when we have eaten the thing will you know peace."

It had taken them many days to stalk the creature. The stag was old and cunning and led them far into the hills and moors to the north. But his new people, the Picts who had once served Nathair, had brought hounds, great savage beasts, closer to wolves than dogs, and they had eventually run the stag to ground. The tall, defiant animal had bellowed again as it was brought down by the hounds. The dogs tore at its flesh and it had struggled and swung its great antlers, snapping the spine of one of the pack, before Acennan had rushed in and pierced its chest with a stout spear. It had looked at him as it had died, and Acennan had known sorrow then. He had slain many men in bloody battles throughout Albion and Hibernia and he had seldom cared for the death he wrought. But on that bleak moor, as the light of life left the eyes of the majestic stag, Acennan had felt sadness for the life he had taken.

He had brought back the venison to Eadgyth and all the people of the settlement had feasted on the flesh. They seemed to enjoy it, and the Pictish hunters told the tale of the hunt and how Acennan had killed the creature. To Acennan, the meat had lacked flavour. It was tough and had stuck in his throat. He had eaten sparingly and had been pleased when the feast was over.

When his new hall had been finished, there was no question of what would adorn the lintel of the building. Whenever he returned to the hall, he would look up at the massive skull with its spreading antlers and offer silent thanks that it now watched over his family and folk.

Acennan looked into the north, narrowing his eyes against the bitter wind. The crows cracked and cawed, flapping and buffeted by the wind. How he wished that Stagga, with its stag's head watcher, were just over the next rise and not many days' ride to the north and east.

Some way off to the north, the lowering sun picked out the crumbling stone remains of a building atop a scarp. It was a fort, built many generations before by the men from the south who had once ruled this land. Such fortifications and buildings dotted the landscape. The crows flew ahead of them towards the ruins. Acennan looked back over his shoulder and his heart lurched. Some distance behind them, coming out of a stand of trees, Gwalchmei's white cloak stood out, stark and brilliant. And suddenly as water flows from an overturned cup, all hope of escape fled from Acennan.

As if in answer to his despair, his mount slowed, its easy gait gone, replaced by a staggering lurch. It made a deep, bellowing sound that reminded Acennan of the great shaggy stag. Ástígend pulled his own mount to a halt and turned to watch Acennan.

He did not speak. There was nothing to say. They both knew what came next.

Acennan swung his leg over the saddle and dropped to the ground with a grunt. His shoulder, back and ribs all ached from the fall. Blood rimed the horse's nose and mouth now, colouring red the foam that bubbled there. The horse rolled its eyes and lowed again, more like a rutting deer or a cow than a horse.

"Easy there," Acennan said in a soft voice. He gripped the reins tightly and, with his right hand he stroked the neck, soothing the animal. It whinnied in pain, and more blood speckled the foam at its mouth. Acennan slid his seax from the sheath on his belt. In the distance, approaching fast, came Gwalchmei and his band of Waelisc warriors.

"You have been a good mount," Acennan said, "brave and proud. And you have carried me from danger. I give you my thanks." He plunged his seax into the pulsing throat of the beast, driving the sharp blade deep into the flesh. Blood gushed hot onto his cold hand. The animal stared at him, its eyes full of fear and sorrow. It dropped to its knees.

"I'm sorry," said Acennan, feeling his throat close with emotion. It was foolish, he knew. It was only an animal.

The horse lowered its head, letting out a shuddering breath. Acennan pulled the seax from the horse's throat with a great glut of blood. Quickly he pulled his shield, sword, and helm from where they had been tied to the saddle.

"What now?" asked Ástígend. His voice scratched and croaked like the crows in the distance.

Acennan looked to the south, gauging the distance to Gwalchmei. There was little time.

"Let us see if your horse can carry the two of us just a little further," he said.

Ástígend raised an eyebrow, but said nothing.

Acennan clambered awkwardly up behind the wounded man. Ástígend winced as Acennan gripped his shoulder for support. The horse whinnied in disapproval at the extra weight.

"Don't worry, girl," Ástígend said, "we won't be riding far now." And, without waiting for instruction from Acennan, he kicked his heels and sent the horse up the hill, following the crows towards the crumbling stones of the long-abandoned fort.

"We could have ambushed them," said Ástígend. He sat on a large heap of fallen masonry, gazing down into the valley below. The Waelisc had passed Acennan's dead horse and were now riding up the hill towards the fort.

"No time for that now," said Acennan. There had been no further to ride. Ástígend's horse would not have been able to carry them any further even if they had yet believed they could outrun their hunters. Acennan pulled his sword from its fur-lined scabbard and rested it against the stone column that made up one side of the doorway into the ruin. This would be where he and Ástígend awaited their wyrd.

Acennan sighed. The end of their tale would be short. In the west the sun had slid beneath the cloud and the red orb would soon touch the horizon. The wind whipped across this hilltop and it was cold in the shadow of the fort's entrance. Acennan shivered.

He rubbed a hand across his face. By God, he was tired. He picked up his helm from where it rested on a stone and he placed it upon his head. With practised ease he quickly tied the cheek plates in place. The familiar muting of the world around him focused his mind.

Beneath them, on the rock-strewn hillside, the Waelisc rode on. He could feel the thrum of their hooves through the earth. He reached for his black shield, grunting at the pain in his shoulder and back from the fall. He was getting old. He smiled grimly, looking at the two dozen horsemen who were almost within a spear's throw distance. He would not be getting any older, that was for sure.

"I'm sure that you would have been ready to prepare an elaborate ambush," he said to Ástígend with a sardonic grin, "but I am weary. And I think the best we can do is to make these Waelisc bastards remember this day." Ástígend pushed himself to his feet with a groan and walked stiff-legged to stand beside Acennan in the stone doorway. "I am proud to have ridden with you, Ástígend."

Ástígend hefted his own shield and planted his feet. To see him thus, nobody would think the man had been injured the previous night and then ridden hard for the best part of a day. And yet Acennan could see the dark stain of drying blood on Ástígend's side and leg. Ástígend nodded. A dozen paces from the fort the white-cloaked warlord reined in the huge black stallion. Behind him his warband drew to a halt with a clatter of harness and hooves.

"And I am proud to die with you here this day," said Ástígend in a low voice that only Acennan could hear.

"Well," Gwalchmei said, his voice loud and clear, "you have led us a merry dance. But now, alas, you will die."

"We will spare you and your men," Acennan replied, "if you ride away now."

Gwalchmei laughed. The harsh sound made his stallion flinch and its ears twitch.

"I like a man who doesn't know when he is beaten." He turned to his men. "Kill them quickly."

Four of the warriors dismounted, pulling blades from sheaths and lifting shields. Acennan cursed silently as one of the men hefted a long spear. The weapon's reach would be hard to counter, armed as they were with only swords. Their position, flanked by the stone walls in the arched entrance to the fort, meant that Ástígend and he would only face a limited number of attackers at any time. The four men of Gwynedd closed in on them.

"This is your last chance, Gwalchmei ap Gwyar," bellowed Acennan. "Call off your men and leave this place and we will allow you to live, despite the wrong you have done to our king and our country."

Again Gwalchmei laughed. The mounted onlookers laughed too.

The four men rushed forward. But their movement was hampered. All four wished to attack the same two men who were protected by the stone columns of the entrance. And so two hung back, hesitating, as the other two moved in close.

The one with the spear came first. He lunged forward with the wicked point, feeling safe at the end of the long ash haft. But rather than hold his ground as the man had expected, Acennan leapt forward out of the shadow of the doorway. He caught the spear on his shield, lifting it harmlessly over his shoulder and thrusting forward with savage efficiency. The man's eyes opened wide in shock as Acennan's sword ripped open his throat. Hot blood spurted over Acennan, adding more gore to the congealing horse's blood that already caked his hand and arm. Without pausing Acennan threw his sword into the fort's entrance and scooped up the dying Waelisc man's spear. He reversed the weapon and drove it into the chest of the next attacker. Twisting the haft, he tugged it free from the man's sucking flesh.

None of the horsemen had yet reacted. They sat their mounts, mouths agape and the laughter dying in their throats.

Acennan spun around. As he watched, Ástígend delivered a scything blow to the third attacker's shoulder. The man screamed and fell to his knees. Ástígend hacked down again and again, and the man crumpled at his feet. The fourth man advanced towards Ástígend, then halted suddenly as Acennan drove the spear's point through the man's back with such force that it protruded a full hand's breadth out of the Waelisc warrior's chest. For a heartbeat, the Waelisc man looked down, aghast at the gore-slick metal that jutted from his body. Acennan tugged the blade free and the man tumbled forward with a whimper onto the bloody corpse of his companion before the stone doorway.

Acennan walked briskly back to take his place once more shoulder to shoulder with Ástígend facing Gwalchmei and his men.

"You should have taken the offer," Acennan shouted. "Now we will have to kill you all!"

Nobody laughed now.

The sun began to sink beneath the edge of the world. Above them the crows croaked, perhaps with joy at seeing the slaughter below. The birds would not go hungry that night.

Ástígend was breathing hard. The blood splatter from the man he had killed was bright and harsh against his pale wan skin.

"How do you fare?" whispered Acennan.

"I am strong enough to kill a few more of those sheep-shagging whoresons." He offered Acennan a thin smile. Acennan believed him.

Gwalchmei barked some orders in the sing-song tongue of his people and half of his remaining warband turned their horses and rode towards the setting sun. The rest of them slid from their mounts and readied themselves to advance on the two defenders.

The Waelisc locked shields and marched towards the fort's entrance. Several held spears over the shieldwall. They came on towards them, less reckless than before, but assured of victory due to their numbers. At their backs, still astride the huge black stallion that had once been Beobrand's, watched Gwalchmei. The horse's black coat shone in the light of the setting sun. Its mane and tail were braided. They reminded Acennan of Eadgyth's night-black hair. He hoped she and the children were well.

With a scream from one of the men, the shieldwall surged forward. The spear-points probed and both Acennan and Ástígend blocked several attacks on their linden boards. The Waelisc formed an arcing line around the doorway, a bristling curved wall of wood and steel. Acennan thrust forward with his own spear, but he only met with the resistance of a Waelisc shield.

An enemy spear-point found his outstretched arm, opening up a deep cut. Acennan pulled his spear back. His arm was aflame with pain. In an instant it was soaked in his warm blood.

"Come on then, you whoresons! Come and die, you goat-swiving Waelisc scum!" Acennan bellowed his ire.

One of the men was foolish enough to react to the taunts and darted forward, probing with his spear. Acennan did not hesitate, deflecting the attack on his shield he punched his spear-tip into the man's face. The warrior collapsed as instantly as a bullock slaughtered at Blotmonath.

Acennan let out a roar.

The Waelisc were wary now and they stood their ground, unwilling to close with the two blood-spattered Northumbrians who stood before a heap of their dead companions.

A sound from the ruins of the fort behind them caught Acennan's attention. Beside him Ástígend grunted, and then, with a sighing groan slowly slid down the stone wall to his knees. For a moment Acennan was confused, and then he saw it. The spear that had skewered Ástígend was pulled free and Ástígend's blood painted the ground as red as the setting sun. What had happened was suddenly clear to Acennan. The remainder of Gwalchmei's warriors had entered the fort from the far side and now formed a ragged line behind them. Acennan glanced down at Ástígend. The man yet gripped his sword and shield, leaning against the wall of the entrance. He might have been resting, but the blood that pumped feebly from the huge gash in his back told the truth of it.

Acennan was alone now and surrounded by a score of Waelisc.

In his mind's eye he conjured up the vision of Stagga as it would look then, in the ruddy glow of the setting sun. He closed his eyes and imagined the faces of Eadgyth, Athulf and Aelfwyn smiling at him. He took a deep breath and flung his spear at the approaching men. He snatched up his sword from where it lay and sprang forward, bellowing the battle-cry that had become so familiar to him over the years in Beobrand's warband.

"For Oswald!"

The crash and clang of metal on metal echoed from the ancient stone carcass of the ruined fort. The crows looked down, with their cold, unflinching eyes, at the battling men. In the west, the sun had vanished behind the rim of middle earth and darkness enveloped the land.

Chapter 45

Coenred splashed cold water on his face. It was yet dark, but enough of the iron-grey light of predawn filtered through the cracks in the walls of the small chapel for him to see. He scrubbed the water against his face with the heels of his hands, rubbing the sleep from his eyes. The chapel was cool, the chill of autumn in the air. Winter would be upon them soon. And yet he had awoken bathed in sweat. His dreams had been filled with Sulis. When he had seen her the day before she had been as she always was: glowering and sullen. She had reluctantly allowed him to see the ragged, raw skin of the scars on her wrists. They were healing well but he applied more of the salve he had made for her. He had revelled in the touch of her soft skin. Coenred had been glad that Cynan had ridden to join Beobrand in the south. The Waelisc gesith had been defensive of the Mercian woman when Coenred had tended her wounds in Deira. But what of it? Cynan was a warrior. He was permitted to lust over a house thrall.

Coenred ran his dripping hands over the rough stubble of his shaved forehead, drying his fingers on the hair that grew long and thick at the back. By God, he tried not to think of her, but the visions of his dream had been so vivid. If he closed his eyes, he could still feel the warm tingle of Sulis' hands on his body.

He remembered a time when he had often woken from such dreams, sticky with his own spilt seed, his manhood throbbing and his groin aching. But it seemed the devil cared less for his temptation in recent years. Or maybe Coenred was closer to God now. He certainly felt a greater understanding of Christ's teachings. He enjoyed talking of the one true God to the people of Bernicia and Deira. Normal, everyday folk like those here in Ubbanford.

He felt at home at the monastery of Lindisfarena. The monks there were his family; his brothers. And Abbot Aidan was a good father to him and to the whole land of Northumbria. Coenred felt loved and nurtured by the brethren and through his prayers. And yet he could not deny that he sometimes longed for the life he had once known at Engelmynster. Ubbanford, with its cluster of houses beside the river, reminded him of Engelmynster. Coenred always looked forward to coming here, to the church that Beobrand had ordered built. It had taken years for Beobrand to give the order, but in the end he had succumbed to Aidan's soft reminders that Beobrand had promised to construct a church for them following Christ's miraculous healing of Attor.

Coenred dried his face on the coarse cloth of his robe's sleeve. Gothfraidh and Dalston still snored in the darkness of the small building. Beobrand had first paid for a cross to be erected in the centre of the village. He had summoned a mason from Eoferwic. The mason, a sombre man from Frankia with a narrow face and huge, burly hands, had chiselled intertwining images of marvellous animals and the Christ himself into the stone rood. They still preached beneath the cross when the weather was good, but far too often it rained and was too cold to be standing under the sky for any length of time.

"It is all very well," Aidan had said to Beobrand at a feast in Bebbanburg one Eostremonath, "for the monks of God to suffer the hardships of the weather. But I find it does not help the ceorl, the thrall, the goodwife or," and here he had smiled archly at Beobrand, "the thegn, to concentrate on the stories of

Jesu Christ when they are shivering and wet and worried that they will fall ill."

And so it was that eventually Beobrand had ordered his gesithas to build the small chapel. It was a simple building, at the side of the settlement furthest from the Tuidi. When a strong wind blew, it creaked and groaned and, if they lit a taper, the flame would flicker in the breeze that whistled through the knotholes and gaps between the planks of the walls. But it was sheltered and dry enough beneath the thatched roof. Beobrand had never intended it to act as sleeping quarters for the monks when they visited, but Gothfraidh insisted that they not sleep in the hall. He said there was too much temptation there. Coenred wondered at times whether Gothfraidh could read his thoughts the way he could read words scratched onto vellum.

Coenred had not felt temptation when visiting, until now. He did not crave mead or rich meats. And, since the passing of Lady Sunniva, he had scarcely thought of women. But somehow, this new Mercian thrall, with her wounds, her pale flesh and her anger, had enthralled him.

They came to Ubbanford once a month to offer the people a chance to hear the word of God. Gothfraidh usually led the sermons. He was good at recounting the tales of the scriptures and, despite some reluctance from a few of the older people, almost all of the folk of Ubbanford attended the church, or sat beneath the stone rood and listened to the stories of Christ and his father, the one true God. Sometimes Gothfraidh allowed Coenred, Dalston or one of the other monks to lead the service, but Coenred was content to listen and join in when called on to respond. He did not much care to feel the eyes of the gathered people upon him. He would stumble over words that were usually easy for him, forgetting things that he well remembered at other times. No, he was happy enough to be there with his brothers, and to help the people of Ubbanford with their chores and tasks. For it was not only with words that the monks provided aid to the folk of the settlements they visited. There was always work to be done and the brethren of Lindisfarena would offer their strength and hard labour to help in whatever way they could.

"This is the best way that you can show them who Christ is," Gothfraidh would say, when any of the novices complained of toiling in the fields. "By offering your sweat for others, you show them that Jesu gave his own sweat and his blood for them."

Coenred walked to the door and pulled it open. It creaked quietly, but Gothfraidh and Dalston slept on. Coenred smiled to himself. There was a time when he had always been the last to wake. Now, he was often the first to rise. He stood in the doorway and listened to the quiet of the dawn. A light breeze rustled the treetops in the distance, but here, on the floor of the valley it was still. Mist curled, sinuous and serpent-like from the earth. The twitter and chirping of birdsong filled the air, welcoming the dawn. He enjoyed these moments of total peace and solitude. Aidan would sometimes have some of the other monks row him to one of the small, barren Farena islands where he would remain alone save for the gannets, guillemots, puffins and the seals for days or even weeks at a time. Coenred admired the abbot for his devotion to prayer and to God. Yet he could not imagine such a solitary life. A moment of still solitude such as this brief respite from chores and offices was enough.

He stared at the shadowy shape of the great hall on the hill. Sulis would be sleeping still. The thought of her made him shudder.

Give me strength, Lord, to do what is right.

And yet he had done nothing wrong, he told himself. For was it not one of their duties to offer succour and aid when one of Christ's flock was sick? And Coenred had a particular skill for healing. Aidan had taught him some of the skills needed to heal different ills. He had learnt how to balance the natural spirits of the body and how to treat common ailments. The abbot had also taught him how to lance boils and clean and bind cuts so that they might not fester. Leechcraft was what Coenred most enjoyed about travelling the land of Northumbria. To apply the knowledge Aidan had imparted and, through the grace of God and his providence, to set the bones that had been broken in accidents, or to draw out the poison from a suppurating wound, or to banish an elf-shot fever from a child. These were to him some of the clearest ways that God had chosen to work through him.

He had sometimes rebuked himself for the sin of pride when he had caught himself grinning with pleasure at curing some sad wretch. He loved the hearty welcome he received from those he had helped in the past, and those who knew of his skills as a healer. Of course, there were still those who turned to the old ways of the dark gods of the forest and the land. Here in Ubbanford, Odelyna, the old woman who had always helped the people with their ailments, would spit at his approach. She would mutter curses under her breath and at such times Coenred's skin prickled as he was reminded of that dark cavern in Muile and Nelda's shrieking spite from the bowels of the earth.

Well, perhaps the old gods had power still, but it was the Christ god who offered eternal life. And it was the one true God who helped Coenred to heal those who came to him. He would check on Sulis again after Prime. It was true that her wounds seemed healed now, but surely it would do no harm to apply the salve one more time.

Someway off to the west a dog barked. Ubbanford would be stirring from sleep soon. The time had come to rouse Gothfraidh and Dalston. Coenred turned to once more enter the gloom of the chapel.

A sound, harsh and hard, and yet somehow stealthy and cautious, brought him to a halt. What was that? Coenred held his breath, straining to hear again the sound that had caused fingers of dread to scratch the nape of his neck. He could make out the low rumble of Gothfraidh snoring and further off in the distance the trees still sighed with the wind-whisper of the breeze.

But gone was the birdsong.

The dog began to bark again, loud, insistent. A moment later, it yelped and was silent in an instant.

Coenred was suddenly cold. Memories of a night long ago in Engelmynster flooded into his mind. For a moment he stood in the doorway of the chapel, unsure how to proceed. Save for the murmur of the wind in the trees, all was quiet. If the wind picked up, the tendrils of mist that eddied and swirled around the buildings would quickly tatter and dissipate.

He made his decision and offered up a silent prayer.

Lord watch over me now.

Making the sign of the cross – forehead, chest, shoulder to shoulder – he stepped outside.

Barefoot and only wearing his simple woollen robe, he crept as silent as thought around the edge of the chapel. Dawn was very close now, the great hall on the hill silhouetted against the lightening eastern sky. The buildings of Ubbanford loomed dark and shadowed yet familiar all around him. He peered into the gloom. The breeze had died again and the dawn was silent. The mist hung in the air, shrouding the earth. Coenred stood still listening and straining his eyes.

He was being foolish. There was nothing here. Nothing untoward to frighten him in this way. The attack on Engelmynster had been years before, and it always surprised him just how quickly the memories could rush back to terrify him again. Gothfraidh said he allowed his imagination to rule him. He would not tell Gothfraidh of this, he decided. He would awaken the old monk and Dalston and they would perform Lauds, the first office of the day. Shaking his head at his own foolishness, Coenred turned.

And then he saw them.

Dark shapes of men flitted between the buildings. They did not speak, and they made no sound. The shades bore shields and Coenred spied the dull glow of steel reflecting the dawn sky.

He did not move; did not breathe. They had not seen him. He was in the dawn-shadow of the church and he must be invisible to them there, in the darkness. He had a sudden urge to piss. He began to shake, but clenched his fists and willed himself to remain still.

He began to recite the Paternoster silently, offering up the calming words to God. The Lord would protect him. But what of Tata? What of the countless dead all over middle earth? Did God truly care for any of his flock? Coenred raised his right hand to his mouth and bit into his finger, hard, dispelling the dark thoughts of doubt with the pain. He must have faith. For without it, what would matter then?

He did not count how many men passed, but there were enough that he knew this day would end in bloodshed. Almost all of Beobrand's gesithas were far away in the war with Mercia. The few warriors in Ubbanford would not be able to stand against so many intruders. And if these men who skulked in the dawn had their wish, Coenred was sure the men of Ubbanford would be killed where they slept.

When the last man had passed, Coenred moved quickly and quietly back into the church. He ran to Dalston's side and shook him awake. He placed his hand over Dalston's mouth as the monk awoke, struggling, eyes wide in the darkness.

"Quiet," he hissed, "don't ask questions. There are men here in Ubbanford. Warriors. You must run to Bassus. Silently." Dalston ceased his fighting, his eyes bright in the gloom. Coenred removed the hand from Dalston's mouth. "They looked to be going towards the river. You should be able to reach Bassus in Ubba's hall, if you run now."

Gothfraidh was awake now too. He sat groggily, but appeared to have heard enough of what Coenred had said to understand.

"But what do they want?" asked Dalston, his whispering voice tremulous with fear.

"There is no time for questions," said Coenred. "Run to Bassus. The attackers expect to surprise us. But if they see you, flee from them and raise the alarm."

Coenred stood and ran to the door.

"And you?" asked Gothfraidh. "Where do you go?"

Coenred thought for a moment of Tata, his sister, and the horrific fate she had suffered at the hands of the Waelisc raiders. And then he thought of Sulis, fragile and beautiful, slumbering in the great hall atop the hill.

"I will go to Sunniva's hall. Reaghan and the Lady of Mercia must be warned."

Without waiting for a response, Coenred slipped into the cool, mist-filled morning and sprinted towards the hill. His bare feet squelched on the dew-soaked grass and wet mud of the path. He gasped for breath, as he pushed himself faster, faster. He would not allow anyone else to die as Tata had.

He left the main settlement behind him, his breath ragged. Again, he wondered whether he was being foolish. The night seemed yet still and quiet behind him. He began to labour up the steep incline towards Sunniva's hall. Could it be that he had imagined these things? Was it possible that Gothfraidh was right about him and this was a fancy; a waking dream?

And then, with a sickening realisation, he knew his fears had been all too real. For the mist behind him was suddenly aglow with the flare of flames. And the silence of the dawn was shattered with the first screams of that horror-filled day.

Chapter 46

Beobrand stared down at the dead horse. His men did not speak. He spat and looked to the north. The great peaks were hidden in a dark mass of clouds. As he watched, light flared within the clouds, as if two mountains had been struck together to produce a spark. He took a deep breath and listened. A long while after the lightning flash came the muffled rumble of thunder. The gods were speaking, but he was no priest who could decipher their meaning. If there were words being spoken in the distant storm, Beobrand could not hear them.

He cast a glance at his gesithas. They were downcast and tired. They may not be able to hear the words of the gods, but as they stood around the stiffening body of the horse, it was clear to them all that the gods did not smile upon them.

The sack that was tied to Bera's saddle was dark, damp from the rain as much as from what oozed within. And to think you called me lucky, Beobrand said silently to Oswald's head. A cold wind rustled the pines under which they had rested for the night. Rain spattered Beobrand's face, bitter and chill. Whatever luck he may once have possessed, it seemed to have vanished like morning mist with the death of Oswald.

After losing Eadgard's and Grindan's horses they had made slower progress than he would have liked. And yet, for a time, as they'd ridden northward towards the mountains of Rheged, things had gone well. There had been no sign of pursuit and the clouds that brooded before them had not brought the rain they promised. Beobrand had dared to believe they might ride free of this western land and deliver Oswald's remains without further difficulties. They had pushed the horses as hard as they could throughout the day. They had spoken little, but Beobrand had noticed he was not the only one who turned in his saddle to scan the horizon behind them. They saw no warriors. No Waelisc galloping behind them. And Acennan and the others were nowhere to be seen. Beobrand worried for his friend, but there was nothing he could do but hope Acennan fared well.

As that long muggy day drew to a close, the wind had picked up, whipping their cloaks about them and throwing grit and dust into their faces. The dark clouds had finally released their burden of rain and in moments the small band had been drenched by the pelting downpour. They had sought shelter in a small stand of pines, where they had cowered beneath the rage of the storm. Lightning and thunder had filled the night and at some point, when the storm was at its height, Elmer's horse had broken its tether in fright and careened madly into the darkness. Such was the ferocity of the wind and driving rain that there had been no point in going after the animal. And so they had waited, cold and wet, until Thunor's chariot had rolled over them and the storm rumbled and flickered into the distance.

In the morning, the watery light of dawn showed them a sodden landscape. Leaves had been ripped from the trees and the long grass of the valley had been flattened. They had set out after Elmer's frightened horse only to find it no further than a spear's throw from their camp. It lay, solid, still and unmoving, in the shadow of an ash tree. Its neck was twisted, distorted and unnatural. It had galloped headlong into the tree's thick trunk. Beobrand shuddered. It was as though the beast itself had offered its own fateful sacrifice to Woden beneath the god's sacred tree.

Like so many times before Beobrand wondered whether Nelda's words yet held sway over him.

Could he be cursed? He spat again, this time onto the horse's head. Curse or no curse, he must lead them from this place.

"Well," he said, forcing any trace of anxiety from his voice, "there's nothing to be gained from standing here. We have yet far to travel. Elmer, you will ride with Gram. But first butcher that horse. Cut enough meat for us to carry, but be quick about it." He fixed Elmer with a stern gaze and the older man nodded, pulling his seax from its sheath and kneeling beside the dead animal.

Beobrand climbed into his saddle and surveyed the land to the south and west. Black specks, the distant forms of crows, flecked the iron-grey western sky. There was no sign of any man. And yet his skin prickled. The Waelisc were out there somewhere.

Beobrand waited until Elmer had cut enough meat from the carcass with Gram's help. Without speaking, he tugged his horse's head to the north and kicked the beast into motion. His gesithas were quiet, sombre and subdued. They mounted their horses and followed him into the north.

After a while, Beobrand looked back at the ash tree beside the path. There could be no denying that any luck he had once had was now gone. If they were indeed being followed, it would be impossible for their hunters not to find their tracks. For there could be no clearer indication of their passing than the bulky horse corpse that rested beneath the tree for any that travelled this way to see.

Chapter 47

Reaghan awoke slowly. She stretched her fingers out, caressing the thick bearskin that covered her. Her sleeping chamber was dark and cool, but she was warm beneath the furs, her body languid and relaxed. She listened to the night and wondered why she had awoken. All was silent and she sighed with contentment. She ran her hand over the side of the bed which was empty, cold. With a dull pang she thought of Beobrand. It had been so long since he had slept at her side. She missed him, but gone was the sharp agony of loss she used to feel whenever he rode away from Ubbanford. Now his absences produced a blunted ache, a small pain that could be easily pushed aside, buried. Forgotten.

She held her breath for a moment. She thought she had heard a sound. A dog yapping far in the distance perhaps. But no, all was still. Judging from the pressure of her full bladder, it must be close to dawn. She had drunk more than was good for her the night before. She had sat up late talking to Cynethryth, long after the Lady of Mercia's gesithas had wrapped themselves in their blankets beside the hearth. In Cynethryth, Reaghan had found the friend she had longed for. Despite their differences, they understood each other as well as any sisters. Where Reaghan's days had previously been filled with monotonous chores and a yearning for Beobrand's return, now the long summer days were times of merriment and laughter. There was still work to do. The hall needed to be swept, bread baked and pottage prepared, but she had Sulis to help her now, and Cynethryth had chided her that it was not the lady of the hall's place to clean or cook or to brew ale. Cynethryth was talented at weaving and sewing, tasks which had never come easily to Reaghan. Cynethryth had laughed at Reaghan's clumsy efforts but Reaghan had not been offended as she had been whenever Rowena had criticised her in the same way over the years. She watched Cynethryth's dainty fingers as they worked the threads and she sought to copy her. Cynethryth was a patient teacher and whilst Reaghan had no natural talent, her weaving improved. Rowena would often come to the hall, sitting with them both, clearly relishing the proximity to Mercian royalty. Reaghan was happy to listen to the old woman's chatter and Cynethryth was ever gracious.

Some days, when the weather was warm, Reaghan and Cynethryth would take the children down to the river's edge where they would splash and play in the shallows of the ford. Cynethryth would talk of her own hall in Snodengaham. There was always a sadness about Cynethryth, a shadow on the edge of her words as she recalled her home. For weeks had gone by without word of Eowa. Reaghan knew that her new friend fretted over the fate of her husband. It was a bond between them. They had both married strong men whose lives were governed by war, power and battle-play. It was their lot to watch their children grow, to tend to their halls and to see that their husbands' lands were well governed.

One day, when the sun was warm and high in the sky, setting the Tuidi flickering like polished steel, they had spoken of their fears. Cynethryth had surprised Reaghan by saying that sometimes she wished that she were a man, that she could take up spear and shield and join her husband in battle.

"Would that not be better than these endless days of worry and fear?" Cynethryth had asked.

"But it must be terrifying," replied Reaghan. She'd thought of the night that Nathair's sons had taken her. Of the horror and the fear. And of how Beobrand had come to her through the flames, gore-drenched and wounded, surrounded by death. "Waiting for our men is torture," she said, "but I would not wish to fight as they do."

The boys had shrieked with laughter, drawing both the women's gaze. As they'd watched, Octa scooped up a pebble from the beach and flung it as hard as he could towards the far bank. It landed some way short, vanishing with a plop into the slow-moving waters. Alweo picked up a stone and threw it with all his strength. It too landed short of the bank, but a movement there showed Reaghan what the boys were aiming at. There, like a grey shade amongst the shadows of the bushes at the water's edge, stood a heron. Perhaps the very same bird that Beobrand used to talk about. Reaghan watched as Osmod picked up a stone and threw it at the bird. For a third time, the stone fell far short and disappeared beneath the waters of the Tuidi. Reaghan was glad. She did not wish to see the bird harmed. And a smile had played upon her lips as the heron, clearly deciding that fishing would be better elsewhere, spread its huge wings and flapped noisily into the air.

The boys had screamed and yelled, throwing stones after the huge bird, but they were yet children and their throws were weak. None of their stones struck home. And the heron had soon been lost to sight behind the trees and the curve of the river as it flew towards the west.

"Perhaps you are right," said Cynethryth, who had watched the boys in silence, her face impassive, "men are not that much different from boys. Everything for them is about strength. How far can I throw a pebble? How much land can I conquer? How many men can I kill? We womenfolk have more power than the men, do we not?"

"How so?" Reaghan had asked.

"Men send others to their deaths. We bring life into the world. Surely there is more power in creating life than in destroying it."

Reaghan had grown sombre and silent then. She remembered all too clearly the terrible, griping pains, as her body had voided her unborn child. Cynethryth, ever sensitive to Reaghan's moods, had reached out a hand to gently touch her arm.

"Octa may not be your flesh," she had said quietly. "But are you not his mother? Do you not love him, nurture him, feed him and clothe him?"

Reaghan had said nothing, merely nodding in agreement.

Behind them Sulis and Saegyth, Cynethryth's gemæcce, had watched in silence. Reaghan had almost forgotten they were there at all, so engrossed had she become in her conversation with Cynethryth and in the boys' antics.

But in that moment, she had suddenly become aware of Sulis' presence. It was as though the Mercian thrall's gaze had a weight of its own.

Now, lying snug under the bearskin and staring into the impenetrable gloom of her sleeping quarters, she clearly recalled the expression on Sulis' face when she had turned to look upon her. Her eyes had brimmed with tears, and her mouth had been set, lips pressed firmly together. There was sorrow there. Sorrow at her plight and a consuming sadness for her loss. And yet there was more, and Reaghan was not blind to it. Sulis' delicate features had been twisted by simmering anger.

Reaghan shivered in the darkness of her chamber, pulling the furs up close under her chin. It always saddened her to think of Sulis. The woman's pain was evident in her haunted eyes and down-turned mouth. Reaghan pitied her. She hated to see suffering and, despite Bassus urging her to have Sulis thrashed for her insolence, Reaghan was pleased that she had resisted. She did not wish to inflict more pain upon the woman. She doubted the thrall would ever love her, but she hoped that Sulis would come to look upon her as a fair and just mistress.

After the thrall's terrible outburst at Cynethryth's welcoming feast, Reaghan had been shocked and furious. But when she had gone to her chambers that night and confronted Sulis she had been pleasantly surprised to find her contrite. Sulis had begged her forgiveness. She would never again speak to her mistress in that way, she had said. Reaghan had allowed herself to be easily mollified, but before her anger had fully burnt away, she had snapped at Sulis, "You know that Bassus would have me beat you? He says you should never be trusted."

Sulis had lowered her gaze and mumbled another apology.

After that night, Sulis had performed her duties well and without complaint. The summer days had been warm and peaceful. It had been easy for Reaghan to push the thoughts of war far into the recesses of her mind; to dark places where her thoughts seldom ventured.

A sudden harsh noise ruptured the stillness of the night. Something pounded repeatedly on the doors of the hall and, outside in the dark, someone was shouting breathlessly. A man's voice raised in anguish, high-pitched.

Terrified.

Reaghan leapt from the warm bed, shuddering as her feet touched the cold rushes. In the dark she fumbled with the latch of the door. The shouting grew louder, more insistent. The hammering on the hall's door suddenly ceased. More voices joined the first. Urgent, questioning. Dread prickled Reaghan's skin. The hairs on her arms rose in the cool air.

What was happening? Could it be that Picts had crossed the Tuidi to attack the hall? Word would have travelled that Beobrand was far from home with his warband. Maybe the tidings of his absence had reached the ears of his enemies in the north. He was no friend of the Picts.

"Sulis," Reaghan said, her voice shrill and sharp, small against the loud voices of Cynethryth's gesithas and the door wards within the hall. "Sulis, wake up, girl." Sulis slept on a small pallet outside Reaghan's chamber. Reaghan peered at the crumpled blankets there, trying to make sense of the shapes in the darkness. But there was no sign of the thrall.

A pale shape loomed in the gloom.

Reaghan started, terrified to think that perhaps a Pict may have reached her chamber. She recoiled from the hand that reached for her. Beyond the partition the voices continued to shout. Something crashed, hollow and booming, and a man cursed.

"Mistress," said a familiar voice in the darkness, "it is I, Sulis."

Reaghan let out a shuddering breath, cursing her own terror. She must not forget that she was the lady of the hall. She pulled her shawl about her. Her hands trembled, but she was sure that Sulis would not be able to see her fear in the gloom. Reaghan forced herself to speak calmly, imagining how Cynethryth would talk to her maid servant.

"We must see that the lady Cynethryth and the children are well," she said.

Before Sulis could reply Cynethryth stepped from behind the partition that led to her own chamber. She had struck a light and carried a taper. The guttering flame distorted her fine features. Her hair was tousled with sleep, wreathing her shadowed face. The rush taper threw enough light to show that Cynethryth's face was drawn and pinched with the same fear that gripped Reaghan.

The clamour within the hall continued.

"Come," said Reaghan. She was surprised at the firmness in her own voice. "Let's see what this noise is all about."

Cynethryth turned to Saegyth.

"See that the boys are well. If they have not woken, awaken them. And dress them. Quickly."

Reaghan led the way into the main hall, followed by Cynethryth and Sulis. There was more light here. Someone had thrown a fresh log onto the hearth and flames licked the wood, casting dancing shadows into the darkened corners. All around them was chaos. The men were all on their feet. Some were already shrugging on their byrnies, hefting shields, buckling on sword belts. Their faces were grim and blank, partway between the slack-mouths of slumber and the clenched jaws of killers of men.

More light filtered in from the open doorway. She had been right, it was close to dawn, the sky was the colour of cold iron. She moved further into the hall and the men finally noticed her and the other women. They turned to face her, expectant, awaiting her command.

For several heartbeats she said nothing. She knew not what to say. Then Cynethryth touched her shoulder lightly, awakening her from the spell of her fear. Reaghan took a deep breath, straightened her back.

By Danu, Mother of all, she told herself, you are the lady of the hall. You must lead these men.

"What is the meaning of this?" she said, raising her voice.

Several men started speaking at once, their words confused and tumbling like stones kicked down a hill. She raised her hand and they fell silent.

"You," she pointed at Lanferth, the door ward. "Speak."

"Brother Coenred has come to the hall to warn us," Lanferth said. "Ubbanford is under attack." Reaghan searched the faces of the gathered men and found that of the Christ monk. He was flushed, his face beaded with sweat. His bare feet were splattered with mud. Beyond him, through the open doors of the hall, the day was brightening. No, she corrected herself, seeing her mistake with a sickening twist of her stomach. The red light she saw came not from the rising sun, but from flames. And what she had taken for clouds tinged with the ruddy hue of dawn was thick, roiling smoke, billowing up from a conflagration. In the valley below Sunniva's hall, the houses of Ubbanford were burning.

Reaghan shivered and her words dried up in her mouth.

Fire in the darkness brought death. Unbidden came the distant memory of the night all those years before when she had been snatched from her village by the Angelfolc. She had seen her loved ones murdered on that night of terror. On another flame-riven night, the sons of Nathair had stolen her away. She had been certain that she would surely die at the hands of those brutal Picts. Beobrand had saved her then, stepping from the flame-flicker darkness and carrying her back into the light. Reaghan shivered again, despite the warmth from the freshly rekindled hearth. Beobrand was far to the south and she knew not who would save her this time.

She was paralysed with fear. Dark thoughts smothered her mind like a frantic murder of black-feathered crows. She could not speak. They would all die here.

Cynethryth stepped forward, taking charge.

"Who are they?" she asked in a steady voice. "And how many?"

Coenred turned to her. He was recovering from his run now, his breath returning. And, whilst he still had the look of fear about him, he appeared to be in control despite his obvious agitation.

"There are many of them, lady," he said, nervously running his long fingers through his hair. "It was dark and misty. I could not be sure of their number."

"Come, lad," snapped Lanferth, "that is of no use to us. Were there five or fifty? A hundred?"

Coenred swallowed and nodded.

"I cannot be sure, but I would judge them to be more than a score. Perhaps as many as two score."

The hall fell silent. With the few men left in Ubbanford, they could not hope to stand against so many. Reaghan's mind reeled. What could they do? Death was coming for them with fire and steel. A thin sound of wailing drifted through the open door. Lanferth ran over, peering down towards the houses below.

Reaghan trembled, wrapping the shawl more tightly about her shoulders, as if the wool could somehow protect her.

"Who are they?" asked Lanferth. "Picts?"

Coenred shook his head.

"I know not who they are, but they are Angelfolc. I heard them shouting to one another once the burning started..." His voice trailed off. Perhaps he was picturing in his mind what was happening to those left down in the valley. Then, as if he had suddenly recalled something, he said, "I do not know them, but I am sure I would not have forgotten them if I had seen them before."

"Why?"

"Their leader is a giant. I looked back as I ran and saw him..." Again his voice drifted into silence. He swallowed. "He is bigger even than Bassus or Eadgard. And he has a great beard and head of flame-red hair."

Cynethryth paled.

"I know this man," she said, her voice small now. Her face was as pale as the linen sleeping kirtle she wore.

"His name is Halga, son of Grimbold. He is one of Penda's men. He must have come for me..." Her face crumpled at the realisation of who the red-bearded giant must seek. "My sons!"

Reaghan knew she must act. To stand like this, silent and unmoving, served no purpose. She may as well welcome these death-bringers that had come with the dawn into the hall with open arms.

"We cannot face them, lady," said Lanferth. He spoke his words to both Reaghan and Cynethryth, unsure who was in command.

Reaghan took a long, ragged breath. This was her hall. Her home. She was the lady of Ubbanford and she must lead the people from danger.

"We will run," she said. "Lanferth, take everyone to the ford as quickly as possible. Go around behind the hall where we won't be seen from the valley. The rest of you," she turned to the gesithas, both Beobrand's and Cynethryth's, "you will protect us as we flee. We will cross the Tuidi and make our way to Stagga. Let us pray that there we will find enough people amongst Acennan's folk to stand with us against these Mercians."

Glad of firm guidance, Lanferth nodded and began shouting orders. The hall was once again filled with noise and motion.

Reaghan turned to her thrall.

"Sulis, go and help Saegyth with the boys. There is no time to waste."

Sulis did not move. Cynethryth frowned.

"Go on, girl," snapped Reaghan, "this is no time for your insolence."

"I will not," said Sulis. She spoke in a quiet tone, but the words were clear enough.

"We cannot tarry here. The men will be upon us soon. We must flee." Reaghan's voice was tinged with despair.

Sulis shook her head. Her face was as cold as stone.

"No," she said. "I am Mercian and I will be a thrall to you no longer."

All around them the men were donning their battle-harness. None save Cynethryth and Coenred seemed to notice the exchange between Reaghan and Sulis.

Reaghan reached for Sulis. She meant to take her by the shoulders and turn her towards the sleeping quarters.

"There is no time for this, Sulis," she pleaded, desperation entering her tone. "Come now, we must run. Think of the boys. They will be killed." Sulis winced at the words.

Cynethryth let out a small cry and pushed past Sulis, running back towards the sleeping chambers. Reaghan could feel her body shaking like a tree caught in a great storm now.

"And think how we will suffer at the hands of those warriors. We both know what will befall us. Please..." she implored.

"No!" screamed Sulis, her ire sudden and searing. The warriors around them glanced over at the sound.

Reaghan recoiled from the heat of that rage. And yet she felt her own anger ignite.

"Sulis," she shouted back at the thrall, "do what I say now." Again she reached for Sulis, to push her towards the rear of the hall.

"No!" shrieked Sulis once more, shoving Reaghan hard.

For a moment, Reaghan staggered back. Anger and outrage flared within her. Then, she gasped as a searing agony filled her belly. Confused, she glanced down. Blood was blossoming beneath a ragged tear in the cloth of her kirtle. She pressed a hand to her stomach. It came back hot and wet with blood. Wide-eyed and shaking, she looked at Sulis in amazement.

At her side, clutched in her white-knuckled fist, Sulis held a blood-slick knife. Absently, Reaghan wondered where she had got the blade from. The room seemed to shift around her, and Reaghan stumbled. Coenred gripped her arms, held her upright. His face was as white as whey, his eyes reflected the horror she felt.

"No," Sulis said for a third time, but now her voice was small, as if she was shocked at what she had done.

"Sulis..." stammered Coenred.

The Mercian ignored him.

"Bassus was right," she hissed at Reaghan. She pushed past Coenred, who watched her go, open-mouthed and staring. Sulis ran quickly towards the doors of the hall. Lanferth seemed bemused at what was happening, but, recognising that something was amiss, he made to grab the thrall before she could flee. Sulis dodged his outstretched hands, lashing out with her bloody knife. Lanferth cursed and retreated, blood welling from a deep cut to his right palm.

Without hesitation, Sulis dashed past him and out into the dawn.

Chapter 48

The sun was low in the west when at last Beobrand saw their destination before them. They had ridden for two more days, plodding northward beneath the low, brooding skies. After the storm and the death of Elmer's horse, the weather had remained cool and overcast. The leaden skies suited Beobrand's mood and most of the time they'd ridden in silence. Only Cynan and Beobrand had their own steeds now and so, for much of the journey, they'd found themselves riding at the front of the small band of horsemen.

Beobrand reined in his mount and pointed.

"There is the peak I spoke of," he said. "Ástígend told me its name is Carrec Dún. There are walls up there, broken and old now, and earthworks too. We rested there on the journey to Caer Luel. It is a castle of the old folk who lived here before the Angelfolc. Before the men of Roma even."

Beobrand glanced over his shoulder. The remaining riders of the group were not far away now and Beobrand gave silent thanks that none of the horses had grown lame from bearing two riders. Still, they had not been able to keep up a fast pace. He had hoped to have arrived at this place sooner. He turned his attention back to the looming hill and the old earth mounds, ditches and walls that adorned its summit. The clouds were heavy, dark and brooding. And low in the sky. They were draped about the hills like a bearskin made of mist. The dense fog on the hilltop obscured the earthworks from view.

"You think they will come?" asked Cynan.

"Bearn will not let me down. He will come." He spoke in a firm, self-assured voice. Now was not the time to show his doubts. They had suffered too many setbacks already.

Again Beobrand scanned the hills but saw no sign of Bearn and his gesithas. He wondered for a moment whether perhaps Bearn had decided to camp elsewhere within sight of Carrec Dún rather than within the crumbled remains of the ancient fortification. He looked east, but saw no sign of movement save for the small shapes of sheep and goats that dotted a far hillside. He could see no shepherd, but he was sure they were being watched as they sat there astride their horses in the dreary valley. Turning to the west once more he saw no indication of a campsite, no telltale smudge of smoke and no sign of Bearn and the rest of his warband. Still, it was no matter. Despite the loss of the horses, they had reached this place without further incident. Acennan too knew where they were to meet. Perhaps he and the others were already there on that bleak hilltop, hidden from view by the low-lying cloud. The thought cheered Beobrand. He hoped that soon they would all be seated around a fire, exchanging tales of how they had stolen Oswald's remains in the dark of night. He would hear tell of Acennan's exploits and how he had led Gwalchmei and the Waelisc away. It would be good to see his friend soon. He missed him.

"Come, men," he shouted to Eadgard, Grindan, Gram, Elmer, Fraomar and Dreogan, who approached slowly on their three mounts, "soon we will be at the agreed meeting place. There, at Carrec Dún is where we are to meet Bearn and the others. You have done well, and we bring with us something of the greatest value..." Beobrand's words faltered and he fell silent. A movement had drawn his gaze. His heart clenched and he felt a lurching sensation in his gut.

To the south, cantering over the brow of the hill they had just crossed, came a warband of some twenty men. At their head rode a warrior on a great black steed. The leader's white cloak fluttered behind him.

Gwalchmei.

For a heartbeat Beobrand's thoughts swirled like leaves caught in a storm. Was it possible? Was Gwalchmei riding Sceadugenga?

Beside him Cynan cursed. Beobrand watched as the six remaining riders of his band lumbered on their three horses towards them. The horses were tired. There was no way they could outrun the Waelisc who, having spotted their quarry, had kicked their mounts into a gallop and pounded down the hill towards them. Beobrand quickly looked around them. There was nowhere where they could easily defend themselves. The land was open, dotted with stunted trees, but there was nothing that could provide them shelter. If they could have reached the old earthworks on the hilltop to the north, perhaps they might have been able to make a stand, but here, in the open, Beobrand could see no way they could prevail against so many.

And yet was he not Beobrand, Lord of Ubbanford, thegn of Bernicia? And were his men not the famed warriors of the black shields, feared throughout Albion? He would not despair so soon.

Leaping from his horse, he bellowed at his men.

"Our enemy is upon us. To me! Shieldwall!"

Beobrand felt a sliver of pride as his men did not falter. They urged their horses forward and, with only the merest glance back at the approaching horsemen, his gesithas jumped from their mounts and readied themselves for battle. In moments, the eight of them had pulled shields and helms from their saddles. They let their horses scatter. There was no time to tether the animals before the Waelisc would be upon them. Beobrand cursed to himself. Oswald's remains were yet attached to those horses. He pushed the concern from his mind. If they survived this fight, there would be plenty of time to worry.

Beobrand pulled his great helm onto his head and was enveloped by the false calm and quiet of its protection. The thunder of the approaching horses' hooves was suddenly muted, the wind no longer caught at his hair.

With the ease that comes from countless days of hard practice, his warriors fell into position beside their lord, forming a strong wall of linden and iron. Not all of them bore spears, but half of them carried long ash hafts tipped with wicked steel points. These they brandished menacingly, pointing them towards the galloping riders. The message was clear. Any horse that got too close would feel the savage sting of the spear-tips. All men knew that a horse would not ride into a strongly formed shieldwall, and so it was no surprise to them when the Waelisc reined in their mounts some distance away.

The distance was well-judged. It was further than even Garr could throw a spear, had he been with them.

"When they decide to surround us, things will get interesting," said Cynan, the Waelisc lilt of his words making it sound as though he were laughing. Beobrand glanced at him. There was no mirth there. The young man's face was hard, his mouth and jaw set firm beneath his open-faced helm. Beobrand said nothing. Cynan was right. Given the numbers of their foe, it was only a matter of time before they were surrounded and cut down.

The last of the Waelisc riders pulled their horses to a halt and sat in a wide line. They slid weapons from scabbards and untied helms that had been hanging from saddles. Beobrand fixed his gaze on their leader. There was no mistaking the Waelisc lord now. Gwalchmei ap Gwyar met his stare for a moment, and then turned to his own saddlebags. And now there was no doubt in Beobrand's mind. Gwalchmei was mounted on Sceadugenga, the great stallion with skin as black and sleek as a raven's claws.

In a matter of moments, the Waelisc who had followed them north from Maserfelth would dismount and form their own shieldwall. Or perhaps they had other plans. Beobrand drew Hrunting slowly into the grey daylight, tugging against the gentle resistance where its nicked blade caught the fur that lined the leather-bound wooden scabbard.

"Forward," he said, and stepped decisively towards the waiting horsemen. He would give them no time to make plans.

He felt his mouth twist into a savage grin as his gesithas fell into step with him as if they were controlled by his own thoughts.

"Do not forget who you are," he said. "You are the bearers of the black shields. Bringers of death. Feeders of the wolf and the raven. You are men of Bernicia. You are my gesithas!" He raised his voice, and quickened his pace. His men surged forward with him. "Do you fear the likes of these goat-swiving Waelisc?"

"No!" his gesithas shouted.

"And what do we bring them?"

"Death!" his warriors roared.

The mounted men before them jostled nervously, uncertain perhaps in the face of the approaching warriors. One horse shied away from the noise of the marching Bernicians.

Gwalchmei, however, seemed calm. He nudged Sceadugenga forward a few steps and then halted. He held up his hand. The men behind him did not move.

Beobrand and his gesithas were still some distance from Gwalchmei. Perhaps close enough for a spear-throw, but it would be no certain thing.

Beobrand raised Hrunting and halted. Without need for a word of command, his gesithas stopped as one.

For a long while they stood like that, the Bernician shieldwall glowering silently at the score of mounted Waelisc. Beobrand was about to urge his men forward once more, when Gwalchmei kicked Sceadugenga another few steps on, towards him. Beobrand tensed. Did the lord from Gwynedd plan on leading his men in a charge against their small shieldwall?

But before Beobrand could react, Gwalchmei reined in once more. His warband had not moved. He held something in his left hand that hung at his side. It was partially hidden by

Sceadugenga's broad neck and Beobrand could not discern what the object was.

"It has been many years since last we met, Beobrand of Ubbanford," Gwalchmei shouted. Beobrand remembered clearly the man's self-assurance. The tinge of contempt in his voice was familiar even after all this time.

"I would be content for many more to pass without seeing you again, Gwalchmei of Gwynedd," said Beobrand in a loud, firm voice. "Though I see you have something of mine still."

Gwalchmei smiled broadly.

"You mean Taranau? But no, I told you back in East Angeln, this stallion is mine, not yours. But you do have something that belongs to me, I believe. Something I would be willing to trade you for."

"Indeed?" asked Beobrand. "And what would that be?"

"You stole something from beneath the great tree at Maserfelth. Something that I had been tasked with protecting. Penda is not a forgiving man and I do not mean to return south without that which you stole. But still, I am reasonable. We can make a fair exchange. You have the head of your king, so shall we exchange heads?"

With that, Gwalchmei lifted aloft the object he held in his left hand. The thin, watery light of the afternoon fell upon a pallid, gaping-mouthed, plump-faced severed head that the lord of Gwynedd held by the hair. Beobrand recognised the face at once, despite the pallor of death and the lack of the lively expression he had known so well.

Acennan.

His most loyal gesithas.

His closest hearth warrior.

His friend.

Gwalchmei's mouth continued to move. He spoke, but Beobrand heard nothing past the rushing in his ears as his rage burst forth and engulfed him with terrible ferocity. Gone was thought. Plans for how best to defend his men in the face of so many enemy horsemen were burnt away in the immolating fire of his anger. Unknowing and unthinking, Beobrand sprang forward and sprinted towards Gwalchmei, bellowing his inchoate ire at the man who had stolen Acennan from him.

Beobrand sped forward, his long strides covering the distance quickly. He was not aware of his gesithas surging after him. Their order was lost, but to a man, they charged forward to protect their lord. All Beobrand saw before him was Gwalchmei, the sneer fading from his face at Beobrand's sudden, careening rush. Beobrand fixed the lord of Gwynedd in his stare and pounded forward.

Gwalchmei, realising he had miscalculated, dropped Acennan's head to the earth and tugged hard on Sceadugenga's reins, attempting to turn the stallion's head, to flee from Beobrand's precipitous attack.

"Death!" screamed Beobrand. "Death!"

Gwalchmei's face paled as he struggled to control his mount. Beobrand was almost upon him when the black stallion leapt forward, bunching its great muscles to send it flying towards Beobrand. The gap between them closed in an instant. Then, as quickly as the beast had lunged forward, it dug its hooves into the earth and came to an abrupt halt. At the same instant, the steed lowered its head. Gwalchmei lost his balance, tumbling forward, over Sceadugenga's head and onto the ground.

He landed hard, with a bone-shaking crash, on his back. The fall must have knocked the wind from his lungs, but he did not stay down. With the speed of a cat he pushed himself to his feet to face Beobrand. Drawing his sword, he swung it before him in a fluid motion that showed skill and a bravado that the onlooking warriors approved of.

But Beobrand cared nought for his enemy's prowess or his bravery. And nothing could stand before his fury. Gwalchmei lunged at his throat. Beobrand did not slow his charge. He swatted the blade away on the edge of his linden board and swung Hrunting's blade down with all his strength and anger.

The patterned blade found the flesh of Gwalchmei's arm, passing easily through sinew and bone. Beobrand punched his shield boss into Gwalchmei's face. The lord of Gwynedd fell back onto the earth, face battered and bleeding. Dark, fresh blood gushed from his severed sword arm. His face was the white of sheep's wool now.

For a moment, Beobrand was confused, as if awakening suddenly from a dark dream. Then he saw the back of Acennan's head where it lay someway behind the dying Gwalchmei and the great black stallion.

This was no dream.

"That is my friend!" Beobrand screamed, hacking down again. Gwalchmei raised his shield, cowering beneath the blows. Sceadugenga stood, head lowered, unflinching and patient behind him.

"And I told you!" Beobrand kicked Gwalchmei's shield aside. He smashed Hrunting into the Waelisc lord's exposed shoulder. "That is my horse!" He swung a final scything cut into Gwalchmei's neck. Blood, hot and dark, fountained in the air. Gwalchmei's head tumbled back and his body slumped.

Beobrand looked up, panting, searching for his next foe; the next man who would feel the bite of Hrunting's blade.

Behind Sceadugenga, Gwalchmei's warband were turning their mounts, kicking them into a gallop. But not towards their fallen lord and the black-shielded warriors of Bernicia. They swung their steeds away. They were fleeing southward and away.

Beobrand was dazed. He could make no sense of it. He looked to the grim faces of his gesithas. They stood a few paces from him in a ragged shieldwall. He saw confusion on their faces too. Surely his defeat of the Waelisc leader had not been enough to send his warband running in fear.

And then, he understood.

Riding out of the clouds that yet brimmed and rolled atop Carrec Dún, hiding the old stronghold from sight, came two score mounted warriors. Spear-points and helms caught the dim sunlight with a dull glow. Many of the riders bore the black shields of Beobrand's gesithas, but a banner also fluttered above the riders as they galloped down the slope out of the mists. It was Fordraed's black bull's head on red and it flapped and snapped as the horsemen approached.

Beobrand had known Bearn would not let him down. He had come with the remainder of Beobrand's warband, and it seemed he had brought an unlikely ally with him in Fordraed. Beobrand nodded and the others turned to follow his bleak stare. Eadgard smiled. Elmer heaved a sigh of relief. He would see his family again.

Beobrand closed his eyes and let out a long sigh. He felt empty and lost. He stepped over Gwalchmei's blood-soaked corpse, absently dropping Hrunting beside the body. He tugged at the ties of his helm and let that fall to the ground beside his sword.

As if from a far distance he heard Fraomar and Gram call out to the approaching Bernicians, but he could not bring himself to meet the gaze of any of the warriors there. Instead, he reached for Sceadugenga. The horse snorted softly and nuzzled its great snout into Beobrand's shoulder.

Beobrand wrapped his arms around the stallion's massive neck, entwining the fingers of his half-hand into the greasy mane and rubbing his right hand over the sleek, muscular, trembling flesh.

He pushed his face into the warmth of the stallion.

"Welcome back, my old friend," he whispered.

Then, with a shuddering sob, the tears began to flow.

Chapter 49

"Your man defied my order," shouted Fordraed. Spittle flecked his chubby lips and Beobrand had a fleeting memory of how it had felt to strike that flaccid face with his fist. But there was no fire of rage in him now. All his fury had left him as quickly as water drains from a smashed pot. In its place was a cold, empty lethargy. It was as though that part of him that rose up to confront battle and conflict with savage glee, the animal within that he so often struggled to hold in check, had fled. As if it had broken its bonds and after that last violent killing of Gwalchmei, there was no reason for its existence. Or perhaps the beast that frequently consumed him with rage now lay whimpering and shaking in a dark corner of his being, like a kicked hound. No amount of violence would return his friend to him.

Acennan had been avenged, but Beobrand felt nothing save for a hollow emptiness. He had sought vengeance often in his life and he had grown to know this feeling. Despite what the scops would sing in the mead halls, when they stood before laughing and boasting warriors, of the joy of revenge, the regained honour and battle-fame, with the death of his enemies he never felt anything save despair. The shedding of their lifeblood would never bring back those they had wronged. Those they had slain would never return.

They were yet dead, those he had loved. His brother, Octa. Sunniva. Acennan. Slaying Hengist, Wybert and now Gwalchmei had not brought him peace. And yet, he knew he could do nothing else. Perhaps they looked on from the otherworld of death. If they did, he hoped vengeance pleased them.

"Well?" yelled Fordraed, half-rising from his finely carved seat. "You are his lord," he said the word as though it were as bitter as an oak gall, "do you have nothing to say?"

The leather walls of the tent slapped and billowed against the wooden frame. The wind was fierce up here on the crest of the hill of Carrec Dún. Most of the men cowered with the horses in whatever shelter they could find in the wind-shadow of the ditches and mounds raised long generations before by men now lost to memory. Fordraed never travelled without this tent. He had it carried on several horses and it was constructed each evening by two thralls that rode with him. It slowed them down, and seemed a waste of effort to Beobrand, but he cared not for Fordraed's foibles.

The inside of the shelter was cramped and dark. Fordraed had commanded rush lights to be lit, yet their feeble flames cast but a dim light. They flickered and danced with each gust of wind. To either side of Fordraed were gathered his closest warriors, his comitatus. They glared at Beobrand from beneath shadowed brows. He ignored them.

He had ignored Fordraed too when he had attempted to speak to him in the valley at the site of Gwalchmei's death. Beobrand had scarcely heard Fordraed's angry words. He had swung himself into the unfamiliar saddle on Sceadugenga's familiar back and had followed Bearn and the others back to the encampment on the hill.

There, he had known a brief moment of respite from the overwhelming sense of gloom that had settled upon him. Garr and Attor, both hollow-eyed and travel-weary, but seemingly unharmed and whole, had rushed to his side as he dismounted. He had embraced them both, and Attor had stuttered through the tale of how Acennan and Ástígend had led their Waelisc pursuers away. Beobrand's eyes had again filled with tears, and he had looked into the wind, blinking away his sorrow.

He had been summoned soon after to Fordraed's tent.

"The lord Beobrand is to come alone," Heremod had said. The gruff warrior had approached Beobrand and his men with three others of Fordraed's hearth-warriors. They were all dour and taciturn, perhaps expecting a fight.

His gesithas protested that he was not a ceorl to be called like a dog to stand before Fordraed, but Beobrand had gone with Fordraed's men without complaint. The feeling of emptiness was upon him. It was as though he were in another man's dream.

Or a nightmare.

He thought of Acennan's face, mouth hanging open, above the ragged cut of his neck and shuddered.

Gods, what would he tell Eadgyth and the children?

Another widow to whom he would need to impart the most bitter of tidings. The oppressive weight of the responsibility to Acennan's and Eowa's kin pressed upon him, causing him almost as much anguish as his own grief.

Now, standing silent and sullen before Fordraed in the overcrowded tent that stank of sweat and burning pig fat, he noticed with a start that Gram and Attor had both defied Heremod and had followed their lord. They flanked Beobrand. He sighed. They were good men, steadfast and true.

"What do you say in defence of your man Bearn?" Fordraed asked, his voice rising as he grew increasingly angry at Beobrand's insolent silence.

"I do not need to defend him," Beobrand answered at last. The tension that had been building within the tent like a thunderstorm shifted somewhat. Whether it lessened or increased was not clear. "Bearn is my man, as you say. And he follows my commands, not yours."

"But Oswiu commanded me to patrol these western lands of Rheged," Fordraed blustered. Beobrand thought that the flapping of the tent appeared to be caused by the wind of Fordraed's words. "But Bearn would not listen to me. He demanded we head to this place. He ignored me and in the end I was forced to bring my own men here too, rather than split the force left under my control. Bearn was left under my command."

"But he is my oath-sworn man, is he not?" asked Beobrand, his voice quiet and dull. He could not summon the energy to fight with the fool.

"He is," stammered Fordraed, off balance. "but—"

"Then there is nothing for him to answer for," interrupted Beobrand. "He was obeying his hlaford. For I commanded that he come here." Beobrand wished to be done with this. He wanted to find some mead or ale and to drink himself into a dreamless sleep where the faces of his failures could not reach him.

"But I speak with the voice of the king!" screamed Fordraed. Perhaps he had expected some apology from Beobrand, or a recompense, weregild from Beobrand's fabled coffers of treasure. He would be sorely disappointed.

As quickly as it had fled, Beobrand's rage returned, like a great wave crashing onto the rocks below Bebbanburg, lifting pebbles and flotsam with its force. The strength of it shocked Beobrand. With a shaking hand he reached down to the dark, stained sack he grasped in his left half-hand. He had held it with reverence and as they had ridden from Maserfelth none had gazed upon that which lay within. He hesitated for a heartbeat, not wishing to touch the object in the bag, but his anger dispelled his dread, his fear of unsettling Oswald's spirit. Clenching his jaw, he thrust his right hand into the dark opening of the sack. The sour stench of corruption billowed out of the gloom and his fingers recoiled at the damp, slick texture of the lank hair.

Everyone within the shelter was silent now, captivated by his movements, awaiting to see what he would produce. Attor and Gram tensed beside him. Next to Fordraed, Heremod took a pace forward, as if he expected Beobrand to pull a blade from the sack.

Turning his face away from the sack's opening and the sickly, stomach-churning scent of death, Beobrand fixed his gaze on Fordraed and tugged on the hair that was now entwined in his grip. He raised Oswald's head from the sack and, as one, Fordraed and his gesithas let out a gasp. Heremod stepped backwards, colliding with his lord.

"You say you speak with the voice of the king," Beobrand said. "Behold my king!"

Oswald's face was sunken, drawn and devoid of colour. The dark eye sockets stared blindly at Fordraed and the gathered men, the once bright orbs within now shrivelled and dark.

Outside, the wind died as if the gods held their breath. The rush light flames burnt straight, sending their thin streams of foul-smelling smoke straight up in trembling lines to the stretched leather of the tent's roof. For a long while, nobody spoke.

At last, Fordraed recovered and pushed himself up out of his chair. He squared his shoulders and looked at Beobrand with difficulty, barely able to draw his gaze away from Oswald's grim corpse-face.

"Oswiu is your king now," he said, his voice small and timid, like a child. As though he were scared that Oswald's head might overhear him and reply in a voice from the afterlife. Fordraed shuddered. "You swore your oath to him, Beobrand. Do not forget that."

"I never forget an oath. My word is iron."

Fordraed nodded.

"Then you will do as I command." He smiled in triumph. "As will your men."

"I have sworn my oath to Oswiu," Beobrand said, the words tasting like bile in his throat, "but until the Witena Ġemōt has been convened, he is not my king. Nor yours."

Fordraed's eyes flickered nervously from Beobrand to Oswald's deathly pallid, rotting face.

"You riddle with me, Beobrand. You know as well as I that the wise men of the moot will declare Oswiu king."

"Perhaps, but we are here and Oswiu has ridden east. To Bebbanburg."

"Then," said Fordraed, his voice rising once more as his impotent anger bubbled up within him, "we will ride to Bebbanburg and there you will hear what the Witena Ġemōt has surely already proclaimed."

Beobrand carefully returned Oswald's head to the sack, closing the opening and once again hiding the terrible reminder of their king's death. The stink of death hung in the air, but the men in the shelter visibly relaxed. As soon as the head was once more concealed, the wind gusted outside, buffeting the tent walls and causing the tapers' flames to gutter and dance.

"No," said Beobrand, "I will ride to Ubbanford and to the hall of Stagga. I must give the grievous news of two great men's deaths to their wives and children." He stepped forward and thrust the sack towards Fordraed. "You can take the head of this great king to his brother and the wise men of the moot."

The corpulent thegn blinked and stared at the sack, but did not reach out to take it.

"You should heed me, Beobrand," he said, his tone growing strident, "I have the ear of Oswiu. Gone is the favour you found under Oswald. Oswiu is not like his brother."

"No," said Beobrand, shoving the sack at Heremod, who reluctantly took it. "He is not."

He did not wait for a reply. He could no longer bear to be in this noisome tent. If he remained here, nothing would stop him from throttling the bag of piss who stood before him. Turning, Beobrand pushed the leather tent flap aside and stalked out into the wind-blown night.

PART FOUR
SLAUGHTER FOR THE SLAIN GOD

Chapter 50

"That doesn't look good," Cynan said. Beobrand glared at him before turning back to stare into the distance. Cynan felt foolish. Of course the smudge of smoke beyond the hills was not good. Good seldom came from a column of smoke on the horizon.

Looking back over his shoulder Cynan saw that the warband were not far behind. He had ridden ahead to join Beobrand.

As they had ridden from Rheged into the east, back into the heartlands of Bernicia, Beobrand had taken to riding at the head of the band of horsemen. He seldom spoke and the men had grown cautious in his company, scared of setting a spark to his infamous anger. At night Beobrand sat apart from them and whenever Cynan had approached him, to offer food or drink, he had found his lord staring away from the fire, peering into the night sky as if searching for something he had lost. Each morning Beobrand roused them with the first light of dawn, urging them to ride hard and not allowing them to set up camp until their shadows were long before them as the sun sank into the west.

They were all wary of him, feeling keenly his grief and sorrow. And yet this silent brooding unnerved them. Beobrand's ire was a savage thing that scops had spun into tales told throughout the halls of Albion. If their lord had raged and screamed, swearing vengeance and death upon his enemies, they would have felt more at ease. This sombre, all-consuming sadness had cast a pall over them all.

"Acennan was his closest friend," Gram had said to Cynan one evening as they sat beside the fire whispering in hushed tones for fear that Beobrand might overhear them. "But that is not all of it. He pushes us to ride hard as he carries the burden of dire tidings for Eadgyth and Cynethryth. He knows it is his duty to bring the tale of their husbands' deaths to them and so we hurry forward, back to Ubbanford. And all the while we ride closer to the moment he must face those women."

They had sat silently for a time, listening to the crackle of the campfire and the murmured conversations of the other men. Eventually Gram had broken the silence. "Beobrand is one of the bravest men I have ever known," he said, "but it is one thing to rush at a shieldwall where you can rely on your strength and sword-skill to slay your enemies. It is quite something else to face grieving widows and orphans."

As each day had passed, Beobrand's mood had grown darker. He rode some way ahead of his gesithas astride the majestic Sceadugenga and his men trailed in his wake. Sometimes he would spur the black stallion into a gallop, disappearing from view into the distance. The first time he had done this, Cynan had ridden after him. Following a brief pursuit where it had become clear that Cynan would soon catch up with his hlaford, Beobrand had reined in his mount and spun round to face the Waelisc warrior. A flash of his fabled fury had played across his features.

"I ride to be alone," Beobrand had growled, "not to be followed. Go back to the others."

Cynan had pulled his horse to a halt.

"If you wish, I will ride at a distance. But I will not leave you to ride alone."

Beobrand had glowered at him and for a time Cynan had thought his lord would scream at him, unleashing the rage that surely burnt just beneath the surface. Or perhaps he would even strike him. He had gritted his teeth, ready for whatever punishment Beobrand flung at him. But in the end, Beobrand had merely spat and, without speaking further, he had kicked his heels into Sceadugenga's flanks and galloped away. After that day Cynan had become Beobrand's shadow. He always kept Beobrand in sight, but never rode close enough to disturb him.

Until today.

Cynan had seen Beobrand halt on the brow of a hill. Beyond him, further to the north, a grey, feathered line of smoke rose high into the afternoon sky. They were close to the Tuidi now. Close to Ubbanford.

"What do you think it could be?" Cynan asked.

Beobrand did not answer. Some way off in the distance Cynan made out a speck of movement. A rider, galloping towards them. He recognised the gait of the rider, how he leaned to one side in the saddle.

Attor.

Without responding to Cynan's question, Beobrand kicked Sceadugenga forward and galloped down the slope to meet the scout.

"Wait, lord," Cynan called, "it may be dangerous."

Beobrand did not slow his progress and Cynan once again felt foolish. Danger would not deter Beobrand.

Cursing, Cynan waved at the column of horsemen who were still some distance behind them, beckoning for them to hurry. He hoped they would understand his signal, but he could not wait to see if they responded. He would not leave Beobrand and Attor to ride towards that smoke alone. Tugging his horse's head to the north, he galloped after Beobrand.

He had been right. No good ever came of smoke on the horizon.

As they breasted the hill to the south of Ubbanford, they had already known what they would find. The air was redolent of smoke and crows flecked the sky above the bend in the Tuidi where Ubbanford nestled. Beobrand, Attor and Cynan slowed their panting steeds for a moment as the extent of the horror in the valley came into view.

Smoke billowed from the blackened bones of Ubba's hall. Flames, small and almost sated now, yet licked at the charred beams. A few of the other buildings had also been destroyed by fire. Looking up at the hill, Sunniva's hall was also a smoking ruin. This was no fire caused by a stray spark or a dropped rush light, Ubbanford had been attacked and its buildings razed.

Cynan's stomach turned and he felt suddenly sick. Apart from the birds, those black corpse-feeding ravens and crows that gathered on a battlefield, all was still in Ubbanford. Cynan did not wish to ride down that slope. Ubbanford had been his home now for six years. These were his people. And he was scared of what he would find.

Unbidden, and with surprising ferocity, one name sprang into his mind.

Sulis.

Gods, please let her be spared.

As if on some unspoken signal, all three riders urged their mounts forward. The rest of the gesithas had caught up now and they rode behind them into Ubbanford, grim-faced and silent.

They made their way between the buildings warily, expecting an ambush at any time. But no attack came. Ubbanford was unnaturally still. Death had come to this place and had left none living after its passing.

In front of the small chapel that Beobrand had ordered built for the Christ followers, they found Gothfraidh. His head had been smashed, his brains splattered on the packed earth before the door. A crow had been gorging itself on the oozing matter from the monk's shattered skull, its black beak slick and shiny with gore. Attor leapt from his horse, chasing the bird away and it flapped onto the roof of the church, croaking angrily at being disturbed.

Near Ubba's hall they found signs of a fight. Two of Beobrand's warriors, who had remained behind to defend the village, lay dead before where the doors of the hall used to stand. The men wore no armour and bore no weapons.

"They probably came at night," said Gram.

They all knew how devastating a hall burning could be. Anyone trapped within would die from the fire or, if they were lucky enough to break out into the cool, life-giving air, they would meet with the iron and steel of those who had set the blaze. The gesithas had either rushed into the night without donning their battle-harness, or their bodies had been stripped by their killers.

Bearn stepped towards a third corpse. The man lay face down, pallid and blood-splattered. Again, he wore no armour. Bearn rolled him over onto his back. The man's throat had been cut and his head lolled at an impossible angle. Bearn shook his head.

"I do not recognise this one," he said.

The men gazed intently at the man's pale face. He had a thick beard of dark, wiry hair streaked with grey and there was an old, puckered scar on his left cheek. None of them knew him.

"At least those who attacked our folk felt the bite of their blades," said Fraomar. He hawked and spat into the stranger's face.

They found three more bodies in the settlement. Old Hunlaf's chest had been pierced with a spear that had been lodged so firmly between his ribs that its haft had splintered, leaving the weapon still buried within his flesh. A pang of sorrow stabbed through Cynan. Seeing the shepherd thus, mouth gaping in agony, his kirtle soaked crimson, saddened him terribly. The old man had always been kindly to Cynan. Where others had sometimes derided him for his Waelisc blood, Hunlaf had always offered Cynan a smile and a wave when he passed with his dog and sheep.

On the path that led down to the Tuidi were the twisted bodies of two young men. Not much more than boys, they were both well-known to the warriors. They were inseparable friends and had dreamt of joining Beobrand's warband when they were of age. But they had yet been too young to fight. Their fathers had bade them to wait one more year until they were old enough to carry spears for their lord. Cynan turned away from the boys' corpses. Their pale limbs were thin and weak. Their blood was bright against their corpse-pallor. They may have been too young to stand in the shieldwall, but they had been old enough to be killed.

One of the gesithas, a burly man with thinning, straggly straw-coloured hair, let out a wail of anguish. He jumped from his horse and collapsed beside the boys. For the first time since they had ridden into Ubbanford, Beobrand spoke.

"We will avenge your son, Ulf," he said and his voice was as brittle and cold as the ice that forms on the Tuidi in the deepest of winter. "We will find who did this, and we will slay them all. You have my word."

Beobrand left the man to his grief and spurred Sceadugenga up the hill towards the smouldering remains of Sunniva's hall. Cynan rode beside him, his stomach twisting and clenching with the fear of what they would find there. Was it possible that those from the village had sought shelter in the new hall? Would they find the rest of the people of Ubbanford slaughtered like so many cattle at Blotmonath?

They climbed the hill in silence. Again he offered up a silent prayer that Sulis would have escaped the horror that had descended upon Ubbanford. He knew she cared nothing for him. She was but a thrall and she despised him. And yet he could not bear the thought of her suffering more than she already had.

Heat still wafted from the embers of the hall. The roof had collapsed and most of the structure had been consumed by what must have been a terrible conflagration. Flames yet flickered around the few remaining pillars that jutted from the blackened debris. How many corpses did the rubble hide? Were the rest of the folk buried there? Had Sunniva's hall become the funeral pyre of Ubbanford?

Two bodies lay on the grass near the building. One was Lanferth, a man they all knew to be strong and dependable. Like the others, he too was devoid of weapons and armour. Beside him was the corpse of a man none of them recognised.

Beobrand dismounted and walked around the charred, smoking remains of his great hall. His face was thunder. His half-hand gripped Hrunting's pommel tightly while his right hand grasped in a white-knuckled fist the hammer amulet of Thunor that he always wore at his neck. His lips moved, but if he spoke aloud, the words were too quiet for Cynan to hear.

Cynan slid from his saddle and moved as close as he could to the wreck of the hall. The heat and smoke prevented him from getting too close. The acrid smoke stung his eyes. Peering into the debris, straining his eyes to pick out any detail, Cynan searched for a sign of people within the stricken building. But he saw none. At last he turned from the hall and walked to stand beside the great oak that grew some way off. He had often sat in the shade of this tree on summer evenings. He reached out and ran his hand over the rough bark. Its touch comforted him. He drew in a deep breath. Here, away from the smoking ruins, the air was clear and sweet in his lungs.

A sudden commotion drew his attention back to Ubbanford. The men had dispersed throughout the settlement, each checking for survivors or any other grisly reminders of the attack they had missed. Now Attor galloped up the slope towards the new hall. He reined in but did not dismount.

"What is it?" snapped Beobrand. His voice cracked in his throat, as raw as a crow's croak.

"They fled, lord," said Attor. He was breathless, panting.

"Fled?"

"Yes," said Attor, allowing a small smile to play on his lips, "they are not all dead, lord. I have followed their tracks across the Tuidi. There were many of them. They crossed the river and headed towards Stagga. Many of our folk, your folk, may yet live."

For a moment Cynan thought that Beobrand would not respond. He stared down at the charred remains of his hall, the home he had built with Sunniva, for a long while but then, with the alarming speed that made him such a formidable warrior, he turned and sprinted towards Sceadugenga. Springing up onto the stallion's back, Beobrand shouted in his battle-voice.

"We ride, men!" he bellowed and Cynan thought that even those far below in the valley must have heard him. "We ride to defend our loved ones, our people. And when we have found them and we have seen them safe, we will ride to slaughter their attackers."

The men mounted quickly and followed their leader as Beobrand rode down the hill towards the ford. Gone was the sombre, silent Beobrand of the past days. In his stead was the fury-fuelled, savage, death-dealing thegn of Bernicia, Lord of the Black Shields. Beobrand had once again found an enemy, and Cynan pitied them. They may yet be breathing, but Beobrand and his warband would hunt them down. And they would find them. And they would kill them.

Chapter 51

The hall was filled with misery. Coenred wiped the sweat from his brow on the sleeve of his robe. The hall was hot and the air felt thick. Coenred did not believe there had ever been as many people in Stagga as there were at that moment. Most of the population of Ubbanford and the major part of Acennan's folk, those who had once sworn allegiance to Nathair, were inside the dark confines of the hall. Those men hale enough to bear arms were near the entrance. Bassus and Cynethryth's men had positioned themselves by the double doors, watching the path that came from the forest in case the Mercians decided to pursue them.

It seemed unlikely now to Coenred that their purpose had been to kill. For the Mercians had outnumbered their warriors many times over. And yet they had allowed the people of Ubbanford to splash across the ford and to flee into the shadows beneath the trees on the northern bank. It was true that the door wardens and gesithas who remained in Ubbanford had put up a doughty resistance, slaying at least one of the Mercians. But it still seemed to Coenred that their attackers had allowed them to escape when it would have been all too easy for them to have cut them down, or to have enslaved them.

In the darkest corner of the hall, some of the children were crying. Coenred felt like weeping too. He looked down at his hands. They were covered in blood, crusted and brown now that it had dried. There had been no time yet for him to scrub them free of the gore. Much of that blood was Reaghan's. He could still barely believe what he had witnessed. Sulis' treachery had been sudden and desperate. She had plunged her knife into Reaghan, leaving her for dead. Coenred thought of how his fingers had slipped against the bubbling blood that swelled in the deep gash to Reaghan's midriff. He had done his best. There had been no time to pause, to heat water and to make poultices, but he had bound the wound as best he could, putting pressure on it as Aidan had shown him. He looked over to where she now lay surrounded by the women. The old woman Odelyna was there with them, burning her wyrts and whispering her ancient incantations. Coenred was tempted to chase her away from Reaghan. The foul-smelling smoke from the sage and mugwort would bring no benefit to Reaghan. But he was too tired. His hands trembled and he could not face the old witch. He frowned. The stench of the herb smoke would do Reaghan no good, but he was sure it would do her no harm either. Whether she lived or died would depend on his skill and on God's will. He prayed he had done enough. Reaghan's life was in God's hands now. There was nothing more that he could do.

"Do you think they will come for us?" asked Dalston, his voice tremulous and high-pitched.

Coenred sighed. Dalston's whining always irritated him. Coenred knew that his feelings were not those of a good monk. Gothfraidh always told him to think how Jesus would have reacted. "It is your duty to seek the strength of God and to behave more like Him. To put aside your petty annoyances." Gothfraidh had always been good at telling Coenred what he should do. Coenred felt tears welling and cuffed at his eyes with his already damp and stained sleeve. No longer would the old monk be there to guide him, to make him act more like Christ.

One of the men had told Coenred how he had seen the old monk struck down by the Mercians. Coenred had hoped that perhaps the man had been mistaken, that perhaps Gothfraidh was only injured and would yet find his way here to Acennan's hall. But the warrior had shaken his head. "No, Coenred," the gruff man had said, with an unusual tenderness in his voice, "the good monk has gone to sit with God in his Mead Hall in heaven." Coenred had not replied that he doubted that God drank mead; that the Almighty was not Woden, not one of the old gods. He was touched that the man had thought to console him with words that he must have half-remembered from the preachings he had heard from Gothfraidh and the other monks.

"Will they come for us?" asked Dalston again, his voice scratching yet further at Coenred's frayed nerves.

Coenred took a deep breath of the heavy air of the hall.

"No, Dalston," he said, fighting to keep the frustration from his voice, "I don't think they will follow us here. They let us go easily enough."

"Easily?" squeaked Dalston. "They killed Gothfraidh..."

"I know and I mourn him. But had they been intent on killing us, they would not have allowed us to cross the Tuidi."

Dalston's brow furrowed. He did not seem convinced, but he fell silent.

A strident voice cut through the hubbub of the hall, drawing Coenred's attention to the men gathered in the doorway.

"I would never have thought you craven, Bassus!" shouted Nothelm, a tall man with black hair and close-cropped beard. "And yet you would have us remain here with the women and children."

Bassus stepped forward, towering over the man.

"Do not forget yourself, boy," he said, his voice a deep rumble, like the grumbling of an angry boar. "I was a king's champion while you were still sucking on your mother's teats. I may only have one arm, but I am no coward and could still send the likes of you to the afterlife without breaking a sweat."

Nothelm glared at Bassus for a moment and Coenred worried he would strike the one-armed warrior. But at last, he took a step back and lowered his gaze. Bassus nodded, but did not speak.

"Then why are we to remain here?" Nothelm asked. The sharp edge had gone from his tone. "With Acennan's few men, ours, and Cynethryth's, we would number as many as those Mercian bastards. And this time we would not be surprised. We should return to Ubbanford and slay them. Shieldwall to shieldwall, as warriors."

"And who would protect our folk? What if the Mercians came here? Or perhaps a band of Picts?"

Some of the listeners scowled at Bassus. They had been Nathair's folk. They may have sworn their oaths to Acennan and Bernicia, but they were still Picts.

"No Picts have attacked us for years," said Nothelm.

"And when was the last time that Mercians raided into the north of Bernicia?" asked Bassus, raising an eyebrow.

Coenred had overheard many whispered conversations all that day questioning how it was that Mercians came to be so far north. There seemed to be only one conclusion and it was not a pleasant thought. If Beobrand was known to have fallen in battle along with his comitatus and warband, the Mercians would know that his famed treasure would be left unguarded.

Nothelm frowned.

"Those Mercians surely came in search of Beobrand's hoard. By now they will be riding south, bound for Mercia once more."

"You may well speak the truth," answered Bassus, "but I know that the people of Ubbanford are more precious to our lord Beobrand than his gold and silver. We cannot leave them unprotected."

Nothelm spat into the rushes in disgust, but said no more.

Coenred let out his breath. Thank the Lord that Bassus would not abandon them. It seemed most likely that Nothelm had the right of it and that Halga and his Mercians would have taken all they were able to carry and set off southward once more. And yet the thought that they might once again descend upon them here in Stagga to finish what they had started in Ubbanford filled him with terror.

"All will be well," he whispered to Dalston. "We are safe here."

Dalston was pale, but offered Coenred a small nod of gratitude.

And then, as if God sought to show him humility, to test him with yet more trials, a sudden shout once again shattered the subdued, hushed quiet of the hall.

"To arms," yelled one of Cynethryth's gesithas who had been left outside watching the forest path. "Armed horsemen approach!"

Chapter 52

Beobrand kicked Sceadugenga forward. He wished to push the stallion into a gallop, but he held back. The gods alone knew how much further he might have to travel this day. The beast was strong and seemed always willing to run, but Beobrand was wary of exhausting the animal.

The stench of burning and death still caught in his throat and clung to his clothes. As they had ridden from Rheged, Beobrand had dreaded reaching his home, for he knew that then he would need to give the darkest tidings imaginable. And yet he had also longed to be home in his hall. To see Reaghan and Octa. To be surrounded by familiar things and to be far from the stink of death and war. Each night he would sit and wonder how he would speak to Eadgyth and Cynethryth of their husbands' deaths. The men would try to talk to him, but he could not bear to speak. How could he? How could he tell his gesithas that he was done with death? It seemed to him he had carried so much anger within for so long that he had forgotten all else. And what had that ire brought him save pain? Oswald, the man who had given him everything was slain, his head rotting in a sack.

As he rode through the dappled light of the forest path north of the Tuidi, he reached down with his left hand and reassured himself that the sack attached to his saddle was yet secure. Gods, he could not believe that Acennan too had left him. The stocky warrior had always seemed invincible. Solid and stable, like a rock in a storm-swept sea. And yet, nobody could escape the cold clutch of death. When the Sisters of Wyrd cut a man's life thread, no matter how great the man, there was no way to avoid the inevitable. But gods, if only he had not sent Acennan with the others to lead away the defenders from the tree at Maserfelth. He told himself on those dark nights, staring at the unblinking eyes of the stars, that Acennan had come up with the plan and had said he would lead the small band of men that would act as a diversion. Beobrand had not sent him to his death. Acennan had chosen his path and would have wanted it no other way. But his loss had left Beobrand hollow, devoid of anything but despair and gloom.

The closer they had got to Ubbanford, the more anxious he had become at having to deliver his terrible tidings to women who would soon discover they were widows. But he also vowed to himself that he would embrace the small pleasures of life. He would talk with Reaghan. Perhaps he could rekindle the passion they had once felt. He would take an interest in Octa, rather than brushing him aside. His son was his only blood kin and he would grow into a man all too soon. Then he would look upon his father as a burden and not as someone to be revered. Beobrand would not send the boy away again to be fostered, no matter what Oswiu might order of him. He would see that the boy was well-trained with sword, shield and spear.

Reaghan and Octa were his future and he wished to look to them, to lighter times. The past was dark, a land he did not wish to visit again in his thoughts.

Cynan cantered up beside Beobrand. The Waelisc warrior had given him no peace on the ride homeward, seeming to have taken it upon himself to follow his lord wherever he went. It had irked Beobrand at first, but he had come to accept Cynan's presence. The erstwhile thrall had looked upon Acennan as a father, or perhaps an older brother. He too must be hurting at Acennan's death.

"We are almost at Stagga," Cynan said.

Beobrand nodded. He knew this path well. Soon they would leave the dense forest behind and the houses clustered around Stagga would be before them.

"Ready yourselves, men," Beobrand shouted. "We know not what awaits us."

He touched Hrunting's hilt. If the men who had destroyed Ubbanford were even now assaulting Acennan's folk, they would regret not having fled from these lands. Beobrand clenched his jaw and frowned. It would ever be thus, he thought grimly. He would wish to be rid of killing and death, but battle and blood would always seek him out. When the scops sang of him, they told tales of a great lord of war, but Beobrand wondered whether he was truly the master of anything and not merely a slave to battle and slaying.

He shook his head to clear it of such thoughts. He may wish to be done with death, but it seemed death was not yet done with him.

"Come, my brave gesithas," he bellowed, at last kicking Sceadugenga into a gallop. "Let us see whether any of our folk's slayers have been foolish enough to remain where our spears and swords can reach them."

Sceadugenga surged forward, carrying him out of the tree-gloom and into the bright, late afternoon sunshine. Cynan rode at his shoulder, a savage grin upon his face. Behind them, ready for battle and vengeance, came his warband of black-shielded warriors.

Beobrand strode into the hall. It stank of sweat, smoke and the bitter iron tang of blood. It was the stench of battle and fear.

"Father!" came the cry from within the gloom at the rear of the building where too many people cowered.

Octa ran forward, his face tear-streaked and pallid. For a moment Beobrand thought his son would launch himself upon him, embracing him. But the boy slowed his rush, looking up at Beobrand with a sombre expression on his round child face.

Beobrand's heart swelled to see Octa alive and hale.

"Well met, son," he said, awkward in the gaze of so many.

Stagga was crammed with the folk from Ubbanford, Acennan's people and also some of Cynethryth's retinue. There had been a moment when Beobrand and his warband had approached the hall when he had thought they would need to fight, that the attackers of Ubbanford had taken Acennan's hall. The warriors who had stood outside the great doors had been unknown to him. They had raised their shields and spears defensively. Bravely, Beobrand had thought, given the numbers in his band and the handful of defenders before the hall. He had been prepared to order the attack when a giant figure had emerged into the sunlight. Beobrand had recognised him at once.

Bassus.

Seeing the huge, one-armed warrior had shone some light into the darkened recesses of Beobrand's mind where for many days only gloom and despair had resided. He had jumped from Sceadugenga's back and run to Bassus. He had surprised the man by wrapping his arms about him, so glad was he to see him. Beobrand felt a thin pang of regret that Octa had not leapt into his arms. He could not recall when he had last held the boy. Before he had been able to walk, most likely.

Looking upon all the people gathered in the hall, he turned to Bassus now.

"You have done well, my friend."

"Not well enough," Bassus grumbled. "Those bastard Mercians caught us by surprise."

Beobrand noticed the stiffening in the faces of Cynethryth's men. These were proud Mercian warriors. They would soon hear that their lord was slain. Beobrand would do well to tread carefully here.

"But by Tiw's cock," continued Bassus, "it could have been much worse. Or perhaps I should thank the Christ, for without His servants, brave Coenred and Dalston, we might all have perished, sealed in our halls and roasted."

"Coenred is here?" asked Beobrand.

In answer, the young monk stepped forward. He had a dark smudge on his shaved forehead. His eyes were shadowed and pinched. Beobrand saw his hands were encrusted in dried blood.

"I am glad to see you well," Beobrand said. "So how is it you saved the folk of Ubbanford?"

Coenred frowned and Beobrand wondered whether he would weep.

"Not all the folk escaped," he said. "I did nothing. I was awake early and saw the warriors. Dalston and I were able to raise the alarm."

"Then once again I owe you," said Beobrand, forcing a smile onto his lips. "And this time it is not my life that I must thank you for, but something of much more import. The life of my folk," he reached out for Octa and pulled the boy to stand at his side, " and my son." He scanned the faces of the people in the hall. He spied Rowena and Eadgyth towards the rear.

"Where is Reaghan?" he asked, and he heard the tremor in his voice and felt the prickle of fear scratch his neck.

The hall was hushed and for several heartbeats nobody spoke. In that moment, Beobrand knew he had not heard the last of the bad tidings that day. His guts squirmed, anxiety making him feel sick. He opened his mouth to speak into the silence. His voice cracked. Octa's tiny shoulder trembled beneath Beobrand's hand. Beobrand cleared his throat with a guttural cough and managed to utter, "Is she killed?"

Eadgyth stood. She was a beauty, with raven-black hair and ice-blue eyes. Acennan had been smitten the moment he had seen her. He had been lucky indeed to convince her kin to allow her to wed him. Beobrand thought of his friend's head, staring blindly into the darkness of the sack tied to Sceadugenga's saddle. He blinked back the sting of tears.

All the while he had feared bringing the news of Acennan's death to Eadgyth, and now, to judge from the solemn expression on her face, she was about to tell him that he had lost his woman. He gripped Octa to him tightly and tried in vain not to think of a cold cavern on Muile where Nelda the cunning woman had cursed him to die alone.

Eadgyth's eyes shone in the gloom. They had known each other for years, and each seemed to be sensing the words the other was about to speak. But then Eadgyth surprised him by saying, "Reaghan lives, lord." A great shudder racked his body. "But she is sorely wounded," she continued. "She may yet succumb to the wound."

He thought of Reaghan as he had last seen her, watching him ride away from Ubbanford. Her long hair had blown about her features, the wind had pressed her dress against her slender form. She had been angry with him and had not smiled as he'd waved farewell. He could not remember now why they had argued.

For a moment, Beobrand knew not what to say. He had prepared the words in his mind over and again as he had sat staring into the darkness each night and as he had ridden Sceadugenga over the hills and vales of Bernicia. But now, when faced with Acennan's widow, he was lost.

"And my husband?" Eadgyth whispered.

Beobrand's mouth was dry. He daren't speak. If he spoke the words, he knew that he would be unmanned before all his folk. And he was their lord. Their hlaford. He was Beobrand of Ubbanford, thegn of Bernicia and he must not weep before his people.

He stared into Eadgyth's eyes. Tears brimmed there.

He shook his head and cast his gaze down, unable to watch her misery. As if they had been waiting for his command, Eadgyth's tears fell. She turned away from him and gathered her children to her. Their shoulders shook and their sobs were loud in the still that had fallen over the hall.

Beobrand wished he could cry with them. Acennan had been his friend, closer to him than any kinsman he had ever known. But no. He had shed his tears back in Rheged. Now was the time for strength.

Besides, there was further sorrow he had to bring to this place.

Steeling himself, he sought out Cynethryth amongst the womenfolk at the rear of the hall. There she was, standing tall and proud, her sons, wide-eyed and pale at her side. He was ashamed at himself for not offering the words he had prepared to Eadgyth. Cynethryth was the wife of an atheling. She deserved the respect of hearing the dire news from Beobrand's mouth.

He squeezed Octa's shoulder briefly, signalling to the boy to remain where he was. Then Beobrand stepped solemnly towards Cynethryth. The hall was as still as a barrow mound, and silent save for the muffled sounds of grief from Eadgyth and her children. Beobrand clenched his fists and squared his shoulders. He must be strong. He opened his mouth to speak, but before he made a sound Cynethryth spoke in a clear voice.

"Do not say the words, Beobrand," she said, her voice calm and controlled.

"But, Lady—" he stammered.

"No," she cut off his words, "I do not want to hear. There is too much sorrow and pain here this day. My husband is yet fighting his brother far to the south. I told you to protect him." Cynethryth stared into Beobrand's eyes. He could not hold her gaze.

"You did," he whispered.

"And did you?"

"I did my best," Beobrand said, his tone desolate.

Cynethryth nodded.

"Very well. Now, come and see your lady. She is drifting in and out of slumber, but your presence will surely bring her some comfort."

*

"You are sure they were Mercians?" Beobrand asked, his tone sharp, brittle.

He had drained two horns full of strong mead, but the potent brew had not appeared to have dulled any of the jagged edges of his suffering. The hall was subdued. People talked in hushed tones as though they half-listened to the night outside the hall, for sounds of another attack from the darkness. Beobrand was confident they would be safe that night. He had positioned guards all around the settlement and there was no way an enemy could approach without the alarm being raised. Besides, if the attackers were truly Mercians, they were surely heading back south. He still found it hard to believe.

"Cynethryth knew the leader," said Bassus, picking up a hunk of bread and tearing off a piece with his teeth. He paused to chew, picked up his horn and drank deeply. "He was a huge brute of a man. Taller than me even, and looked to have the strength of a bear."

"Could she not be mistaken?"

Bassus shook his head.

"He was the kind of man you would never forget. A giant with a thick beard as red as fire."

"Halga," breathed Beobrand.

"Aye, the same," said Bassus.

Beobrand frowned. How could this be? He had seen the son of Grimbold at the battle of Maserfelth. Why would the Mercian risk riding so deep into Northumbrian territory? If Beobrand had returned home directly after Oswald's death, Halga would have found Ubbanford thick with Bernician spear-men. And yet… Beobrand had not come home, because he had been sent south once more on an errand as likely to see him killed as to succeed. And who was it who had sent him on that foolhardy mission into the jaws of the wolf?

Beobrand thought back to the last time he had faced Halga in combat in the forest glade near Grimbold's hall in Mercia. That had been years before, but he still recalled the giant's speed and prodigious strength. And how he had needed to use all his guile to best him.

And he remembered Wybert's last whispered word to him before he had delivered the thrust that had sent Sunniva's defiler to the afterlife.

He had thought that Oswiu had ordered him south not to find his brother's head, but to die. Now he wondered. He lifted his horn to his lips and found it empty. Eadgyth, face sombre and strained, made to refill it with mead. Beobrand shook his head.

"Ale, please, dear Eadgyth," he said. He was surprised that she had not retired to her sleeping quarters, but she was a strong woman who knew her mind, and he would not send her away. She lifted a second pitcher and poured ale. "My thanks," he said, "I will be needing my wits about me tomorrow."

"You will ride then, lord?" she asked.

He nodded and took a draught of the ale. It was bitter after the mead, but it was good. He had no appetite, but he picked up a piece of the bread and some cheese and ate. He needed to keep strong. Grief threatened to engulf him in its black wings, but he must fend it off. He had wished to be done with death, but that had been before he had seen the smoking, crumbled and charred ruin of his home, the pale corpses of his people. And the tiny, deathly white face of sweet Reaghan, sheened with sweat. To see her thus, in a slumber so deep from loss of blood that she was more in the otherworld than on middle earth, had filled him with dread. Would he lose her too, as he had lost so many?

And then he had heard the tale of how she had been struck down by one of the very women he had rescued from Fordraed. He had grown morose, gulping down great mouthfuls of mead in the hope they would wash away the taste of his failure.

"You cannot change wyrd," Bassus had said, placing his hand on Beobrand's shoulder, "but you can put up a good fight."

Bassus had grinned, despite the sadness in the hall. Beobrand had not smiled, but he had listened to the old warrior's words and heard the truth in them.

"Wyrd may be inexorable, Beobrand," Bassus had continued, "but you will never lie down and give in to your fate. It is not in your nature."

Beobrand had nodded, silent anger burning away the sorrow within him, replacing it with a raging furnace of fury.

He reached out and gripped Eadgyth's hand tightly.

"Yes, we will ride at first light," he said. She held his stern stare for a long while.

"It is almost harvest," she said, her voice so quiet that he had to strain to hear. Her words surprised him. He was consumed by the all too familiar need for vengeance and she spoke of bringing in the crops for the winter.

"We will return before harvest, Eadgyth. Do not fear."

"The winter will be long and food is always scarce ere spring comes."

"Do you hear that, men?" Beobrand bellowed, startling the people of the hall with his sudden shout. "We ride at dawn. We will seek out the cowards who attacked our home, and we will kill them and be back before the reaping. There may be fewer mouths to feed now, but there are Mercians to slay before the harvest."

Chapter 53

Beobrand wiped the rainwater from his face and surveyed the horizon. He saw no movement in the valley to the south. The hills in the distance were hazed by the rain that had fallen constantly for the last two days.

"Any sign of them?" asked Bearn, also peering into the distance.

Beobrand swung around in his saddle, looking behind them, back into the north. The clouds were black, and the wind drove the cold rain into his face. In the valley below, on the old road, his warband travelled on. He saw nobody else abroad on such a day. Most men would be in their halls. Men who rode in this rain did so out of necessity. Men who journeyed in such weather were up to mischief.

Or in search of revenge.

"I see nobody but us on this path," Beobrand said.

"You think the plan will work?" asked Bearn.

Beobrand cast him a sidelong glance.

"If the gods and wyrd will it," he replied. "I trust Attor. I know of no one better at reading sign."

Bearn grunted. Beobrand knew Bearn didn't much like Attor, but there was no questioning the man's tracking skills.

When they had left Stagga, they had returned to Ubbanford just before the rain had begun to fall. Attor had walked around

Ubbanford, kneeling from time to time, pressing his hand into depressions in the earth, examining patches of ground that looked like any other to Beobrand. He had taken so long that the men had grown restless and impatient.

"We are wasting time here," Ulf had snapped at the tracker. "The bastards who killed my boy are riding ever further from this place."

Beobrand understood the man's anguish, he too felt the pressure of time passing. In his mind's eye he could see Halga and his warband making their way southward, towards Mercia, and sanctuary. But Beobrand needed to know what they would face when they ran the Mercians to ground.

And they needed a plan.

Eventually, Attor had come to him. He had read the tracks and had a proposal.

Beobrand had thought it a good one.

Now, sitting astride Sceadugenga next to Bearn on the hill, drenched beneath a leaden sky, he began to question his decision to send Attor, Cynan and eight others away. His mind tugged at the memory of Acennan riding from the main body of his warband. Beobrand spat. He could not dwell on such things. The plan was good.

"Attor will send word soon," he said, forcing confidence into his voice. Bearn nodded and the two of them rode down to rejoin the horsemen in the valley below.

It continued to rain and the men trudged on through the day in grim silence. Soon after they had halted for a brief rest, there was a sudden commotion in the rear ranks. Beobrand tensed, reaching for Hrunting, before sighing in relief to see a lone rider galloping through the sheets of rain. It was Cynan.

The Waelisc rider brought his mount to a skidding halt before Beobrand. Cynan was mud-spattered and as wet as though he had swum in his clothes, but he still rode with an elegance and control Beobrand could never hope to know.

"Well met, lord," Cynan said, his tone serious, but with the edge of excitement Beobrand recognised in those men most naturally suited to warfare. He knew that feeling well. The thrill of impending battle.

"What news?" Beobrand asked.

"We found them easily enough. It was as Attor said it would be. They number a score of men, and they have two heavily laden carts with them. Filled with your treasure, I'd wager."

"Where are they?"

"On Deira Stræt. They would be slow enough without this rain, but as it is, they are progressing at the pace of a snail."

Beobrand frowned.

"And they ride openly on the road?"

"Aye, they have made no attempt to conceal themselves, not that they could with those carts. But no, they ride as if they were Northumbrians."

The brashness of Halga's raid smacked of treachery.

"Well, we will show them what happens when they meet some Northumbrians, won't we, lads?"

The gesithas let out a desultory cheer.

"And they did not spot you, Cynan?"

"No, lord, we have been as invisible as wraiths. And this weather has helped."

"How long until they reach the Wall?" Beobrand judged their own position. They were on a road less-travelled, but without carts to slow them, they would be at the Great Wall by dusk.

Cynan shrugged.

"Perhaps before nightfall tomorrow. Maybe the next day."

"Good. We will be in position well before then. They will regret the day they crossed Beobrand of Ubbanford."

Chapter 54

It continued to rain, a seething, bitter downpour that soaked the land turning the earth to thick cloying mud. They arrived at the Wall near Hefenfelth as the sun coloured the clouds in the west red and gold, so that they looked like billows of smoke from a blazing bone-fire. Beobrand ordered the men to set up camp on the southern side of the massive stone barrier that stretched both east and west until it was lost to sight in the rain-misted distance. They traipsed, bedraggled and tired after the long ride, through the great, crumbling fortified gate. The tall structure provided them with some shelter, but they passed a miserable, chill night, as Beobrand forbade them from lighting fires.

When Eadgard had grumbled, Beobrand had replied that it was better to be cold than to warn their enemy of their presence with trails of smoke. Eadgard had wrapped his sodden cloak about his shoulders and slouched down to sit with his back against the hewn rocks of the Wall. Nobody else questioned Beobrand's order.

Beobrand had posted men on the crumbling ramparts with a warning that they were there to see, not to be seen.

All the next day the rain fell. Few people travelled in such weather, but a couple of drovers with half a dozen cattle came up from the south, wishing to push their animals through the gate and on towards Stanfordham where they said Lord Merehwit was waiting for them for his daughter's wedding feast. Beobrand knew of Merehwit. He was a fat, choleric man, with a sour-faced wife and an unhappy household.

Beobrand turned the men away. He would not have them warning Halga of what awaited him at the Wall.

The older of the drovers raged at him.

"If I don't get those beasts to Lord Merehwit in time, he'll likely string me up. I need to be paid, not killed by the likes of you," he said, clearly placing Beobrand into the same group of nobles as Lord Merehwit. The drover may well be right, but Beobrand would not allow him to pass. In the end, Beobrand gave the man a chunk of hack silver in exchange for the cows with a promise that he would deliver them to Merehwit as soon as he had concluded with his business at the Wall. The man had grumbled and groaned, but had snatched up the silver quickly enough. The younger of the two men had gawped at the shiny metal in the older man's hands.

"That is so much silver, pa," he had said, mouth agape. "More than I ever did hope to see in this life."

The old man had cuffed him hard about the head and shoved him away from the warriors and the Wall.

"When we have done with the Mercian scum and can safely light a fire, we will slaughter one of these kine and feast our victory," Beobrand had told the men and that had cheered them for a spell.

All that long day, as the rain blurred the distance, Beobrand paced and fretted. He climbed up onto the Wall and gazed out northward. He had sent Cynan back to join Attor and to tell him they would be waiting. Looking over to the north-east, Beobrand scanned the dense woodland of aspen and oak. There was no sign of the men who hid there. The forest lay someway distant from the gate. The men who had built this fortification had cleared the land all around so that they would never be taken by surprise. Some shrubs and trees had sprung up over the generations since they had left Albion, but their mark on the land was yet clearly evident.

The plan was simple, but relied on timing. He had placed Bearn in charge of the warriors in the trees. The remainder of the men, some fifteen strong, were with him behind the Wall.

Beobrand clutched his mutilated hand to the Thunor's hammer at his throat.

Thunor, please grant me victory this day. I will give you blood and mayhem. Woden, All-father, I offer to you the lives of my enemies.

A sudden bluster of wind shook his heavy, water-logged cloak and he realised it had stopped raining. He wondered whether the gods truly cared for anything that men did. When he had left Stagga, Coenred had surprised him. He had pulled Beobrand to one side and offered him his Christ god's blessing. Then, as Beobrand had pulled his cloak about him, ready to step into the rain that had started to fall in the night, the young monk had clutched at his arm.

"Find them, Beo," he'd said, the intensity of his emotion causing him to shake.

Beobrand had nodded, his face grim.

"I will."

"Find them," Coenred had repeated, "and…"

Beobrand had paused, waiting for Coenred to find the words.

"Avenge Gothfraidh," he'd said at last. And then, as if the words had hurt him, Coenred had let out a sob and fled back into the dark of the hall.

Beobrand had stared after him for a time. To hear Coenred asking for revenge saddened Beobrand almost as much as anything else that had befallen him in the last weeks. Coenred was ever forgiving, always seeking peace. Beobrand had grown to expect Coenred's reprobation whenever he spoke of battles or vengeance. For the monk to speak of revenge was to feel the solid earth shifting like a quagmire beneath his feet. Nothing was as it should be.

A flock of birds fluttered into the sky in the distance, where the road came from between two bluffs. Beobrand fixed his gaze on the road but he could not make out anything. His eyes were not the best.

"Fraomar," he barked, "what do you see there?"

Fraomar shaded his eyes with his hand and stared for a long while before turning to his lord and nodding.

"They are coming," he said.

"Down from the Wall," Beobrand shouted. He looked at the sinking sun in the west, gauging how much daylight was left. Gods, he prayed that the plan would work. Scrambling down from the ramparts, he snatched up his helm from where he had left it beneath his saddle, out of the rain.

"Prepare for slaughter, my brave gesithas," he shouted at the men who were busy shrugging on their rusting byrnies and hefting their black shields. "Ready your weapons. They will drink of Mercian blood before night falls."

After readying themselves for battle, Beobrand and his gesithas stood in the shadow of the Wall and waited. As is so often the way, time seemed to pass more slowly as the moment to fight approached. They had been standing for so long, shivering from the damp clothes cooling against their skin, that Beobrand began to wonder if somehow Halga had scented the trap and had outsmarted them.

Beobrand closed his eyes and pictured the land north of the Wall. The Roman road passing between the two hills. The woodland where his men were hidden. The Wall and the fortified opening where once a great gate would have stood, but now yawned open and inviting. What had he missed? He checked again that Hrunting was safely in its scabbard and that his seax was secure in its sheath, then rubbed absently at his right leg. He recalled how Halga's hunting dog had leapt out of the forest in Mercia and clamped its jaws onto his thigh. He had been blinded by his desire for vengeance then. Had he been blinded again?

"What do you see?" he called up to Fraomar. He had left the keen-eyed man on the Wall, where he watched from a crack in the masonry.

For a moment, Fraomar did not reply and small teeth of worry gnawed at Beobrand.

"Fraomar," he hissed.

"Soon, lord," came the whispered response. "The Mercians are close. Attor and the others have just shown themselves. They are riding towards them along the road. The Mercians are in confusion."

Fraomar fell silent again and Beobrand tried to imagine what the young warrior could see. He was tempted to poke his head out and look for himself, but if the Mercians saw him, they would get wind of the ambush, and their defeat would be all the more difficult. He waited, breathing through his mouth and straining to hear any sound that might filter through the rock of the Wall and give some clue as to what occurred to the north.

Everything relied now on Bearn's timing.

Beobrand held his breath.

Woden, bring me victory and I will heap the corpses in your honour.

"Bearn has come from the wood," came the excited whisper from Fraomar.

There was a long pause. Beobrand gripped the Thunor hammer amulet at his throat so tightly that his knuckles showed white in the shadow of the Wall.

What was happening? No sound reached him. Nothing to indicate whether the trap was going to work.

"They've seen them." Another pause as Fraomar peered through the gap in the stonework. "The Mercians are not standing to fight. They are hurrying towards the gate."

Beobrand let out a long breath and then filled his lungs with the cool, wet, earthy air. He offered up a silent prayer to Woden then. The All-father was ever thirsty for lifeblood. Beobrand would give him a glut of the stuff before sunset.

"You know what to do, lads," he said, his voice low. Around him, his gesithas tensed, flexing muscles that had grown stiff from inactivity. Ulf caught his gaze and nodded urgently, his eyes wide and crazed with the prospect of spilling the blood of those who had taken the life of his beloved son.

Fraomar dropped down from the ramparts and scooped up his spear and shield from where they had been propped against the stone.

"How far are they from the gate?" Beobrand asked him.

Before Fraomar could answer, the first of the Mercians clattered through the opening in the Wall. And the chaos and joy of battle swept over Beobrand like a wave.

Chapter 55

Beobrand waited until several Mercian riders had passed through the gateway before giving the order to attack. Each of the horsemen reined in their steed, clearly readying themselves to dismount. The sixth rider must have seen the warriors waiting stealthily in the shadows behind the Wall, or perhaps he saw something in the faces of the lead horsemen who were casting about them, eyes wide in surprise, beginning to realise that they had ridden into a trap. Whatever the reason, the sixth man yanked the reins of his stallion hard, turning the mount in a scraping slew of mud. He was quick-witted this one, and a good rider too, for he kept his seat.

"It's a trap!" he shouted at the same instant that Beobrand bellowed for his warband to attack.

"Now!"

At the order, his gesithas surged forward from both sides of the gateway. They bore their spears high and the sharp points found the flesh of beast and man alike as the Mercian horsemen attempted to turn and flee. The screams of wounded horses were drowned beneath the roaring battle-cry of Beobrand's black-shielded killers. Beobrand was closest to the gate's opening and he sprang forward, thrusting the leaf-shaped blade of his spear at the sixth rider, who, for an eye-blink had his back to the lord of

Ubbanford. The Mercian's horse's hooves slipped and skidded, churning up the mud beneath the Wall. The beast struggled to gain purchase on the wet ground and almost toppled over. Its eyes were white-rimmed as it sent up great splashing clods of muck into the air. Beobrand marvelled at the rider's skill. Most men would have been unseated by such a manoeuvre, and yet this man remained atop his mount and would surely have escaped and ridden away had not Beobrand's probing spear found the nape of his neck. The steel point, bearing the full weight of Beobrand's charge, entered the man's flesh as easily as if it were smoke. The metal sliced through sinew and bone and instantly the Mercian was dead, a limp corpse where a heartbeat before had ridden a vital warrior filled with vigour. Beobrand twisted his spear and pulled it back. Blood gushed red and hot from the man's neck as he tumbled from his terrified horse. The animal, its hooves finally gripping in the mud, sprang away in the direction from which it had come. Beobrand let it go.

On the south side of the Wall the other five Mercians were all dead or dying. One lay pinned beneath his horse. A broken spear jutted from the animal's chest and it bellowed and thrashed its legs in agony. As Beobrand watched, Fraomar plunged his spear into the trapped Mercian's chest.

Another horse, riderless, eyes rolling in terror, galloped towards the gate. Beobrand leapt aside to allow it to pass.

Judging that his gesithas were in control, Beobrand turned his attention northward.

Closer than he had imagined, barely a spear's throw distant, two carts lumbered, pulled behind brawny, hang-horned oxen. Beyond them, in the distance, Beobrand recognised Attor, Cynan and the small band of riders who had trailed Halga's steps all the way from Ubbanford. Off to Beobrand's right, and further away still, galloped the band of warriors led by Bearn. The thin sounds of their hollering war-cries reached Beobrand where he stood in the gateway.

Halga's men were in disarray. They milled about the carts, unsure of what to do. They had fallen into the trap perfectly. Believing themselves pursued from the north and with the defensible position of the gate in the Great Wall invitingly close to hand, they had hurried to make their stand there. But now, having seen their comrades slain by Beobrand's hidden force, they were confused, unsure how to proceed.

But these were trained killers, not brigands that could be easily frightened. Halga's gesithas were proud spear-men who had stood in battles in the service of their lord and their king. Their shock and surprise would not last long. Beobrand's gaze fell upon the bright red beard of the giant who led the men. Along with the remainder of his men, he had reined in his mount close to the waggons. Halga, his eyes burning with fury, stared back at Beobrand. He may have been caught momentarily off guard, but Halga showed no sign of fear.

"Shieldwall!" Halga screamed, his voice cutting through the distant sounds of the galloping men and the cries of the dying that emanated from south of the Wall behind Beobrand.

In an instant Beobrand could see that neither Attor nor Bearn would reach Halga's men before they had been able to dismount and form a shieldwall around the waggons. If they were allowed to form a strong defensive position, although outnumbered, the Mercians might yet be victorious. The fight would become a long, drawn-out, bloody affair. If Beobrand's gesithas were not able to press home the advantage of their numbers, a strong shieldwall of Mercians would exact a heavy toll on them.

Even as Halga and his men began to dismount, Beobrand sprinted forward. Dragging Hrunting from its scabbard, Beobrand let out a roar.

"For Oswald," he screamed, invoking the familiar battle-cry. "Black Shields, with me!"

In an instant his fears and concerns fled, replaced by the terrible thrill of battle. He felt his mouth twist into a wolf-like grin, baring his teeth as he loped towards his enemy. At the sudden turn of speed, Beobrand was once again reminded of when he had last faced Halga. His right thigh gave a twinge of pain but he ignored it, willing himself on to greater efforts. He knew not whether Fraomar, Eadgard, and the others had heard his cry and were following behind him. There was no time to look. If it was his wyrd to die here this day, so be it. But that red-bearded bastard would be going to the afterlife with him.

"Now you die," Beobrand yelled.

Halga's warriors were still in the process of dismounting. Beobrand would be upon them in moments. But Halga was as calm as he was fast. Leaping from his huge horse, he unslung the shield that had hung on his back and, turning to face Beobrand, drew his sword.

Beobrand let out a scream of rage. When faced with Beobrand in his war harness, bellowing his ire, wielding the famed sword Hrunting and hefting his crow-black shield, foe-men would often hesitate, or even turn and flee; something that would always spell their death. Beobrand had broken many shieldwalls simply with his weight, courage and the battle-fame that went before him like an unseen shield. The sight of the huge thegn, blue eyes burning cold beneath his great helm, mouth twisted into a feral snarl was enough to cause most adversaries to flinch. But Halga had faced Beobrand before and he was no ordinary foe.

The fire-haired giant bellowed his own roaring scream and rushed forward to meet Beobrand.

Beobrand ducked beneath Halga's wild swing, catching the sword blade on his shield's rim. His own thrusting attack slid harmlessly past Halga, as their shields connected. Beobrand grunted. It was as though he had collided with a boulder, as if he had run into a cliff. Gods, but the man was strong. Beobrand shoved against his linden board and jumped backwards, giving himself room to move. The last time they had fought, Halga had been armed with a spear and Beobrand had suffered from being held at bay by the longer weapon. This time, they both bore swords, and whilst Halga was taller and Beobrand knew him to be lightning quick, if he could move freely, Beobrand felt he would be able to best the Mercian.

Halga grinned over his shield rim, holding his sword loose and ready in the warrior stance.

"It is about time I repaid you for slaying my hound," he said. He swung his sword in a flourishing arc, before bringing the blade back to rest upon his shield's edge. "And for breaking my arm."

Fraomar and the rest of Beobrand's gesithas sprinted past them. They ran around the two massive warriors the way river water splashes around rocks in a rapids. Behind Halga, Beobrand saw his men meet the hastily forming Mercian shieldwall with a clatter of weapons and boards.

"I meant to kill you back then," Beobrand said. "I will put that right before the sun sets."

Halga laughed, a mad sound, like the cackle of a magpie.

"I have your wyrm's hoard, Beobrand. Wybert took your woman, now I have taken your gold."

Beobrand knew that he must not let his ire consume him. He would need all his wits and cunning to beat this beast of a man. But at the mention of Wybert and Sunniva, he felt the raging anger within him throw off its shackles. Springing forward he rained blows upon Halga's shield. Splinters flew, but Halga hardly seemed to notice attacks that would have downed a lesser man. He soaked up Beobrand's attack. Beobrand saw nothing but Halga now. His focus had become as sharp as Hrunting's patterned blade and he watched with a detached admiration as Halga deflected strike after strike. Then, with the incredible speed Beobrand remembered, Halga flicked out an attack of his own. Beobrand saw Halga's sword point clearly as it glittered in the dim light of the dying day.

Halga's blade would have taken him in the throat, if Beobrand had not thrown himself backwards, reversing his forward motion with a supreme effort. He felt the whisper of the metal as it passed not a finger's breadth from his unarmoured neck. Now it was Halga's turn to press the attack. Beobrand was dimly aware of his Bernician horsemen arriving at the waggons, as he was pushed ever further back by the giant Mercian.

Halga smashed great overarm swings of his sword into Beobrand's shield with such ferocity that with each blow Beobrand's forearm throbbed. In a matter of moments his left arm was numb from elbow to wrist and he was glad of the straps he used to reinforce his grip on his shield.

A sliver of fear worked its way through Beobrand's anger. By Woden, the man was a monster, his strength and power incredible. With each crushing blow that rang through the hide, wood and iron boss of his shield, Beobrand would see an opening where he might send Hrunting's blade into Halga's arm, or leg, or throat. But such was the power of the Mercian's hacking strikes that it was all he could do to block the attacks, and each instant passed before he could act. Beobrand tried to skitter back, using his famed speed to put some distance between him and Halga.

And yet Halga was just a fast as him. Perhaps faster, whispered a dark, sibilant voice in Beobrand's mind. As Beobrand shuffled quickly back, seeking to distance himself, Halga used the momentary shift in their stances to send a slicing blow at Beobrand's leg. Beobrand had been so intent on the overarm hammering from Halga's blade, he had failed to anticipate the giant's low attack. Using all his skill and prodigious speed, Beobrand twisted his body and flung Hrunting's blade downward in a furious attempt to parry the blow. Steel met steel with a clang and the shock thrummed in his hand and arm. A heartbeat later, he felt a burning sting in his thigh.

Cursing silently, Beobrand jumped backwards, once more trying to escape Halga's savage sword.

This time, seemingly satisfied at having landed a blow at last, Halga allowed him to retreat a few paces. Beobrand's right thigh was hot and wet. He chanced a quick glance down and saw it was drenched and dark, his breeches sliced open in a long gash. Blood bubbled up from the deep cut.

"Does that pain you as much as my hound's strong bite?" asked Halga.

"It is but a scratch," snarled Beobrand. "I killed your pup of a dog and I will kill you just the same."

His words were empty bluster and, in the smiling eyes of the Mercian, Beobrand could see that Halga knew as much. The red-bearded giant laughed.

"I see the fear in your eyes, Beobrand," he said. "You have never been a match for me. Now you will die."

Halga leapt forward then, as quick as a cat. His sword flickered towards Beobrand's head. Gritting his teeth against the searing agony that now engulfed his leg, Beobrand raised his shield, catching the attack on the rim and taking another quick, shuffling step backward.

Too late he realised his error as his feet connected with something that lay in the mud. He lost his balance and tumbled to the earth. Halga had pushed him all the way back to the Wall, to the fortified gateway, and even as he sprawled onto the ground Beobrand understood what had happened. Years before, when they had fought in that faraway Mercian forest, Beobrand had tripped Halga in just this way on the corpse of the giant's dead hunting dog. Now Halga had done the same to him using the body of the rider he had slain as his horse churned the mud in the gateway.

Crashing onto his back, the air rushed from Beobrand's lungs. He knew what came next. When the situation had been reversed, he had hammered down a blow aimed at Halga's neck. The huge warrior had only prevented the slicing attack from killing him by halting Hrunting's blade with his forearm. Halga would step over him now and with a quick downward thrust, the Mercian would take his life.

Halga closed the distance. Beobrand gripped Hrunting tightly. If he could strike Halga as the giant delivered his killing blow, he might yet snatch victory. All warriors knew that they were most vulnerable from a blade beneath the shield. Many a good man had died from a thrusting seax or sword into the soft, unprotected flesh of groin and inner thigh.

Woden, even if I am to die here, let me take this whoreson with me.

Beobrand grasped Hrunting and prepared himself to drive the blade deep into Halga's groin. Halga strode forward and Beobrand lunged. Halga laughed, clearly expecting the attack and with savage speed he smashed his blade into Beobrand's right wrist.

Hrunting flew from his grip and Halga kicked the blade away, far from Beobrand's reach. Beobrand's eyes widened in dismay. After a moment of searing agony, he no longer felt his hand. He looked down, expecting to see the horror of a blood-spurting stump.

His hand remained attached to his wrist. He blinked stupidly for a moment, unable to comprehend how Halga's sword had not severed his limb. Then he saw the splints of iron he wore strapped to his wrist and offered up a silent prayer of thanks to whichever god looked over him.

Halga's shadow fell on him. It was no matter that Beobrand yet had a hand, he would be dead in a moment. Desperately, Beobrand made to lift his shield, to ward off the attack he knew would come, but Halga stepped on the wood, pinning it to the earth with his bulk. Beobrand's right hand throbbed and ached now, and it would not obey his commands. He reached for his seax, but his hand would not grip, the fingers clumsy and numb.

"I've longed for this moment for many years, Beobrand of Ubbanford," Halga said. "The moment when I kill you like a cowering cur. And this is better than even I had hoped for. Woden All-father has smiled upon me. First Oswiu gifts me your treasure, and now Woden grants me the taking of your life. A fair blood-price for slaying Wybert and my hound."

Beobrand's mind reeled. His body screamed with pain. Had he heard Halga's words? Was it possible? But, he would never know the truth of it. Halga turned his sword in his hand to aim the point at Beobrand's throat.

Beobrand looked up into the shadowed, leering face of the red-bearded giant. Death was there in Halga's eyes. Beobrand's throbbing hand would not grip, but he dropped it onto the antler hilt of his seax where it lay sheathed on his belt. He hoped that Woden would see him and take him into his corpse-hall.

Halga's eyes narrowed as he lifted his sword, ready for the downward thrust that would slice into Beobrand's flesh and soak the earth in his lifeblood.

Beobrand closed his eyes and felt the sharp pain as the wickedly keen patterned blade of Halga's sword sliced into his exposed throat.

Chapter 56

The pain in his throat was not as bad as Beobrand had thought it would be. But he had never died before, so he was unsure what to expect. He kept his eyes tightly closed and tried to feel his hand on the cool ridged smoothness of his seax handle. His fingers were still numb. They felt nothing. And yet his forearm ached where Halga's sword had struck against the iron splints of armour he wore there. And his thigh was a searing agony, throbbing with each beat of his heart.

Taking a deep breath, he focused on his throat. He thought he could make out where blood trickled down the side of his neck. Surely all the pain would cease soon, as his heart gave in and his spirit left his body. Or perhaps the dead felt forever the agony of their final wounds. He shuddered, gripped by a sudden fear of an afterlife of endless suffering.

His body throbbed and hurt. From the distance he could hear the sounds of battle. The clash of blades against shields, the shouted taunts and insults of men intent on killing. How long would it take him to die, he wondered?

He was just about to open his eyes to see what had happened, when something solid and hard crunched into his face. Beobrand's nose was crushed and he heard, deep and loud from within his head, his cartilage smash and grind. Fresh blood gouted from his broken nose.

Grunting, he opened his eyes. They were filled with tears that blurred everything. He could make no sense of what he saw. A huge shadow was falling towards him and he tried to roll to the side, out of the object's path. Perhaps Halga had decided to have fun with him before delivering the killing blow. Mayhap this was all a game to the Mercian.

Before he could move far, the shape crashed into him, forcing the breath from his lungs, leaving him gasping. The metal-stink of blood filled his nostrils. His face and chest were suddenly awash with hot, sticky liquid. Was that his blood, spurting from a great gash in his throat that he could not truly feel due to some twisted magic that befell the dying?

"Beobrand," a voice said.

Beobrand groaned and blinked, trying to decipher the shape that swam against the rolling grey clouds above him. Was this the Grey Wanderer, the one-eyed Ruler of Gallows, the grim All-father? Had the Chooser of the Slain come to claim him?

"Woden?" Beobrand croaked.

Something heavy weighed him down, crushing him. Blood stung his eyes and he pulled his numb right hand free from beneath the weight to rub clumsily at his face.

"Lord," the voice said, and the weight was suddenly lifted from him.

Beobrand gulped in a great lungful of cool, moist air and saw at last who it was leaning over him.

"Cynan?" he said, his voice cracking. He sat up and spat blood onto the earth beside him. Lying there, eyes wide and unseeing, was the red-bearded head of Halga. Blood seeped from the neck where it had been severed from the body. Beobrand shook his head, clearing it of the fog that had come with the certainty of death. He scrubbed with the heel of his hand at the thick blood that coated his face. He clenched and unclenched his fist. Slowly, some sensation was returning to his fingers. His arm still ached.

Blood flowed freely from his nostrils, and tears, brought on by the sharp pain to his nose, ran unbidden down his blood-drenched cheeks.

Reaching his hand down to his throat, he found no gaping wound in his neck. His touch brought a thin licking of pain and his fingers came back slick with yet more blood, but it seemed Halga had not rammed his sword through Beobrand's throat after all.

Beobrand shook his head again. On the earth to his left, beside Halga's head, lay the giant's fine sword. To Beobrand's right was the rest of Halga where Cynan had rolled the headless corpse.

Blinking away the blood and tears, Beobrand gripped the hand that Cynan was proffering. The Waelisc warrior heaved him to his feet. Beobrand groaned at the renewed pulse of pain in his leg. He tottered for a moment, leaning on Cynan for balance.

By the waggons, the fight yet raged. The Mercians had formed a strong, tightly packed square of shields that bristled with spears. They were surrounded by Beobrand's Black Shields who had more than twice their number.

"Gods, I thought you were dead, lord," said Cynan.

Beobrand spat again.

"So did I. Truth be told, I feel I have enough blood on me to be a corpse."

"Aye, but most of it is not yours."

Beobrand wiped the blood that yet poured from his nose on the back of his hand. He held it up for Cynan to see.

"This is mine," Beobrand said.

"I am sorry about that," Cynan said, not sounding sorry at all. "It seems that Halga had one last attack left in him, even in death."

Beobrand stared at him enquiringly.

"I took his head from his shoulders," said Cynan. "He was so intent on taking your life, he never thought that someone else might take his. His head fell into your face."

"Gods, but it smarts," Beobrand said and spat a fresh gobbet of snot and blood onto Halga's pale features. "A brawler to the end, eh?"

Beobrand shook his left arm free of the straps that held his shield in place, letting the board clatter onto Halga's splayed legs. Then, scooping up Hrunting from where it lay, he reached for Halga's head. Absently, he hoped this was the last severed head he would need to touch for a long while. Halga's helmet had toppled off, so Beobrand wrapped his fingers in the man's shaggy, fire-red hair. Hefting the head high into the air, Beobrand bellowed in his battle-voice, "Your leader is killed! See the face of your lord, Halga, son of Grimbold."

The fighting faltered as the warriors on both sides gazed upon Beobrand's grisly trophy.

"Your oaths are done," Beobrand yelled. He could feel the blood welling in the cut to his leg with each beat of his heart. His right hand prickled and throbbed. A wail of grief came from Grimbold's gesithas at seeing their hlaford slain. Nobody moved.

"Throw down your weapons or fight to the last man," Beobrand shouted into the momentary hush. "I care nought."

One Mercian suddenly screamed in rage and sprang forward. He was of middling years, tall, and yet somehow seeming to hunch, such was the breadth of his shoulders. In his hand was a wicked-looking langseax. The blade was as long as some swords, but the man swung it as if it were as light as an eating knife. The metal caught the watery light of the westering sun, glimmering pale and grey, like the Whale Road on a still day.

Perhaps the Mercian had expected the rest of Halga's men to follow him in a mad, frantic welter of blows. Maybe he believed he could avenge his lord's death. If all of the Mercians had pushed the fight to the Bernicians at the same moment, they might have had a chance, despite their numbers.

But none of the others moved.

Dreogan stepped forward to meet the man. The dark soot-stained lines on his face gave him a savage, grim aspect. Everybody there watched as the two men clashed. The Bernicians stepped back to give the men space to fight.

Again there was a moment when the Mercians could have attacked, perhaps surprising the Bernicians who gazed upon the duel between Dreogan and the crazed man wielding the langseax. But again, they did not move, and the moment was lost in a heartbeat as Dreogan parried a vicious downward strike from the langseax on his black shield, pushed it aside and hacked into the man's unprotected neck. Blood, bright and shocking in the dull grey afternoon light, blossomed in a spraying sheet as the man's heart laboured to keep him alive. The langseax fell from his fingers, he looked surprised and horrified as he dropped to his knees, then slumped onto the churned mud. Dreogan stepped close, snatching the dying man's weapon from where it had fallen and pressing it into the Mercian's grasp.

The Mercian warband seemed to let out a sigh, as if whatever fight was left in them had fled, carried away with the spouting lifeblood of their comrade.

"Throw down your weapons," Beobrand shouted, stepping forward, shaking Halga's gore-dripping head to reinforce his words.

For a moment he thought that he might have misjudged them, that the Mercians would rally at the sight of their dead lord's face, but the instant passed and, one by one, the warriors flung their spears, swords and seaxes to the ground between the two shieldwalls.

Beobrand strode towards them, his leg screaming with each step. He met the gaze of each of the Mercians in turn. Some looked away, unable to meet the ferocity of his stare, others fixed him with murderous fury. Those men wished for his death and would not hesitate to avenge their lord. These were the men who had ridden to Ubbanford. The men who had put Sunniva's hall to the flame; destroyed his people's homes and stolen his treasure. These hard-faced killers had come in the dawn light and slaughtered his folk.

Beobrand threw Halga's head onto the pile of blades, spears and shields. It clattered on the wood and metal, rolling away from him to rest looking at the Mercian warriors accusingly. One of Halga's gesithas moaned in anguish.

"Bind them all," Beobrand said to Dreogan.

It did not take them long to tie the hands of the Mercians. They did not resist now, seemingly broken and resigned to their wyrd. They stood sombre and grave as their hands were bound tightly behind their backs. These were proud men. Beobrand once more gazed at each one in turn. Cynan had helped him to staunch the flow of blood from the wound in his leg, pulling the lips of the ragged cut together and binding a strip of cloth about it. Beobrand hoped that the wound had not been elf-shot. Perhaps Coenred would be able to work his leechcraft magic on it if he yet remained at Stagga. The thigh yet pained him, sending throbbing stabs of agony through his leg. But the bandage was good, and Beobrand could no longer feel blood running down his leg to fill his boot.

The eyes of the Mercians burnt with a hatred Beobrand understood well. These men lived to kill, to seek out battle-glory with their swords. To serve their lord and to protect him. In turn he would give them wealth and lead them to greater victories. Beobrand had taken all of that from them. Their lord was just another cooling corpse and the treasures they had stolen from Ubbanford had been lost.

Beobrand took in a deep breath, turning away from the line of proud, defeated warriors. Ulf was staring at him. The burly warrior did not speak, but Beobrand knew what he was thinking. One of those men had killed his son. Beobrand nodded to him and looked at the Great Wall.

Bearn barked orders at some of the men, directing them to round up the Mercian horses. They were setting up a makeshift corral against the Wall.

A harsh croak, loud as a splintering shield, drew Beobrand's attention upward. Atop the gatehouse perched two huge black birds.

Ravens.

One of the night-black birds rested to the east of the entrance, the other on the west tower. They each appeared to be watching him with their dark, emotionless eyes. The one to the west let out another rasping croak. Claws of unease scratched down Beobrand's back. The birds reminded him of Nelda and her curse. But Nelda was dead. These birds were surely sent by another.

Before engaging with the Mercians in battle Beobrand had promised Woden All-father great slaughter and the blood of many men.

The eastern raven squawked. A sudden chill breeze ruffled its sooty feathers and tugged at Beobrand's cloak. His blood-soaked breeches were cold and clammy against his skin.

Woden. Frenzy.

Beneath the ravens Bearn and the others were intent on the horses. Beobrand looked to the rest of his men. Cynan stood close by, watching him with a curious look on his face. Dreogan, flecks of blood streaking the black tattoos on his cheeks, was grim, awaiting his lord's command.

Beobrand looked back to the two onlooking birds with a shudder. Was he the only one who saw them? He wished to ask, to utter the question, but feared to hear the response from his men. With a pang he longed for Acennan and his words of calm. He could hear his friend's words in his mind. They're only birds, he would have said.

And yet Acennan was dead. His voice silent. From the crumbling ramparts of the Wall gate tower, one of the ravens croaked again. Woden's birds had spoken. Their voice was hard, imperative. It must be obeyed.

The ravens stared down at him implacably. You gave your word, they seemed to be saying. Woden heard your call and granted you victory. Now you must repay him the blood-price you promised.

Beobrand closed his eyes and rubbed his hand over his face. He winced when his palm glanced against his broken nose. He could feel the men watching him. Their gaze was heavy, pressing on him the way Halga's corpse had fallen upon his battered body.

In his mind's eye, he pictured the smouldering bones of Ubbanford's halls, the smoking ruins of the buildings, the fish-pale flesh of the dead who lay strewn upon the grass and earth that had been their home.

"Lord?" Cynan's voice shattered the dark memory. His tone held an edge of concern.

Beobrand opened his eyes and turned to the Waelisc warrior.

"Kill them all," he said, his voice empty and hollow.

From their perch on the Wall both ravens cawed as one.

Chapter 57

Beobrand did not wish to watch the slaughter. But he was lord here, and this was his command. He could not turn his face from that which he had ordered.

His gesithas were grim-faced and as efficient as ceorls killing sheep before winter. But these were no sheep. These were warriors. Shield-man. Spear-men. Bearers of many warrior rings. One of the Mercians rushed forward, screaming suddenly. Taken unawares, Fraomar was knocked sprawling to the ground. The Mercian ran several paces until Grindan tripped him with a spear. Grindan and Eadgard dragged the man. He spat and raved in anger and fear.

Beobrand remembered a distant yew tree when he had been little more than a boy. The Mercian's screams brought back the whimpering cries of Tondberct. Tondberct had been his friend, but that had not stopped Beobrand ordering him hanged from the tree for his crimes.

The Mercian spat and blubbered now. Eadgard hit him hard, pushing him to his knees.

Beobrand clenched his jaw. These Mercians were not his friends.

"Kill him first," he said, his voice as final as death itself.

The man's screams intensified before being quickly silenced by a vicious cut from Grindan's sword. The Mercian's headless corpse crumpled, the head rolling a few paces towards Beobrand.

Beobrand scanned the rest of the men with a gaze as cold as the North Sea at Geola. They were pale and one of them twitched as Beobrand stared at him, clearly unable to keep his nerves in check. But none of them begged for mercy or screamed and raved. These men were not his friends, but they were warriors and they had their pride.

"I could have you slain like nithings, like men of no honour and no value. But if you give me your word that you will go quietly to the afterlife, I will see you each have a weapon in your hand when you breathe your last. Maybe Woden will see you and remember your past deeds and offer you a place in his corpse-hall." Beobrand looked up to the Wall. The two huge ravens yet sat there, eyeing the proceedings below with great interest. "Though why," Beobrand continued, "the All-father would wish for company of the likes of you, child slayers and as soft as women, I cannot say."

None of the Mercians responded. They merely glowered at the Bernician lord. They knew no words would save them now.

"Well," Beobrand said, "do you give me your word, such as that's worth?"

The oldest warrior, a tall, broad-shouldered man with streaks of grey in his thick beard nodded.

Beobrand glared at him.

"Do I have your oath?"

"Aye," the greybeard said, his voice gruff, "you have my word, you Bernician bastard. Now stick a sword in my fist and have done with it."

Beobrand nodded to Grindan, who picked up a seax from the pile and handed it to the man. The old Mercian held the weapon behind his back and, without a word, knelt awkwardly. Beobrand nodded again and Eadgard struck the man's head from his shoulders, stepping back too slowly to avoid being sprayed in the great fountain of blood that gushed from the old warrior's neck.

Beobrand felt sick at the spectacle. He balled his hands into fists at his side to stop the shaking that always came upon him after a fight.

"And the rest of you," he said, addressing the remaining Mercians, "do you give me your word?"

"Aye," they replied.

Beobrand waved forward more of his gesithas to carry out the sacrifice. Ulf had tears in his eyes, but his expression was keen, eager for vengeance for his son.

"Slay them all quickly," Beobrand said to Cynan, "and see that each one has a weapon in his hand."

Beobrand watched as the men knelt, but turned away before the blades chopped down. He had seen enough killing. He walked, stiff-legged and aching to the nearest waggon. The oxen yoked to the cart stared at him with their stupid bovine eyes. He recognised the nearest animal as one of Rowena's plough oxen. He stroked the beast's neck as he walked past. The ox flinched at the sound of swords hacking into flesh. In quick succession several more blades chopped into the kneeling Mercian warriors. The butcher-sound of slaughter filled Beobrand's ears, but he did not turn. He knew what he would see. He continued to the rear of the waggon, nodding silently to himself.

There had been no other sound but that of blades cutting into meat. The Mercians had kept their word. He was glad. He had not wished to hear their tormented cries. Above him flapped the two ravens, flying north into the low clouds that rolled there, heavy with the promise of more rain. They had seen the blood-price paid. He sighed, wondering what further mischief they were flying to see.

From the lack of noise, the killing was over now, and Beobrand turned to see his men dragging bodies to the side of the road and piling the heads together into an awful bleak mound of hair, staring eyes and gaping mouths.

"Kill one of those cows that were meant for Lord Merehwit," Beobrand said. "And light a fire. I would eat meat and be warm this night. In the morning we ride north. Back to Ubbanford." A couple of younger men, helping Bearn with the horses, let out a cheer at the prospect of meat, warmth and the return home. Those of Beobrand's gesithas who had dealt death to the kneeling Mercians did not smile.

Reaching the rear of the cart, Beobrand made to peer beneath the leather coverings that sheltered the cargo from the elements. But as he lifted the flap, a figure surged from the darkness within. The iron of a knife flashed, catching the dimming light of the sun. Beobrand was caught off guard, but he still had his speed. He leapt backwards, avoiding the blade. His feet slipped in the slick earth and he almost lost his footing. A stab of pain radiated from his thigh. The figure, long dark hair a tangled mass of madness, clambered from the cart and threw itself at Beobrand.

It was a woman, face distorted by fear and rage. She swung her knife at him in frantic, crazed ire-filled attacks. She was fast and erratic, but she was no warrior and Beobrand swatted away her knife easily. He pushed her backwards and she clattered against the wheel of the cart. The oxen lowed as the waggon rocked behind them.

"Enough, woman!" Beobrand snapped. "Put down your knife."

But she did not heed his words. With a snarl, the woman launched herself at him again.

"You are a nithing," she shrieked, "a craven." She aimed a slicing blow at his face and he swayed out of reach of the gleaming blade. There was something familiar about this woman. Her savage anger reminded him of Nelda. That long-dead cunning woman had come at him with a knife in the darkness of her cavern on Muile. She had raved at him for the death of her son, spitting her fury and curses in the gloom.

And then he knew who this woman was. She was the Mercian thrall he had rescued from Fordraed's men. She too had lost her son. Lost everything. And it was she who had struck down Reaghan. Sweet Reaghan who had offered her kindness and received treachery in return.

Another wild swing almost opened his throat. He dodged her attack and once more shoved her back.

"Woman, put up your knife. I do not wish to kill you. Gods, I did not save you for this."

"Save me!" she screamed. "Save me! Your Waelisc whore tried to save me too. I cannot be saved, there is nothing to save."

Her eyes were full of madness and violence as she leapt towards him again.

Beobrand was done with this. He did not wish to kill the woman, but she deserved death. She had raised her hand against Reaghan and the gods alone knew if his woman yet lived. The image of Reaghan lying in the overcrowded hall of Stagga, sweat-drenched and trembling, came to him unbidden.

Beobrand could feel his own anger mounting, rising like water behind a beaver dam. Ready to burst forth in a torrent of violence.

Too often he had shown leniency to his enemies.

Anticipating the Mercian woman's downward swing with the knife, Beobrand blocked with his forearm and punched her full in the face. She was flung backward and sprawled in the mud beside the waggon.

Beobrand dragged Hrunting from its fur-lined scabbard.

"Perhaps death will save you," he said, his voice as sharp and cold as Hrunting's patterned blade.

He stepped towards her. A movement on the cart caught his attention and he was not surprised to see the ravens fluttering down to land atop the leather cover. One of the birds croaked. It seemed Woden wished for yet more blood. Would the god never be sated?

So be it, thought Beobrand. What difference the blood of this treacherous thrall? He raised Hrunting.

"Go on then," the woman spat from where she lay in the mud. "Show me what a strong man you are, you Waelisc-loving whoreson."

The muscles of Beobrand's jaw bunched. He could no longer hold back the wave of anger. Gods, he would silence the bitch. He lifted his blade. She would learn soon enough not to cross Beobrand or his kin.

Without warning Beobrand was pushed away from the prone woman. Strong hands shoved against his chest and he was forced backwards.

"You cannot kill her, Beobrand," said Cynan.

The Waelisc warrior had positioned himself between Beobrand and the slave woman.

"She is my thrall," Beobrand said. "I can do with her what I please. Perhaps the men would like a plaything while they feast tonight."

"No, lord."

"No?" replied Beobrand, his tone growing as frigid as a winter's night. "You dare defy me, boy?"

Cynan's face grew pale, but he did not step aside.

"This bitch stabbed Reaghan in my own hall," said Beobrand. His voice trembled as he fought to control his rage. "I gave her life, but she deserves nothing but death. Better if I had left her to Fordraed. Get out of my way."

Cynan did not move.

"Get out of my way!" bellowed Beobrand, suddenly full of such fury that he raised Hrunting above Cynan and was ready to slay him for his temerity.

For a terrible moment Beobrand knew that he would kill this fool who would dare stand before him. He was Cynan's lord. Gods, Cynan had been but a thrall when he had taken him into his gesithas. And this is how the sheep-swiving Waelisc repaid him? He was surrounded by treachery. Well, if he could not count on Cynan's obedience, the boy was of no worth to him.

Beobrand made to swing Hrunting down. Cynan flinched, but he did not defend himself, or move away.

The ravens croaked again and their voices sounded like the cackling of bitter laughter.

Beobrand stayed his hand. In that instant he recalled a lightning-flickered night when he had rained blows upon Acennan because his friend had dared defy him. With a flash of regret he remembered pummelling his fists into Anhaga's face. His steward had done nothing wrong, and for his loyalty all he received was violence and then death at Beobrand's hand.

He stared into Cynan's eyes and saw the fear there. Cynan knew that Beobrand would kill him in an instant. But something else flickered there in Cynan's hazel eyes.

Disappointment.

Shaking, Beobrand lowered his sword. His chest heaved as though he had run a great distance.

"You will not stand aside?" asked Beobrand in a quiet, unsteady voice.

"I cannot, lord," replied Cynan, who yet held Beobrand's gaze with his own.

"I have your oath and yet you would defy me?"

Cynan swallowed.

"If you wish to kill me, Beobrand, then so be it. But I will not stand aside and let you kill Sulis. She has suffered much and I fear her mind is broken and twisted. But to slay her would bring no good."

"She sought to kill Reaghan," Beobrand whispered, his anger yet pushing at its shackles. "Mayhap my woman is already dead and cold in the hall of Stagga." The thought of it made his voice crack. "This woman must be punished."

"She has lost her son and been made a thrall. Has she not been punished enough?"

"Her death is my weregild. My right by the dooms and laws of the kings of Bernicia."

"Do not do this thing, lord," said Cynan. "I am one of your Black Shields. Have I not always fought for you with honour? Do I not seek to serve and obey you? To protect you?"

Beobrand said nothing.

"You know what other men are capable of. When the battle-lust is upon them and the joy of victory flows in their blood. You have seen too often the horrors of war. But you have always commanded us not to harm women and children, lord. Even when others take their pleasure from the wives and daughters of the men they have slain in the shieldwall. You will never allow it of us. You think we would rather take our share of the spoils? No. We love you for your strength. You are a better lord than others and you have made us better men. Do not do this thing. You will forever regret it."

Beobrand gripped Hrunting so tightly his fingers hurt, the knuckles showing white. Cynan's words rocked him as if he had been struck. He took a step back, away from the Waelisc gesith. Away from the woman who cowered and shook, panting in the mud. Her pretty face was bloody. As he watched, fresh blood oozed from her nose and ran into her open mouth. He had done that when he'd punched her. His knuckles yet stung from the force of the blow.

Sulis stared at him from beneath the wreath of her unruly hair. There was hatred in those eyes. And a terrible sorrow. But no fear. She was beyond fear now. For what else could be done to her?

Unbidden, the image of Hengist came to him then, smiling at the pain and anguish of others. Beobrand's mother had told him he was not his father's son, but now he knew he shared the same father as that monster, Hengist. He could feel the same blood coursing through his veins. The same fury and lust for violence. He had believed it came from Grimgundi, but now he knew otherwise. He had vowed he would never abuse the weak as Grimgundi had.

But, in the darkest corners of his mind, he knew that he could all too readily become a man such as Hengist. He shared the same blood, and he harboured the same rage.

He sheathed Hrunting. Such was the shaking of his hand that he missed the scabbard on the first attempt. Beobrand was suddenly aware of the hush that had fallen over the men.

"You," he said, pointing at Sulis, "have raised your hand against my woman and me. Your life is mine by right of law." He hesitated. The ravens eyed him, but were as silent as the men now, as if they too listened to his words. Beobrand hawked to clear his throat and spat. "But instead of death, I give you your freedom." The woman's glaring expression did not change and Beobrand wondered if she had understood him. "Go," he said. "Return to Mercia. But know this," he fixed her with a hard stare that at last caused her to flinch, "if I see you again, I will kill you."

He turned his back on Cynan and the Mercian thrall and walked towards the Wall.

Chapter 58

Cynan stood for a long while and watched the small shape of Sulis until she was lost to the distance and the gathering dusk.

After Beobrand had walked away, Cynan had drawn her to her feet. Awkwardly, he'd tried to dab at the blood on her beautiful face, but she had pulled away from him, hissing like a wild cat.

"It is all well now," he had whispered to her. "Nobody will harm you now."

She had let out a harsh laugh then.

"You are a fool, Cynan," she'd said. She'd reached out her hand and for the briefest of moments her fingers had caressed his cheek. He could still feel the thrill of her touch.

There had been tears in her eyes, but she had not cried. She'd wiped the blood from her bleeding nose and stuck the knife she carried into her belt. Cynan had fetched a cloak from one of the slain warriors. It was a fine garment, made of the best wool, thick and heavy and dyed a rich blue. It would keep her warm and dry. Sulis had taken the cloak without a word of thanks and he had pressed a lump of silver into her hand. Again he had thrilled at her touch. She had remained silent. She glanced down to see what he had given her and then slipped it into a pouch that hung from her belt.

All about them, the rest of Beobrand's warriors were busy with the horses, the carts and oxen and preparing a fire and food for the night. Cynan knew they glanced at him and the slave woman. They probably thought he was a fool too. Standing before Beobrand like that had been madness. And yet, he could not bear the thought of Sulis being slain. For her life to be taken by the lord he revered had been a horrific prospect.

As he watched her go, walking westward, into the watery red light of the setting sun, Cynan imagined leaping onto his horse and riding after her. Perhaps it would be best for him. Beobrand would surely despise him now for his audacity and defiance. What life would he have now with the lord of Ubbanford? Perhaps he could make a life for himself with Sulis. Maybe he could find a new lord to serve. Or he could simply build a small house for her somewhere out there in the western wilds where no lord truly held sway. They could raise a family and live a quiet life, eking out a living from the land.

Two ravens that had been perched on the carts both flapped into the sky, as Fraomar goaded the oxen and the waggon lurched forward. The birds croaked angrily as they flew northward. Cynan shuddered. Had those ravens been there before? He had not noticed them until now. Their cawing sounded like harsh chuckles at his foolishness.

Of course he could not follow Sulis. Even if he had thought she might allow him to. He had given his oath to Beobrand, and the thegn of Ubbanford had given him everything in return. A life with meaning. Wealth. A family of oath-sworn warriors.

Cynan glanced towards the gatehouse in the Great Wall. Beobrand stood there watching him. Cynan could not make out his expression. Beobrand met his gaze and held it for a moment, before turning and walking through the gate and to their camp south of the Wall. Had Beobrand offered him the slightest of nods of approval? It was hard to say in the dim light.

Cynan looked back westward, hoping for a final glimpse of the woman who had suffered so much and caused so much pain. He longed for her, and yet he knew she would never willingly be his. His stomach clenched and he felt a pang of sadness when he realised he could no longer see her. She had been swallowed by the distance and the gloaming.

"Come on, Cynan," Gram said, cutting into his reverie, "it will be dark soon and there is still much to do if you have finished pining for your wayward thrall."

Cynan turned, a flicker of anger rippling through him. But he saw no malice on Gram's face. In fact, the older man offered him a twisted smile of commiseration.

"Bearn could use your help with the horses if we are not to lose some of them in the night," Gram said.

Cynan saw that some of the Mercian mounts had galloped away from the road and needed to be rounded up. As the best horseman of Beobrand's warband, it made no sense for him to be standing idle while his comrades struggled to catch all the mounts before nightfall.

With a sigh, Cynan nodded to Gram and stalked off to where his horse stood, waiting patiently for its rider.

He could never turn his back on his oath. Or his friends.

Swinging lithely up onto his horse's back, Cynan pulled the animal's head in the direction of the furthest wayward horse and dug in his heels. The beast carried him forward at an easy lope.

Despite himself, Cynan smiled. He rode away from Sulis and the confusion he felt and towards a simple task. One he knew he could easily fulfil without the need for killing or having to confront the maelstrom of emotions that broiled within him.

He could never ride away from his lord and this group of men. His family.

Kicking his steed into a gallop, Cynan rode into the gathering gloom to do his duty.

Historical Note

The period of history depicted in the Bernicia Chronicles is distant and veiled in mists of uncertainty. As with the previous books in the series, in *Warrior of Woden* I have taken some historical events which are recorded in *The Anglo-Saxon Chronicle* and Bede's *History of the English Church and People* and I have woven Beobrand's story around the few facts available. As always, I see my role as storyteller, not historian. This is primarily a work of fiction, but it is firmly based in the historical setting and around the real events and lives of kings, priests, thegns and peasants of seventh-century Britain.

The battle at the beginning of *Warrior of Woden* alludes to a confederation of southern Saxons that is mentioned in the *Annals of Ulster* under the title "The Battle of Oswald". It is possible that the entry in the *Annals* refers to the later battle of Maserfelth (Maserfield), but I have imagined a confederation between different nations against the rising power of Oswald of Northumbria and the sons of Æthelfrith. Lindsey was a small kingdom that had long been subject to Northumbria and it seems possible that the royal line of Lindsey would side with other enemies of Northumbria, such as the pagans, Penda of Mercia and Sigeberht the Little of the East Saxons, in an attempt to overthrow Oswald. I have envisaged them amassing troops in Lindsey, near the capital of Northumbria, Eoferwic (York) and launching a surprise attack whilst the Christian Oswald is distracted celebrating Easter, that most holy of Christian festivals. In the Prologue, Oswald has been alerted to the attack and has succeeded in leading his own warhost to the field to meet the uprising before they reach Eoferwic, at Tatecastre (Tadcaster).

Whatever happened in reality, Oswald continued to rule the most powerful kingdom in Britain until AD 642.

Perhaps it was in such a battle that Eowa turned his back on his brother, Penda, effectively splitting Mercia in two.

The battle against the Picts, Cair Chaladain, is fictional, but loosely based on the earlier battle of Raith in AD 596, where the Angles defeated an alliance of Scots, Britons and Picts.

I have Oswald's son, Œthelwald, being born in AD 636, soon after the king's marriage to Cyneburg. It is not known when Œthelwald was born and it has been postulated that he was from an earlier marriage and thus older than I have made him.

The location of Eowa's hall in Mercia is unknown. I chose Snodengaham (Nottingham), in northern Mercia, with Eowa ruling the land thereabouts and his brother, Penda, ruling the west and south of Mercia.

The fostering of noble children was commonplace. Having Octa fostered by Eowa, the atheling of Mercia, provides an elegant solution for Oswald to keep an eye on his reluctant ally through Beobrand's visits to his son.

The names of both of Eowa's children are known. Eowa's proud line was strong and the boys, Osmod and Alweo, both survive to have children of their own. Osmod's line leads to that most famous of Mercian kings and builder of a great dyke, Offa. Alweo's line leads to another king of Mercia, Æthelbald.

Eowa's wife's name is not known. I decided to use Cynethryth, the name of the queen of the later king, Offa.

The attempt to assassinate Eowa is based on an event that took place in AD 626 to another king: Edwin of Northumbria. A West Saxon attacked Edwin with a poisoned blade and the king only survived as a result of one of his thegns, Lilla, interposing himself between his lord and his would-be assassin. Lilla was slain and Edwin barely made it through the night after being injured with the envenomed blade.

I could find no record for a name for the Roman road from Manchester to Carlisle, so I decided that the Anglo-Saxons would refer to it as Weatende Stræt. Weatende means the furthest west part of something in Old English. Similarly, the Roman road from York to Manchester has no recorded Old English name and so I chose to have the locals call it Hēah Stræt. There are of course many other High Streets in Britain, some of which are Roman roads.

One of the defining events of the novel is the battle of Maserfelth, where Penda slew Oswald and broke Northumbria's stranglehold over Britain. The location of the battle has long been traditionally accepted as Oswestry in Shropshire. The town even derives its name from Oswald's death (Oswestry comes from Oswald's Tree and the name in Welsh is Croesoswallt, which translates as Oswald's Cross). However, there has been much conjecture over this location and when the facts are analysed it seems possible, likely even, that medieval clergymen decided to propagate the story of Oswald's death there, to capitalise on the saintly king's burgeoning cult. There are several other contenders for the location of Oswald's final battle. In the end, I settled on a site just north of the Mersey, with Oswald defending his kingdom from Penda's attack, rather than attacking deep into Mercian and Powys territory.

Eowa did die at the battle of Maserfield. It is not known whose side he was on, but it has been conjectured that he was a client king to Oswald.

Animal sacrifice was common practice in many religions. Stallions were particularly prized for the powerful magic their blood invoked and were used in rites conferring kingship. At the pagan temple at Gamla Uppsala in Sweden, Adam of Bremen wrote in the eleventh century that every nine years, nine males of every living creature were sacrificed and their corpses hung from the limbs of trees to placate the gods Woden, Thunor and Freyr. Adam also writes of a practice of throwing a human sacrifice into a spring. If the unfortunate victim did not resurface, the gods accepted the offering and "the wish of the people will be fulfilled".

Adam was a Christian monk, so his accounts may have been exaggerated or invented to further the Christian religion over the old Norse gods of Sweden, but there is plenty of evidence for sacrifices elsewhere, such as the remains of animal and human sacrifices being excavated in Trelleborg, Denmark, predating the tenth-century Viking fort there.

Human sacrifice, whilst certainly not as common as animal offerings, was the ultimate blood gift to the gods. Bede describes how Penda had Oswald slain and "ordered that his head, hands, and arms be hacked off and fixed on stakes". The impact of this image, offering a kingly sacrifice to Woden in a grisly parody of the crucifixion of Christ, cannot be underestimated for both pagans and Christians alike.

The retrieval of Oswald's remains from the battlefield is documented in Bede's history, though it sounds like the stuff of legend. I have compressed the timeline and altered the protagonist of the action. Bede has Oswiu returning the following year with his army to bring back his brother's head and limbs.

The names of Hyfeidd the Tall and Mynyddog, are plucked from the Old Welsh poem, *Y Gododdin*. The poem tells the tale of the tragic last stand of the native Britons against the Anglo-Saxons at Catraeth (Catterick) around AD 600. It is an epic tale somewhat akin to Custer's famous last battle at Little Bighorn in its futility and reckless bravery, which ends with the deaths of all of the valiant warriors who ride to war against the Anglo-Saxon invaders. Hyfeidd the Tall's name stands out as a warrior of legendary status, "a champion in the charge in the van of the armies; there fell five times fifty before his blades, of the men of Deira and Bernicia a hundred score fell and were destroyed."

For his brave sacrifice in battle, the author of the *Y Gododdin* poem says that "Hyfeidd the Tall shall be honoured as long as there is a minstrel". When I read that, even though the battle of Maserfelth takes place some forty years after Hyfeidd the Tall's death, I had to use his name, keeping his memory alive in some small way 1,400 years later.

The kingdom of Rheged is all but lost to history, with little being known of the location of its borders or its main power bases. Recent evidence could point to Trusty's Hill, in modern-day Galloway, being the site of a royal hall, but details of who Rheged's people really were, how they lived and even where they lived, are scant. At some time in the 630s, Oswiu married Rhieinmelth of Rheged, great granddaughter of the famed Urien. This political marriage must have seen Rheged fall under the control of Bernicia. In effect, Oswiu's marriage to Rhieinmelth spells the end of Rheged's power and its royal line. I think it likely that the fortified Roman town of Carlisle would have been the location of at least one of Rheged's royal halls.

The Roman fort where Acennan and Ástígend face Gwalchmei and his warband is the ruin of Mediobogdum, the fort located in the Hardknott Pass in Cumbria.

The iron age fort where Bearn awaits Beobrand's return with Oswald's remains is Carrock Fell. I have called it Carrec Dún, as Fell comes from the Old Norse, Fjall, making the name later than seventh century. Carrec is Cumbric for rock and Dún is the Old English for hill or mountain.

Although royal dynasties were evident in each of the kingdoms of Britain, kings were not decided by birth, but rather by a gathering of the wise men (Witena Ġemōt, later known as the Witan). The new king was frequently the brother or cousin of the deceased king and certainly not always the eldest son.

At the end of *Warrior of Woden*, Oswiu has returned to the east of Bernicia and convened the Witena Ġemot, but the power of the realm of Northumbria is now in the balance. Will Oswiu be crowned king? And, if he is, will he be able to again unify the two kingdoms of Bernicia and Deira as Oswald had?

As the kingdoms of Albion continue to vie for supremacy and the followers of the Christ preach their teaching of forgiveness and eternal life over the dark sacrifices of the old gods, one thing is certain: Beobrand will be in Oswiu's service, and will do his bidding, however much he might wish he could follow a different lord. For Beobrand has given his oath and Beobrand's word is iron.

Beobrand's path is never easy. He will go on to stand in more shieldwalls. He will again know great friendships and suffer terrible losses. And who knows? Perhaps he will even find that love and sense of peace he craves.

But that is for another day, and other books.

Acknowledgements

First, I must thank you, dear reader. Without you, there would be no point to writing these stories. I really appreciate the time you have invested in the Bernicia Chronicles, especially if you have read the series up to this point. I don't take it for granted that the novels will sell, and I do my utmost to create stories that will excite and satisfy you. If you have got this far in the saga, hopefully you have enjoyed the stories and *Warrior of Woden* has been a satisfying read.

No novel makes it into print without many people being involved. Thanks, as always, go to my cadre of dedicated test readers, Rich Ward, Shane Smart, Graham Glendinning, Mark Leonard, Emmett Carter and Simon Blunsdon.

Special thanks to my great friend, Gareth Jones, who not only reads an early draft of each novel and provides valuable feedback, but also meets up with me regularly to drink copious amounts of beer, discuss all manner of things and generally set the world to rights.

Thanks to Alex Forbes for the continued support, for always believing and being a steadfast friend.

Robin Wade, my agent, has been a constant supporter and is

an invaluable guide through the sometimes rough waters of the publishing industry. For this he has my gratitude.

With each novel's publication, I realise how lucky I am to be published by Head of Zeus. The entire team, and everyone at Head of Zeus, are as passionate about books as they are professional. Special mention must go to my editor, Caroline Ridding, and my copy editor, Paul King, without whom the book you are holding would be a lot less polished.

Finally, but by no means least, I am, as ever, indebted to my family and especially my gorgeous wife, Maite. I really wouldn't be able to write without her endless support.

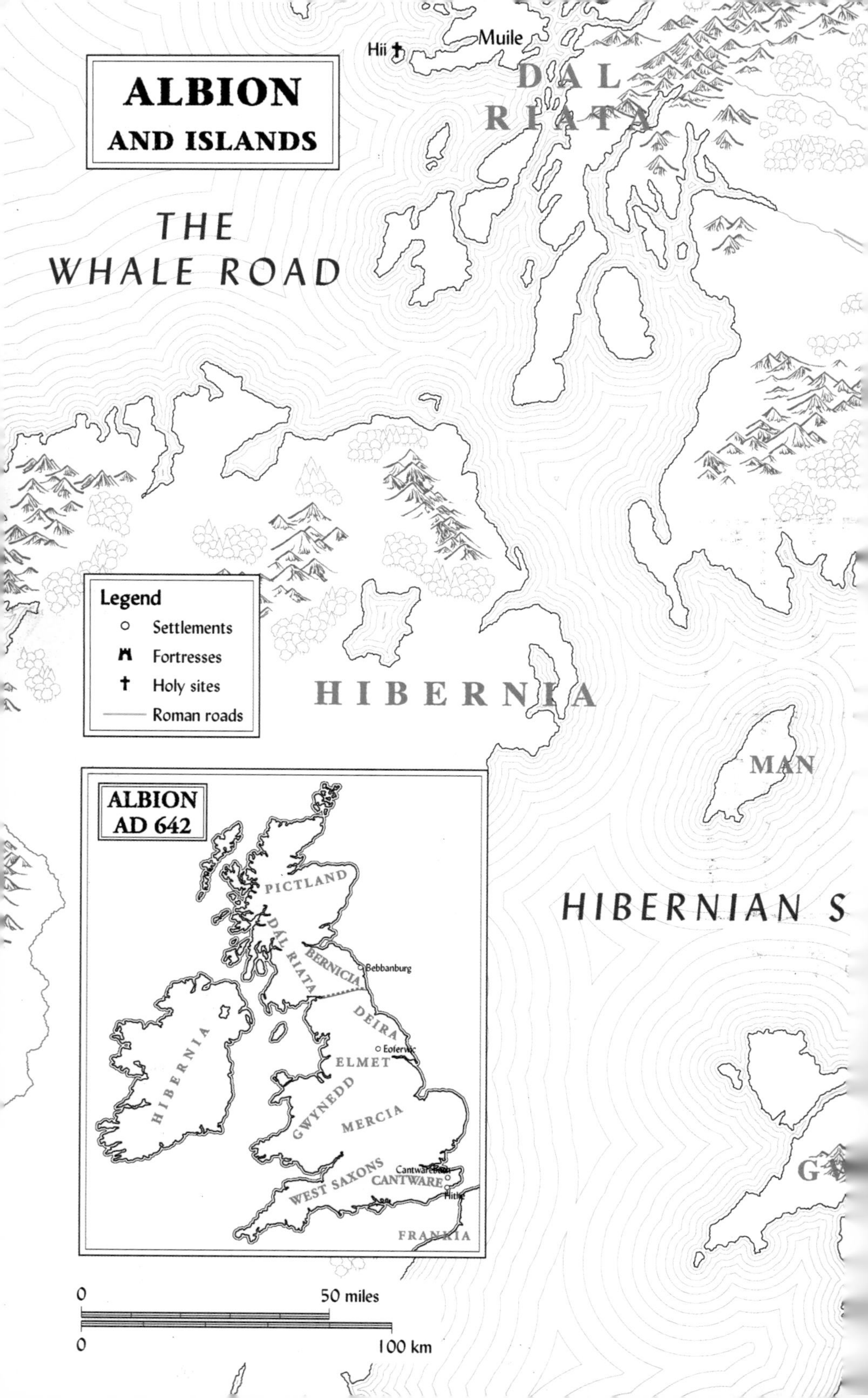
ALBION
AND ISLANDS
THE
WHALE ROAD
Hii
Muile
DÁL
RIATA
HIBERNIA
MAN
HIBERNIAN S
Legend
Settlements
Fortresses
Holy sites
Roman roads
ALBION
AD 642
PICTLAND
DÁL RIATA
BERNICIA
Bebbanburg
DEIRA
Eoferwic
ELMET
HIBERNIA
GWYNEDD
MERCIA
WEST SAXONS
CANTWARE
FRANKIA
0
50 miles
0
100 km